MW00984613

The Gods
Time Forgot

The Gods
Time Forgot

《 *A Novel* 》

Kelsie Sheridan Gonzalez

alcove
press

This is a work of fiction. All of the names, characters, organizations, places, and events portrayed in this novel are either products of the author's imagination or are used fictitiously. Any resemblance to real or actual events, locales, or persons, living or dead, is entirely coincidental.

Copyright © 2025 by Kelsie Sheridan

All rights reserved.

Published in the United States by Alcove Press, an imprint of The Quick Brown Fox & Company LLC.

Alcove Press and its logo are trademarks of The Quick Brown Fox & Company LLC.

Library of Congress Catalog-in-Publication data available upon request.

ISBN (paperback): 979-8-89242-032-7
ISBN (hardcover): 979-8-89242-233-8
ISBN (ebook): 979-8-89242-033-4

Cover design by Corinne Reid

Printed in the United States.

www.alcovepress.com

Alcove Press
34 West 27th St., 10th Floor
New York, NY 10001

First Edition: April 2025

10 9 8 7 6 5 4 3 2 1

Here's to never putting Rua on the shelf.

Pronunciation Guide

Badb—bive (like *hive*)

Bealtaine—bee-yowl-tinna

Cú Chulainn—koo-kullen

Imbolg—im-bol-g

Lúnasa—loo-nah-sa

Macha—mah-kuh

Medb—may-ve

Nemain—nevin

Oweynagat—oen-na-gat

Rathcroghan—rath-craw-hin

Ríastrad—ree-ah-strad

Rua—roo-ah

Samhain—sow-wen (*sow* like *cow*)

One

Somewhere between the light and the dark, a woman got lost, and as the earth closed in around her, she wondered what she'd done to deserve it.

She wriggled her fingers, loosening the dirt, feeling it burrow between her nails as she searched for release.

"Emma? Emma, are you out here?" Distant muffled calls came from somewhere aboveground.

She stopped struggling to listen.

"Emma, where are you?"

She considered answering but wasn't sure they were talking to her. Her stomach knotted. Why couldn't she remember her name? She closed her eyes, retreating into the vacant depths of her mind. Why couldn't she remember anything?

"Emma?" The voice sounded closer.

Her name could be Emma, she supposed, and certainly they wouldn't be against helping a woman out of a hole even if she wasn't the one they were looking for.

"I'm here," she answered, choking on the dirt. "I'm here!"

Wedged so tight into this narrow passageway, she could hardly breathe. Digging her knees deeper into the dirt, she tried to push herself forward. Pebbles and bits of clay fell all around her. It was so much effort for such little reward. If she didn't free herself soon, she was going to suffocate.

"Where are you?" the voice called to her, sounding closer.

"Here," she coughed out, unsure if she'd even made a sound.

This time she drove her elbows into the dirt, her body moving infinitesimally closer to the slip of light that would offer her both freedom and a deep breath.

She wondered what this hole looked like to people not in it. Would they even notice it in the ground? Or would they walk right past her body as she lay rotting with her feet dangling above the cave she'd tried to crawl out of?

No, she wouldn't let that happen, she told herself. Buried and forgotten was not to be her fate. Her hands clawed at the dirt while she shimmied herself upward with her knees, her elbows chafing against the soil that enclosed her.

She pulled and pushed until finally the pressure on her chest started to lift. The dirt and gravel loosened beneath her. She was almost out. One last desperate pull and she was free.

Gasping for the air she'd recently taken for granted, she rolled onto the grass and faced the darkening sky. How did she end up here? She turned her head to glance at the triangular hole she'd just crawled out from and the mound of grass above it. From the outside, one would never suspect a massive cave rested beneath.

She hadn't a clue what would have prompted her to enter such a thing.

Her body still trembling from the exertion, she sat up. Her shaking hands as dirty and bloodied as her tattered dress.

While her breathing steadied, she took in more of her surroundings. The forest around her was lush and thriving. A creek cut through the trees. Upon seeing the water, her throat burned with need.

She rose to her feet, shuffling to where the creek had pooled, backed up against the rocks. The water was still, a perfect mirror image of the woods around her. It called to her, offering to quench her thirst and cleanse her soul.

She knelt before it, cupping the cool water with her hands and lifting it to her lips. At the same moment an image flooded her mind.

"My darling sister, ever the fool."
She looked up to find who had spoken.

"Have you no sense of self? No respect for our sisterhood?"
Languid, the sable-haired woman lay against the rocks, letting her
fingers dance in the water.

The fairer woman frowned upon hearing the harsh words but did
not offer a rebuttal nor speak up in her defense.

She took another sip, the image of the women still clear in her
mind. They were draped in long flowing gowns, belted at the waist,
sitting by the water, and she was one of them.

The water trickled down her chin and the length of her arms as
the forest came back into focus. She sat back on her knees, looking
around her, noting the similarities of the world she saw now and the
one she saw in her mind. The pool of water was the same, but the
fauna was different. The trees here were taller, the brush thicker but
still so eerily similar.

Thinking about the sisterhood the woman had mentioned, she
dipped her hands in the water once more. She didn't know of any
sisterhood. At least, she couldn't remember one.

"No! You cannot touch the water! It's cursed," a woman shouted
at her, the same voice she heard calling for Emma.

She turned to find a petite woman with a pallid complexion
wearing a terrified look and a drab gown much different than the
garments of the women she had seen in her mind's eye.

"Oh, Emma." Relief washed over the woman's face as she ran
toward her. "You're all right." She let out a deep breath. "What happened? What are you wearing?"

"I'm not Emma." She shook her head, though she wasn't sure.
She wasn't sure about anything.

Concern filled the woman's eyes. "It's all right now. Just come
with me." She took a small step forward with her hands out, speaking the way one would to a frightened child.

The sound of men's voices carried through the trees as they
crashed through the underbrush. "Emma Harrington?" they yelled.
"Where are you, Emma?"

She went rigid at the sound of their menacing shouts.

"She's over here," the woman called.

There was chaos in the trees. Snapping branches, grunting and
panting. They were coming for her.

She took a step backward, her heels dipping into the cool water behind her, her vision growing cloudy once more.

She hovered on the water's edge, wishing for a way to go back and undo it, to prevent what was yet to come.

He came up behind her, settling his arms around her waist. She leaned into his embrace, pressing her cheek against his, wondering if this would be the last time.

"Rua, love, what's on your mind?" he whispered, his warm breath tickling her ear. Playfully, he nipped at her earlobe while his right hand slipped beneath her tunic, gliding across her collarbone.

Guilt gnashing at her insides, she answered, "Nothing of consequence."

He stopped, hearing the lie.

She could not turn to face him. He took a step back, removing his warmth.

Rua dove under the water, absorbing its power, feeding her misguided soul.

"No! Stop! What are you doing?" the woman shouted.

She came back to reality, finding herself standing in the water, submerged from the waist down, her filthy gown clinging to her legs. The temperature was cool but welcome against her sweaty skin.

"Emma, get out of there!"

"My name's Rua," she said, lifting her head as she stepped out of the water. Her body moved slowly, jolting with every labored step as though the water could not bear to let her leave.

The woman gave her an odd look. "Okay, Rua, I'm Mara."

Rua didn't care that Mara didn't believe her. When the name left her mouth, she felt in her bones it was the truth.

Half a dozen men approached them, out of breath and burly, flanking Mara on both sides. Rua's heart raced at the sight of them all.

Their collective shouts of, "Here, she's here!" quickly turned to grimaces and looks of horror. "What in the bloody hell is she doing out here?"

Cornered between the men and the water, there was nowhere for her to go.

"She's wounded!" one man shouted.

Confused, Rua looked down at her half-soaked gown, covered in a mixture of blood and earth. She touched her stomach. Her hands didn't drip with blood, but they were stained. Her body was sore, but she wasn't hurt.

Forgetting his hesitance, a man rushed toward her, the rest following in step.

"It's going to be all right," Mara said, stepping aside to let them pass.

"No," Rua said, trying to keep the men back from her. She wasn't Emma. She didn't need to go with them. "Don't touch me," she snapped, yanking her arm back as a man tried to grab hold of her.

He reached for her again, careful not to step on the slick rocks, and she swatted him away. Irritated, he nodded to the others. They skulked toward her, trapping her between them and the water.

"Let's not make a fuss now. Your mother's waiting for you," the closest man said.

Mother? She didn't have a mother.

Flustered, she retreated farther into the water. The men looked on with terror in their eyes, as though she might burst into flames and drag them all to hell.

Using it to her advantage, she splashed the water at them with a quick swipe of her hand. A sizzling sound filled the air, followed by a collective roar as the water made contact with their flesh. Alarmed, she looked at her own skin, wondering why it didn't affect her the same.

She waited a moment, watching the man closest to her writhe in pain. The water had burned through his shirt and blistered his skin. She looked at her own hands. Nothing but the remnant tint of blood.

And then she ran.

"Don't let her get away!"

She ran and ran, unsure of where she was going or how she was going to find her way out of the woods. She was exhausted, drained, and hungry, and desperately racking her brain for answers.

A hollow ache drummed in her chest. Why couldn't she remember anything about her life? She thought of the blurry memories, of the woman with two sisters and a man who seemingly loved her. Was that her life, or was it this one?

And then the woods cleared, immediately and without warning.

Rua stumbled onto a freshly mowed patch of lawn, expansive and luxurious. She stepped forward, taking cautious steps toward the tremendous mansion that abutted the garden. So out of place in her disgusting gown, she felt like she was dirtying the grass.

As she approached the home, she noticed the many servants who'd stopped to stare. They pointed and whispered.

"Emma!" a woman standing on the limestone veranda shouted down to her with a coldness that sent a chill down Rua's back. "Heavens above, what happened to you?" The woman glided down the dozens of steps toward her, past the fountain and the statues. She was serene in a cream-colored gown and a sleek bun. Not a wrinkle in sight. "Where have you been?" Her face was stern, her tone the same.

"I believe there's been a misunderstanding. I'm not sure who Emma is, but—"

The woman's eyes widened as she looked around to see who might've heard the admission. "Do not utter another word."

The men who'd been searching for Emma emerged from the forest. The one with the severe burn marks on his chest was being propped up by two other men, his feet dragging on the ground as they walked.

The servants had returned to busying themselves, though Rua guessed their ears were wide open.

"You're not well. You need to lie down." The woman waved someone forward. Rua turned to see that it was Mara.

"Get her up to her chambers immediately. Let no one see her, and keep her quiet. Burn these clothes."

"Yes, Mrs. Harrington." Mara nodded, waiting for Rua, but she was glued to the spot.

"My name is not Emma." Could they not see that she was a different person?

"Yes, you said that, and I advise you to stop," Mrs. Harrington said, as though Rua's very existence were an inconvenience.

Rua turned back to face the woods and thought of the hole she'd barely managed to crawl out of. The way it constricted her every breath, squeezing tighter and tighter until there was no more air.

She looked down at the blood on her hands. Was it hers? She couldn't remember what had happened. Her heart began to beat a little faster, and her pulse drummed in her ears.

What were her choices but to run or to find out why they thought she was Emma?

"Your imprudence is a disease." Mrs. Harrington's lip curled in disgust. "Get up to your bedchamber. Now."

Rua bristled at Mrs. Harrington's apparent distaste for who she thought she was—her daughter, Emma.

"A word, Mrs. Harrington?" an older gentleman in a dirty suit and sweat on his brow interrupted as he walked up the steps toward them. Rua recognized him from the woods. He eyed her nervously, then stopped.

"Oh, for heaven's sake," Mrs. Harrington huffed, turning to Rua. "This is what you've done to this family." She gestured toward the man too afraid to come any closer. "This is the effects of your pestiferous reputation," she snapped before walking over to him.

Rua watched as they talked, whispering and casting sidelong glances her way. She wondered if she shouldn't just run and take her chances in the woods. The water, however poisonous, soothed her. She longed to dive beneath its surface, to be weightless and calm, but as she thought the words, a dark fog crept into her periphery. Its cold grasp settled over her senses as she began to sway, pulling her toward oblivion.

Rua's eyes flew open as a loud crack of thunder shook the room. She stared up at the ceiling, a ceiling with a glittering chandelier covered in gold detail and little painted flowers, a ceiling that she'd never seen before.

She sat up and scanned the massive, unfamiliar room. With every sweep of her gaze, she grew more disturbed.

All possible surfaces, save for the wood floors, were a pink-flowered spectacle. The sheets, the walls, the light fixtures, the furniture—all of it. Nothing had ever looked so heinous.

Jumping off the bed, Rua ran over to the tall, rectangular window, whose panes were pushed outward. The heavy curtains obstructed most of the narrow frame. There was no breeze, only stagnant, humid air. She tucked the curtain behind the gold-braided tieback and glanced at the garden below her, guessing it was morning. The birds were quiet, slow to begin their chirping, the sun not quite up. Surely this intangible sense of stillness marked a new day.

She had a clear view of the woods. The full memory of her ordeal weighed heavy on her chest. Anxious, she turned back to the room with no idea of what she was going to do next.

Rua walked back to the bed, tracing her hand along the white oak frame. As her mind tried and failed to come up with a plan, a half-completed painting on an easel caught her eye. She approached the sad-looking subject with red hair, freckled pale skin, and vacant green eyes and hesitated. A portrait of her. No, not her, but someone who looked just like her. Exactly like her.

A duplicate.

She reached out to touch it.

"Emma, I'm so glad to see you back. I was so worried."

Rua pulled her hand back.

Hovering on the fringes of the doorway was the maid, Mara. "Your mother asked to be informed the minute you woke," she said, her tone apologetic, as she left to fetch the matriarch.

Rua said nothing and turned back to look at the painting, understanding now why they called her Emma. The resemblance was uncanny, and she was suddenly unsure of why she thought she wasn't Emma. She couldn't remember a thing about her life, as though her existence prior to this moment was so inconsequential that she'd simply forgotten it. Her fingers grazed Emma's portrait, sliding gently down the painted hair. Could she be Emma?

Unsettled, she turned to the gilded mirror resting on the vanity, praying that looking upon her reflection might reveal some answers.

Disappointment flared in her chest.

She looked like the woman in the painting, from the auburn streaks to the green of her eyes, but she herself was altogether unfamiliar. A hollowed-out version Rua didn't recognize.

She tugged at the high neck of her itchy sleepwear. Her skin was red from the irritation. She noticed that her hands had been cleaned as they traveled over her bodice, getting lost in the multitude of layers.

She lifted her skirt, feeling the weight of the rich fabric, and noticed a mark on her ankle. An odd shape, it was silver from age and had a swirling pattern. She wondered if it was intentional or a pretty scar.

Hurried steps rushed toward the room, and Rua dropped her skirts as though caught red-handed. But what reason should she have to hide a mark on her ankle?

"Emma, darling, you're up." Mrs. Harrington's voice was soft and new, as if the last time she'd spoken to Rua she hadn't been snarling. "Might we start by you telling me where you have been?" she asked while also directing Mara to a chair by the doorway.

"What do you mean?" Rua mumbled as she looked back at her reflection in the mirror, lost in a room that wasn't hers with only the vague feeling that she was somewhere she wasn't supposed to be.

"What do you mean, what do I mean? You disappeared two nights ago," Mrs. Harrington snapped.

Had Emma gone missing the same time Rua had appeared?

"I don't remember." It was the truth, but it wasn't good enough—for either of them.

Another servant stopped outside the room. "Dr. Bloom has arrived, Mrs. Harrington."

"I don't need a doctor," Rua insisted.

"And the sky isn't blue," Mrs. Harrington scoffed before leaving.

Rua groaned and leaned against the bed. All of this—she glanced around the decorated room, at her nightgown, at Mara the maid—it didn't belong to her. It wasn't her life. And it was this innate knowledge that left her flooded with a terrible sense of unease.

Mara spoke up from her post by the door. "The doctor will be round any moment, but tell me what happened?" She reached out her arm and pushed the door shut.

There was a gentle presence about Mara. No judgment, only genuine concern.

Rua wanted to ask her how it was possible that she'd taken the place of another woman, but she settled on, "Tell me where I am."

"Your country estate."

"But where?" Rua begged.

Mara's eyes widened with concern. "Conleth Falls, New York."

"New York," Rua repeated. She closed her eyes and tried to remember something about her life. Something that would tell her why she was here.

She forced herself to recall the women from that brief memory, the one that mentioned sisterhood. But she was already losing the image her mind had conjured; their features were nothing more than a blur. She was beginning to doubt she'd even remembered it correctly. What if she'd been seeing the women through Emma's eyes? Or if it was all a dream and none of it real?

No. She looked around. Everything here felt wrong.

But she remembered the feel of the man's arms wrapping around her waist as she stared into the water. The water that burned everyone but her. She closed her eyes. She could still feel him now. A shiver crept up her back. She couldn't even picture his face. How could she think it was real?

Rua moved to the chair beside the window and watched as a butterfly fluttered past her window.

The unfinished painting depicted a woman who had been restrained to the point of obedience. That was not who Rua felt she was, though how could she really know? She had no tangible memories of her past.

More troubling, how could Mrs. Harrington not know? Wouldn't a mother know her daughter? Unless Rua was her daughter.

No. Rua pushed the thought away. She wouldn't entertain it.

The door swung open, and through it came an unfamiliar man carrying a brown leather bag, followed by Mrs. Harrington.

"Hello, Miss Harrington. How are we feeling today?"

Rua looked at the doctor, who set his bag down on the dresser, and then back out the window. She shut her eyes.

"Badb, you must leave her be."

"And why must I do that, Nemain?" Badb *pushed past her, knocking her shoulder into their gentler sister's side.*

Nemain looked apologetically to Rua as Badb approached. Rua bristled, riddled with contempt, devastated by the loss.

"There is nothing that can come between us, sister." Badb *stretched her arms out wide, leering over the hillside.* "We are all that matters in this world. I love you. You must see that now."

After what they'd just done—after what Badb had made Rua do?
How dare she speak of love. Rua let out a sob.

"I have done this for us," Badb *said, desperate to make Rua*
believe it. She cupped Rua's cheek, blood lust swirling in the gold of
her eyes. "I will protect you, always."

Lies. Rua jerked her head away.

"Miss Harrington." The doctor cleared his throat. "I said take
these." Rua was surprised to find him standing in front of her.
"These will make you feel infinitely better," he said, holding out two
pills.

"I don't want them." She folded her hands in her lap, her mind
too fixated on the women she'd seen in her mind, the ones she'd
considered sisters.

Mrs. Harrington's nostrils flared as she pursed her lips and
glared at the doctor. "Do you see?"

He frowned, nodding in agreement. "She has suffered a great
deal of trauma. This kind of confusion is to be expected after a fall
down such a flight of stairs. I don't doubt that with a few more days
of rest, your daughter will be right as rain."

"A fall down the stairs?" Rua looked to a despairing Mrs. Harrington, wondering why she was lying to the doctor. "I didn't fall
down the stairs." Or was this something that had happened to
Emma?

"My daughter hit her head so hard she's lost all her sense."
Mrs. Harrington cut her off. "I'm beginning to think a sanitarium
is our only option."

"Perhaps she just needs some sleep, Mrs. Harrington, like the
doctor said," Mara was bold enough to interject on Rua's behalf. "I
will sit with her."

Mrs. Harrington's eyes narrowed, her lips twitching, as though
Mara had offended her by speaking.

"I'm not your daughter. I am not Emma," Rua blurted out, tired
of repeating herself. Mrs. Harrington had no authority to commit her.

"Emma!" Mrs. Harrington was seething. "You are my daughter.
On that you cannot argue."

"I'm telling you that my name is Rua." She wouldn't let them
take the one thing she knew to be true. "I'm not your daughter. I

have never met you before." Her raging frustration fueling her disorientation.

"Mrs. Harrington, this is a very delicate situation. You must do your best not to upset the girl," the doctor warned.

"I can hear you, you know," Rua snapped, with half a mind to smash the miniature vase sitting on her side table.

The doctor muttered something under his breath, rummaging through his bag.

"Emma." Mrs. Harrington's voice was a low whisper, a warning. But Rua didn't care. She didn't care if the doctor thought she was crazy. She didn't care about Emma's reputation. She was not her.

"Stop calling me Emma!" Rua shouted, standing up from her chair.

"Enough!" Mrs. Harrington shouted back. All pretense of sympathy was gone; her expression had turned indignant.

Rua noted the change in the air. It was instantaneous. There was no masking the hostility.

Mrs. Harrington and Dr. Bloom exchanged a glance, prompting a nod from a sorry-looking Mara. Mrs. Harrington gestured to someone outside in the hallway, and two male servants entered.

"What's going on?" Rua took a nervous step forward, but Dr. Bloom pushed her back down with a firm grip, his hand digging into her shoulder. Anger flared at the uninvited touch. "Get your hands off of me," she hissed, jerking herself away, but the doctor squeezed tighter.

"Hold her arms," he said to the men. "She'll need a sedative," he muttered.

"No! What are you doing?" she screamed, thrashing against their grip.

Mrs. Harrington gave a little yelp as a crack of thunder ricocheted around the room.

A flash of lightning, then more thunder. The windowpanes rattled outside, swinging open and shut, sending the curtains from their ties and the drapery ends tossing about the room. In all the commotion, the vase was knocked from the side table, shattering against the hardwood floor.

A sweet whiff of almonds filled Rua's nostrils. The familiar scent like a dagger in her chest. She struggled against the men to find the bouquet of meadowsweet lying on the floor. She hadn't noticed it in the room before.

"Hold her steady," the doctor said as he laid a medical tool kit flat on the vanity.

Terror coursed through her. Something horrible was coming. She could see it in Mrs. Harrington's sudden relief.

Rua admonished herself, wishing she'd been level-headed enough to stay silent. She'd seen the portrait of Emma with her own eyes, so why had she thought she could convince Mrs. Harrington she was anyone else? Pure thickheadedness.

And now Rua was going to be sedated because she'd been combative, but she needed Mrs. Harrington to understand that she knew better now. She wasn't going to fight her on this any longer. She had learned her lesson.

Desperate, she turned back to Mrs. Harrington, tears filling her eyes. "Please? Don't let him do this. I'm sorry. I just want to go home." Rua's voice trailed off in a whimper as she realized she didn't know where home was.

Mrs. Harrington looked down at her with horror. "You are home. My god!"

The harshness reignited Rua's panic. Like a wild animal, she kicked and screamed, anything to save herself.

"Hurry!" Mrs. Harrington cried, turning to the doctor.

Oxygen left Rua's lungs as her fear incapacitated her. She couldn't breathe. She couldn't speak. All she could do was watch as a terrifying brass syringe hovered above her.

Every muscle in her body tensed. She wanted to cry out, to tell them she could be their Emma, but it was too late.

The needle pierced her skin, taking with it her consciousness.

Two

"I am Emma Harrington. I live here. This is my house." Even as she repeated the lie, she was unconvinced. How could she expect to convince the rest of them?

Rua stood in front of the gilded mirror and smoothed out the folds of her day dress.

"If you're making a case for why you should be sent to the asylum, I'd say you've got it," a soft voice spoke from the doorway.

Rua spun around. "Mara, you scared me."

She eyed the maid, still trying to decide if she would forgive her for the part she'd played in Mrs. Harrington's sedation tactics.

"You need to be more careful," Mara said, walking over to the windows and pulling back the curtains. Rua shielded her eyes, not ready for the light. "You're lucky it was me and not your mother," she continued as she pushed out the windowpanes. The stagnant summer air forced its way in.

"I can usually hear the approach of Flossie and her imperious footsteps. You, on the other hand, are a touch more sneaky," Rua said, fidgeting with her high collar, feeling the fabric chafe against her neck.

For now, Rua would let it go. Mrs. Harrington was Mara's employer; the maid likely had little say in the matter. And more importantly, Rua needed an ally.

"You shouldn't call her Flossie, you know. She wouldn't like it if she heard," Mara said.

"Then I won't let her hear me," Rua said with a smile. The last thing she was going to do was call Florence Harrington *Mother.*

Mara shook her head and continued turning over the bedsheets. "She means well and cares only for your safety." Rua rolled her eyes, and Mara frowned. "Considering everything that's happened, I'd think her overexcitement is to be expected."

"If that's what you'd call it." Rua hardly thought having servants pin her to a chair while a doctor forcibly injected her with a syringe constituted overexcitement.

It had been six days since she'd stumbled out of the woods without her memory. And she'd spent all of them hiding away, but she could no longer endure the confines of Emma's bedroom, nor could she pretend everything was fine. She needed to understand how she'd ended up here, living another woman's life.

"I've never seen you so rattled before, Emma. I'm concerned."

Sweat slicked the back of Rua's neck. She closed her eyes, allowing her thoughts to give life to the malaise that stayed with her always. It lived in this room and clung to her skin like a balmy sheath.

She'd never get used to pretending to be Flossie's daughter, but for now, she was Emma Harrington or she was no one.

Her gaze shifted out the window, toward the woods, whose presence loomed on the periphery of the Harringtons' splendid house. That's where her answers lay, and that's where she needed to go.

"Do you remember what happened?" Mara asked.

Rua shook her head, getting the sense that there were things Mara wanted to share but that, like Rua, she was unsure.

A friendship had existed between Emma and Mara, that much was clear, but Rua's actions this past week had shifted things. Mara was cautious, likely even wary, of her friend who had crawled out of a hole in the middle of woods and demanded to be called by another name.

"None of it?" Mara pressed gently.

"No," Rua said. "I just remember waking up here in my bed."

"Nothing of the woods? Or the hellmouth?"

Rua shook her head, trying to hide her interest as she learned of the word hellmouth for the first time. The less she knew, the more

Mara might tell her. She wondered if the hellmouth was where she crawled out from or if it was the pool of cursed water.

"Perhaps that's for the best; it was a gruesome sight. Though no one else is likely to forget that anytime soon."

Rua groaned and tossed herself onto the pink chaise. She didn't know how or why any of this had happened. She was as much a victim as Emma had been, but that didn't matter. Emma's sins belonged to her now.

"Has Flossie said anything new about the asylum?" she asked Mara.

Rua would reap the benefits of whatever relationship Emma and Mara had forged. She had to be careful not to push too far, though. Mara was a member of the Harringtons' staff, so their friendship likely had limits. But so far, Mara had been a great source of comfort.

Mara gave her a sympathetic smile. "She's considering it. She's always been considering it. With your recent expulsion, and you . . ." She stopped, busying herself with Rua's bedsheets.

"Me what?" Rua asked.

"You now insisting that your name isn't Emma," Mara said.

That was damning, Rua couldn't argue with that. "But I didn't mean it. I was just confused after . . ." She hesitated.

"After what?" Mara asked, eager to understand.

Rua shook her head. "I don't know. I'm not sure what I was thinking." After being manhandled and sedated, she was done arguing with Mrs. Harrington about her name until she found out what had happened to her. From here on out, she was on her best behavior. What choice did she have? A woman with no memories. No resources. Where could she go?

"Even so, you said it, and the doctor was a witness to it. Your mother is unsettled."

Rua let out a heavy breath. All she needed to do now was convince Flossie that she was fine, that things were fine. Removing the threat of the asylum would give her time to figure things out. "Maybe I should join Flossie for tea this afternoon?" she suggested.

"She's reading on the veranda. You can join her for tea now," Mara said.

Rua grimaced, and Mara laughed.

She hadn't spoken to Flossie, or anyone besides Mara, since she'd woken up after the doctor knocked her out. Nor had she stepped foot outside her bedchamber.

Flossie had of course checked in on her, according to Mara, but she'd never lingered and she hadn't asked questions. Rua didn't mind. She was ill prepared to handle the matriarch and her authoritarian gaze, but she could endure the four pink-flowered walls of her room no longer.

She followed Mara out of her room and was blown away by the grandeur of the house.

With every click of her heels against the hard floor, she grew smaller. The vast white ceilings were at least fifteen feet high, the walls covered in embellished plaster surrounding sunflower medallions spaced every few feet. Rua counted six white pedimented doors not including her own, and between each one and the next hung magnificent pieces of art.

She paused at the top of a grand staircase. More marble, but this time swirled with dark brown and gold.

As they descended the steps, her hand slid along the thick limestone railing, which seemed more frivolous than purposeful. She did her best not to trip over her dress as her gaze traveled upward to the heavenly mural painted on the ceiling.

They continued down another marble hallway furnished with more artwork and gold benches conveniently placed in case one should need a rest as one traveled downstairs.

A pair of young women servants approached them, their eyes widening when they spotted Rua. One clutched the other's arm, whispering, as they hurried to get past.

"What was that about?" Rua asked Mara. If she didn't know better, she'd say those women were frightened of her.

"Everyone's heard about what happened," Mara said in a low voice. "The servants are all talking about it. Your mother is doing everything in her power to keep them from leaving."

"Why would they leave?" Rua asked, stopping them both.

Mara turned to her, confused. "You were covered in blood when we found you and knee-deep in cursed waters." Her eyes darted around the empty hallway, making sure they were alone. "They think you're a devil worshipper."

Rua's stomach dropped. Devil worshipper? "Does Flossie know that part?" she asked.

Mara's eyes narrowed. "Why do you think she wants to send you to the asylum?" She leaned in closer. "Are you sure you're well enough for tea? Questions like these will only provoke your mother."

"No, no, I'm well enough. I can handle it," Rua said, waving her arms in front of her as if the small movements were enough to push away her troubles.

They continued walking toward Flossie, the woman who wanted to commit her daughter to a life of internment. Tea was certainly a bad idea, but Rua reminded herself she was not her daughter. She would not suffer Emma's fate.

When they neared the end of the hall, she felt the subtle change in humidity. Mara guided her onto a limestone veranda. "Don't bring up anything unsavory," she warned.

"You're not staying?" Rua turned, but Mara was already gone.

Nerves bundled in her stomach when she saw the distinguished Flossie Harrington sitting at a little table drinking tea and reading a paper, statuesque with her high cheekbones and sleek coiffure, her expression unreadable.

A different maid waited idly by the wall.

Rua cleared her throat. Flossie's eyes lifted slowly.

"Oh my." She dropped the paper. "What a delightful surprise!"

Her reaction was so startlingly genuine that Rua almost smiled in return.

Flossie rose from her seat like a queen in her bright-yellow gown. It wasn't the cheery kind of yellow that filled a room with joy but rather the kind that would take your eyes if you stared at it too long.

"Thank the heavens you're looking so well. Perhaps a few days' rest was all you needed." A relieved Flossie turned to the servant. "Get my daughter some tea." She gestured for Rua to sit down beside her.

Rua looked at the paper Flossie was reading. The *New York Daily News*.

Flossie noticed and smirked, pointing to the stack of papers on the empty wrought-iron chair beside her. "I've been very well read since your incident." Her face wore a smile, but her words were thick with malice. "I have to make sure it hasn't reached any of the papers. To think we're finally on the brink of greatness and here you are, doing your best to undermine it."

"I'd hardly say I'm trying to undermine it," Rua answered, noticing the rapid shift in Flossie's demeanor.

Flossie leaned forward. "Then what is it you're trying to accomplish by disappearing into the woods like some demented child? Sneaking off at odd hours, befriending the locals?" she hissed. "I mean, really, Emma, have you no pride?"

Rua had not been prepared for a verbal assault of this caliber, so wicked and pointed. She hardly had time to realize she'd been struck. How long had Flossie waited to unleash on her daughter— or was this a daily occurrence?

Unruffled, Flossie smiled while the maid poured Rua's tea and then kindly asked her to bring around some more sandwiches. Rua had the worrying feeling that this was par for the course with Flossie. A beautiful snake, luring you in with its bright colors, only to attack when you'd come too close.

"But fortunately for you, there's been no mention of anything in the papers." Flossie rested her hand atop Rua's, and she stiffened. "I do not want to send you away—your absence this fall would be noticed—but make no mistake, I will do what is necessary to protect this family's interests." She squeezed Rua's hand a little tighter. Rua wanted to pull away, but she remained still. "Have I made myself clear?"

"Perfectly," Rua said, gritting her teeth, and Flossie let go.

"Excellent. Now, would you like to help me comb the rest of the papers for any mention of your name?" Flossie asked, but before Rua could answer, she gave a delighted squeal. "Oh heavens above, look at this." She shoved the paper under Rua's nose.

The clip read:

THE CENTRAL PARK HOTEL BREAKS GROUND

Longtime friends Richard Fitzgerald and Ned Harrington strike deal bringing about what's sure to be Manhattan's most prestigious hotel.

"Can you believe it, your father's name next to Richard Fitzgerald's? Oh!" She squealed again. "They've always been friends, but now people will *know* it. We've finally been extended an invitation to Mrs. Fitzgerald's ball. Now there will be no doors we can't walk through." Flossie was frenetic as she imagined her future.

Rua could barely manage a grin. She didn't know which way to look, where to turn, which side of Flossie's mouth was going to talk next.

Flossie rose from her chair, beaming. "I must excuse myself. There is much to be done. Enjoy your tea, darling." The maid hurried after her.

"Holy hell," Rua muttered when Flossie was out of earshot. She leaned back in her chair and let out a deep breath. The whiplash was severe. She wasn't sure how she was going to stay on Flossie's good side, if she even had a good side.

The matriarch wanted to climb the social ladder, and Emma's apparent devil-worshipping behavior was a threat to that ascension. A major threat. And then there was Emma's father to contend with. If he was anything like Flossie, Rua was doomed. She needed to figure out what was going on and fast.

Rua looked on through the screened-in marble archways, past the manicured lawn and toward the forest. The garden's rows and rows of colorful flowers were no match as they came to a dead stop, drawing a sharp line between splendor and unknown threats.

What had a wealthy socialite been doing in the woods? A better question: What had Rua been doing in them?

A hand touched her shoulder. Rua jumped, swallowing back the rising lump in her throat.

"Are you all right?" Mara asked, looking worried.

"Yes," Rua said, "just thinking."

"Your mother seemed to be in good form."

"Did she?" Rua plucked a strawberry from atop a pastry and took a bite, savoring the sweetness.

"We're leaving for Manhattan first thing tomorrow." Mara eyed her curiously. "She wants to join your father as soon as possible."

"Really? Tomorrow?" Rua reached for another strawberry, wondering why Flossie hadn't bothered to mention it.

"That's odd," Mara said.

"What?" Rua asked, tearing the little green leaves off the berry.

"I've never known you to eat strawberries."

Rua stiffened before quickly placing the half-bitten strawberry down on the table.

She flashed Mara a smile, reminding herself that no one suspected she wasn't the real Emma, because that would be an outlandish idea to entertain. It simply appeared that Emma was acting out of character. But Rua would have to be more careful.

Emma Harrington was on thin ice. One wrong step and they'd both fall through. Rua needed to make sure "Emma" appeared as normal as possible, and that included liking everything Emma liked.

"I wanted to see if my tastes had changed." Rua played it off with a shrug. "So, we're going to Manhattan tomorrow?"

Mara nodded. "Your mother told me not to say it to you yet, so I would appreciate it if you kept it between us?"

"Of course," Rua said, unsurprised. Flossie likely didn't want to give her the chance to disappear again. But she needed to go back to the hellmouth. She needed to see if anything could trigger her memories and save her from this gilded prison.

"She's just worried that you'd run if you knew," Mara added unnecessarily.

"Why are you so sure that I won't?" Rua asked, wishing to understand the limits of Mara and Emma's friendship.

"I think you know by now that your mother's threats are no longer just that. She's made inquiries."

Rua looked up at Mara. "And what did Flossie have to do to convince you not to quit?"

"Convince me? I don't understand." Mara shook her head, looking around her, always checking to see if someone was listening.

"The devil-worshipping rumors don't bother you?" Rua's question was a harsh whisper.

"Why would they? I know they're not true."

Rua pressed her lips together, waiting for her to elaborate.

"It doesn't matter what the others think," Mara continued. "We know better. We have the Morrígan."

The name Morrígan sparked a note of familiarity, but Rua couldn't remember where she knew it from.

This conversation confirmed two things: Emma and Mara were much closer than Rua had realized, and the two of them were heretics. No wonder Flossie was at her wits' end.

Rua sighed as she evaluated her situation. She could wait for her memories to return and risk setting off the high-strung matriarch, which, in light of this new information, seemed probable. Or she could run away and see how she did on her own with no money and no friends.

She supposed it was better to uncover her past from the comfort of the Harringtons' palatial home than to live hand to mouth on the streets. And even if she did run, the family would likely send someone after her, thinking she was Emma.

"Would you like to come inside and pick your favorite books from the library? I doubt you'll be coming back." Mara frowned. "If all goes according to Flossie's plan, you'll be engaged by the end of September."

"I can guarantee that will not be happening," Rua said, rising from her seat. The last thing on her mind was a man. "But I think I'd like a turn about the garden."

"I advise you to keep to the garden, hmm?" Mara warned, suspecting Rua's intentions. "Your mother will have people watching the windows, waiting for you to do this very thing."

Mara was right, but this might be Rua's last chance to visit the hellmouth, the probable source of all her problems.

"We're leaving tomorrow. I want to visit it once more," Rua said.

"Don't go into it again. We don't know why that happened. You were gone for almost a day."

"Em . . . I went into it?" she asked, surprised to hear that Emma had willingly ventured into the dark hole that Rua had fought so desperately to climb out of and that Mara knew about it.

"You truly don't remember?" Surprise flittered across Mara's face, as though she hadn't believed Rua the last time.

"I don't remember."

"Then that is what's for the best," Mara said.

Rua disagreed but asked, "Will you make sure Flossie doesn't find out?"

"Be quick about it. Your mother has gone in for her late-morning nap, but if she catches you . . ." Mara shook her head. "I dare not even think it."

Rua nodded; being forcibly sedated had not left her mind. Fake daughter or not, she was living in Flossie's world, and Rua needed to fall in line. At least until she remembered who she was.

She walked down the steps of the veranda into the open garden. There was a fountain with a stone lion standing up on its hind legs, water spitting out of its mouth. Once or twice, she circled it to see if anyone was watching. There were so many windows that she supposed she couldn't really know for sure.

Rua moved to the edge of the garden, walking along the border, doing her best to look aimless. Her hand floated atop the flowers while she tilted her face toward the sun. If the situation weren't so dire, she might've enjoyed it.

Finally, she reached the bushes she and all the others had trampled through as they exited the woods the other day. Taking one more look around, Rua slipped between the trees.

Her intuition was her guide as she walked through the woods. In the daylight, it wasn't so frightening, the sun's rays casting an enchanted glow on the forest floor.

As she continued, she noticed a path. It wasn't wide, but it was obvious enough, meaning someone was traveling it regularly. She followed it.

The forest hummed around her, pulling her forward, taking her where she needed to go.

She arrived at the hellmouth a few moments later. The sight before her filled her belly with a nervous rush of excitement. Cascading gently over a small cliff of rock was the waterfall that trickled into the water basin. It continued flowing down the creek, hardly noticeable because the current was so weak.

She ran toward the water, knelt before it, and scooped some into her hands. Cool to her touch, it did not hurt her the way it had hurt those men; it nourished her. She closed her eyes and splashed it onto her face.

She wondered what about the water had harmed those men. Why people called it cursed when it did nothing but invigorate her. She stared through the crystal-clear water to the smoothed-out stones on the basin floor. She put her arm partially under the water and in slow, rhythmic motions moved it backward and forward, letting it glide over her fingers.

When she was done, she rose to her feet. For the first time in days, she felt like herself. If returning to the house in a sopping-wet gown weren't a problem, she'd have dived under the surface.

Rua turned her attention to the mound of grass adjacent to the water. Blanketed in bright-green moss, it hardly looked like a threat. She walked around to the front, something in her chest tightening as she looked at the part she wanted to avoid.

The endless black hole, triangular in shape, cut into the earth and not wider than her shoulders. A stone slab lay across the top. At the center of the stone was a carved symbol that resembled inter-locked swirls. A symbol she'd seen before, on her ankle.

Slowly, she stepped toward the hole, its narrow entrance taunt-ing her, reminding her of her fear as she struggled to climb out. What lay at the bottom was as much a mystery to her as the reason she was in it. She stared at it, feeling the sharp pain of despair as her mind drifted further away.

Sweat prickled her forehead. The air was thick with laughter.

She was spinning under a canopy of trees with just enough sun-light to warm her face. Her head dipped backward, and her arms floated up. She was flying. Until she remembered the feeling of some-one's hands holding her. He was laughing, too.

They stopped.

Her hair stuck to her neck as she leaned forward, resting her hands on his shoulders and her forehead against his. "Run away with me," she whispered.

"Why?" He set her down on the grass but held tight to her, clasp-ing his hands behind her back.

"I cannot tell you," she said, pressing her chin against his chest to stare up at him.

He frowned, shaking his head. He never spoke it aloud, but it was there—the mistrust embedded into the very fibers of their existence. As long as they were who they were, they would never know peace.

"Then I cannot go," he said.

And then it grew dark. He was ripped away from her, leaving her empty and hollow.

When Mara came to find Rua for dinner, hours had passed and no one had said anything about her trip into the woods. She thought it unlikely that no one had noticed, but again, she didn't understand how this household operated. Perhaps they were used to avoiding Emma, or perhaps she often ventured into the woods, and what was one more trip before she left Conleth Falls for good?

Rua followed Mara into the dining room. The table had room enough for twenty-four, but there was only a setting for one.

"Will I be eating alone, then?" Rua asked.

"Your mother has already supped."

"Without me?" She wanted to get a feel for how things worked around here, how strained Flossie and Emma's relationship truly was.

"Well, it was her turn to host the book club, and—"

"And she didn't want me there. That's understandable, I suppose," Rua said, wondering how often Emma ate alone.

Mara smiled. "Things will turn around in time, you'll see. Once you're away from Conleth Falls, your mother will come around. There's so much to look forward to. No one needs to know what happened, and if I know Mrs. Harrington, no one will."

"Of course." Rua smiled and plopped herself into the massive dining chair, which required two footmen to push it in and out for her. The decor was dark-mahogany floors and walls. The windows were hung with rich burgundy curtains and thick tiebacks.

Dinner was plated in front of her, but she had no appetite. Her mind was on the stranger from her memories. A man she could not place, the image in her mind blurry beyond recognition. Whoever he was, he must be important enough that his memory could resurface in her otherwise unoccupied mind.

With what she assumed was the incorrect piece of silverware, Rua took a bite of her vegetables. It was the best she could do with her mind working hard to piece together her past.

Not wanting to sit alone in the dining room any longer, Rua left to find her bedchamber. Following the sound of women's laughter, she walked toward the main entrance. She wondered which room held Flossie's guests. She was near the base of the staircase when Mara intercepted her.

"Let's use the back stairs," the maid said, guiding Rua away from somewhere she might be seen.

Rua was at a loss. She wasn't even allowed around houseguests. What would Manhattan be like? She couldn't help but feel like she was trading one hell for another.

Reading her worry, Mara said, "Under normal circumstances, you wouldn't have to take the back stairs, but your mother is in rare form. One of the men your mother hired to find you has been hospitalized with his injuries, and one of the ladies has canceled her attendance tonight because of it. He's a servant in her household. Mrs. Harrington is trying to keep the damage to a minimum."

Rua swallowed back the lump in her throat, remembering the sight of the man being dragged out of the woods. "All from the water I splashed on him?" she asked quietly.

"I told you it's cursed," Mara said, keeping her voice low.

Rua shook her head in disbelief. "There has to be another explanation," she said, recalling the sizzle and the way the man had rolled around in agony, screaming about the burns on his chest. "Why didn't it do anything to me?"

"I don't know," Mara said, worried. "Perhaps it was a protective gift from the Mothers after we honored the feast day? You must be cautious going forward."

Rua wondered what feast day fell on the first of August as she and Mara entered Emma's pink bedchamber. Two maids were already waiting to dress her for bed. It was a strange feeling, letting someone else dress her.

"I've left your favorite books on the table there." Mara smiled from the doorway. "Good night."

Rua glanced at the stack of books sitting by the window. Emma was an avid reader. Rua supposed there wasn't much else to do around here in the middle of the woods. She went to examine the titles.

She lifted the first book, *The Lady's Manual of Fancy-Work*, and set it down. A book on embroidery was not something she considered entertainment. The next, a novel, looked more interesting—*The Romance of the Forest.* Perhaps she would bring it to the city.

She skimmed through the rest of the titles and picked the ones she thought she might like. Something told her she'd need the book on embroidery to impress Flossie, along with anything else that might teach her how to be a society lady. She lay back on the bed and flipped through *Godey's Lady's Book* for some tips.

It took all of thirty seconds before her eyes glazed over. Giving up, she closed the book and put her head on her pillow. She'd have enough time to learn the ways of the society women. For tonight, she would dream of nothing.

Three

No one had told him that getting into business with Americans would require so many leisurely afternoons spent at the club.

"What do you say, Donore? If I throw in my daughter to sweeten the deal, will you sell to me then?" Richard asked.

Finn leaned back in the brown leather chesterfield chair, tapping the tips of his finger against the arm. The club was crowded, full of Manhattan's sharpest and wealthiest capitalists, trading stories, making deals.

And Finn was, for lack of a better word, happy to be a part of it. But he wasn't one of them. He never would be.

"The lot downtown is spoken for," Finn said with the usual amount of politeness he reserved for Richard's questions. Though the offer of his daughter was new.

All he needed was a foot in the door, and he'd make his own way after that. And so far, Richard's partnership was opening all the right doors.

"Whatever they're paying you for State Street, I'll double it."

Richard Fitzgerald was a prick, but he was a shrewd businessman, and that's exactly why Finn had left Ireland to go into business with him.

"They're not paying me," Finn said. "It's a charitable donation for a hospital." One that would provide free health care for the city's poorest. Whatever funds he was out by donating, he would recoup tenfold with the hotel he was planning to build at Central Park South with Richard.

"Charitable donation," Richard scoffed. "Those disease-ridden criminals don't deserve it, if you ask me."

"I didn't." Finn winked and took a sip of his drink. "Is Harrington on board?"

Richard shifted in his seat, not meeting Finn's gaze. "I've given him the first two floors and the rest contingent on his performance."

"Performance?" Finn sat forward. "Christ, Richard." He shook his head. "I thought we'd chosen the subcontractor based on their expertise."

"Don't trouble yourself with the details, Donore. It's why you've brought me on board. You can focus on your charities." Richard said the last word with a heavy layer of condescension.

Finn took another sip of his drink in an attempt to curb his irritation. He hadn't quite gotten over the sting of his name not appearing in the paper next to Fitzgerald's. Harrington wasn't even signed on for the whole project and the *Daily News* had written it like it was his business deal, but this was Finn's deal.

"Back to the subject of my daughter," Richard said, "we can have this squared away before the season starts. No trouble at all. It'll do wonders for your reputation."

"My reputation?" Finn leaned back in his chair, setting his near-empty glass on the side table. "What of it?"

Richard nodded toward the copy of *Harper's Weekly*, which featured a simian-faced Irishman wielding a baton in one hand and a pint in the other.

Bollocks.

"If my reputation was in question, Richard, you wouldn't be throwing your daughter at me." And that was a fact.

Finn's reputation was pristine. He took great care to select the company he kept. Moral failings were contagious, and he could not afford to fall ill. There was strength in his name, and he planned to keep it that way.

Richard let out a laugh and rose from his seat, wagging a finger at Finn. "I'll see you this evening. A small affair at the house. You can formally meet her then."

"Fine." He would be a fool to turn down a match like this. Marrying into the Fitzgerald family would do more than open doors; it would cement his foothold in Manhattan.

Richard wandered over to the group of men sitting to their right and didn't invite Finn to join them.

Finn was above the gossip and the petty squabbles of small men, but he glanced once more at the publication on the table, feeling his blood boil. It sickened him to see the way his countrymen were portrayed and mocked. The anti-Irish sentiment ran deep and bled out.

But he would not let it hinder his goals. He was going to establish himself in this country as he had at home.

He'd already begun his search for parcels of land stateside when he'd heard about an American man looking to purchase the Lord Riverton's Manhattan property. It was pure happenstance and a brilliant stroke of luck, but he saw it for the opportunity it was.

Lord Riverton, the ornery bastard, had shared many a night nursing a sore head on Finn's London doorstep. The rancorous drunk could never get the numbers to his townhome right. But one evening, in a stupor, Riverton shared a story about how an American had offered six hundred thousand dollars for his plot of land and how he'd refused to sell it to him.

It didn't matter that Riverton had no use for the land and that it'd go to rot. Said he'd be damned if he let a bloody Patriot take it.

When Riverton sobered up, Finn brokered the deal. He bought the property off Riverton for half the price and contacted an eager Richard Fitzgerald.

And so began his life in America. The Irish were as welcome in New York as the gutter rats, but Finn, the Lord of Donore, partnered with a man like Fitzgerald, could make a place for himself among the city's elite. They pushed back, skeptical of a man who tied his nobility not to the English monarchs but to the ancient Irish kings. The laws of tanistry.

They didn't want him in their circles, but he didn't care. He was wealthy in his own right and owner of the most desirable plot of land in all of Manhattan. They'd come around quick enough, and so had their daughters.

Finn wasn't seriously considering any of them except Richard's daughter, Annette. As much as he disliked Richard's approach, his connections were a necessity.

Finn checked his watch. A quarter past two. Surely St. Brigid's Home could do with a visit. Without saying a word, he left the Union League and walked downtown.

The walk was quiet, off the beaten path, away from the bustling fanfare that Broadway offered.

He approached the unique redbrick three-storied building. Established in the 1700s, it was the only building in the neighborhood with a castle turret and a garden, Gothic inspired and quite ominous on the otherwise dainty street.

"There's great drying out," Sister Mary called from the front steps of the orphanage, shielding her face from the sun. She walked toward him, smiling. "I must thank ye again for the books. The wee ones are delighted."

Sister Mary was from County Mayo, and she, with a few others, ran an orphanage that assisted forsaken immigrant children. Like thousands of others, they arrived on South Street without a penny to their name or a hope for their future. The nuns took them from the streets, where they would have surely perished, and offered them a chance to thrive.

When Finn happened upon St. Brigid's, it was underfunded and understaffed, and he had worked to remedy both. The children, who spoke mostly Irish, were taught English, given daily lessons, and were generally well cared for.

"Not at all." He leaned on the front gate.

"Will ye stay for a cup of tea?" Sister Mary asked, but he promptly refused.

"I've only come to see how you're getting on. There's a steamship arriving at Castle Garden tomorrow. Do you have enough beds?"

"Sure, we're grand. I'll go down in the evening with Sister Eve." A loud crash echoed from indoors. "I'd better go. The wee rascals run circles around Sister Kelly when I'm out."

Finn smiled and waved her off.

He was privileged enough that he hadn't had to pass through the overrun Castle Garden like the rest of the immigrants arriving in Manhattan. Richard had arranged everything—proof of the man's hooks in this city and his clout with the politicians in Tammany Hall.

Finn checked his watch. He'd killed an hour, but he needed to get back to his hotel apartment to get ready for Richard's impromptu dinner.

Finn walked back uptown, disliking the muggy August afternoon. The sun beat down on him, and the footpath offered little reprieve. The trees, few and far between, granted no shade. Gentlemen's clothes did not suit New York's summer weather.

He quickened his pace, desperate to get out of the heat.

Courting Richard's daughter would be no issue at all. He was almost looking forward to it. He'd seen her in passing; she was a beautiful woman with all the airs and graces of someone born into this world. It was the logical next step. And it would grant him the assurances he needed to make this hotel a success.

"Good afternoon, my lord," the white-gloved doorman said as he opened the door for Finn.

"Afternoon." He continued through the lobby toward the elevator.

"Will you be needing a transport this eve?" the doorman called after him.

"Bernard, you know I prefer to walk," Finn answered.

Finn approached the elevator, standing behind an elderly man and woman. He cast a long shadow over them. Noticing the sudden darkness, they turned around, their gaze level with his chest, slowly moving up to his face.

"Afternoon," Finn said with a nod, and the couple turned back to the elevator attendant, who offered them an apologetic shrug.

"My lord," the attendant said, opening the ornamental iron gate.

The attendant entered the car first, then the elderly couple, and then it was Finn's turn. He dipped his head under the frame as he stepped inside the ornate box. The floor bounced and screeched under the weight of him.

"Lord bless us and save us," the old woman muttered.

Finn let out a sigh. "I'll take the stairs."

Promptly at five, he arrived at the Fitzgeralds' mansion on the corner of Thirty-Fourth and Fifth Avenue. Finn looked upon the impressive residence, often touted as the grandest home in Manhattan, and found it careless. What did three people need with a home that size?

"My lord, I'm so happy you could make it," Mrs. Fitzgerald greeted him at the door. "I've warned Richard about inviting guests over with such short notice, but he never listens." She glared at her husband.

"It's quite all right, Mrs. Fitzgerald. As it turns out, I was available." Finn was always available. He did not have friends, nor did he have any family. He was a solitary man, and he preferred it that way. But perhaps Richard's daughter might offer a glimmer of a different future. One where he settled down and reared a handful of children with an adoring wife.

"Donore, I'd like to introduce you to my daughter, Annette," Richard said. The young woman stepped forward, her pale-blue gown swishing at her feet.

She was half the size of him—most people were—but she greeted him with a warm smile and twinkling blue eyes.

"A pleasure to meet you," Finn said honestly.

"Likewise, my lord," she said.

"Dinner will be served shortly," Mrs. Fitzgerald said, guiding them toward the drawing room. Annette stayed by Finn's side, her movements so subtle she could almost go unnoticed.

Richard handed Finn a drink, and the four of them sat down. Finn glanced at Annette as she sat beside him and observed a rush of color flood her cheeks. He smiled, and she looked excitedly across to her mother.

The walls were covered in rich golden-yellow paper with massive paintings over top. The chairs they sat in matched the walls and the flowers on the table. He presumed it was in fashion, but it was too much for his taste.

"I passed by the Harringtons' new residence this morning on my back from the park." Richard raised his brows and shook his head. "Unsightly."

"Are these the same Harringtons that we're to go into business with?" Finn asked.

Richard nodded. "Ned and I attended Columbia together."

"Ned Harrington is a darling man," Mrs. Fitzgerald cut in. "But his wife and that daughter of theirs . . ." She shuddered. "True menaces to society."

"That's enough, Gloria," Richard said halfheartedly to his wife, and Annette giggled.

"And this was our best choice?" Finn asked, not wanting anything to undermine the legitimacy of his business.

"It's been handled. My wife is a gossip."

Gloria pushed Richard's arm and shook her head. "My husband doesn't want to admit that he made a mistake. He'd already offered Ned the job before we'd learned of what happened. He has a soft spot for his old friend, you see." She mocked her husband with a frown.

"Gloria," Richard warned.

"A mistake? What happened?" Finn was reeling. Annette looked expectantly to her mother and then her father. He didn't care what had transpired so long as the embarrassment did not reach his door.

"Nothing you need to be concerned with, Donore. The story has been buried, and the Harringtons have been warned."

Finn understood now why Ned Harrington had been contracted to do only the first two floors of the building. Richard was preparing for scandal.

"When are they returning?" Annette asked.

"Tonight? Tomorrow, perhaps?" Richard answered.

"Well, let's just hope they'll do the right thing and lock the girl up," Mrs. Fitzgerald quipped.

"Lock her up? For Christ's sake, Richard." Finn was beside himself. He couldn't imagine what the girl could have done to earn such a reputation as that.

More concerned with his wife, Richard waved him off. "Gloria, I'll remind you again to keep your feelings about their daughter to yourself. We've signed contracts. It's in the papers. You'll only drag our name through the mud along with theirs."

"Don't you think I know that already?" she snapped.

"And that goes for you too, young lady," Richard said to Annette.

"Of course, Father," she said.

"I'll be polite and entertain the foul little upstarts," Gloria said with a smile.

Richard let out a hearty laugh.

"It really makes you appreciate what you have." Gloria reached across the high table and cupped her daughter's cheek. "Our darling girl has a lovely voice and is quite skilled at the pianoforte."

Finn smiled, unsure of the appropriate response.

The butler entered the room. "Dinner is served."

"May I?" Finn offered Annette his arm.

"Thank you, my lord." She smiled. It was shy, sweet even. He smiled back.

Yes, this would be a pleasant, no-fuss courtship.

"I've heard the weather is supposed to cool down a bit over the next few days," Annette said. "I do love a crisp afternoon walk."

"I have to agree with you there, Miss Fitzgerald. I'm not accustomed to this heat," Finn said. His skin was prone to sunburn.

"The summers are uncomfortably hot," she agreed. "But I'm certain it's an improvement for you. I've heard the weather in Ireland is quite unfavorable."

Finn gritted his teeth. "I prefer it, actually."

"You haven't been downtown in the summer, daughter," Richard interrupted. "The stench would water your eyes. If the heat doesn't let up soon, it'll make its way uptown too."

Annette grimaced. "I should hope not."

"Perhaps if the poor weren't shoved in on top of each other in dilapidated hot boxes, they'd fare better?" Finn suggested.

"Not likely," Richard remarked. "And where would you have them go?"

"Your home is certainly large enough," Finn said, disliking Richard's flippant attitude.

"That's enough, boys," Gloria cut in, and Richard laughed.

Finn bristled, tilting his head to one side and then the other, hoping it might release some of his irritation.

Set for four, the dining room was luxe and well appointed. Finn found himself seated beside Annette.

"Well, isn't this lovely," Gloria said, smiling at them.

"Perhaps after dinner, I can play you something on the pianoforte?" Annette asked.

"I would enjoy that very much," Finn offered politely, though he didn't much care for the pomp and circumstance the wealthy relied upon to draw lines between them and the rest of the social classes.

Richard was nodding with a smile. "Very good, very good. Now, let's eat."

If all Finn's evenings went this smoothly, he'd be a very happy man. A union with his business partner's daughter would ensure his success. He had nothing negative to say about Annette, only that there wasn't the hint of a spark between them. But not everything needed to burn brightly to be worthwhile. Perhaps in time, if things went well, they could learn to love each other.

For Richard, this was just a feather in his cap. If things went wrong, he'd buy another building or another plot of land. But for Finn, this deal was everything.

Four

The Conleth Falls train station was as unimpressive as it was outdated, though Flossie had assured her that it was newly built—perhaps to convince herself that the Catskill region was a worthwhile place to summer.

They stood waiting in the dirt along with thirty other men and women as the massive train car rolled into place. Rua wasn't quite sure the train would make it under the wooden pavilion that served as the boarding station. The words CONLETH FALLS R. R. STATION were displayed proudly in bold black-painted letters.

She was shocked to find that Mrs. Haughty Harrington was willing to stand on the ground, letting her satin boots gather dust. They were now so far removed from the stateliness of the country estate.

Rua wasn't sorry to be leaving the property, but she was worried that she was moving away from the place that held her answers. She couldn't explain it, and perhaps it was all in her head, but since drinking the water at the hellmouth, she'd felt surer in her thoughts and choices. She only hoped that the effects might linger.

"Oh, why is the station so crowded today?" Flossie muttered. "Speak to no one, look at no one. We're almost gone."

"Why don't I just cover my face altogether, then?" Rua said, tipping her white parasol forward so that her face all but disappeared.

"Much better," Flossie answered.

At that moment, Rua realized she might be making a mistake. She'd only known Flossie a week, and already she found her unbearable. What was she thinking, moving to a new city with her? A place where she might not be allowed to leave the house at all for fear of damaging Emma's reputation?

Rua looked to Mara beside her, who offered an encouraging smile. No, this was the right choice. She could not live alone in Conleth Falls. She'd have had herself labeled a runaway and carted off to the nearest asylum the moment she was caught. Moving to Manhattan had been her only option. For now, she would have to put Conleth Falls behind her.

A few minutes later, the horns blew, and the conductor began shouting for the patrons to board.

Rua climbed up the stairs to the enormous passenger car without bothering to look back. She didn't need to. The bad feelings were climbing on board with her.

The scent of vanilla and cigars enveloped Rua as she entered the car. The thick maroon carpet cushioned her steps, and the oak paneled walls breathed warmth into the air. Tables and sofas lined the sides of the train, but Flossie and her party appeared to be the only passengers in this first-class car.

Rua took a seat by the window and opened Emma's mind-numbing book on embroidery. If Emma knew how to embroider, then Rua should too, though she wasn't sure how easy it would be to learn. Mara sat across from her, just staring out at the slow-passing landscape as the train departed.

Rua read the same sentence three or four times over without ever seeing the words. All she could think about was the growing distance between her and the hellmouth. Like she was leaving the very place that could save her.

She glanced across the train car at Flossie, who had one eye on the waiter talking to her and the other on Rua. Rua sighed, knowing she had invited the matriarch's attention.

Flossie glided over to her. "Put your book down," she said, sitting in front of Rua, folding her hands in her lap.

Rua meant to groan inwardly, but a slight squeak escaped. Flossie's nostrils flared.

"I must impress upon you the seriousness of what I'm about to say. One more misstep, one more toe out of line, and you will be dealt with accordingly."

Rua sat in silence as Mara and Flossie's lady's maid pretended not to listen.

"Your father's deal with Richard has catapulted us right to the top of all the important invite lists, and I will not have you ruin that."

Rua nodded and wondered what additional secrets of Emma's might pop up and undermine her efforts to stay on Flossie's good side. The train began to pick up speed, forcing Rua to adjust in her seat.

"Well, if you don't mind, Mother." The word stuck to the roof of Rua's mouth. "I'd really love to get back to my book." The criticisms coated in delicate dictation were wearing her patience thin.

Rua caught the warning look Mara gave her a second too late.

Flossie's face expression turned dark. "Have I not made myself clear?"

"You have," Rua said quickly.

Flossie leaned forward. "Do you see that?" She pointed out the window.

Through the fog, in the middle of the river, Rua could make out the shape of a large, ominous structure—an island connected by a road so narrow it was barely visible. As the train rolled closer to the island, Rua could see the dilapidated brick building and the massive iron fence that surrounded it. In rusted letters, she read the words BOA ISLAND SANITARIUM.

Without thinking, she moved closer to the window, hands pressed against the glass. She couldn't peel her eyes away. Fear slithered down her throat and coiled itself around her chest, squeezing tighter and tighter.

Flossie moved beside her, speaking low so the train attendants wouldn't hear. "I've already made the necessary inquiries. They're all but expecting you at this point. Give me one more reason, darling."

Rua's blood turned cold as she swallowed the lump in her throat. That building looked like it couldn't keep itself from collapsing, never mind house patients. Surely Flossie could afford better?

"Might you bring us some tea?" she heard Flossie ask. "My daughter is simply beside herself at the thought of leaving Conleth Falls."

Stunned, Rua moved back to her seat. Mara looked just as rattled as Rua felt.

For the remainder of the journey, Rua was silent. Flossie had made her point. Driven it home in the most efficient way possible. And Rua wondered if she might not have been better off if she'd just run.

By the time they arrived in Manhattan, night had fallen, but the Thirtieth Street station was bustling.

"Don't make eye contact with anyone," Flossie warned as they deboarded the train. "We don't need our luggage stolen."

The Harringtons' driver met them at the station doors, and they entered their carriage.

Rua fell in and out of sleep as they rode to the Harringtons' home. Nightmares filled with the memories of being trapped in the narrow passage of the hellmouth, coupled with the threat of the asylum, left her feeling the worse for wear.

The streetlamps cast a dull glow over the sidewalk as they arrived in front of the massive neoclassical home. As far as Rua could tell, it took up the entirety of the block.

"Good evening, Mrs. Harrington, Miss Harrington. I trust your journey back was pleasant enough," a woman with an air of authority greeted them as they walked through the door. She was tall, with square shoulders and rigid posture. Rua guessed the housekeeper was nearing Mrs. Harrington's age.

"Mrs. Smith, we have much to discuss," Mrs. Harrington said, getting straight to business, not minding the late hour.

"The vases were delivered this morning. I've unpacked them and put them in the breakfast room," Mrs. Smith said.

"What about the artwork?"

"Hung in your husband's office."

"I must have a look," Flossie said excitedly. Rua wondered if Flossie single-handedly decorated the Harrington residences. An amazing feat, if so; the country estate was curated to perfection, and Rua could already tell that this home was the same.

"Take her right upstairs. We have a full social calendar. And that girl needs all the rest she can get," Flossie said.

As Rua's eyes fully adjusted to the light inside, she couldn't help but wake up and admire everything. The entire foyer was made of marble. The floors, the walls, the staircases—everything. And yet it wasn't cold. The heat from the fire hugged her as she followed Mara and Mrs. Smith up the stairs.

When they reached the top of the second staircase, they turned right and walked down a long corridor lined with portraits of people she didn't know.

Mrs. Smith opened the door to her bedchamber. "Your personal effects have already arrived," she said before leaving and taking Mara with her.

The bed was raised on a carpeted platform and had an ornate white oak headboard, with a ceiling-height curtain resting above it. The curtain and the comforter were made of matching silk in a glistening shade of pale purple and ornamented with pearls and other embroideries.

In front of the bed stood a marble desk with white oak legs and a matching white oak chair. A chaise matching the lilac embroidery rested in the corner under a massive window. Chandelier sconces had been placed on every wall, and each one was lit with candles. All of it was one thousand times better than the pink room in Conleth Falls.

A chambermaid Rua didn't recognize entered the room to dress her for bed. While she wrapped Rua's worn gown to take it to be laundered, Rua remembered a piece of chocolate she'd left in the pocket. "Wait!" she shouted, and the woman jumped.

"Sorry," Rua whispered, and gave an awkward smile. "I left something in the pocket."

When she stepped forward to retrieve it, the maid took a panicked step backward. Rua frowned and took another step. The maid gasped, dropped the gown altogether, and fled.

"Wonderful," Rua groaned as she took the sweet treat out of the pocket of the gown. It seemed all the servants were privy to Emma's transgressions.

She left the chocolate on her side table, climbed onto her new plush bed, and slid under the sheets.

Relief washed over her as she sank into the pillow. Tomorrow was a new day and a new start. She'd put Emma's Conleth Falls mess behind her, and she'd be the picture of perfection while she worked to uncover the truth of her past.

The next morning, Rua woke before dawn. Excitement coursed through her as she gazed out the window, knowing she was in Manhattan. At least in the city, if she decided it was all too much and she needed to run, she could beg, borrow, and steal to find her way. In Conleth Falls, she'd have been left to the wolves.

A small garden sat below her window, and she decided she'd like to sit there and watch the sun rise.

She opened the armoire and slipped what she hoped was a morning dress over her head. Forgoing the eighteen layers of under-garments, she opted for a shawl to cover her shoulders on the off chance there was a chill in the air.

Rua wandered around the massive residence until she found the veranda. The house was mostly quiet, save for a few servants mulling about who either didn't see her or were ignoring her outright.

The doors were heavy and stuck with the humidity, but she managed to get out without making too much noise. There was no warm summer breeze to greet her as she descended the steps, only putrid city air.

She moseyed around the garden, admiring the fullness of the blue and purple hydrangeas. A charming white table and chairs sat tucked among the flower bushes. This was where she should plop herself down and enjoy the morning. But across from the table set, roses crawled up a wrought-iron lattice connected to a gated path-way that she assumed led to the street.

On one hand, she should stay put, but on the other, Flossie was still asleep, and how much trouble could Rua really get into on a morning walk?

Rua lifted the latch and pushed open the gate. The part of her that knew she should be more considerate of Flossie's warnings all but disappeared as she gazed upon the cobbled streets. The world was quiet, lending itself to her belief that all would be fine.

She walked a few blocks until she reached Central Park, the charming natural oasis at the top of a crowded city. Flossie had mentioned the proximity to their home only a few dozen times in the last day.

Rua wrapped her shawl around her head and walked along Fifth Avenue until she found an accessible entrance to the park. She followed the steps down to a large castle-like brick building.

With the break of daylight came a chaotic symphony of animal sounds. Squawking, bleating, growling. Perturbed, she followed the noise around to the back, where she read the words CENTRAL PARK MENAGERIE. She watched with revulsion as handlers fed and prepped the poor animals. Hippos, bears, lions, peacocks, just to name a few, all within a few strides of one another. Displaced and held captive by their small cages and narrow enclosures. The smell was rife. The situation bleak.

At the sound of a lion's roar, she decided she'd seen enough of the zoo.

She continued along the manicured path, enjoying the lush gardens against the backdrop of the violent red sky. Caught up in her reverie, she hardly noticed when she'd somehow exited the park.

Horse trolleys and couriers flooded the street. Men appeared as if out of thin air as they pushed past her, hurrying to get where they were going. They were not the sort of men Flossie would approve of. None of what she was doing was on Flossie's list of acceptable activities, a fact that both delighted and worried her. Perhaps she'd done enough exploring for one morning.

A sudden throng of people shuffled her across Fifty-Ninth Street.

Maneuvering between the men speed-walking past her was all but impossible. They were so focused on where they were going that they didn't seem to notice they were bouncing her around like a play toy.

"Move out of the way!" one man shouted at her, while another plowed his shoulder into her as he rushed past. She stumbled forward, doing all she could not to fall on the ground and be trampled. She caught herself on a lamppost and clung to it.

On the other side of the sidewalk was an abandoned-looking construction site that promised a respite from the hurried crowd around her. Rua hung on to the lamppost, waiting for a small break in the swarm, dreading walking perpendicular to the flow of traffic. Finally seeing her chance, Rua pushed through.

She was too determined to notice that she'd crossed through a barricade, but at least it was quiet.

Rua walked beside the makeshift railing, the only thing blocking her from falling into the massive pit that had been dug. She paused, amazed at the sheer size of the hole, which implied a future enormous building.

"What is it that you think you are doing?" a man shouted.

Instinctively, Rua reached for her shawl.

"I'm speaking to you," he said, his Irish accent pronounced.

Clutching her shawl tighter around her face, she regretted ever leaving the Harringtons' garden.

The man walked around to Rua's front, stopping mere inches from her, overwhelming her with his size. She could tell from his pressed morning coat and condescending tone that he was a person of means.

Her heart battered against her rib cage. Flossie was going to kill her. Her first day in the city and she'd already ruined everything.

She should make a run for it back to the house. Now was her chance. The man didn't know who she was, and she doubted he'd chase after her. But his harshness had her feet firmly planted.

"Are you mute?" he asked, not caring for the answer. "It is no matter. Prostitutes are not permitted on these premises. You must take your services elsewhere." He reached for her hand, gently placing a large coin in her palm.

As the money settled in her hand, she realized what he'd just said.

"Prostitute?" She glanced down at her gown. She'd forgone changing into the proper walking attire this morning and her arms were bare, but was her being a prostitute truly the only logical conclusion?

She craned her neck upward to glare at him, the money heavy in her hand, and her shawl fell to her shoulders.

He looked at her then—really looked at her—and his offense melted into confusion. His dark brows furrowed as he examined her face. She felt a rush of heat under the scrutiny.

He was handsome, devastatingly so.

Pushing aside the unwelcome fluttering in her stomach, she reached for his hand. She swallowed hard, stunned by her own boldness.

He gave it to her freely, no doubt curious to see what she was going to do next.

Unprepared for the way touching his skin would make her feel, her heartbeat quickened. Slowly, she turned his hand over so that his knuckles rested against her palm, the tips of her fingers brushing his wrist under the hem of his sleeve. She could have sworn she heard him suck in a harsh breath, but she couldn't look to see, couldn't meet his gaze, because her own breath was faltering.

It was far more intimate than she'd intended it to be. She had only wanted to give the money back to him the same way he had given it to her. But here she was, holding him with one hand while her other worked to relax his fist, lifting one finger at a time, tracing the length of it until it was flat against hers. She stared at it, forgetting her purpose, admiring his palm, coarse with scars. His skin was warm against hers; she couldn't breathe.

Wishing to break the spell, she looked up. But when she met his eyes, she realized that was a mistake. His gaze bored deep into hers, knocking what little air she had left from her lungs. She couldn't place the look on his face. Bewilderment, longing, irritation? They all melded into one.

She was frozen, caught in a haze of almost recognition, the answer there on the tip of her tongue but, like everything else, indefinitely irretrievable.

Recovering herself, she cleared her throat and put the coin in his hand. Severing any lingering tension, she said, "I demand an apology."

He stared at the coin a moment, a smirk tugging on his lips, then tucked it into his breast coat pocket. "An apology for what?"

"I thought as much." She had no expectations for the men in this world. They kept their women in corsets and confined to the home.

She turned her back to him and continued walking along the perimeter of the construction site, toward what she thought was the way to the Harrington house. This morning had gotten so far out of hand. She needed to get back before Flossie caught wind of it.

"Tell me, then, what other reason is there for a woman to be walking alone at this hour of the morning?" he asked, catching up to her.

"Rather than admit you're wrong, you'd pretend your mind cannot comprehend the possibility of another motive for a woman on a walk?"

"Not before the sun is up, I can't," he said.

She glanced up at the morning sky, confirming that the sun had yet to rise.

She frowned. "Well, just so you're aware, you're wrong," she said, looking sideways at him. He was a Goliath of a man with perfect proportions and a face she could almost place.

"Tell me, then, if not for work, then where is it that you were going at this hour, Miss . . . ?" He waited for her to fill in her name. She didn't.

"I'm afraid that's none of your concern. And come to think of it, I'd prefer if you stopped following me now." She needed to return and pretend this never happened. She couldn't imagine what Flossie would do if she heard about the interaction.

When he did not respond, she looked behind her, finding him yards away, arms folded across his chest. A flicker of disappointment flared in her chest, though she didn't know why. He'd done as she'd asked.

She continued walking, flexing her palm, wondering why she could still feel the touch of his hand on her skin.

Five

Finn stood speechless as the brazen woman floated away from him. He tapped the coin in his chest pocket, the heat of her touch still fresh on his skin.

So unexpected. He'd been prepared to see a weathered hag hiding behind that silky shawl but never a face covered in freckles with enchanting green eyes. And that spiraling blaze of auburn hair—she was like something out of *Grimms' Fairy Tales*. Were he not immune to such notions, he would've ceased breathing at the sight of her.

And were it a different time entirely, under different circumstances, he might've chased after her. Lord knew he wanted to. She'd ignited a spark inside him, and he hated to douse it. He wanted to remember the way it felt when her hand caressed his own, teasing him with the tips of her fingers. A rush like no other, so unexpected and physical—he wanted to explore it.

But he could smell the trouble a mile away, and he needed no distractions, no scandals. Nothing unsavory that could threaten the life he was trying to make for himself.

The woman hadn't made it past the side of the work site when Ned Harrington walked over in a panic. Finn watched as Ned reached for her arm, and she ripped it away.

Concerned for her, Finn ran over. He'd only just met Ned for the first time this morning.

"What's wrong? Are you all right?" Ned asked the woman, his voice laden with worry.

She looked at Ned, utterly bewildered, then turned to Finn as if for help.

"Is everything all right here?" Finn asked, stepping between her and Ned.

"I was only out for a walk," she groaned from behind him. "This man grabbed me."

"This man?" The blood drained from Ned's face. "Darling, perhaps it's time I get you home?"

Finn stepped aside, understanding setting in.

"Your mother must be beside herself with worry," Ned said, reaching for her, but this time she didn't move.

Ned Harrington's bloody daughter.

Finn watched as she registered the information, as though learning it for the first time, before being whisked away. It was as bad as Gloria Fitzgerald had said. Worse, even.

The laborers started to gather, and with them their murmurs. It hadn't gone unnoticed that Miss Harrington did not recognize her own father.

"Such a pity that is," the foreman said. "I knew there was truth to those rumors."

"What rumors?" Finn asked, feeling foolish for believing Richard when he said he had this handled.

"Went missing one afternoon. The Harringtons sent a search party out after the lass. Thought she was dead, they did. Reappeared in the woods the next day like nothing happened."

"And what did happen?"

The foreman, a man from home, made the sign of the cross. "Mixed up with the devil himself, she is. Lad in the search party turned up dead. Imagine, that wee girl there did it?" His head jerked toward the Harringtons. "Didn't want to be found, I suppose."

Finn's chest tightened. These rumors were more than damaging. They were career killing. He took the foreman to the side. "How do you know all of this?"

"My sister minds a family in the village there. The man she killed worked for them. He went as a favor to help the Harringtons bring the lass back."

"But how did she kill him?" He couldn't imagine that slip of a woman, feisty and all as she seemed, to be a murderer.

Finn wondered if Richard had heard about this part of the story—or were there other things he was keeping from him? But it wasn't too late; work hadn't started. Ned Harrington could still be removed from the project.

"It was the water that did it."

"The water?" Finn repeated, feeling as though he'd just been taken for a ride.

The foreman looked around and leaned in closer to Finn. "Sure, you've heard of Oweynagat?"

"In Rathcroghan?" Finn inquired about the ancient archaeological site in Roscommon, a supposed residence of the famed Irish warrior Queen Medb and the setting for many famed legends. Oweynagat was the cave located in Rathcroghan and known as Ireland's gate to hell.

The foreman nodded.

"For Christ's sake, what does that have to do with Miss Harrington?" It was nothing more than folklore designed to scare children. The bloodthirsty Morrígan goddesses who crept out of their cave dwelling in the dead of night, unleashing monsters on unsuspecting victims during Samhain, were the stuff of legend, but clearly his countrymen had brought the tales with them.

"Oweynagat's not the only cave."

"Are you taking the piss?" Finn was incredulous.

The foreman's eyes narrowed. "The hell caves are everywhere, if you know where to look for them."

"Get out of my sight." Finn waved the man away. He would not tolerate that nonsense another minute.

"The water at the cave, that's what did it, and she's responsible." The foreman pointed a finger at Miss Harrington, who was being shoved into a carriage. "Only someone touched by the devil could touch it and come out unharmed."

Whatever the real story was, that girl was going to drag the Harringtons' name through the mud and Finn's right along with it if he wasn't careful. Good businesses had been toppled for less.

"Donore, a word?" Richard approached him.

Raging, Finn turned to face the business mogul.

"I see you've met Ned's daughter."

"For fuck's sake, Richard." He shook his head. "Your wife wasn't wrong."

"Hardly ever is." Richard frowned.

"They told me what happened to Miss Harrington this summer. Apparently, the story got out before you had a chance to handle it. A man died. Did you know that?"

"Who said that?"

"The foreman," Finn said, nodding back toward the men.

"Ah." Richard waved a hand. "Nobody cares about what a few laborers have to say. You just stay away from her."

"Our paths had not crossed before this morning."

"Keep it that way."

Finn clenched his jaw and nodded.

The Fitzgeralds ran New York. They'd be able to weather a possible fallout from a Harrington scandal. It would be nothing but the topic of discussion over dinner one evening, and then it would blow over. But Finn, the foreigner, had to work that much harder to prove himself and dispel any stereotypes. He could not afford to get caught up in whatever mess the Harringtons were involved in, but he couldn't shake the feeling that perhaps he already had.

The men moved inside to their provisional office and spent the next few hours mulling over drawings and punch list items.

Richard checked his watch. "I'll see you tonight, then?"

"For what?" Finn asked, his eyes bleary from his work.

"Good one, Donore. My wife would have both of our heads if you weren't there. Save the first dance for my daughter, hmm?" Richard winked and walked off.

Finn ran his hand up and down his face, then checked his own watch. The Fitzgeralds' ball—it finally came to him. It was the last event he wanted to attend. He hated large gatherings and the fuss that went with them.

He felt unsettled. The sensation was unfamiliar and all consuming, like something trapped inside his chest was fighting to get out. Perhaps it was the aftermath of meeting Miss Harrington and understanding the very real threat she posed.

Following Richard's lead, Finn locked the office and left.

He tilted his head back to the sky and rolled his shoulders, trying to relieve the tension. It was most definitely Miss Harrington. But there was something else weighing on him. The story the foreman told. What did Oweynagat have to do with New York or Miss Harrington? It was such a bizarre claim to make.

Frustrated, Finn walked to the New York Athletic Club on Fourteenth Street. Some physical exertion would clear his mind, and he had enough time for a quick match. In the city, he was limited to the offerings of the sports club. Though he liked boxing and fencing well enough, the men here weren't a match for him. They were professional leisure seekers, not competitors.

He strode through the well-appointed lobby with its six center columns and scattered armchairs and went straight for the gymnasium.

Dressed in his shorts and headgear, a sparring partner similar in size to Finn, was there at the ready. Finn was grateful that the man looked like he could hold his own because he wasn't going to hold back. Finn didn't bother to get his sparring partner's name nor did he bother changing his clothes. All he wanted to do was rid himself of the feeling eating at him and fight.

"Look at the two bulls in the ring." A man roared with laughter as a crowd gathered around them, hanging off the ropes.

"Money's on the Mick," another said.

The pair tapped gloves, and before the other man even had the chance to blink, Finn had him flat on his back. One blow to his right cheek was all it took. The pure power in Finn's arm as his fist made contact with the man's face was strength like he'd never experienced. It pulsed through his veins, sparking and short-circuiting until there was nowhere to go but out.

Finn removed his gloves and bent down to see if the man was all right, but the referee pushed him back. He was looking at Finn like he'd done it on purpose. Everyone was.

"Is he dead?" a man in the crowd asked.

"Out cold," the referee called after checking the man's pulse.

Embarrassed, Finn dropped his gloves and rushed out of the club, avoiding the pedestrians as he made his way back to his hotel apartment. He hurried, his strides double the length of a normal man's. He squeezed his fists together a few times, trying to understand where that power had come from. He couldn't concentrate, couldn't get his thoughts together. A fight at the club should have helped him to release this energy, but as he was now, it might have made things worse.

In this moment, he was agitated and volatile. A man unfit for this world. Too large for their dainty dinner parties and the restrictions of their rigid rules. He was spiraling, momentarily losing sight of everything that mattered. He wanted to run free. Feel the wind at his back, the sun in his face. But he was here. He looked up at the buildings towering above him, trapped in a concrete cage. A cage he'd willingly entered.

A man walking the opposite way knocked into his shoulder. Between the speed of Finn's gait and the breadth of his shoulders, the poor man didn't stand a chance. He fell to the floor with a thud.

Finn tried to help him. "My apologies, sir. Are you all right?"

The man shook him off and got up on his own. "Watch where you're walking, you oaf."

Finn rushed back to his hotel, feeling out of sorts and entirely unlike himself. There wasn't time to dwell on this feeling. As he splashed cold water on his face, he reminded himself what was a stake—his future and the futures of those who depended on him. He could not build his hospital or maintain his charities if he was caught up in scandal. This was the world he lived in.

He lifted a towel to dry his face, his mind wandering to Miss Harrington, the supposed murderer. Richard had said he had it handled. Finn needed to trust that, though he wouldn't trust the man himself as far as he could throw him.

His mind had wanted to paint a different picture of Miss Harrington, one in which she would be easy to dislike, but something told him the opposite was going to occur. She was sharp as a tack and, truthfully, the most beautiful woman he'd ever seen. He almost believed his eyes were playing tricks on him. How could something so remarkable cause such trouble?

Finn stared into the mirror, not recognizing the unsettled man before him. He preferred order and precision in his life. With a deep breath, he walked to the bar cart and poured himself a spot of whiskey. He tilted the glass back, swallowing it quickly. He would be fine in a minute. It must have been the stress of the season's events picking up.

Six

Rua waited all morning for Flossie to stomp into her bedroom and declare she'd ruined everything and was being sent away.

Mr. Harrington must have tattled on her after he put her into the carriage. She wouldn't have blamed him, of course. But here she was, a whole two hours later, still watching the clock. Perhaps Mr. Harrington was waiting until Flossie had her midmorning nap to spring the news.

Rua tossed her head back on the pillow.

The man hadn't said anything at all on the short carriage ride back from the park. He was pensive as he helped her in and out of the transport. Then they'd walked indoors and simply parted ways.

The mind games of the Harringtons were not to be outmatched. Rua glanced at the clock once more. Any minute now it would happen, she was sure of it.

She braced herself as her door opened.

"Hello," Mara said with a smile. Two more maids filed in after her. "We've much to do today. The Fitzgeralds' ball is tonight."

"The Fitzgeralds' ball?" Rua sat upright. "Are you sure?"

"Quite sure. I've just spoken to your mother. She wants you to forgo breakfast and get started setting your curls."

"Did you happen to see Mr. Harrington this morning?"

"Your father, you mean?" Mara corrected. The other maids exchanged glances.

Rua rolled her eyes. "Obviously, that's who I mean."

"He had tea with your mother a short while ago. Is everything all right?"

"Yes." Apparently, everything was just fine. Relief washed over her. A confusing sort of relief but relief nonetheless. Rua disliked Flossie tremendously, but her well-being depended on her.

Rua sat in her chair as the chambermaids began their preparations. It was only then that it sank in that she was going to a ball. An event where she'd have to interact with Emma's peers and all the people that mattered to Flossie.

Her stomach bundled into a knot. She'd known these were the kinds of things she had to look forward to as Emma Harrington, but thinking about it and doing it were two very different things.

"Will there be many people in attendance?" she asked Mara.

"I assume so. It's the Fitzgeralds."

Rua nodded, accepting her fate, drowning in a sea of nausea. She wasn't even sure she knew how to dance.

"Are you sure you're all right?" Mara met her eyes in the mirror.

Rua considered her, deciding what she should and shouldn't share. She hadn't had enough time to acclimate to this world, and she needed someone thoroughly on her side.

"To be honest, I'm nervous. So nervous. I don't know if I'm up for it," Rua admitted.

She didn't understand the intricacies of the upper class and all their social graces. She hadn't had any real time to even learn anything about herself yet. What was the point of all this if Flossie was just going to send her away after tonight? She supposed she should have put this kind of thought into her excursion this morning, but regardless, it wasn't enough time.

"I know you're not fond of social engagements, but you'll be fine. Don't speak unless spoken to, and even then only the most mundane answers. Demure smiles. Little movements."

Rua groaned. "This is going to be a disaster."

The maid putting curls in her hair snickered, and Rua thought about growling at her. Saving her the trouble, Mara sent her away.

"Out," Mara ordered the maid, and took over. "If you do not engage with anyone, then they'll likely not engage with you."

Being ignored was the best Rua could hope for.

"Do you think anyone knows about what happened in Conleth Falls?"

Mara frowned, peering at her through the mirror.

Rua groaned. "I thought Mrs. Harrington wasn't going to let the story out."

"She fired the maid that spread the gossip. But, truthfully, they were all talking about it. Though I think the message was received loud and clear. No one else wants to be let go without recommendation. It will be all right." Mara smiled, doing her best to reassure her. Rua gave her a small smile back.

"You've so much hair, you know. I'll be at this for hours," she said, running the comb down the length of it.

"Can't you just stick some pins in it? I don't understand what has to take so long if it's going to be pinned up anyway."

"The curls have to set," Mara said.

"It's already curly," Rua argued, though she was just being difficult. Her curls were not tight, smooth ringlets but rather frizzy waves that tangled.

Mara opened her mouth and then closed it.

"What?" Rua asked.

"Well, I thought this was your favorite part of getting ready. You've always loved seeing the result."

Of course Emma Harrington loved having her hair set. "I'm just experiencing a little stress today."

"Yes," Mara said as she untangled a curl, "but this is the part that calms you, mostly because your mother never bothers you while it's happening."

"Well, today it's not enough," Rua snapped, and immediately regretted it.

Mara pursed her lips and raised her brows as she continued rolling Rua's hair.

Mara couldn't know she wasn't Emma. This conversation wasn't some secret ploy to trick Rua into admitting the truth of who she was; she was simply remarking on why Emma didn't want to do something she typically loved.

After a long moment, Rua sighed. "I'm sorry." She met Mara's eyes. "I'm anxious about what people are going to say. I don't want anything to upset my mother. The threat of the asylum is wearing on me."

"I understand," Mara said, "but it won't come to that. We'll make sure of it."

Rua wished she could take Mara's word for it, but she doubted Mara held any sway when it came to Flossie's decisions.

The process of dressing for a ball was tedious, lengthy, and invasive.

Forced to soak in a hot tub for far longer than she thought necessary, she was beyond irritable. If it had been a cool winter's day, perhaps she might have appreciated it, but the day was muggy and the boiling-hot water an assault on her skin.

Her fingernails were clipped, her toenails too, and perfumed lotion was rubbed on her entire person.

After that came her undergarments and the powders for her face and décolletage. She didn't recognize herself, but she was too tired to fight it.

Hours later, Rua was dressed and ready to go. She left her bedroom, catching a glimpse of her gown in the full-length mirror. She paused in momentary shock. The bright-purple silk was a sight to behold and most definitely not her color. She'd felt the awkwardness of the bustle when it was first put on, but now, seeing how it all came together with the pinched waist and the ruffled petticoat, she disliked it even more.

She spotted Flossie and Ned from the top of the staircase.

"Finally," Flossie called from the bottom of the stairs next to Ned. Both were dressed handsomely.

Rua wondered if Ned would choose this moment to tell Flossie about her morning jaunt. Had she suffered this day for nothing?

She offered a weak smile, and Mr. Harrington lifted a finger to his mouth in a shushing gesture and winked. Flossie didn't notice, because she was busy scolding a servant for offering her the wrong shawl. "It's impossible to find good help these days!"

"The carriages are waiting, my dear," Mr. Harrington said, guiding his wife out the front door. Rua followed behind them, pleasantly surprised.

As they rolled out of their front gates, a crowd was gathering on the sidewalks along Fifth Avenue.

"Oh, look!" Flossie squealed. "Look at them all, coming to gawk! I knew it was going to happen."

Flossie wasn't wrong. They were bending their necks to get a look inside the carriage.

"Why are they staring?" Rua asked.

"Should the lower classes not be allowed the privilege to look upon their betters?"

Rua thought she might like to kick Flossie in the teeth.

They'd only pulled out of their drive when they were stopped.

"Hurry up!" Flossie banged on the carriage wall behind the driver's head.

"Flossie, darling, there's nothing he can do about the traffic," Ned said, unaffected by his wife's scathing look.

"Couldn't we walk?" Rua offered. Mara had told her that all the important people lived sequestered together uptown, most not even a five-minute walk from each other.

"Do you see what I'm talking about?" Flossie looked to Ned. "Do you see now? She is going to ruin us."

"My dear, it was only a question," Ned soothed.

"It was an absurd one, which only further proves my point. She should not have been brought back to the city."

Rua stared out the window. If Flossie only knew where she was this morning.

Flossie continued talking as if Rua weren't right there, confined to the insides of the same small carriage. "We could have told everyone she was still at boarding school."

"They all know she's been expelled, darling," Ned said. "Our hands are tied. Not having her here wasn't an option."

"Is it an option now?" Flossie asked eagerly.

For god's sake. Rua sat back and tried to tune the two of them out. She needed to come up with a plan and fast.

Though Rua had never met Emma, she had been of the opinion that the other young woman was quiet and unassuming. Perhaps it was the subdued depiction of her in the portrait in Conleth Falls, coupled with Rua's own experience with Flossie's overbearing personality. Enduring a lifetime of Flossie would crush anyone's spirit. But what could she have done to be expelled from boarding school?

And was that where Mara and the Morrígan came in? Had Mara offered Emma solace in the form of worship? While Rua wasn't certain what the Morrígan was, it wasn't a leap to assume there was some sort of religious aspect involved. Others called it devil worshipping; Mara called it the Morrígan. Whatever it was, it must have influenced Emma, and maybe that was why she had been expelled. She'd crawled into a hellmouth, after all.

After forty-five minutes, their carriage was next to drop off the Harringtons in the Fitzgeralds' half-moon drive.

Flossie and Ned exited first, giving Rua ample time to view the outside of the house. It was smaller than the Harringtons', but she assumed most homes were.

Mrs. Fitzgerald welcomed them through the front doors. She looked every bit the picture of wealth in all her jewels.

Rua took a deep breath as they were shuffled away from the foyer to socialize with the others before the evening's entertainment began. She hadn't time to admire the portraits and the tapestries hanging on the walls, but she did notice the massive bouquets of summer flowers placed on every side table and open space available.

Ned took his leave of the women while Mrs. Fitzgerald guided them into the salon where the rest of the women were.

"Ladies." Mrs. Fitzgerald addressed the room, gesturing a gloved arm in their direction. "Mrs. Flossie Harrington and her daughter, Miss Emma Harrington."

All at once, two dozen eyes assessed Rua. The best she could do for herself was to force her gaze out of focus so she didn't make eye contact with anyone. She was ill prepared for such concentrated scrutiny.

"Care for some lemonade?" Mrs. Fitzgerald asked Rua.

Rua shook her head. Flossie flashed her a warning look.

"So, tell me, what has prompted your return from your country estate so soon?" Mrs. Fitzgerald grinned, wasting no time wielding her social power to sway the room's opinion. "I wasn't sure you'd make it this evening."

Rua ground her teeth together to keep from telling her that her devil-worshipping cult had disbanded early. Or that she'd already drunk the blood of a lamb and was free to leave the Catskills.

Fortunately for the Harringtons, Flossie answered first.

"Truly, it's not as soon as it seems. It's quite typical for us to return near the end of August. This was the first year that my daughter's not been away, so we thought we'd return a few days sooner than norm."

"I see." Mrs. Fitzgerald's smile never faltered.

Rua waited for her to bring up Emma's expulsion at the boarding school to make sure she was as uncomfortable as possible, but instead she asked, "Miss Harrington, have you met my daughter, Annette?"

Rua shook her head again, words still being too tricky to come by.

Annette was attractive, her fair complexion and blonde hair accentuated by a blue gown. "I wasn't sure I'd get to meet you at all after what happened," she said with a grin.

Rua's heart was in her mouth. *After what happened?* she wanted to scream. What were they referring to? The man she'd splashed poison water on at the hellmouth? Or the fact that she'd crawled out of a hole in the ground and was now living someone else's life?

"You know, it's really quite a shame they wouldn't keep you at the Devonshire Academy. My father is well connected, if you need him to step in on your behalf. We're always looking to help those less fortunate." Annette's subsequent smile cut Rua to the bone.

The air in the room was cloaked in spite as everyone waited to see how she would respond.

Rua turned to Flossie, who met her with a disapproving look.

"Now, now, darling." Mrs. Fitzgerald rested her hand on Annette's shoulder, no doubt proud to see that the apple didn't fall far. "Let's keep the conversation light. I'm sure the Harringtons don't want to discuss their personal troubles with a roomful of strangers," she said, wearing a smug grin.

Rua's throat tightened as she watched the mother-daughter pair sharpen their tongues. She didn't take kindly to being belittled, but she kept a wary eye out for Flossie, who would be quick to reprimand her if she spoke out of turn.

"I'm so looking forward to the promenade tomorrow," Flossie said, astoundingly unbothered by Mrs. Fitzgerald's remark. "I believe your husband has invited mine to share your marquee."

"Has he now? The generous man." Mrs. Fitzgerald feigned surprise as she looked around to the other women. "We might as well open it up to the public at this point." The women all snickered.

Rua watched Flossie's face, waiting to see if Mrs. Fitzgerald's sting had landed, if she had the capacity to be embarrassed, but Flossie never flinched. Instead, she focused on the woman to Mrs. Fitzgerald's right, who looked to be just as eager for her approval as Flossie was.

"Marisol, will I see you in the Fitzgeralds' marquee tomorrow?" Flossie asked.

The room fell silent. Marisol's tawny cheeks turned scarlet, and Mrs. Fitzgerald's eyes narrowed as she addressed Flossie. "No, she will not."

"Not quite so public, then," Flossie said with a triumphant smile. Rua had to hand it to her—she was well cut out for this world.

A sudden outburst of delighted squeals and giggles broke the tension.

Rua turned to see what was causing the commotion and immediately wished she hadn't.

It was the man who had scolded her at the construction site this morning, who had acted as witness to her not knowing her own father. More embarrassing than that, she had caressed his hand.

Looking at him now, so dashingly self-assured in his evening wear, she didn't know where she had gotten the nerve to touch him. To hold the heavy weight of his hand in hers. Her cheeks burned at the memory. Quickly, she turned away, ready for the ground to open up and swallow her whole.

All pretenses and decorum went out the window as mothers and daughters alike shuffled forward, bumping crinoline, all so they could be the one to catch the man's momentary attention.

Trying to be subtle and not wanting to give him the satisfaction of her looking, Rua moved away from the commotion. The man was far more attractive than she had realized. Perhaps it was the three-piece suit, or maybe the lack of a scowl. She could certainly see what the fuss was about, though she'd never admit it.

"What are you doing over here?" Mrs. Harrington growled through her teeth. "Come and let us say hello to the Lord of Donore."

Of course he was a lord.

"You want us to wait in that line?" Rua asked, pointing to the throng of women at his front. "Do you think perhaps he would autograph my gloves?"

"He is in business with your father. He will be expecting us to say hello. Now"—she gave Rua a push—"do not embarrass me, darling." Flossie had a knack for keeping a beautiful smile while snarling.

Rua doubted he'd even noticed they were in the room. How could he with this fuss?

"Don't you think it's more embarrassing to wait in line to greet him?" Rua asked. Ned might not have told Flossie about what happened this morning, but what was to stop this man from mentioning their run-in or saying *Nice to see you again*? Flossie would wonder how he could possibly know her and start her inquiry.

Flossie gave Rua another nudge. "As it turns out, I do not. Now, get over there."

As Rua reluctantly made her way to the cluster of women clamoring for the Lord of Donore's attention, Mrs. Fitzgerald announced that they were to make their way to the ballroom.

Flossie glared at Rua as they followed Mrs. Fitzgerald's instructions. "Do not do that again. The next time I tell you to do something, you do it," Flossie hissed.

Rua didn't respond; she was relieved to have avoided one possible disaster. She trailed after Flossie as they entered the ballroom, grandiose and dazzling. Her eyes danced around the room.

The well-to-do women whispered as they passed, blocking their malicious words with their embellished fans as their eyes stayed fixed on her and Flossie.

Rua had known society would be difficult, but never had she expected the upper tens to be so up front about it. They were practically spitting.

Flossie appeared indifferent, or she was just too thickheaded to notice, but Rua was incensed. She wanted to snap every last one of those little fans in half, but she reminded herself of where that would lead her—destitution.

If she wasn't Miss Emma Harrington, heiress to Ned and Flossie's vast real-estate fortune, she was no one. For now.

Rua tried to focus her attention on the crystal sconces that lined the walls and the polished floors that glowed with their reflection, but Flossie wouldn't let her. "Pick up your head. You're embarrassing me."

Indignant, Rua did as she was told. It was no small feat having to meet the eyes of the peers who would sooner show her the door. But Flossie didn't care about that. She was too busy pushing her way in.

Despite the hostile expressions the women wore, they all looked glorious. It wasn't possible to say one was more beautiful than the next.

The men were the same, in their trousers and evening coats, but far more subtle about their contempt. They would use Rua's reputation to their advantage and assume she was desperate for a man. The rumors about her didn't bother them, because she was fresh meat and they were above reproach. Collectively they ogled her like lamb on a rack, wondering who was going to get the best cut.

And still none approached her. They would wait until the women handed down their judgments.

She searched the room, moving from one unfriendly face to the next, wondering how she'd ended up here. What series of life choices doled out this form of punishment? The constant chatter was grating, the air thick with whispers and hearsay. She needed a repose.

Flossie stopped to speak to a woman who did everything to avoid acknowledging that Rua was there. Since Flossie had no objections to this rudeness, Rua slipped away to a satin-cushioned chair she spotted tucked in the corner.

Warding off the relentless glowers was tiresome. She wondered if everyone could see through her charade. If they knew she wasn't who she was pretending to be.

"Don't you even think about it." Flossie startled her, grabbing hold of her arm midsit. "How is the Lord of Donore supposed to find you all the way over here?"

"It hadn't crossed my mind," Rua said honestly.

"That much is clear," Flossie snapped as the orchestra began to play. The focus in the room shifted toward the center of the dance floor, where a few couples were dancing. "Look at what you've allowed to happen," Flossie huffed as Rua spied the Lord of Donore and Annette dancing. "You'll never measure up to Annette Fitzgerald."

Perhaps a comment like that might have bothered Emma, but Flossie would have to do better than that if she wanted to hurt Rua. They all would. Rua cared only for her continued survival, however that looked. If it meant putting on gowns and ignoring the sycophant's insults, so be it.

A flash of blue caught her eye. Rua looked upon the darling couple gliding across the dance floor, a match made by the heavens, and found she was bothered. More bothered than she had any right to be.

The man was quarrelsome and arrogant, born to be her adversary. But there was something else there, something warm and familiar, and it felt like hers.

Seven

When the dance concluded, Finn glanced around the room at all the matchmaking mothers waiting to pounce—smiling broadly, pushing their blushing young women toward him.

Three hundred of Manhattan's wealthiest individuals huddled under six glittering chandeliers, thanking their lucky stars that Gloria Fitzgerald deigned to think of them. The money spent on this event alone could feed the entirety of the city's poor for a year. He was ashamed to be a part of it.

A ruffled Ned Harrington approached him. "This corner of the room is wedged. I see why now," he said, nodding back to the cluster of women standing in what resembled a line. "Fear I may have a few daggers in my back, seeing as I've jumped the queue." He laughed.

"Is it always like this?" Finn asked, taking a sip of his brandy.

"I wouldn't know," Ned said. "We're new to these circles. I've only recently reconnected with Richard. He married into Gloria's family, and our paths had not crossed for quite some time."

"Well, he's brought you into the fold now," Finn said. However short lived it was likely to be.

"Tentatively, I'm sure. I know my daughter isn't helping things."

Finn was surprised to hear Ned acknowledge it so freely.

"I know she means well, but she's just so . . . lively." Ned knocked the liquid in his glass back and signaled for another.

Finn thought back to the way his daughter had sparred with him just this morning. *Lively* wouldn't be his first choice of words, but he chose his next ones carefully. "Seeing as we're going to be working together, I thought it prudent to inform you that I've heard some damaging rumors regarding your daughter."

Ned's red face blanched, but he nodded, understanding. "My wife kept it from the papers, but you can't keep the servants from talking."

"Is there any truth to any of it?"

"Depends on what you heard," Ned said.

Finn didn't have the stomach to tell her father that people were calling her a murdering devil worshipper.

Another servant returned with Ned's drink. "That bad?" he asked.

"Well"—Finn hesitated—"yes. That bad."

Ned closed his eyes and finished his drink in one swallow. "I don't know what happened. Emma was doing well; she was at the Devonshire Academy, in her final year. The next thing we know, she's been expelled. We brought her to the summer estate—Flossie couldn't bear to have her return to the city, of course. We thought we might wait it out while handling the news of her expulsion. All that money I spent to keep it out of the papers, and for what? Everyone knows." He shook his head but continued.

"She was unsettled at home. Acting strangely. She and my wife were always at odds. It was quite precarious. And then one afternoon she went missing." Ned's words were flowing like a ruptured dam, rapid and scattered. And he was somewhere else entirely, watching it all play out.

"We searched everywhere. A maid was with her in the garden. She could have only been gone a minute, but she vanished. Nowhere to be found."

After a long moment of silence, Finn asked, "And what happened?"

"The search party found her in the woods a day later, and nothing more was said about it, but she's different now, changed somehow. I can't quite put my finger on it."

"I heard a man died. Is that true?"

Ned looked at Finn, horror-struck with the realization that he might've said too much.

"I'll keep this between us," Finn assured him, though most of these details were already out.

"She didn't do it, but a man that went to help her died. Fell into a hot spring, and the burns were too severe. Couldn't be saved. Of course they'll blame my daughter, though."

A hot spring? Finn supposed it was plausible. And more believable than what the foreman had suggested, that it was Oweynagat, the Cave of Cats. Though Ned was right: they would blame his daughter regardless.

Finn scanned the ballroom for Miss Harrington.

Impossible to miss, she was the first woman he'd seen when he first arrived and walked into the salon. And now, through the crowded ballroom, without any effort at all, he found her. His eyes were drawn to her in the back corner, bickering with her mother.

"I feel she'll never garner the acceptance her mother so desperately seeks," Ned said.

Finn knew how difficult it could be to infiltrate society circles. He'd had a devil of a time entering London society. No one wanted anything to do with the unknown lord from Ireland. They had a dim view of the Irish there in general, but fortunately for Finn, he was a man, and he was rich. And of course, here in New York, he was an exotic lord, Irish or not. That was all it took to have the ladies of the upper ten clamoring for his attention.

"Well, perhaps a dance with me would help." Finn was offering before he realized what he was doing or why he was doing it.

"Let us find her, then." Mr. Harrington perked up. "And if you wouldn't mind, keep this morning's events between us? It'll cause unnecessary drama with my wife."

Finn nodded, understanding.

They shuffled through the throng of partygoers to the back of the room to find Miss Harrington sitting in a chair while Ned's wife chatted with another mother and daughter.

It was a true shock to the senses to see someone as stunning as Miss Harrington relegated to a chair at the back of a ballroom. Under any other circumstance, he had no doubt she'd be the center of attention, the woman everyone wanted. He almost didn't believe she was the threat they described. Almost.

Watching her stare out at the other guests with a narrowed gaze, scanning, observing, assessing as though impervious to her own indiscretions, he sensed she was more mischievous than benevolent. A harsh judgment, certainly, but he could not deny his immediate instinct.

When Mrs. Harrington spotted their approach, she beamed. Her daughter, on the other hand, looked ill. He wondered if she was worried about him bringing up what happened this morning.

"Good evening, my lord." Mrs. Harrington rushed forward, then turned back to her daughter, motioning for her to stand up. Miss Harrington peeled herself from her chair.

As she rose to her full height and rolled back her shoulders, he was caught under a brief spell, mesmerized by her movements. Poised and unaffected, with her long slender fingers, she brushed loose curls from her face. He'd never seen such beauty. A single strand stuck to the corner of her mouth. Her lips parted slightly as she used her index finger to free it, pulling gently on her bottom lip. A perfect pair of lips.

Remembering himself, he cleared his throat. "Good evening, Mrs. Harrington, Miss Harrington. A pleasure to meet you both."

Miss Harrington looked at him, relief flooding her face, presumably because he hadn't acknowledged their meeting this morning. She gave him the smallest of smiles, and he found himself happy to be the one to have solicited it.

"My lord, here is my daughter's dance card." Interrupting their moment, Mrs. Harrington shoved the small card in his face and then handed him a pen.

Irritated, Finn flipped it over, finding it empty. He looked again to Miss Harrington and back at her empty card. None of it added up.

Mrs. Harrington grabbed her husband's arm, dragging him away. "I must steal my husband momentarily. I assure you I will return him. Darling, stay with the Lord of Donore."

Mrs. Harrington's behavior was mortifyingly obvious, as Gloria Fitzgerald had mentioned it would be.

He and Miss Harrington were left standing alone. He could feel the room watching them where they stood. He loathed the attention, especially that it was negative. This was the threat Miss Harrington posed: she was a social pariah. And the longer he stood by her side, the more his own reputation was at risk, but he'd foolishly given Ned his word.

Miss Harrington glanced around her and then up at him. He did as was expected and offered her his arm, wondering if she knew how far out on the limb he was going for her.

She stared at it, looking thoroughly uninterested, then walked away.

He stood motionless as he registered the slight, and then he went after her.

Pushing through the nosy spectators, he hoped they couldn't see the embarrassed flush of his cheeks. He'd be damned if he'd let her take him down with her.

"Where are you going?" he asked, catching up to her.

She didn't answer, instead continuing her misguided march to ruin.

"Miss Harrington, if your intention is to further sully your reputation, then by all means, keep walking." He knew it was a low blow, but both of their reputations were at stake. To be seen engaging in conversation with her was precarious enough, never mind having her publicly rebuff him.

She stopped, turning slowly, as she asked, "What do you know of my reputation?"

If he were a lesser man, he would have crumpled under the weight of her ire.

"I know more than I ever cared to." And because of that, and his connection to Ned, he now felt responsible. Culpable. Her actions would have consequences that would affect them both.

Miss Harrington considered him a moment, regarding him with her bright-green eyes, and then nodded, both of them coming to a silent conclusion.

In one swift movement, he moved to her side and tucked her arm around his.

He saw her breath catch, felt his own quicken. It was a reckless sense of satisfaction, having her on his arm, as if they belonged to only each other. She was the most beautiful woman in the room, and she belonged at his side.

A paradox if there ever was one.

He pushed the wayward thoughts away. By his side was the last place he should desire her to be. He'd worked hard to establish himself and would not throw it away because he found himself attracted to the last woman he should be.

"I trust you know how to waltz." He guided them toward the dance floor, trying to remain indifferent.

"I believe so." Her voice was unsure.

He looked again to see that it was the same woman on his arm. "You believe so?"

"Well, this is the first ball I've been to. I'd hardly say I'm an expert," she said, her right hand pulling at her skirt while she scanned the ballroom, meeting one resentful glare after another.

"Wasn't that the point of finishing school?" He couldn't imagine someone of her age and wealth to have been sheltered in such a way.

The movement was subtle—he doubted she even realized she'd done it—but she shrank into him, pressing her body tighter to his, as though he might shield her from the scorn. Part of him wished he could.

"Didn't they tell you?" She raised a brow, a smirk tugging at her lips. "I was expelled."

"You seem awfully pleased with yourself," he said.

"I'm certainly not displeased." She grinned.

He felt his own mouth fighting a grin. "Why on earth would your mother hand me your dance card, then?"

"Please do not allow Flossie's request to confuse you, my lord. Nor should you look further into the meaning behind it. You're simply a handsome means to what she hopes to be a very illustrious end. I can assure you that I would prefer to be sitting in the cushioned chair you plucked me from rather than be displayed in front of a roomful of people that would sooner burn me at the stake than offer me a smile."

If not for the fact that she'd just called him handsome, he might have asked why she referred to her mother as Flossie. She was giving herself away with every word. But the more she spoke, the more he needed to know. Not because he wanted to save himself from scandal but because he'd never met anyone like her.

They lined up along the edge of the floor with the other couples.

Miss Harrington continued, not caring that people might overhear their conversation. "I don't see how not knowing a dance should have any reflection on my character. It is one of the more ridiculous rules. Damned if you do, damned if you don't."

"You need not dance to ruin your character, Miss Harrington. Merely opening your mouth should do the trick. But your mother was right about one thing: a dance with me will do wonders for your reputation."

"Awfully impressed with ourselves, aren't we?" She glanced up at him.

"No more than you," he challenged.

An airy chuckle floated from her lips. He relished her approval.

"But I am a lord, and as such, I am the most sought-after man in this ballroom. One glance around and you'll see that I'm right. Every eye is upon us."

"It's a wonder anyone else can even fit into this ballroom with the size of your head."

He swallowed a laugh, and with the change of music, he released her arm, moving his right hand to the small of her back. As his palm grazed the silk of her gown, he hesitated, noting a pull so singular in its urgency he feared that if he held her, he might never let go. Flexing his fingers, he took a quiet breath, until finally he rested his palm flat against her back.

Her body relaxed into the pressure, but at the same moment, she looked up at him, unsure. Holding her gaze, he took her other hand. Her fingers curled around his, and he pulled her closer. A warm rush filled his chest. He was muddled, reeling from the closeness. The cosmos could've separated them, and still it wouldn't be enough space to clear his mind.

"Just so we're clear." Her words were a devastating interruption to his musings. "I would prefer not to dance with you, my lord."

"Afraid it's too late for that." They began to glide. Not that he would have given her up anyway. For this moment, she was his.

"I should think a gentleman would have at least given me the choice."

"Well." He dipped his head lower, wearing a devilish grin. "I am not a gentleman."

She opened her mouth in disbelief, then closed it.

Apprehension flashed in her eyes as they began to move, her nerves making her squeeze his hand tighter. She looked up at him, vulnerable, almost pleading, though he doubted she'd ever admit it. He'd wager she'd bungle the dance before she'd ask him for help, but he would help her anyway.

He gave her an encouraging nod and began to whisper, "One, two, three, one, two, three, one, two three," until he could see she had it. She was a quick study, picking up the steps in no time.

"Would you have truly declined my invitation, given the choice?" he asked as they danced across the ballroom.

"Of course I would have declined. You're not as appealing as you think you are."

"But you do find me slightly appealing?" He cocked a brow. He couldn't stop himself.

"Why should it matter if I find you appealing, my lord?" She fluttered her lashes. "I'm sure your moral superiority would not allow you to be flattered by such a base compliment from a woman with a reputation like mine."

The guile glittering in her eyes did not betray her thoughts. A formidable opponent.

"Finally, we are in agreement, Miss Harrington. Your flattery would only wound me."

"I thought as much. A man of your stature could never stand to listen to the wicked things I might say."

He covered his shock with a cough. She offered a satisfied smile. Bloody hell. He wanted nothing more than to find the darkest corner of the ballroom so he could hear more of those wicked words tumble out of her rosy lips.

Before his mind wandered any further, he stopped himself. He needed no distractions while he was in New York. Most definitely not when they came in the form of discerning redheaded beauties on the fringes of polite society.

Finn cleared his throat in an attempt to return some normalcy to the conversation he had willingly guided off track. "Tell me what brought you to the worksite at such an early hour today?" Perhaps if he could remind himself of the devil-worshipping rumors or the man who had died trying to find her, his own good sense would kick in.

"As much as you might wish it otherwise, my lord, my choices and motivations are none of your concern," she said, as though she could see past his polite facade right to his very soul, to the part of him that wished to know everything about her.

He searched for clever words that could act as a rebuttal, but there were none.

"What's the matter?" she asked. "Surely, you cannot be done reprimanding me."

His eyes found hers once more. They were full of life and full of wonder, taking in the room around her, as though she were seeing it all for the first time.

"If you must know, I was wondering what it's like inside that head of yours," he said.

She smiled. "I daresay you wouldn't like it. Far too many thoughts and considerations for a man to keep pace."

He let out a laugh. She was exquisite. He almost didn't care that there were hundreds of eyes on them and they'd been carrying on a conversation for far longer than was appropriate. Almost.

"You should smile more," she said, wearing a thoughtful look.

As if prompted by her very words, his smile grew. Embarrassed, he looked away.

He made eye contact with Ned Harrington, who looked nervously at the two of them laughing and chatting away as if they were familiar. He and Miss Harrington were under enough scrutiny already. It was time he had a care.

"I would prefer if you would refrain from giving unsolicited advice regarding my personal appearance, Miss Harrington," he said sternly.

"Is that so?" she asked, catching his sudden change in tone. "I would prefer to stop dancing right this very minute." She pressed her body closer to his. He cursed the garments between them. "But we can't always have what we want, now, can we?" she whispered up to him. "Perhaps I'll be the first to teach you that lesson?"

"I beg your pardon," he said, swallowing hard.

A smile tugged on her lips. "Close your mouth, my lord. You might catch a fly."

He snapped his mouth shut. He couldn't think straight. He needed to get away, but this waltz was never ending, and the music would play in his head forevermore.

"Do not mistake my shock for desire," he warned her, yet he held her tighter, lying to them both.

"I hardly think I'm mistaken. Look at you." She smiled; her lips parted slightly as she tilted her head upward. A glutton for punishment, he bent to meet her, letting the warmth of her breath tickle his ear. "You can scarcely breathe."

The hair stood on the back of his neck. The music stopped. She stepped back, and he cleared his throat in an attempt to appear collected.

"There, that's done," she said over the room's customary applause.

"Let's find your parents." He ground the words out, offering his arm, wondering if she were affected at all the way he was.

The crowd parted as they walked together. Rather than adulation, they were showered with glowers and murmurs.

He glanced down at Miss Harrington, lovely and impenetrable, and was struck with a terrible sense of déjà vu. As though in another life they'd lived this exact moment, or at the very least, one just like it.

Sensing his focus, she looked up at him. In her gaze he found none of that fiery frustration he was growing accustomed to but instead warmth and a gentle curiosity. She searched his face, and a lifetime passed between them.

Somewhere along the way, her hand had slid down his forearm and was dangerously close to intertwining with his. He wasn't sure she was even aware, but he didn't have the fortitude to stop her. He allowed his desires to best him as he waited to see how it would play out. At what point he would stop her, he didn't know.

In a moment of horrifying clarity, she yanked her hand away and shoved it behind her back. "I—" she started to say, but stopped.

He said nothing as they found the Harringtons standing with the Fitzgeralds. Here he was, caught red-handed, doing the one thing he was warned not to, in the most public way possible.

Miss Harrington walked up to them without him, and he let out a deep breath.

He heard Mrs. Harrington ask Miss Harrington where he had gone to, but he slipped away before she could catch him.

He had done what Ned had asked and then some. She was far more trouble than Ned realized, and he was going to have an impossible time keeping her from the scandal sheets and off Mr. Fitzgerald's radar.

If the Harringtons ever wanted to make it in this world, they would do well to keep their daughter confined to the inside of their home. Though, deep down, he hoped they wouldn't.

Eight

Rua was glad to be rid of the Lord of Donore. At least, that's what she told herself as she entered the cloakroom.

The doors shut behind her, drowning out the collective chatter of the three hundred guests.

She needed time to collect herself and get him out of her head. She rested her hand against her stomach, trying to catch her breath. Something had come over her. An all-consuming moment of madness where she could focus on nothing else but him. In his presence, she felt a spark. A twinge of excitement in an otherwise bleak existence. More than that, she felt familiarity.

Perhaps it was too much for one day. She wasn't prepared for this, and she was acting foolish out of her desperate need to blend in.

She paused at the mirrors, looking exactly as she felt—flustered. Red cheeks, sweat in her brows, hair falling out of place. Perhaps this was the cause for the dirty looks. She leaned in closer, noticing unusual gold flecks in her green irises. She blinked a half dozen times. Did her eyes always look like this?

She thought back to the portrait of Emma hanging in Conleth Falls. Those eyes were green and subdued. Surely an artist would have picked up on a shimmering gold color, if only to bring out an ounce of life in Emma's morose face.

There were so many other things Flossie was ignoring about her daughter. What was a slightly different eye color when the rest of the body looked the same?

Rua moved past the mirrors and found a comfortable chair behind a floral three-paneled room divider. The fresh roses lifted her spirits. Despite the tall ceilings and gilded edgings, the room was intimate. A side table with a stack of books sat beside her, and a lovely painting of a woman drawing under a tree hung above. She could feel her stress beginning to leave her.

Maybe she'd stay here for the rest of the night. After all, she had danced with the self-proclaimed most important man in the room. What more could she do?

She smiled to herself. If she was lucky, that dance would catapult her right into high society's frigid arms and the Fitzgeralds' good graces. Then she could retreat to the Harringtons' library and never come out again. She was already tired of trying. Being a debutante was exhausting.

Ballroom babble and cold air filled her sanctuary.

"Can you believe he danced with her, of all people?"

"Shut the door."

The door shut, but the chill never left. Rua sat forward to listen.

"His first ball and he dances with that filthy, pagan potlicker."

Pagan potlicker? Rua mouthed the words. She recognized Annette Fitzgerald's delicate voice instantly.

"I overheard Mr. and Mrs. Harrington practically beg the man to dance with their daughter. Quite pathetic, really. And what choice did the Lord of Donore have? They're in business together."

"Exactly right," Annette said. "You heard how she disappeared this summer while attempting to sacrifice herself in some sort of satanic ritual?" There was a pause. "Yes, well, apparently, she killed the man hired to help bring her home. Her mother thought she could keep it a secret, but how dare she! Letting her evil infect us all."

They were talking about Rua, that much was clear. But killed a man? She shook her head in disbelief. She knew the man had been hurt, but killed? Because of the water?

She couldn't very well have that spreading around, but now wasn't the time to defend herself. All she could do was hope these women didn't come behind the divider and discover her eavesdropping.

"How did you learn of this? She should be turned over to the authorities," another woman said.

"Servants know everything that goes on in a household," Annette said.

"It's preposterous that she should even be let into these parties. The entire family is a disgrace. Remind me again of why your father is in business with them?" someone else chimed in, her question sounding more like an accusation.

"Unlike your father," Annette spat, "mine is a man of his word. Mr. Harrington was involved before we knew of his daughter's affliction."

"Well, at least the Lord of Donore danced with you first."

"I'm not worried. It was all out of pity and really is indicative of the kind of man the lord is. Can you imagine that he would risk his reputation to dance with someone so unfortunate?"

Rua's body shook with an indecent amount of temper. So much so that it gave her pause. She sat back, took a breath, and thought of Flossie. A well-behaved woman would never raise her voice. She would not engage. She would become a doormat.

"Let's just hope the lord knows to keep his distance going forward. My father has already warned him," Annette said.

"What does anyone really know about the Lord of Donore anyway? My aunt says he showed up in London declaring relation to an Irish king. A bit suspect, wouldn't you say?"

"No, it's not," Annette snapped. "He's wealthy and he's handsome. I wouldn't be surprised if we were married by next summer."

"Wait," someone said, followed by hushed voices and whispers. Rua feared they were about to discover her, but then there was a shuffling sound and the door opened. "Gather yourselves, ladies; I must find the lord before that heathen can do any more damage."

The sounds of the women's voices disappeared out the door. Rua considered going after them, but what would be the point? She wouldn't change their minds about Emma or the Harringtons, that much was obvious.

It must be so nice for the Lord of Donore to be above their scrutiny. She wondered what they meant about him showing up in London out of thin air. Was there something unscrupulous about everyone's favorite Irishman? Or perhaps she was just looking for excuses to explain the effect he'd had on her. Either way, something was off.

Rua stilled, hearing the door open once more. She listened as quiet footsteps approached. She braced herself, sensing that she was about to be exposed.

"Ah, Miss Harrington, I was hoping I'd find you here."

Rua said nothing as a young woman with dark-brown hair and a stunning pink ball gown smiled down at her. She didn't remember meeting her, but she could have been in the salon when Mrs. Fitzgerald first introduced her. The many faces were a blur.

"I'm sorry you had to hear all of that. My friends can be a bit boorish when they're threatened."

"I never threatened them," Rua argued.

"Certainly not directly, but it does not change that they are, in fact, threatened." The woman raised a knowing brow. "I'm Lily Stevens."

"Emma," Rua said, hating the lie.

"This might come across as a bit odd, but I am part of a women's group, a society really, and we meet every couple of weeks. I think you'd be a perfect candidate for membership."

"How do you figure?" Rua asked, mistrustful of Lily's intentions. Especially after claiming Annette and those other vipers as her friends.

Lily smiled. "It's a club for strong-minded women. Unique individuals with interests beyond the marriage mart. Not for the likes of Annette Fitzgerald," she added, as though that might sway her, and it might have if Rua weren't already suspicious of her motives.

"I appreciate your consideration, but I don't think—"

Lily cut her off. "My group does not judge women as harshly as the world does. You don't have to give me an answer now. The next meeting is in a few weeks."

Rua nodded, mustering a fake smile.

"Well, Emma, I shall leave you to your solitude," she said, smiling back at Rua. "Oh, and keep this between us, would you?" Lily winked and left the cloakroom.

What a strange invitation.

With no intention of leaving, Rua riffled through the stack of books and decided on *Godey's Lady's Book*, Vol. 80. Maybe it would teach her how to act, though that was unlikely, seeing as her mind was flat out rejecting the printed words. Every other sentence she felt herself nodding off and having to reread the section before. Eventually, Rua shut the book altogether and closed her eyes.

As the dark grew around her, so did the pull of the water. She ran faster, knowing it was the only way.

She couldn't let him see her. There was no coming back from what she'd done. What she was going to do.

Tears pooled and burned her eyes.

A tangled mess of vines took her to the ground. She lay there, wondering why the earth wouldn't just swallow her whole.

"Rua!" The voice of hope and reason called for her.

She closed her eyes tight.

There could be no more hope; there were only her sins.

Guilt fueled her resolve. She lifted herself up and kept running.

"Is this where you've been all evening? Napping!" Flossie's shrill voice cut through her slumber.

Rua's eyes flew open. "I wasn't napping." She stood up too quickly and grabbed the table for balance. "I was resting my feet."

"You've been gone for hours." Flossie glared at her.

Rua's eyes flew to the clock. It was well after midnight. "Have you been searching for me all this time?" she asked, worried that she might have sent Flossie into a tizzy.

Flossie shook her head. "Out of sight, out of mind, my dear. I thought it was best for everyone. Let's go. The carriage should be here any minute."

Rua had to admire Flossie's obstinance.

She wondered how many people had wandered into the room and seen her passed out on the chair. That should garner some goodwill among the women.

The ballroom had almost cleared out. The remaining guests were making their way out through the front doors.

She searched the crowd to see who was left, not willing to admit there was only one person she was looking for.

Ned, looking a shade of red she hadn't thought possible and smelling of drink, approached and hurried them toward the door. "I don't want to wait another minute. Our transport is here."

The Harringtons filed into the carriage, fake daughter and all.

"I think that went well, all things considered." Ned took a flask from his breast coat pocket and emptied the last remaining drops onto his tongue.

"Well? Our daughter took a nap in the cloakroom."

Rua contemplated asking Flossie if she knew who Lily Stevens was but decided against it.

"I said 'all things considered,'" Ned corrected his wife.

Rua groaned and turned her body away from the couple. She couldn't wait to be alone. The ball had not been as bad as she was expecting and yet had somehow been worse. The party guests seemed more than happy to ignore Rua's presence, a detail that would make all events going forward tolerable. Her problem, however, lay in the Fitzgerald women's extreme distaste for her.

And there was the Lord of Donore. It would probably be the last time she ever came in contact with him; Annette would make sure of that. She batted down the unwelcome swell of disappointment and ignored the sharp prick of jealousy.

"We have big plans for tomorrow," Flossie said. "We must continue to show everyone we're not to be dismissed."

"This one feels a bit snugger," Rua said as the maids fit the whalebone corset around her middle. While she adored the look of the hourglass shape, she despised wearing the garment that made it possible. Rua sucked in as the maids fastened the front busk. Slowly, she let her breath back out. There was no fear of ripping the garment. It was as if they'd dipped her in cement.

"Where is it that we're going today?"

The maids pulled the beige skirt over the slight bustle and fitted the jacket on Rua's arms. There were no ruffles on her underskirt today but a white embroidered design all along the edges that she couldn't make out because it was so faint against the cream color of the fabric. She didn't understand why she was wearing a jacket in this hot August weather.

There must have been two dozen buttons from top to bottom, constricting her further with every snap. The buttoning stopped when they reached the middle of her neck. She wanted to pull at the fabric, loosen its hold on her neck, but her movements were stilted. The final touch, a bonnet pinned to the top of her hair, covered her tight ringlets.

"Why am I being dressed like this?" Rua choked out. It was different from her other gowns.

The chambermaids giggled, and Mara dismissed them with a stern, "Leave." She turned back to Rua. "You look lovely. And your mother insisted."

Rua strained her neck backward and lifted her arms, hoping to loosen the jacket a bit.

"Here, you'll also need these." Mara handed her a pair of gloves.

"But these are leather." Rua gaped. "It must be ninety degrees outside."

"They're kidskin and essential."

"Essential to what?" They'd have to cut the gloves off her when she returned home.

Instead of answering, Mara laughed as she shuffled Rua out of the room.

"There you are, darling!" Flossie cooed from the bottom of the stairs. Ned stood beside her. "The promenading will begin shortly. We will meet the Fitzgeralds by their tent."

Rua would rather eat knives than spend the afternoon in a shared space with Annette and Mrs. Fitzgerald.

"Are we going to the park, then?" Rua asked, unsure of where the tent would be set up.

"Where else?" Flossie snapped, looking at her as if she should know better. And she should, she supposed. Emma would.

They spent more time packing into the carriage than actually traveling to the park. The upper tens appeared to enjoy wasting their time on frivolous things, because to do so was a privilege in and of itself.

Rua couldn't believe the amount of people in the park. She and the Harringtons walked along a wide path lined with elm trees and wooden benches, not one of them vacant. Families and couples were out lying in the grass, having picnics, with children running wild. Topless carriages carried well-to-do ladies while others rode bikes.

Then there was the more formal crowd, the one Flossie was rushing toward, who were strolling with their parasols and bowler hats. The promenade in Central Park was nothing more than an extravagant parade of wealth.

"Darling, come here. Come and say hello to Mr. and Mrs. Fitzgerald," Flossie said as she pushed and shuffled them through the crowd.

Rua forced down a rising wave of antipathy as she approached the couple. She wasn't in the mood to dodge insults this afternoon. Her dress was too tight, and she'd had only a scone for breakfast.

But as she glanced around the mass of wealthy men and women, she understood that things were not going to go her way. Everyone was staring at her, whispering back and forth.

She wondered what they were saying. Did they suspect she was an impostor? Had they heard about the devil worshipping? Or did they simply not like her?

"Ned, good to see you," Mr. Fitzgerald said, ushering them under his family's white marquee.

"How's the head?" Ned asked.

"Not as sore as yours, I imagine." The two men laughed and went to get drinks from the table.

"Miss Harrington, lovely to see you again," Mrs. Fitzgerald said. "Annette is around here somewhere. Probably still on the Lord of Donore's arm." She looked around and then looked back to Rua, wearing a smug grin. "Your riding habit is darling."

"My what?" Rua looked to Flossie, who was eyeballing Mrs. Fitzgerald as she spoke to a servant.

"Your riding habit." Flossie's voice dropped lower. "Do not make a fool of me."

Mara might've mentioned this when she helped dress her this morning.

"You mean for me to ride a horse, in front of these people?" Rua whispered harshly.

She wasn't sure she even knew how to ride one, and she certainly wasn't going to try to figure it out now. Imagine falling off a horse in front of everyone that mattered. No way would she risk it.

"You have two seconds to adjust your face," Flossie hissed.

Wearing her best smile, Rua whispered back, "I wish you had told me what was happening, because I would have told you that I can't ride a horse."

"Oh, please don't start. So help me, you've been riding your entire life."

"Is everything all right?" Mrs. Fitzgerald asked.

Rua didn't know what to say to change Flossie's mind beyond the obvious—that she wasn't her real daughter.

"Yes, of course," Flossie answered before turning back to Rua. "Go now, find Mara and have her take you to your horse. I want you seated promptly." Flossie shooed her away.

Rua was absolutely not going to go find Mara and her horse. What she was going to do was disappear into the crowded park and stay lost long enough to miss whatever horseback-riding event was going to happen.

She allowed herself to be carried away by the crowd of people, slipping away from the Harringtons and Fitzgeralds. A sense of relief overcame her, realizing she could leave now and never go back. The thought of never seeing Flossie's sour face was tempting.

The scent of roasted nuts and stale beer wafted around her as she made her way around the park. Vendors were haggling over the prices of everything from turkey legs to shawls. If she had some money, she could buy a bigger hat and hide her face.

A large crowd had gathered around the pond. She walked past the mass of revelers, a wide array of cultures mashed together on one tiny island, all in search of the opportunity the city promised them.

As she slipped farther into the swarm, there was a noticeable change in the clientele. Not a top hat in sight, just falling-down drunkards and brawlers. The women were dressed for the warm weather with far less layers than Flossie would deem appropriate. Rua was out of place, and it was obvious.

Not wanting to be caught somewhere she shouldn't be, she continued walking. She didn't have a destination in mind; she only wanted to put space between her and Manhattan's elite.

It was exasperating to pretend she cared for anything other than her own well-being. To cater to Flossie's pedantic whims. She sighed, staring at the Central Park woods in the distance, what remained of undeveloped Manhattan.

She found herself drawn to it. Farther and farther she went until the noise from the parkgoers vanished. The path narrowed, overgrown with brush and shaded by treetops. Tall grass and scrawny bushes guided her way. The world around her was quiet, the way it was meant to be. No blaring horns, no shouts from vendors. No people at all.

She smiled when she saw the meadowsweet, so dainty amid the rest of the undergrowth. She walked toward the sweet-smelling white flower, trying to remember when it had become her favorite.

Soon the path became nothing more than stomped-on grass, the hedges barely pushed out of the way. Dead leaves littered the ground, tangled with low bushes and rocks. She sensed she should turn back, but there was something lingering in the air. A low hum, meant only for her, drawing her forward.

Skirts trailing in the dirt, she chased the sound. The gentle vibration grew louder as she moved, guiding her in the right direction. So determined was she to reach it, she hardly noticed the fuggy air or the way her breathing faltered.

And then a branch snapped, echoing loudly around her.

She spun around, frantically looking for what she couldn't see. High and low she searched, but there was nothing. No squirrels or rabbits. No person lurking behind her. Nothing to account for the sound.

Heart pounding, she kept walking, this time slower, and with the disquieting sense she was being followed. The buzzing sound had all but vanished, permitting the full weight of her poor decision to sink in. If she let out a scream, would anyone hear her?

Slicked with sweat and unable to think, she was no longer confident she was going the right way. What was the right way to begin with?

She paused, her gaze sweeping the trees, hoping for any kind of discernible marker, one that would guide her back to the park and the people she didn't want to see. Though why should the universe offer her one? She'd foolishly followed a strange noise deep into the woods. It was one bad choice after another. Perhaps dying alone in the woods was to be her destiny, if only she'd lie down and accept it.

Hands on her hips, she bent forward, letting out an exasperated groan. But there was no relief to be found while wearing whalebone.

Struggling, she rose back to her full height, lifting her hair off the back of her neck to cool down. The heat was going to kill her before anything else got the chance.

"Enough is enough," she muttered, deciding her next move. She took a step forward and quickly changed her mind. Perhaps she had come from the other direction. She turned around, this time letting out a scream as she did so.

Before her stood a man, tall and broad shouldered, with swirls of golden-brown hair under a bowler hat.

The Lord of Donore.

She stumbled backward. He reached out and steadied her, sliding one hand behind her back and the other around her upper arm. The touch of his hands burned right through the fabric of her gown, sending an onslaught of shivers down her back. He pulled her in tighter, intoxicating her with his scent. What was it? she wondered, taking a deep breath. Sandalwood? Rosewood? Some manly concoction; it didn't matter.

Coming to her senses, she pushed out of his arms and took a much-needed step backward. "What the hell are you doing, sneaking up on me like some feral hog?" she gasped.

"I beg your pardon?" He choked on the words.

"Why were you following me?" She focused her gaze, still trying to catch her breath.

"What are you doing all the way out here?" he asked. She couldn't tell if he was concerned or annoyed, though he had no right to be either.

"It wasn't your business yesterday, and it certainly isn't your business today," she said, wondering how he'd managed to creep up on her like that.

"On the contrary, Miss Harrington." He took a step closer, his gaze lingering on her mouth before moving up to her eyes. "Everything you do is my business."

"What a deranged thing to say," she countered, trying not to let his proximity cloud her judgment.

"I'll ask you again: What are you doing out here, alone, when everyone you know is back there?" He extended a long arm and pointed in the direction she didn't know she needed to go.

She pushed past him, not intending to answer.

He waited a moment, long enough for her to get a few steps ahead, and then caught up to her. "I wanted to see for myself if you're as much of a liability as they say you are. I need to protect my business interests."

The nerve of him. She spun around on him. "I don't care how important you think you are; you are out of your depth with me."

"Is that so?" he challenged, meeting her eyes with a fierceness that drove through the center of her chest. As if he'd looked at her this way a thousand times before, but her mind offered no explanation—only a crack in the wall exposing her damaged foundation.

"Yes," she said, more breathless than she'd have liked.

There was a pull from deep within her core, tethering her to this very spot, to him. She'd felt a pang of recognition yesterday, but confronted with it again, she was sure of it. She knew him and she wasn't supposed to.

"Very well, Miss Harrington." His expression softened, as though he were looking at her for the very first time. "Allow me to start over?"

"By all means," she said, trying to clear her head, but her thoughts could not compete with the warning bells firing off. How could she feel like she knew him when she didn't know herself?

"I am in business with your father," he said.

"And?" she asked, searching the recesses of her mind for any indication that she'd ever known him. His eyes, his physique, his lovely Irish accent. Surely she wouldn't have forgotten someone like him.

"And I will not allow anything to undermine the construction of that hotel."

"So, you've appointed yourself as my keeper?" she asked, mocking.

"No. That's not what I said." He took his hat off, running a hand through his hair, looking flustered for the first time.

"Then what?" she asked. "I'm failing to see the connection between a hotel's construction and you feeling entitled to the knowledge of my whereabouts." Though she saw the connection clearly. A scandal was bad for business. She was bad for business.

"I've encountered you twice now in places you should not be. And, if I'm not mistaken, it's only your second day in the city."

"Who says I should not be here?" She wasn't sure why she was continuing to provoke him.

"If you cannot understand that there are places women simply do not go during certain hours of the day, and most assuredly not alone, then I am afraid we are at an impasse."

"I understand well enough. I simply do not agree." Rua turned away from him again and continued down the well-worn path. He followed suit.

"I do not necessarily agree either," he said, after a pause, "but as a contributing member of society, I find it in my best interest to follow the rules."

"That is because the rules were made with your best interests in mind," she said.

He glanced sideways at her. She saw the smile he was trying to hide. "Fair enough, Miss Harrington."

"If you're going to be following me around all the time, you might as well know my name. It's Rua." She smiled at him, but there was a subtle shift in his posture. It was questioning, defensive almost.

Brows furrowed, he asked, "Rua?"

The sound of it on his lips warmed her soul. Like a secret meant only for them. And then she realized what she'd said. "It's my middle name," she corrected quickly, but not quick enough. "I prefer it to Emma, though no one obliges me."

He nodded, saying nothing more.

She didn't like that she couldn't tell what he was thinking, and that he seemed to scrutinize and judge every word she said. Nor did she like the lingering curiosity he left hanging overhead, taunting her with hidden yearning and misbegotten wishes.

He hadn't intended to follow her all the way out here. Merely curious when he saw her wander off, he assumed she was going to visit the vendors or sneak an ale, but then she kept going. He couldn't believe it when she left the path and continued on into the woods. She could argue it all she liked; it wasn't safe.

But now, upon hearing her call herself Rua, he was at a loss. He was certain her first name was Emma. Perhaps it was her middle name, as she'd said, but her cagey explanation made him think otherwise. But what reason would she have to lie?

"What time is it?" she asked him.

He checked his timepiece. "Quarter to four."

"Good." She nodded, looking ruffled. "I'd better get back now."

"I will accompany you," he offered, eager to get out of the woods. There was a quiet darkness emanating from within. While he normally preferred the solitude of the outdoors, he was on edge and reluctant to travel any farther.

"I'd prefer if you didn't," she said, and walked away.

It had been too easy for him to leave the promenade and follow Rua. She was utterly magnetic, and he her polar opposite.

He'd been in the midst of a conversation with Annette and another young woman, discussing table settings for an upcoming dinner at the Randalls', when he spotted Rua arriving with her parents. Why Annette and her friend were prematurely concerned with seating arrangements was beyond him, but as he was considering a courtship with Annette, he thought it best to at least pretend to share her interests.

He watched as Rua exchanged harsh words with her mother before slipping away, wearing a satisfied grin on her face as she did so.

It was the grin that intrigued him, leaving her looking like she'd just gotten away with something. He had to see what she was up to. For business' sake, of course.

He shook his head, knowing he was lying to himself. If he wasn't careful, Ned Harrington's daughter would bring his world to a grinding halt. Annette, on the other hand, would help it flourish. She was agreeable and reserved. A woman whose life matched the one he wanted.

Rua wasn't even an option. In fact, she had gone out of her way to make sure he knew how uninterested she was. So why was he fighting his courtship with Annette?

Finn kept pace behind Rua, wanting to make sure she was returned safely. Or perhaps, despite his better judgment, he wasn't ready to part with her. He loved a woman that could hold her own, and hell if she couldn't hold hers.

"Rua," he whispered to himself once more. A name so uncommon it wasn't even a name. *Rua* was *red* in Irish. He had a hard time believing Mrs. Harrington had chosen that name for her daughter. But what other explanation was there? Was he so convinced of the rumors about her that he'd jumped to strange conclusions? Or was it something else entirely?

Her hair, her freckles, her smile—all of it so familiar. What was the explanation for that?

In the distance he could see the mall. The crowd had grown livelier as the hours wore on.

"Donore." A man from the Union Club gave him a nod. Finn nodded back, pleased.

"Where have you been?" One of the Harringtons' lady's maids hurried over to Rua. "You missed the ride."

He could see Mr. and Mrs. Harrington standing under an elm, speaking with the Fitzgeralds and their daughter, Annette.

Finn walked toward them, regretting his decision to return with Rua. She made sure to pause long enough to make it appear as though they'd returned together, side by side. Mrs. Harrington eyed them with glee while every member of the Fitzgerald family looked disgusted.

Though he wasn't fond of Mr. Fitzgerald keeping tabs on the company he kept, he understood the sentiment. Rua had already demonstrated her propensity for rule breaking twice now.

"The Lord of Donore intercepted me on my way to the stables, and I lost track of the time," Rua lied to Mrs. Harrington effortlessly.

The look on Richard's face was enough to make Finn consider contradicting Rua's version of events, but whether she was a hellion or not, he was not in the habit of calling women liars in front of their peers.

So Finn stayed quiet.

Rua gave him a subtle nod of appreciation, a small gesture that satisfied something deep within him. He ran a hand through his hair, stunned that it had taken all of twenty-four hours for him to get mixed up with the one woman he had been warned to stay away from.

Needing to salvage the situation, he did the only thing he could think of. "Miss Fitzgerald, would you care for a stroll around the lawn?"

He glanced at Rua, not to taunt her but to see if she cared. He didn't know why that mattered to him. Though he regretted looking instantly, for the scowl on her face could have leveled an army.

Oblivious to his thoughts, Annette responded, looking like the cat that got the cream. "That would be lovely, my lord." He took her arm and left Rua behind him. At least that was what he intended to do. His mind had other ideas.

He'd concluded that the rumors about her might not be far off base. She was bizarre, for one thing, but she was also headstrong, with a quick wit. A lethal combination.

"Do you promenade every day?" he asked Annette.

"Nearly. It's quite fun, isn't it?" Annette smiled.

"Quite." Finn nodded, thinking it was one of the more frivolous habits of the upper class but at least it was done out of doors.

Annette kept her eyes ahead, walking with the all the airs and graces one would expect of someone with her upbringing. She would be a welcome addition to his life, an asset of the highest degree.

Rua was a wild card. Things would be infinitely more exciting, but they would be tumultuous and unstable. He'd never know what she was thinking or what she wanted. She was a force unto herself, and it was no way to build a life.

Christ. How had he circled back to imagining a life with Rua?

Perhaps it was that in all her perceived faults, he found he was envious of her ability to simply do as she pleased. A luxury Finn would not grant himself. But in her freedom lay ruin, and he'd do well to remember that.

He stared ahead, trying to free his thoughts of her.

Everyone they passed smiled and said hello, a far cry from the scowls he'd received with Rua on his arm last night. But this was how it was supposed to be. This was what he wanted for himself. Respect. And he would earn it through the Fitzgeralds.

He'd make a point to invite Annette to his opera box later in the week. And he should send flowers. Yes, that would make clear his intentions.

Nine

The next morning Rua lay in bed going over the events of the day before. She didn't know how it had been spun into something negative. Flossie had even smiled when Rua walked back with the Lord of Donore.

But the moment the lord asked Annette Fitzgerald to promenade on the lawn, Flossie had soured.

"Do you understand the position you've put us in, once again?" Flossie had screeched on the carriage ride back. "He took Annette Fitzgerald to the lawn for all to see. And where was he seen with you? The stables! You're no better than a peasant."

"A peasant? I ran into the lord and thought walking with him would do more for my reputation than a silly horse ride," she protested.

"He obviously found you unpalatable, seeing as he whisked Annette away immediately upon return."

At that point, Rua had stopped responding, and they hadn't spoken since.

Dreading the day ahead, Rua flung off her sheets and climbed out of her bed, remembering her dream.

"You were exceptionally lethal today," Rua said, wiping the blood from her spear.

"It is never without reason." Badb paused, glancing down at the bloodied corpse beside her. "Well, almost never." She ripped her spear from the dead man's gut.

They both smiled.

"Ah, to be rid of them all, sweet sister." Badb gazed longingly over the hillside.

"All the men in the world?" Rua laughed. "I should hope not."

"It is men who have wrought chaos on these green fields," Badb scoffed. "The ill-advised tyrants, waging war over cattle while their women suffer the consequences."

On that Rua could not argue.

"But today it is one in particular that irks me so." Badb turned to face Rua, eyes shining with the power of the sun. "If you knew there was one man that could destroy all of this, what would you do?"

"Destroy what?" Rua asked.

"Us," Badb said impatiently. "The life we have made for ourselves. The life that lets us do as we please. Think of all the good we could do in this world."

Rua wondered what her sister meant by good *as they stood upon the hilltop looking down at the blood-soaked battlefield.*

"The world demands balance, and I am determined to tip it in our favor. I will not allow a man to be our ruin."

Who were these women? And was this a memory or purely fantasy? A trick of the imagination.

On her way to the washbasin, she tripped on the rug that had turned up. Annoyed, she saw that the corner of the carpet showed a crease, as though it had been lifted quite regularly. She bent down to see for herself.

Stunned, she took in the size of the symbol engraved into the floorboard hidden under the rug.

"Holy hell," Rua whispered aloud as she ran her hand across the rough wood. The strokes were frenzied, the edges haphazard, but the symbol was there, plain as day. The same as the one on her ankle and at the hellmouth.

Emma Harrington had lost her mind. *Anyone* could have found this.

Unlike the rest of her wooden floor, this inlay was uneven. Rua pressed a little harder and found it loose.

She looked over her shoulder, making sure her door was closed, then wriggled the floorboard free. The space beneath it was filled with dusty trinkets and leather-bound books.

She took out the larger first, reading the title aloud: "*Ancient and Natural Evils: A Universal Study on Witchcraft and Demonology.*"

The book was like new, the spine hardly cracked. She opened to the table of contents. It was an anthology on the occult. The red-ribboned bookmark had been left in the middle of the book. Rua turned to the page.

The *triskele* or *triskelion* is one of the oldest symbols known to mankind. The three-legged symbol has many interpretations but is most commonly understood to represent the three-in-one Holy Trinity. However, that meaning is misguided, for the spiritual symbol did not originate with the Good Lord. Rather, it is the work of the devil.

Rua rubbed anxiously at her temples, never lifting her eyes from the page. Beside the explanation was an image of the design branded on her leg.

Throughout time, the mark has been left at many sites of great and terrible atrocities, of murder and mayhem, spanning the world over. It belongs to the Irish triple goddess, the Morrígan. The three sister goddesses are evil incarnate, changing their appearance at will: mother, maiden, and crone.

In every bodily form, the Morrígan represent death and the ungodly. Natural-born deceivers, mistresses of the devil, they find their dwellings in caves under the soil, also known as hellmouths, a direct connection to the underworld. Linked and scattered across the world, hellmouths are typically found near bodies of water. The necrotic water is lethal to humans and will eat the soul from the inside out.

Rua's heart raced as she thought of the man she had splashed the water on, the one who had died.

There are those who wish to join the ranks of the Morrígan, worshipping at the feet of false gods. Those in search of eternal damnation do so through the use of the hell-mouths. On unholy feast days, when the veil is at its thinnest, the evil spirits waiting underground lure in the weak minded and devour their souls.

Lost are they to the Good Lord and the gates of Heaven closed to them forevermore.

Horrified and intrigued, Rua couldn't read the words fast enough. Her eyes flew across the page as she tried to absorb their meaning. She wondered how that worked—to co-opt an ancient symbol, then claim the origins evil. Wherever this book came from, someone was trying to guide Emma away from the Morrígan.

Rua set the heavy book down and reached for the other.

This one was much smaller, a journal, perhaps. She flipped through the pages, which were covered in handwritten symbols and words she couldn't make sense of.

As she fanned the pages, one caught her eye. In the center of the page was a circle with a star at the center of it. Dates were scribbled within each section, the entire diagram resembling a pinwheel. Her heart started to race as she read *Lúnasa—August 1*. Both the name and the date were circled multiple times. There were other dates with their respective names: *Samhain—October 31, Imbolg—February 1,* and *Bealtaine—May 1*.

She looked back at the circled date, August 1. The same day she'd come through the hellmouth.

Shutting the book, she listened for any noise outside her bedroom door. Mara would be around to dress her at any moment. But she couldn't just leave all this here.

If Flossie found these—well, she knew what would happen. Rua couldn't live comfortably in this house knowing a maid could trip over the carpet and discover everything at any moment. Or maybe they already had and that's why Emma—now Rua—was one misstep away from being sent to an asylum.

She ran to her desk and found a letter opener in the drawer. She would scrape the symbol from the wood until there was nothing left but straight edges. Anything, even a marred wood surface, was better than the triskele etched into her floor.

She scuffed and scratched, trying to blur out the ancient symbol. Her wrist ached. Wood shavings collected everywhere, and still it wasn't enough.

Muffled voices sounded outside her door.

Rua looked at the mess around her, cursing repeatedly. There wasn't time to put everything back.

"Emma, my dear, I've finally heard back from the modiste," Flossie said from outside the doorway.

Shit, Rua mouthed, frozen on the floor.

"You would think she would have realized who we were a great deal sooner. I sent her the *Daily News* article for good measure." Flossie's voice grew louder as she entered the room. "At any rate, she will see you today." There was a long pause. "Where are you?"

Rua was hidden from view on the opposite side of the platform bed. Out of time, she slipped the blanket off her bed, letting it fall over the plank of wood and the books, and flipped the carpet back in place.

"I'm right here." She stood up slowly, careful not to put her foot where the gaping hole in her floor now was.

"What were you doing down there?"

Rua's heart pounded. What answer could she give that would satisfy Mrs. Harrington?

Flossie took a step toward her. Rua dug her heels in. If she moved, she'd step in the hole and pull the rug down.

"Well?" Flossie's tone was sharp. "And what of this mess?" She gestured to the blanket.

"I—I was praying . . . on my knees."

"Praying?" Flossie eyed the space where Rua stood. "To whom?"

"God," she blurted out, hoping Flossie would believe her.

"If I might interrupt?" Mara walked in behind Flossie.

Rua fluffed her skirts out over the rug.

"Miss Harrington and I have been praying together recently. I thought it might be good for her."

"Oh, well." Flossie touched her hand to her chest, appearing delighted, "I'm glad to hear it. If you're done, perhaps you will get dressed and go to the seamstress? I'm having tea with Mrs. Fitzgerald, so I won't be able to join you, but I would like you to leave sooner rather than later."

It was the first time Flossie had asked Rua to do something rather than told her to do it.

Perhaps she should be caught praying more often.

Rua was being fitted for an entirely new wardrobe upon Flossie's discovery that their latest step up the social ladder had granted them access to the most exclusive dressmaker in the city.

"Mara, come with me. I have a list I need taken care of before you leave," Flossie said as she and Mara exited the bedroom, giving Rua a quick moment to return the books beneath the floorboard before the chambermaids came to dress her.

After what felt like an eternity, she was ready and alone once more. She peeked into the hallway and called Mara's name.

No answer. She hurried back into her room, knowing she only had a few minutes.

She lifted the floorboard to remove the books, then returned it and covered everything with the carpet. Rising to her feet, she tucked the incriminating books among her skirts and exited her room.

Rua waddled to the library with the larger of the books shoved between her thighs and the smaller one tucked under her arm, pausing to look at the paintings anytime a servant passed by. They already thought she was mad, so they didn't pay too much attention to her gushing over the portraits of late Harrington family members.

The tome detailing the Morrígan's wicked immorality was so heavy that by the time she reached the library, she was sweating. She shut the door behind her, and the books fell to the floor.

Before lifting the large text, she flipped through the opening pages and read the note from the author: "Be gone, ye terrible things."

She shut the anthology, then took it and the little journal and shoved them on the bottom shelf behind the encyclopedias gathering dust. Nobody needed to find these. Ever. And at least, if they were out of the bedroom, she could deny she knew anything about them. Though she doubted anyone would believe her.

Rua would have preferred to walk to the dress shop, but Flossie said only servants and beggars would be caught dead walking all the way downtown and promptly put Rua and Mara into the Harringtons' carriage.

Distracted by the passing buildings, Rua wasn't aware of the words coming out of her mouth until she'd already spoken them. "I wonder if we'll bump into the Lord of Donore."

Mara snorted as she glanced out the carriage window. "And why would we do that?"

"It's an exercise of his, monitoring my whereabouts. I find it quite frustrating." And she did find it frustrating, but also a small part of her didn't. He was meddling in her business far more than he ought to be, and she wanted to know why.

"I'm sure you do." Mara smiled and pointed to the corner of Twenty-Third Street. "The shop's just down that street."

The carriage rolled to a stop on Broadway between Twenty-Third and Twenty-Second Streets, pulling in behind a number of other carriages dropping off their well-to-do women.

Flossie thought this would be an excellent opportunity for Rua to be seen and not heard. Nothing like a stroll down Broadway's Ladies' Mile to show off one's personal wealth.

Rua was just hoping that the somewhat fresh air would clear her mind and help her think.

The street was lined with elegant storefronts, Italianate banks and brownstones, and dozens of restaurants.

Street vendors were selling papers, vegetables, flowers, and anything else you could think of. They shouted and haggled over prices while the more refined-looking customers window-shopped. Broadway was every bit the bustling oasis.

She descended the carriage, not realizing people would be watching her. Women passing by craned their necks, while others blatantly stopped. They pointed and whispered, making her feel like it might have been a mistake to leave the house.

"Emma, is that you? Emma Harrington?" Rua was only out of the carriage when a young woman wearing a bonnet over her blonde hair waved at them.

Rua looked at the stranger but was too busy adjusting her gloves to realize she was speaking to her.

Mara nudged her.

"Emma?"

"Oh, yes, hello," Rua answered with a hesitant smile.

"Goodness me, you look so . . . healthy. I almost didn't recognize you." The young woman's words were sweet but laced with poison.

Rua pursed her lips, not appreciating the jab. "Tell me, how is it that you think I looked before?" She glanced in the window of a department store displaying a wide array of hats, thinking she'd like to find one to hide her face behind.

The woman's cheeks reddened.

"Forward as ever, I see! And too good to acknowledge me now that she's mingling with the Fitzgeralds."

Little did this woman know, Rua hadn't a clue who she was. Emma might've recognized her, but Rua didn't, and it was a situation that was likely to keep happening.

Rua took a noncommittal step toward her, and the woman stepped back, bringing her hand up to her neck.

"I must say, the sight of you at the Fitzgeralds' party caught me off guard. I almost alerted the hostess, thinking you came uninvited. Silly me." The woman giggled, then offered a smile so chock full of condescension it spilled over onto the sidewalk. "Oh, but it is so delightful for you and your family to finally be moving up after all these years, even after your little stunt this summer."

The blood in Rua's veins was slowly beginning to boil. Either this was one of the nasty women who had been in the dressing room last night or this was what everyone in the city thought of the Harringtons. She was inclined to think it was both.

"I'm sorry, but could you remind me of your name?" Rua asked.

"My name?" The woman's pretty face scrunched in confusion. "We were the only two New Yorkers boarding at Devonshire before your expulsion."

"Oh, please don't take offense," Rua said. "It's exactly as you said: I've been meeting so many new and important people that it's hard to keep track of the ones who don't mean as much."

She heard Mara curse under her breath at the same moment the woman's jaw hit the floor. Her face recovered almost instantly, her smile pristine. "Send your family my best."

"If I could remember your name, I would," Rua said, and the woman stomped past them.

"Oh, what have you done? Your mother is going to flay you. Not even a wardrobe from Madame Malvina will make up for this. Do you know who that was?"

"No, but I thought Flossie was going to make sure no one was going to find out about what happened this summer," Rua said to Mara, pulling her under a storefront's green canopy, away from the busy shoppers.

"She stopped it from being printed in all the papers."

"But Annette and all of her friends know," Rua groaned, looking at everyone that passed them by, wondering if they'd heard about what happened this summer too.

"The upper class doesn't welcome new money. They're looking for reasons to cast your family out. It's not going to go away, especially not with that man dying."

Rua grimaced, not having realized Mara knew about that, and they resumed walking. This time, Rua kept their arms linked. "How can that be put on me? I overheard Annette tell all her friends about it at the ball."

"Well, it was you," Mara said, keeping her voice low, "but it wasn't your fault. The water should have scalded you the moment you touched it."

They walked north to Twenty-Third Street, keeping pace with the carriages, which were stuck in a long line of traffic. *This is why walking is better*, Rua thought. She winced, watching people weave between the transports trying to cross the road. The scene was chaotic, but Mara seemed unfazed by it. Standard fare in Manhattan.

Rua thought back to the words she'd read in the anthology. The water was lethal to human flesh. She glanced down at her hands. Did that mean she wasn't human? She pushed the thought away, embarrassed for thinking it. No, it had to be something else.

"It was your protection," Mara assured her. "The Morrígan blessed you as thanks for our devotion. You crawled into the hellmouth and returned stronger for it. I'm sure the water wouldn't have burned me either had I touched it."

Rua detected a touch of jealousy in her voice.

"Why didn't you crawl into it, then?" Rua asked.

"She didn't ask me to," Mara said.

"Who didn't ask?" Rua stopped again, bringing Mara to a halt with her. She was alarmed to hear there was a third party involved.

"The Morrígan. I thought we went over this?" Mara's brows furrowed. "Lúnasa was your idea. You said you were ready."

"Right, of course," Rua said, remembering the word she had read in the journal and the date, August 1. "Can I confess something to you?" She knew she could trust whatever relationship Mara had with Emma. It seemed they were friends. At the very least, they were coconspirators, and neither one of them was going to implicate the other in whatever this was.

"Anything." Mara nodded.

Rua looked around her to make sure no one was listening. Noise from the street was overpowering, and as far as she could tell, no one was trying to eavesdrop, though the dirty looks were bountiful.

"I don't remember anything." She was taking a leap by giving this information to Mara.

"Yes, you told me you didn't remember crawling out of the hellmouth," Mara said, looking confused.

"I know, but the truth is, I don't remember anything at all. It's like the power of the hellmouth wiped my mind clean. Perhaps the enormity of what I witnessed was too great for my feeble mind." Rua was laying it on thick, but Mara was eating it up. Surmising that Mara revered the Morrígan to the point of being fanatical, and that she expected, or at least hoped, that Emma would share in her reverie, Rua guessed this was exactly the kind of thing Mara might like to hear.

"Perhaps it will come back to you in time?" Mara squeezed Rua's arm excitedly, proving her correct. "I cannot wait to learn what you saw. It must have been truly wondrous. When the timing is right, all will come back. I'm sure of it."

Rua watched Mara's face as she pieced it all together. "That's why you fought with your mother and the doctor? Why you argued that your name wasn't Emma?"

Rua nodded.

"I have wondered about your behavior," Mara said, searching Rua's face for the truth. "Do you still believe that to be true? That you are not Emma?"

"Of course not!" Rua lied. "Coming out of the hellmouth was disorienting." That part was true.

"And for good reason," Mara agreed. "You met the Mother. You must have. What else could have altered your memories like this? We'll sort this out." She patted Rua's hand.

"Thank you, Mara." Rua smiled.

"We'd better get a move on. You have an appointment."

Rua turned her attention back to the city and the task Flossie had sent them on. As they turned down Twenty-Third, Rua noticed a line of women forming in front of a shop.

Mdme. Malvina Webster was painted in small gold block letters on the front door. There was no need to advertise. According to Flossie, Malvina Webster's luxurious boutique was only for the most dignified and worthwhile women. Her clients were the wives of politicians and foreign dignitaries. If you weren't dressed by Malvina, you needn't bother showing up to the ball.

Flossie had somehow managed to gloss over the fact that she didn't own a single piece made by Madame Malvina.

The line was so long outside the shop's front door, it blocked the view of the elegantly fitted mannequins in the flower-painted windows. Rua's stomach gave a nervous flutter. She hadn't been expecting so many people.

"Did your mother tell you what I had to do to get this appointment? It was mortifying." Mara grimaced. "She sent me down here with newspaper clippings to prove that your father was in business with Mr. Fitzgerald."

Rua groaned as the door swung open. "Miss Harrington! Madame Malvina's been expecting you," said a smiling young woman.

The ladies tattled to their mothers as Rua jumped the queue.

"Please, come in." The woman ushered her and Mara inside. The shop was filled with women and girls, each one attended to by her own personal seamstress. "This way."

Rua followed the woman to the back of the shop into a private room.

Malvina Webster rose from her seat behind her desk. She was every bit as sophisticated as Rua had imagined the owner of such an establishment would be. Her sky-blue gown, while undeniably functional, warmed her dark-brown skin in such a way that even the most handsome of evening gowns could not compete.

"Good morning, Miss Harrington." She smiled and guided Rua to the mirror while Mara waited by the door.

"Morning," Rua said, still admiring her.

Malvina appraised Rua while her assistant took her measurements.

"This dress was not made for you," Malvina said after they were finished.

"What do you mean?" Rua asked. How could she possibly know? How could she see the difference? She and Emma Harrington were exact replicas of each other. Even Flossie couldn't tell.

"The fit, the color, all of it—wrong. They do not suit you, Miss Harrington."

Rua met Mara's worried eyes in the reflection for a fleeting moment before she looked away. Rua shifted uncomfortably. Suddenly the waist was too tight, the neckline too high, the air too thick. She felt wrong. Suffocated.

"You will be outfitted with a new wardrobe entirely."

The number of gowns she would need—morning dresses, walking dresses, tea dresses, evening gowns. And the cost. Would she be around long enough to wear them all?

"Yes, it will be quite extensive," Madame Malvina said, knowing what Rua was calculating. "Miss Harrington, from sunup to sundown, my shop is full of women and their maids. You can imagine the gossip one overhears under such conditions."

Rua grimaced. Malvina grinned.

"There has been only one name discussed in my shop this week. Can you guess whose name that might be?"

"Mine," Rua said with a sigh.

"Yours." Malvina smiled. "Everyone will be looking at you in the coming months, and I have some designs I need someone bold enough to wear." She lifted a burnished green fabric to Rua's skin. "Let's make it impossible for them to turn away, hmm? And perhaps even find a love match along the way?"

Rua's cheeks reddened, hating that the Lord of Donore crossed her mind as soon as Malvina said the words *love match*.

Malvina gave her a knowing smile. "I heard about your dance with the lord this morning."

Rua shook her head to deny it, but there was no point. It was as though Madame Malvina had peered inside Rua's soul and caught hold of her innermost desires. Her aptitude for dressmaking lent her to being an expert in understanding women.

Rua did not care what anyone in this city thought of her, but if she was going to endure this life of falsehoods, she should, at the very least, look better than everyone. And if she could bring the Lord of Donore to his knees in the process, so be it.

Her hands grazed green taffeta fabric. The shade was divine, like it was made for her.

"I suppose if they're going to stare anyway," Rua said with a grin, pointing to a dark-burgundy roll of fabric. She turned back to the mirror, imagining herself in a stunning gown made only for her. She would be unstoppable.

"Excellent," Malvina said, noting her selection.

After more measurements were taken and Rua's taste in dresses had been discussed, they left the dressmaker's.

The carriage was waiting right outside, the driver ready for them with the door opened. She and Mara climbed inside.

"Can you believe it?" Mara gaped. "*The* Malvina Webster is going to make all your dresses! She's only the most sought-after seamstress in New York. Your mother will be beside herself. She dresses Mrs. Fitzgerald and all her important friends. Everyone that matters, really."

"Is it true what she said?" Rua asked, her mind elsewhere.

"About what?"

"That these dresses don't suit me?"

"They fit you well enough, but now that I look at you, Madame Malvina is right. They don't look like they were made for you." Mara frowned. "Which is silly, of course, because they're yours," she added.

If she only knew.

"Tell the driver to take us to the library."

"The library? Now?" Mara appeared just as excited as she was concerned by this request.

"Yes," Rua said.

"Which library? Your mother was expecting us home right after."

"A big one." One that would have the kind of information Rua was looking for. One that wasn't limited to the Harringtons' personal taste.

"While I'm delighted you haven't forgotten your love of books, surely the one in your home is big enough?"

"It's not." Rua smiled, knowing she was wearing Mara down. "How could Flossie possibly object to us visiting a library?"

"You'd be surprised," Mara muttered, but told the driver where to go.

After about thirty minutes, they exited the carriage on Lafayette Street. As Rua was unfamiliar with the city, she had no clue how far they were from the house. It was a handsome building, three stories tall, with arched windows that took up the block. There was a small limestone wall that separated the library from the sidewalk.

"Astor Library." Rua read the name aloud as they walked up the front steps.

They entered a marbled vestibule and walked to the front desk. Beyond it she could see the atrium, open and bright. The upper floors looked down to the main floor by way of a thick marble balustrade. There were rows and rows of shelves and large tables open for reading. It was intimate but impressive.

"Good afternoon," the woman behind the desk said. "Can I help you?"

Rua pursed her lips. She wasn't exactly sure what she was looking for. "I'm looking for anything you have on Ireland and their lords. If you could just point me in the direction I can begin my research?"

Mara gave her a funny look.

"I'm afraid it doesn't work like that here." The librarian tipped her head forward, narrowing her eyes.

"Oh?"

"We pull from the catalogs, and you sit at a table and read. And you can't take them home either."

"Very well," Rua said, though she would have preferred to do her searching alone.

"Abigail, this woman is looking for anything we have on Ireland," the librarian said to the elderly woman who was also behind the desk.

"Follow me," Abigail said, guiding them up to the second floor. Scattered about the library were men and women sitting at tables, quietly reading.

She sat Rua and Mara at a table by the window and disappeared behind the glass where the books were housed. She came back with five books of varying sizes and genres: *Memoirs of Captain Rock*, *The Chronicles and Memorials of Great Britain and Ireland During the Middle Ages: Vol. 1*, *A Tale of a Tub*, *A Guide to The County of Wicklow*, and *Reliques of Irish Poetry*. None of which were remotely helpful.

"Is this it?" Rua asked.

"We close in twenty minutes," Abigail replied with a curt grin. "I'll be back in fifteen to collect these."

"What are you looking for?" Mara asked, opening the smallest of the books.

"I was looking for something on the Lord of Donore." It wasn't the only thing Rua was looking for, but she didn't want Mara to know. She had confided in her the depths of her memory loss, but she didn't want to give Mara an advantage over her. She wanted to learn about the Morrígan and the hellmouths on her own terms, unsullied by Mara's motives, whatever they might be.

"The Lord of Donore?" Mara's eyes widened. "In these books?"

Rua opened the largest text. "I'm looking for anything that mentions his lineage."

"Why would that interest you?"

"Because I'm not sure he is who he says he is," Rua said, as if that were good enough reason.

"Why do you care?"

"I don't care." Rua looked up, "But I'm curious. I find his superiority irksome. And I don't like that he's keeping tabs on me. I think it only right I return the favor. Do you know what county he's from?" She could've sworn she'd heard Flossie mention Meath at some point or another.

"Are you really the one to be digging into someone's background?" Mara asked.

"What is that supposed to mean?" She didn't like the implication that she was doing something wrong. It was so frustrating being blamed for Emma's choices and having to live with those consequences.

"You know exactly what it means." Mara looked around, lowering her voice further. "What you and I believe, it's heresy. You're under enough scrutiny as it is, and that's based on gossip alone. Don't give anyone a reason to go looking into you."

"What more could they possibly find?" Rua asked. "They already think I'm a devil worshipper."

"Proof that you are."

"What proof?" Rua asked, uneasy.

Mara's eyes darted around the room, and she leaned closer. "The real reason you were expelled from Devonshire. I can't believe you don't remember that."

Rua swallowed the lump in her throat.

"They caught you in the midst of your blood sacrifice. You had made an altar in the woods, and a professor followed you. Apparently, they had been wary of your behavior for months. They couldn't stand to see a meek young woman grow into someone assured, no longer afraid."

Rua's mind was racing. Had Emma sacrificed some poor little animal as a form of worship? And been foolish enough to get caught?

"Look at your palms. Haven't you wondered where you got those scars?" Mara nodded toward her hands.

Rua turned her hands over, finding nothing. She balled them into fists and tucked them back under the table, hoping Mara didn't notice that there weren't any scars on Rua's palms.

"How has no one found out about this?" Rua asked.

"Money and the fact that it's in everyone's best interest to keep it quiet. It would damage the school's reputation if word got out about you. They helped to keep it quiet."

Rua let out a deep breath. It was a lot to take in. If the gossip about her and what happened in Conleth Falls was enough to label her a pariah, the truth of her expulsion would certainly be enough to have her condemned.

What Rua didn't understand was why she hadn't been sent away to an asylum then. Why bring her home at all? Perhaps it had all happened around the time the Harringtons were getting into business with the Fitzgeralds and Flossie was afraid of the optics.

"Well." Rua frowned. "These aren't going to have what I need anyway." She piled the books one on top of the other.

"I know you're adjusting," Mara said, leaning in closer. "The move back to the city was quicker than we expected, but there are more hellmouths. We are never far from the Mother. We can help you get your memories back."

"There's more of them?" Rua leaned across the table, closer to Mara. She'd felt off kilter leaving the hellmouth in Conleth Falls, as if it held more than her answers. But if the hellmouths were all interconnected, like the book she'd found in Emma's room claimed they were, then this could be the solution she'd been hoping for.

"There's one quite close," Mara said. "In the northern corner of the park, there is a stone chamber. It only serves its purpose if you know what you're looking for."

Chills covered Rua's arm. The woods in Central Park; the buzzing she'd heard. She must have been near the hellmouth.

"So, the feast days, then." Rua paused, recalling the dates she'd read in Emma's book. She'd assumed they were some sort of calendar of holy days. "That's when the hellmouths work?"

Mara nodded. "I know you're eager, but I think it best you don't visit. You must be on your best behavior. If your mother catches you leaving the house unaccompanied . . ." Mara trailed off. "Well, I'd prefer not to think on it."

"But if we tell her I'm promenading in the park?" Rua offered.

"And let word get back to her that we were seen well beyond where it's acceptable to travel?"

Like where the Lord of Donore had already caught her.

"I suppose you're right," Rua conceded. It was clear that Mara cared very much for Emma's well-being. She wondered how long they'd been friends. "So, will you go and enter the stone chamber for me? Perhaps you can speak to the Mother and find out how I can get my memories back?"

"And risk ending up somewhere else?" Mara shook her head. "No, I won't go in it, but I might visit. And it doesn't work like that. You must pray to the Mother, earn her respect."

"End up somewhere else? What do you mean?"

"Lore tells it that depending on the day and the time, you can enter in one place and exit from another hellmouth entirely," Mara said.

Rua nodded. The caves were connected. She knew in her gut that this was exactly what had happened to her and Emma. The question remained: Where had Emma ended up?

"What would I do without you?" Rua smiled. "Best to steer clear of it all then, hmm?"

"At least for now," Mara said.

Footsteps sounded on the floor before Abigail approached their table. "The library is closing," she said.

Rua rose from the table, and Mara handed all the books to the librarian. "Thank you."

Abigail muttered something under her breath and shuffled away.

As Rua and Mara walked back to the carriage, she couldn't help but wonder about Emma Harrington. Was she living in some other place right now, hoping to get back to her family, or was she finally free?

She'd hate to think she was dragging her back to a place she'd escaped from, but Rua wasn't going to sacrifice her own happiness for some woman she'd never met. This was Emma Harrington's life, and Rua was not going to keep it.

Ten

Finn was inundated with mail. It was astounding to see the kind of doors that opened to him simply by spending time with Annette Fitzgerald.

"Is all of that for me?" He was going to have to hire someone else to go through it.

"It is, my lord," the valet answered.

He picked up a handful off the top of the pile. An invite from the Applegates, another ball at the end of the week, a charity event at the Metropolitan Museum of Art.

He stared down the mountain of mail long enough to let the doubt find its way in and ruin it. Was this what he wanted? A life spent pandering to peers at social engagements?

Shaking his head, he tossed the letters back on his desk. It was tiring, the promenading and the smiling, the drinks before dinner, the cigars at the club. Not a moment of peace was to be found. But he thought of his business aspirations, knowing he couldn't have one without the other.

"The water is ready when you are, sir."

Finn looked to the valet; his shaving kit was laid out at the ready. He had the Randalls' dinner tonight.

"Thank you," he said, dismissing the valet with a nod. He'd never let another man hold a blade to his neck.

Finn bent over the basin and splashed the hot water on his face, then began to shave.

The Randalls' dinner was an event as exclusive as they came, a *Who's Who* of the social set—though Gloria Fitzgerald would argue that they were letting anyone in these days, her remark no doubt directed at the Harringtons.

He'd seen it in action, the way Flossie Harrington quite literally pushed her way into things. She was forward and unscrupulous, impervious to the fact that the social elite did not want her and her new money. Richard had seen Ned's millions and welcomed him in, but money wasn't enough to grant access to their world. True acceptance was imparted by the women, women like Gloria Fitzgerald and her friends.

They were waiting for Rua to slip up—hard evidence to prove Richard had made a mistake in taking a chance on Ned. He couldn't help but feel there would be a domino effect. If Ned toppled, Finn was next.

He paused to look in the mirror, careful as he let the sharp razor glide across his cheek.

Nasty business, the lot of it.

His mind wandered to Rua. It had been days since he'd last seen her, and he dreaded the thought of another event in such close proximity.

The first of the trunks from Malvina Webster's shop arrived a week after Rua had her measurements taken and just in time for the Randalls' dinner. It wasn't a coincidence. The dressmaker was well aware of the social calendar, and she was sending up Rua's wardrobe as it became ready.

Rua didn't know who the Randalls were, but they were important enough for the Fitzgeralds to attend their event, which meant the Harringtons would be tagging along too.

"The dresses from Malvina's are perfect," she said to Mara.

Made for her, not Emma. A simple truth that lifted a thousand pounds off her shoulders. It was almost enough to make her look forward to the dinner this evening.

"Your mother wants you downstairs in the breakfast room," Mara said, organizing the gowns for the chambermaids to put away in their appropriate places.

"Very well." Rua smiled, sliding her hand across the many skirts as she left, excited to have something of her own.

"You're in a cheery mood," Mara noted as they descended the staircase.

"How can I not be? This evening will be different," she said, finally feeling like she was gaining some footing. She'd spent the last few days in the library, out of Flossie's way, reading guidebooks on acting like a proper lady. For once, she felt prepared to venture out of the house.

Reading up on social etiquette wasn't necessarily the best use of her time—she was still memoryless and not Emma—but she hoped it would earn her a reprieve where Flossie was concerned. If the events she attended went well, she would be able to search for the truth without the stress of the asylum hanging over her head.

"I hope so," Mara said, waiting for her to walk into the breakfast room.

Rua sat down at the table alone while Mara stood behind her. A footman set tea and sweet scones on the table.

"Thank you," she said, to no response.

As she buttered her blueberry scone, she wondered if the Lord of Donore would be at the dinner. Part of her hoped so. She wanted to get to the bottom of whatever it was about him that had her so vexed. Though she doubted she'd get within two feet of him, seeing as Annette had her sights on the lord.

"You'd better hurry up with that scone before your mother catches you," Mara said.

"If I wasn't supposed to eat it, it wouldn't be on the table," Rua quipped.

The pastry was on its way to her mouth when Mrs. Harrington burst into the room and swatted it from her hands. The buttered scone dropped to the floor, tumbling under the table.

"Dear god! Whatever were you *thinking*, putting something like that in your mouth? You have dozens of Malvina Webster gowns that you need to fit into! Mara, I've warned you to watch her. I'll have to have a word with Mrs. Smith about your duties."

Eyes downcast, Mara nodded. "Apologies, Mrs. Harrington."

"She tried to stop me," Rua interrupted, but Flossie held up her hand to shush her.

"Have you learned the names of tonight's attendees?" she asked Rua.

"Oh, yes, I memorized every last one of them." Rua laughed, assuming Flossie was joking, but she should have learned by now that the woman didn't make jokes.

Flossie's eyes narrowed. "Go on, then, name them."

Unprepared, Rua pressed her lips together.

"That's what I thought," Flossie said, as though Rua's failures were inevitable. "Tonight's event will be far more intimate. Perhaps you might even have a second chance with the Lord of Donore. If you are prepared." With that final warning, Flossie exited the room, the skirt of her dress sweeping behind her.

"The names of the attendees?" Rua turned to Mara.

"I'll get the book," Mara said, looking flustered. "I keep forgetting you don't remember *anything*." And just like that, Rua's confidence in her abilities to impress Flossie vanished. Not that she'd ever thought she could impress her, but she'd thought she could at least not annoy her.

Rua bathed in record time so she could put on her new gown. The bodice, made of an orange silk faille material, was closely fitted, with boning in the seams, short puffy sleeves, and lace trim around the décolletage. The waist was extended, coming to a point in the front in a ruched basque.

The only part of the underskirt that was visible was the tiered ruffled lighter-orange hem. On top of that was the knee-length overskirt, with more ruffles and ribbons, bunched up in a polonaise style over the bustle.

The final touch was the short white gloves she pulled on as she walked down the staircase.

Rua knew she looked good, though Flossie merely nodded. She was beginning to think it might actually kill Flossie to pay her a compliment.

"You both look magnificent," Ned said, guiding them out the front doors to the carriage.

On the impossible chance that Flossie would forget she was there, Rua sat in silence, staring out the window. She couldn't risk Flossie asking her to rattle off the guest list, because she simply could not.

Rua turned her focus to a woman walking on the dark sidewalk, barely visible under the dim lampposts. For a moment, Rua was jealous of the woman's freedom. Why was she allowed to walk by herself outside but Rua couldn't? But she reminded herself that staying with the Harringtons, and following their rules, was her choice.

She sat forward as they kept pace with the woman. Her gait was familiar, long and hurried. A gust of wind kicked up, blowing off the woman's hood, revealing Mara.

Rua wasn't sure why she was surprised to see her walking on the sidewalk. It had never occurred to her to ask Mara what she did in her free time or that she even had any. Perhaps she was sneaking off to a lover or visiting the hellmouth.

They arrived at the Randalls' home exactly on time. It wasn't as monstrous as the Harringtons', but it was no less elegant.

"Good evening." A butler greeted them at the door. The foyer was empty, but Rua could hear laughter and chatter echoing from the room to their right.

"Mr. Harrington, if you will follow me." Another servant appeared. "The men are on the veranda."

Ned smiled and walked off to join the others.

"Flossie." A woman Rua assumed to be Mrs. Randall found them in the foyer. "So lovely that you could make it." She smiled.

Liar, Rua thought.

"Emma, this is Mrs. Randall."

They exchanged pleasantries and followed Mrs. Randall into the salon.

Luxe tapestries coated the wall, and smartly appointed furniture filled the room with warmth, complementing the well-lit sconces and candelabras.

About a dozen women were scattered about the room, some on couches, others hovering by the floor-length windows. There were a few open chairs nestled nearby where Annette Fitzgerald was making a show of looking at Rua and giggling with her friends. Lily Stevens was among them, though she offered Rua an apologetic smile.

"Smile and say hello," Flossie hissed.

Rua would have preferred to gouge her own eyes out. Fortunately, the rest of the women had collectively decided to ignore her presence, saving her the trouble. They cast their glances sideways and returned to their conversations with their noses stuck up in the air.

Undaunted, Flossie pushed her way in, leaving Rua to her own devices.

She waited awkwardly with her back to the door, looking in on conversations that she'd never be privy to. The women's exclusionary tactics did not inspire in her a desperate need to fit in; rather, they filled her with a simmering hatred that was sure to boil over.

She imagined Emma Harrington, the one they were really trying to hurt, to be timid and softspoken, a woman who likely did want their acceptance. But rather than allowing her the privilege, they'd bully her until her diabolic mother decided she could handle no further embarrassment and send her away. Too bad for them, they had Rua to contend with now.

Out of nowhere, the chatter grew to a fever pitch. Rua looked to Flossie, who was making crazy eyes at her, mouthing and motioning for her to turn around.

But she didn't need to turn her head to know what had caused the commotion. The way Annette's smile softened and her eyelashes flittered told Rua exactly who had entered the room. What was he even doing in here? The men were on the veranda. Perhaps the Lord of Donore just needed a quick boost to his ego.

She could feel his presence directly behind her. Indomitable and imposing. If she took a step backward, she would land in his arms. The thought sent an irritating flurry to her stomach.

Before Flossie gave herself a stroke, Rua gave in, turning to look at the lord. Her heart gathered speed as her eyes traveled upward and found his. The intensity in his gaze left her breathless. And for a brief, mind-altering moment, they were the only two people in the room.

Rua fought hard against the haze threatening her consciousness. The one that offered her bliss in the form of sweet-smelling flowers and masculine strength.

He leaned toward her, turning her own body against her. They were so close she could reach out and touch him. His eyes moved to her mouth, sending her pulse racing and the world grinding to a halt. He was going to kiss her; she was sure of it. Her traitorous lips parted at the thought.

"Miss Harrington," he said, his breath deliciously warm against the nape of her neck. She swallowed hard, anticipating his touch. "Has the cat got your tongue?"

Rua sucked in a mortified breath and faced him. He grinned, leaving her with a wink and a taste for blood.

The lord continued farther into the room, and mothers and daughters alike descended upon him. Incensed for more reasons than she cared to count, she watched disdainfully as he chatted with Annette. They looked the perfect couple, ideal specimens in their own right, she with her delicate beauty and he with his god-like presence. She wanted to strangle them both.

Rua's stomach growled just as Mr. and Mrs. Randall announced it was time to be seated for dinner. She saw the rest of the men had returned to the foyer.

As the room emptied, the snubbing continued with a few sidelong glares and upturned noses. If only these women knew she preferred ostracization to their companionship.

The guests moved to the dining room, which looked impeccable. Not one inch of the tablecloth was visible under all the plates of food and greenery. Servants stood behind each chair, waiting to pull them out so the guests could sit.

The table was set for twenty-four. As one could expect, Annette and the lord were to be seated together near Mr. and Mrs. Fitzgerald and Ned and Flossie by the Randalls at the head of the table. Conveniently, Rua was left out of all consideration and left standing while everyone she knew took their seats.

"Heavens me," Mrs. Randall said, feigning ignorance as she noticed Rua standing by herself.

Rua looked around for an empty seat and found one at the opposite side of the table. A walk so far from where she was standing, she'd likely die from the daggers they shot before she got there.

"A simple oversight, I'm sure." Mrs. Fitzgerald smirked, looking at Mrs. Randall.

"There's room there at the end," Annette offered, wearing a grin that Rua wanted to strike from her face.

"Not to worry!" Flossie jumped out of her seat. "Might you move down a chair?" she asked the woman in the seat beside her.

Rua groaned internally, feeling the brunt of Flossie's outrageous request land squarely on her shoulders.

The woman was so shocked by the request that she did exactly as Flossie asked. The subsequent shuffling of a dozen people as they moved down one chair each had Rua's insides reeling. The angry murmurs turned to proclamations of disgust, and she was no longer sure she was safe to sit down. But how could she not, after that debacle?

Rua was humiliated, a feeling she hadn't thought possible. It turned out disdain was not stronger than ignominy.

"There now, all settled," Flossie said, tapping the chair beside her, oblivious, intentionally or otherwise, to the scene she'd just caused. The empty seat was conveniently across from the Lord of Donore.

Searching for a forgiving face, she found Lily Stevens, the girl who had offered her membership in her club, but she was seated in the middle of the table and of no use to Rua.

Inadvertently, she glanced over at the Lord of Donore, but he didn't see her. He was too busy watching the game of musical chairs continuing at the end of the table.

"Sit down, Miss Harrington. It's the least you can do," Mrs. Randall said sharply.

Rua didn't move, because rigor had set in. Never could she have imagined a scenario as absurd as this one. But as the hostess's words sank in, Rua's mortification quickly melted into offense.

She wasn't the one in the wrong here. They had deliberately seated her away from the Harringtons, and Flossie was the one who had forced the other guests to move. Taking a quick sweep of the room, she saw she had no other choice. It was either sit down or leave.

They all watched as Rua took her seat, no doubt hoping to see if she moved the wrong way, put her hand in the wrong spot, or allowed a slight bend in her back as she dropped into the chair.

Slowing her movements, she tried to remember everything she'd learned about proper etiquette. Head up, shoulders back, no fidgeting. Rua's back was stiff as a board as she sat down.

Posture, apparently, was everything to the upper class. Flossie would go so far as to have her believe that her acceptance was dependent on it, but the way they were all staring, Rua no longer doubted that it was the truth.

Rua placed her hands in her lap and focused her attention on the bouquet of flowers in front of her. It was either that or the Lord of Donore's face.

"Are we ready now?" Mrs. Randall asked, not masking her irritation.

Rua nodded, grinding her teeth to dust in the process.

Dinner commenced as planned, though she didn't know how she was going to endure all ten courses.

The servants leaned over the guests' shoulders, placing a bowl of soup before each of them. And then the chatter began, none of which was directed at Rua.

While Rua enjoyed exclusion from conversation, she was not exempt from creating other problems for herself. Problems in the form of Irish lords too handsome for their own good. It was like a compulsion—every other second she caught herself watching him as he conversed with Annette or the others around him, and on more than one occasion he caught her.

Something about him didn't add up. She had no proof, no reason beyond her own gut feeling, but the Lord of Donore was hiding something. Though, after tonight, she wasn't sure she'd be around long enough to find out.

"Miss Harrington," Annette said, craning her neck over the bunch of flowers that separated them across the table, "I am afraid we never finished our conversation from the other day."

Rua glanced up from her plate, knowing the room was alight with anticipation, waiting to see how the uncouth Emma Harrington would respond.

"Well," Rua said, "I was certainly finished with it." She could not bear to have Annette bring up Emma's expulsion again.

Flossie let out a groan.

Annette's smile never faltered. "I must comment on your gown. I simply cannot wrap my head around it." She paused, her grin widening. "It's so harvest-like. Surely it's a bit early for that, is it not?"

The room erupted into a polite fit of laughter, effectively incinerating her. Rua should have run when she had the chance. This time, the Lord of Donore's eyes were on her, but she refused to meet them. She would not see him laugh at her.

Rua gripped the edge of her spoon, almost believing she'd worn the wrong gown. That perhaps Malvina had sent the later fall gowns by mistake. But she reminded herself of the line outside Malvina's shop and her expertise in dressmaking.

"Your attempt at insulting my gown only highlights your limited knowledge on fashion trends, I'm afraid."

"Excuse me?" Annette tried to hide her surprise.

"We both know Malvina Webster chooses only one woman to display her latest designs each season. You're just jealous it wasn't you."

"Jealous of you? A country pumpkin?" Annette spat while searching the room for validation.

Rather than responding, Rua focused on bending the utensil in her hand and imagined flinging it at Annette's overindulged head.

"Come now. I think Miss Harrington looks delightful."

Rua didn't know who had tried to defend her, but the pity in their compliment was almost worse than the insult. She counted to ten in an effort to calm herself.

"Mr. Larchmont, I never took you for a liar," Annette said with a high-pitched giggle.

Rua set her spoon down gently and leveled her gaze.

"Keep your mouth shut," Flossie hissed at Rua, but she ignored her.

"Whether they'll admit it or not, everyone in this room knows I look divine. So, my point stands: either you have poor taste or you're jealous of me."

Annette's face went scarlet.

"So, which one is it?" Rua lifted a brow.

Flossie gagged on her wine, and Mrs. Fitzgerald looked like she'd love nothing more than to spring across the table and wring Rua's neck.

It didn't matter. Annette would have to find herself a new target if she was looking for someone to bully.

"That is enough," Mrs. Randall warned from her position at the head of the table.

Rua bit her tongue as commanded, but her anger had reached new heights. She was finished with everyone in this room. As though they were all above reproach. If she didn't have more pressing troubles, she'd spend every last minute of her life uncovering the most salacious gossip about everyone in this group, and she'd ruin them all with it. She hadn't memorized their names before the party, but she'd be damn sure to remember them now.

Once more glancing across the table, her eyes found the Lord of Donore, only this time he was looking back. Too irate to be embarrassed, she didn't look away. Instead, she was caught off guard, ill prepared for the softness in his eyes. No pity, no contempt, only understanding.

A silent exchange that offered no words, only a flutter of butterflies. Rua's cheeks warmed, then she looked away.

With expert ease, the conversation switched to business as the men dominated the discussion. They didn't care what the women were fighting about. Mr. Harrington, the lord, and Mr. Fitzgerald were soon lost in their plans for the hotel they were going to build.

Course after course, the men droned on while the women tried and failed to include themselves.

"Now, now, gentleman, you don't want to put the women to sleep before they've had a chance to dance, do you?" a man chimed in.

"Why would that put the women to sleep?" Rua asked aloud before she'd thought it through.

Everyone turned to face her, and she felt a pit form in her stomach.

"Ah, Miss Harrington, you delicate girl." The man pouted.

Rua was sure she heard the Lord of Donore grunt at the term of endearment.

Because one wrong opinion wasn't enough, another man added, "you see, my dear, women have far simpler tastes, and many topics should be left to the men. It would only cause you distress."

"Is that so?" Rua asked, eyeing their ring fingers to see if any woman had the misfortune of being married to them.

The sharp toe of Flossie's laced boot met the side of Rua's ankle in what she assumed was an attempt to get her to stop speaking, but it was too late for that. She was well past the point of no return and not over her exchange with Annette.

"Indeed," the man continued. "For instance, while you would find reading on needlework and homemaking immensely enjoyable, it would be of little interest to the gentlemen at this table. It is the way the minds work, you see. The fairer sex cannot handle anything more than a little light reading on the gentler subjects. It is not good for your hearts. I daresay your brains would not be able to absorb the information. Allow me to demonstrate further."

"Demonstrate what, sir? That my brain is not able to absorb information the same as a man's?"

"If you'll just wait and see," he said with an irritated laugh.

"How will you demonstrate such a thing?" She cut him off. "Are you going to cut my head open?"

The women all gasped their horror, but Rua continued, "I would be very curious to know how exactly you expect to prove such an absurd statement. Are you a doctor? At the very least a scientist? Do you have an operating table?"

"Stop it this instance," Flossie said, slightly louder than a whisper. Rua continued to ignore her protests.

"Young lady, your behavior is abhorrent," the man said.

"What is abhorrent, sir, is that you had the nerve to say something so stupid so loudly." She'd had it with them all.

"Well, I . . . Miss Harrington, I advise you to mind your manners." He turned to Ned and Mr. Fitzgerald and gave them a knowing look.

Anger rushed through Rua, and all she saw was red.

"Please, pay my daughter no mind. She gets carried away," Flossie said, trying to ease the situation. The servants continued plating the next course as though they were used to such raucous affairs.

The corner of Rua's mouth twitched. Leave it to Flossie to openly admit to a roomful of their peers that she thought her daughter was ridiculous. She would be the one to take them all down with her desperate need to reach the top. She should be propping Rua up, not belittling her, but the bigger picture was lost on her.

Rua bent the soup spoon in half and then straightened it once more. Over and over and over until finally it snapped.

They all stared, waiting to see if Ned would scold her or have her leave the table after Flossie's dismissal.

She looked down at the broken piece of silverware clutched in her white-knuckled fist and thought about jamming it down that man's throat. What was stopping her? They all thought she was crazy anyway. If she was going to be sent to an asylum, she should at least do something to deserve it.

"Please accept my daughter's sincerest apologies," Ned said. Rua gaped at him. Ned nodded. "Go ahead, Emma."

She'd sooner shove the spoon down her own throat.

"Foul woman," the man spat. Fed up, Rua jumped out of her seat and leaned forward, placing her hands on the table.

Gasps were heard around the room.

The Lord of Donore rose to his feet suddenly. "Miss Harrington, could I interest you in some fresh air," he said, almost pleading, "and issue an apology on behalf of Mr. Crowley here. His commentary on women would have offended the pope."

Shocked expressions showered the two of them as they towered above the elegant dinner table. Rua was equally confused, but as her anger dissipated and she took one glance around at the Randalls and their appalled guests, she knew she'd crossed a line.

But what she didn't understand was why the lord was throwing her a life raft. A raft that was liable to sink them both, because a turn about the garden in the middle of dinner was certainly not any more appropriate than her trying to maim Mr. Crowley.

But she wasn't one to look a gift horse in the mouth. "That would be delightful, my lord."

Annette let out a little whine, the sound like music to Rua's ears.

Then she turned to Flossie, knowing that her return indoors, to this gilded life of leisure and lies, was dependent on the expression the matriarch wore.

Rua would either go for a walk with the lord, or she would jump the gate and never come back.

Her chest tightened as she looked upon Flossie's stony face. She was going to have to run. Where, though? And how? She had nothing to her name.

And then Flossie spoke. "A marvelous idea, my lord."

Relieved but unsure, Rua began her walk toward the door. On the opposite side, the Lord of Donore did the same. A death march played to the sound of contemptuous silence.

By now, the end of the table would be rehashing the events of her outburst. She could hear them repeating the story, leaving out

and adding details at random. Anything to make it more scandalous than it already was. They should thank her for providing them
with a season's worth of entertainment all in one night.

And still she could not fathom why the Lord of Donore was
here by her side.

"Miss Harrington," he said, offering her his arm when they met
by the door.

"My lord," she said, taking it. A thrill rushed through her as he
tucked her arm protectively beneath his. She rested her fingers on
top of his arm, resisting the urge to squeeze it.

"Please, call me Finn," he said.

Eleven

Finn glanced once more at the woman on his arm and wondered what in the hell he was thinking as he led her out of the dining room.

"Finn," Rua started, as if testing out the use of his first name. "Care to explain what is happening here? While I do appreciate it, I'm not sure I understand."

Hell if he knew. It had all happened so quickly. One minute Rua was putting Crowley in his place, and the next he was certain she was thinking of marring him with the spoon in her hand. Her eyes were glowing, and his instinct took over.

"Well, I was trying to deescalate the situation, though now I think I might've made things worse." He thought of Mr. Fitzgerald and how sour Annette would be. Christ. He'd have some amount of explaining to do.

"On the contrary, my lord, you might've just saved a man's life," Rua said with a laugh, but somehow he didn't think she was kidding.

"I am a hero, then?" he asked.

"Yes, and I the villain," Rua said.

They walked to the veranda with a maid on their heels. He presumed Mrs. Harrington had sent her out after them to chaperone. The back doors were open, letting the warm evening air envelop them.

The terrace was longer than it was wide, being no more than two yards in width. The edge of the property was backed up against another mansion.

Rua moved away from Finn's side.

Like a siren, she called to him, luring him in with the sweet sound of her voice. Herein lay the path to destruction, and he was walking it willingly.

"You can go back inside if you like. I'll be all right." Rua was pensive as she stared at the small patch of grass below them. "I'd say it's not too late for you to return with your reputation intact."

"I'll be fine," he said. But would he be?

He felt like he'd dived headfirst off a cliff without checking to see what lay below, and the chances of him coming out unscathed were near zero. But something about Rua had done this to him. There was a mysterious pull to her presence, wild and challenging, and he couldn't resist.

She smiled. "I'm certain you will be. Me, on the other hand?" She gave a delicate shrug of her shoulder and walked down the steps.

That was his out. His chance to leave her there and return to the dining room with some semblance of his mind intact. He should do just that. He knew he should. He was teetering on the point of no return.

She was at the bottom of the stairs, fading from his view, taking with her all the adventure and clarity. A clarity borne of chaos, but it was clarity nonetheless, because as he watched her disappear, the familiar fog of his reality returned.

Rua set his careful world on fire, and he wasn't ready to let that wane.

He followed her down the steps and walked up beside her, wondering if she felt it too.

He watched her looking up at the moon, wishing he could tell her that the orange of her gown made her look like his favorite part of a sunrise, the part that burned the brightest. But he wouldn't dare. She had no need for his reassurances.

"Rua?" he asked.

She looked at him, her eyes bright. "Yes?"

He had nothing to say. He only wanted to be near her.

A crinkle formed between her brows; she was searching his face for answers. "Truly, what are you doing out here? If you wanted me alone in the garden, surely there were less dramatic ways you could have achieved that." A slight smirk played on her mouth.

"I wasn't trying to get you alone," he countered, looking over his shoulder for the maid who had scurried after them only moments before. She was nowhere to be found. "Where has the maid gone?" He looked around the would-be garden.

"My company is not for the faint of heart," she said.

"I'd wager Crowley would agree. I doubt he'll speak to another woman again," Finn said.

"Nor should he," Rua said.

He laughed. "At last, we are in agreement."

Finn wondered if she was aware of the rumors circulating about her—that a man was dead and she was to blame. Surely, if she knew, she would have refrained from saying anything to that imbecile Crowley. But as it was, he couldn't tell. She seemed the defiant type.

She smiled at his answer. The sight warmed him to his core. And damn if he didn't want to pull her mouth up to his. One taste was all he needed. One taste, and perhaps the spell would be broken. What other explanation could there be for his ability to lay his careful plans aside, all so that he might breathe the same air as her?

She took a small step forward, teasing him with her proximity, daring him to reach for her. They were truly alone now. In one quick movement, he could have her body wrapped in his arms. What must that feel like? Her body pressed against his, intoxicating him with her scent. It'd be like catching lightning.

A gust of wind passed between them, blowing wisps of her hair in her face, blocking the only view he'd ever wanted. He lifted his hand to brush them aside, stopping midway when he realized what he was doing.

Rua watched his hand fall away, her expression inscrutable.

He took a step back. "Perhaps we should return." It wasn't a suggestion but a necessity. Her nearness left him vulnerable. Vulnerable to the deep recesses of his mind where he felt like he knew her.

Without waiting for him to offer his arm, Rua went back upstairs. He followed close behind, thankful for the slight reprieve.

The disaster of a formal meal had ended, and the party shifted to the salon.

"There you two are," Mrs. Harrington cooed as she approached, dragging her husband behind her. Ned was busy apologizing to all the people his wife had knocked into on their way over.

Rua smiled, but it was forced. Finn sensed the shift in her posture, tense and braced for a fight.

"My daughter's dance card." Mrs. Harrington stuffed the card into Finn's face. "Before it's full." *Unlikely*, he thought.

This seemed to relax Rua a bit, but still she stared into the unforgiving crowd. Only a fool would miss the virulent whispers, and a fool Rua was not.

Finn opened the empty dance card and put his name down.

He would prefer never to dance at all. If you danced with one, then you must dance with them all. As he handed the card back to Mrs. Harrington, he noticed the steady encroaching of the mothers, licking their chops, their own daughters' dance cards in hand.

"Appreciate it, Donore," Ned said. Finn acknowledged him with a nod.

Ned was a nice man who didn't seem to grasp how much trouble he was in. Mr. Fitzgerald was certainly not going to take kindly to Rua's outburst at dinner. The ice she was skating on was paper thin.

"Please excuse me," Finn said to the Harringtons. He needed to find Mr. Fitzgerald and assess the damage. His situation was not dire like Ned's, but he still had his reputation to consider. He cursed, thinking about how rash he'd been in whisking Rua to the garden. What must that have looked like to everyone? And now the dance card. He was well on his way to ruin.

"Don't forget." Mrs. Harrington shook the card in the air. Finn looked to Rua once more, but it was clear that her mind was elsewhere.

"I won't," he said, offering a polite smile.

Finn found the Fitzgeralds at the center of the makeshift ball-room. All three of them looked like they wanted to shout at him, and he didn't like it one bit.

"Donore," Richard said.

"My lord, I must warn you, your stunt at dinner was not looked upon favorably," Mrs. Fitzgerald said.

"My stunt?" Finn bristled.

Richard put a hand on his wife's shoulder. "What my wife means to say is that you must consider the situation. Look at the scene that girl caused. Why get tangled up in it?"

Finn couldn't argue with that, though no one was reprimand-ing Annette for her spiteful remarks. Perhaps because Rua had well and truly put her in her place.

But it was true: there was no reason at all that he should've inserted himself into that mess, and yet he had. He was so bloody tangled.

"You'll be written off if you're not more careful," Richard warned.

"Well, it's a good thing I've got my affairs in order, then."

"Never underestimate the importance of an opinion. Now, why don't you two go and have the first dance?" Richard said to Finn and his daughter.

Finn wondered how much Richard's concern had to do with the hotel and how much with his interest in having him marrying his daughter.

Rua wasn't dancing with anyone this evening, especially not Finn. He'd been pressured into dancing with her at the Fitzgeralds' ball, and she didn't have the stomach for it to happen again.

The reception upon their return from the garden was icy cold, though the lord was in the process of being thawed. He was at the center of a small group of women, Annette being one of them, and they were discussing whether or not tomorrow's promenade would be washed out by the rain. Annette scowled at Rua before turning back to Finn.

How Flossie thought Rua would even be allowed on the dance floor after what she'd said in the dining room was beyond her. Life in the matriarch's head must be something to behold—too dense to notice or too stubborn to care. Either way, Rua wasn't going to be the pawn.

Flossie had slipped into conversation with another woman about an event coming up next week, leaving Rua the chance to quietly disappear.

Making sure to keep her steps slow, she edged along the wall of the salon, pausing every time she'd catch someone watching her. She tried to wait them out, for their attention to divert elsewhere, until she realized they would always be watching her.

Then she spotted Lily Stevens, who looked every bit as fashionable as the other women, with her royal-blue gown and layered polonaise. Her dark-brown hair was pinned back from her porcelain face, bunching in tight ringlets at the base of her neck. They made eye contact and Rua stilled, half expecting Lily to look at her with disgust, but instead she smiled and walked over.

"I wanted to tell you that I think your dress is lovely. You mustn't let what Annette says bother you," Lily said.

Easy for you to say, Rua thought. But she responded with a thank-you.

"Have you given any more thought to my invitation?" Lily asked, keeping her voice low. "After tonight's performance, I must admit, my instincts were right about you."

Rua smiled, not wanting to hurt Lily's feelings, but it wasn't exactly what Rua wanted to hear. And she wasn't interested. She had enough on her plate, never mind aligning with a women's group that allowed their friends to torment other women.

"The location changes each week, but we discuss everything we're not allowed to talk about in public. The next meeting will be here in no time. I'll send you the details."

Before Rua had the chance to object, Lily walked away.

Rua resumed inching toward the hall, the area tempting her with its lack of people and proximity to the front door.

The salon behind her erupted into a fit of laughter. She turned and saw Mr. Fitzgerald and another man at the center of the commotion. It was hard to imagine this was the same crowd that had glowered at her through dinner.

Rather than trying to hide, she ought to make nice with the party guests. Let Flossie see her efforts succeed, if only to keep her threats of institutionalization at bay for the moment.

But of course, that was what she ought to do, not what she wanted to do.

Unobstructed, Rua slipped into the foyer, with no real intention of leaving the party, but then the servant opened the front door for her.

"Thank you," she said as she walked out. The door shut behind her with a slam, and she wondered if she'd be let back in.

Finding no other guests outside, Rua walked down the front steps and entered the Randalls' front garden. It was small, not much of a garden at all, more like a strip of grass behind a midsize limestone wall.

She opened the little gate and walked through it. The smell of smoke wafted in the breeze, despite the lack of any fires that she could see.

Fall would soon be here. Rua wondered if she would still be living this life by then. Or would she have made her way back to where she belonged?

She rested her elbows against the wall as she gazed into the night.

What she really needed was another look inside the books she'd found in Emma's room. If she could understand why Emma had gone into the hellmouth in the first place, maybe she could figure out why she was the one to have come out.

She thought of the triskele on her ankle. Was she devoted to the Morrígan the way Emma and Mara were and she simply couldn't remember? Though she had a hard time believing she would feel so moved by a deity as to have their insignia branded onto her skin.

And then there was Finn. A piece to a different puzzle. There was a pull there, even with all their differences. But there was something else too: a boundary, or a line, that she was afraid to cross. Like if she opened that door, they might never be able to close it.

"A word, Donore?"

Rua whipped her head around at the sound of the man's voice. Her heart thundered as she ducked and slumped behind the wall before they could see her.

"Enjoying yourself?" Mr. Fitzgerald asked Finn as they walked closer to where she was hiding.

"Enjoying well enough," Finn said, sounding annoyed. His voice was so close, she presumed he was just on the other side of the wall. If he looked over, he'd catch her huddled in a ball on the ground, trying not to be seen.

"I'll get right to the point so we can enjoy the rest of the evening's festivities. What the hell were you thinking?" Mr. Fitzgerald barked.

Rua winced.

"I beg your pardon?" Finn responded.

"You know exactly what I'm talking about, Donore. Taking that disturbed girl out to the garden? What kind of harebrained act was that?"

She listened closely, equally as curious as Mr. Fitzgerald, though she didn't take too kindly to his description of her.

"Oh, I don't know." Finn's voice was strained. "I felt bad for the girl. It was hard to watch."

Rua frowned, feeling the sharp prick of embarrassment.

"A bloody disaster, but now you're in the middle of it and you've insulted my daughter. I cannot have you picking sides."

Poor Annette. Rua rolled her eyes.

"Picking sides? What are you on about?" Finn asked.

"You have a choice to make. If you want my daughter's hand, you'll have no more to do with that heathen Harrington girl."

Rua took the "heathen" comment in stride; it was the insinuation that Finn would marry Annette that left her breathless. It wasn't a shock to her—she had presumed as much given how much time they were spending together—but hearing it aloud made it feel real.

"Do I have your word that you'll stay away from her?" Mr. Fitzgerald asked.

Rua waited with bated breath for Finn's answer. She didn't understand how she had come to care so quickly. She shook her head. She didn't care; she was merely curious. Curious because when they were together, she felt a glimmer of what it'd be like to be whole.

A long moment passed. Rua's heart lifted when Finn didn't respond, pleased that Mr. Fitzgerald would know someone as esteemed as the Lord of Donore was not so readily discarding her.

"If you cannot bring yourself to answer, Donore, then I'm afraid that's answer enough."

"Bloody hell, Richard, I'm not interested in the Harrington girl, but I've had enough of your vague threats. If you're going to do something, do it."

Crushed. The way he said the "Harrington girl" snatched the wind out of her sails. Like she was nothing more than a nuisance. A social oddity that had interrupted all of their lives.

"Very well, Donore."

Rua listened as the footsteps moved farther away and the front door opened and shut.

Keeping her head below the wall, dejected, she turned herself around. With just her fingers exposed, she pulled herself upright to peek over the ledge.

Before she even had the chance to rise to her full height, her view was blocked by a hulking figure.

"Why am I always finding you in places you shouldn't be?"

Rua let out a startled yelp, falling backward to the ground.

Without delay, she rose to her feet and dusted herself off. "Why does it seem you're always looking for me?" she countered, hurrying toward the gate.

Finn moved in sync, blocking her exit.

"Please, move," she said.

He didn't budge. "Were you listening to my conversation?"

Of course she was listening. She had no other option but to listen. Rather than answer, she turned sideways, trying to fit between the gate and his massive frame. The space was so narrow, there was no choice but for them to touch. She heard his intake of breath as she accidentally rested her hand on his torso for balance.

The desire to linger there a moment with their bodies pressed closed together under the starry night sky overwhelmed her. All she could see was his chest; all she could smell was his cologne. She was overcome with the thought of him.

Needing more, she glanced upward, finding his eyes already on her. Her breath was shallow, his the same.

"Rua," he whispered, his voice thick with longing. The flutters in her stomach were unbearable. She felt warm all over, insatiable, her body showing all the telltale signs of betrayal, its new constant state when he was around her.

She brought her other hand up to his chest, feeling the hard muscle beneath the fabric of his dress shirt. "Yes, Finn?" She toyed with his collar, her fingers brushing against his neck.

He reached his arms behind her back, pulling her tighter to him, and then a terrible shredding sound tore through the air.

"No," she cried, sliding out from between him and the wall. She reached for her skirt, feeling that it was torn from her backside to her knee, exposing the bustle beneath.

"No, no, no. How will I go back inside?" She dropped her hands to her side. "I can't go back inside."

Finn looked abashed. "What can I do to help?"

"I don't know, can you sew?" She looked at him, incredulous. "Flossie is going to kill me."

"Why do you call your mother Flossie?" he asked, brow raised.

"This is your fault!" she shouted, bringing him back to the matter at hand and away from her slipup.

"My fault?" He gaped.

"Yes! Why didn't you let me pass?"

"Why were you in there in the first place?"

"None of your concern, my lord." She felt the skirt again. "Oh god, what am I going to do?" She groaned, trying to put the dress back together, as if the fabric would just magically stick at the seams.

She weighed her options. Running home was preferable to asking Finn for assistance, but could she just leave? Would Flossie punish her for it? Well, it was that or going back inside and feeding herself to the wolves.

"Please, Rua, take my carriage," Finn offered, sounding apologetic.

"But what will I tell my mother?"

"I will take care of it," he assured her, hurrying her toward his carriage.

She wasn't sure he realized he was touching her. Again. The palm of his hand covered the small of her back. It was subtle, delicate but protective, and it filled her with butterflies.

More butterflies that she did not want. But she'd heard what Finn had said. He wasn't interested. She was the "heathen Harrington girl."

He opened the carriage door, and she walked up the steps. "I will return in a moment," he said, before returning indoors.

Though Finn would have preferred not to reenter the Randalls' home at all, he had told Rua he would handle the situation, entangling himself further.

She hadn't been wrong earlier: he could have let her pass in the garden, but he didn't want her to go. There was something about her, something he couldn't resist, and he didn't know how to make sense of it.

"My lord, there you are." Annette approached him the moment he walked into the salon. The room had been converted into a makeshift dance floor. A lively tune played in the background.

"I'm looking for Ned," he mumbled, pushing his way into the room.

"Join me." Annette held out her hand and smiled. Finn hesitated as he glanced around for the Harringtons. Instead, he caught Richard's eye. A few others turned to see Annette's offer hanging in the air. He couldn't rightly refuse her now.

Frustrated, he took her hand, and they made their way to the center of the room.

He hoped Rua had the patience to wait, though he doubted it.

His mind was in pieces—she had him in pieces. When he was near her, he could think of nothing but the desperate ache in his chest. So consumed with his longing, he was free of all his earthly endeavors. When he was with Annette, he could see his future, the one he had planned for. Was he really so irresolute in his choices?

As the music changed, so did the tone of the room. Everyone's focus turned to Finn and Annette. The smiles and the laughter were infectious. He gave in to it, allowing himself a moment to understand what it might be like to truly be "in" with these people. It was what he wanted, after all.

Rua was nothing but a beautiful temptress leading him away from the scrupulous life he was trying to lead. Her presence filled his mind with mayhem and left him wanting. He could not sustain her willfulness without succumbing to it entirely. And he would not do it. He would not throw it all to ruin.

After the dance, he would find Rua's parents, as he'd said he would, and he would send her home and be done.

Mr. and Mrs. Harrington were outside on the terrace, speaking with a couple he hadn't yet been introduced to.

"Good evening. A word?" he said to both of them. A glassy-eyed Ned looked at Finn like he'd never met him before.

Finn turned to Flossie. "I am afraid there's been a bit of a mishap and I've spilled my drink all over your daughter's gown."

"Good heavens, is she all right?" she asked, as though Rua had been wounded.

"Perfectly fine. I've offered my carriage to take her home; I hope that suits. She's outside."

"Yes. I'd like a word with her before she goes."

"There's no need," Finn said, but Mrs. Harrington was already hurrying toward the door.

He wasn't sure how to explain that he'd lied about Rua's dress. It was a stupid lie, but he preferred that to telling Flossie the truth.

He caught up to Flossie when she was outside. The heavy smell of smoke floated around them.

"Where is she?" Flossie asked, looking around for his missing carriage.

The cheeky rascal. She'd taken his transport.

"She's on her way home," he said, hoping it was true.

"I thought you were going to be with her," Flossie said, her eyes narrowing.

"I didn't think it would be appropriate without a chaperone," he said.

Flossie eyed him suspiciously, then she nodded. "Well, seeing as you're without a transport, we can drop you on our way home."

Before Finn could object, a wobbly Ned hurried out the front door.

"Leaving without me, my dear?" he asked Flossie.

"Hardly." She smiled at her husband. "But since you're here, why don't we pull the carriage around? It's late."

And Ned had drunk his fill.

"Well, good night, then," Finn said to the couple, slinking toward the door. He had no intention of being cajoled into a carriage ride with the mother of the woman who spoiled dinner.

"My lord, I will not take no for an answer. The party is over. My daughter has taken your carriage; allow us to repay the favor." Flossie turned to her husband. "Ned, stay here; the lord and I will be right back. We must thank our hosts." Finn suspected she wanted to parade him in front of the others.

"I'll be fine out here with your husband," Finn told her. The Randalls were so deep in their cups that in the morning they wouldn't remember who had or hadn't bidden them farewell.

"You're right; let's just leave. I'll send Beth a note in the morning," Flossie said, and he was positive it was because she didn't want to risk letting him out of her sight.

Flossie sat beside her husband and across from Finn. Ned was snoring within seconds of entering the carriage.

"The Madison Hotel is a fine establishment, my lord, but what are you doing staying in hotel apartments? Surely you would prefer something more permanent?"

Flossie really was the nosiest person he'd ever encountered. This was the last conversation he wanted to have at this hour of the night.

"Indeed I would," was all Finn offered. He turned his attention to the orange glow cast over the night sky.

"That's odd," Flossie remarked as the carriage rolled to a stop.

Not bothering to wait for the driver to open the door, Finn jumped down from the carriage.

"Can't get any closer. Road's blocked off, my lord," the driver said.

And Finn could see why. The Madison Hotel was up in a blaze.

"What is the meaning of this?" Flossie shouted, but at the sight of the burning hotel, she gasped. "Is that the hotel?"

Finn nodded.

"Why, you'll need somewhere to stay!" Flossie exclaimed excitedly.

"What?" Finn looked at her. Everything he owned was in that hotel, everything of importance. Panic struck him at the thought of one item he couldn't replace. He shoved his hand into his pocket, rummaging for the coin, hoping he had it with him.

Relief washed over him as his fingers wrapped around the coin in his left pocket. He held tight to it, unsure why it meant anything to him. It was a half dollar, the one he'd tried to pay Rua with and she'd given back.

"Get back in. You'll come and stay with us," Flossie said. "We've plenty of room."

His lodgings were the furthest thing from his mind. "I'm going to see what I can do to help."

"Help? Good heavens, you can't," Flossie shrieked.

Finn ignored her. He was already on his way.

The last thing he heard from Flossie was her yelling out to him, "We'll see you tonight. Forty-Ninth and Fifth!"

Twelve

"What on earth are you doing?"

Rua's eyes snapped open at the sound of Flossie's high-pitched voice. Disoriented, she looked around her and at her nightdress, realizing she'd fallen asleep in the library, but not before her chambermaids had helped her into her nightclothes and gawked at her ruined gown.

When she remembered she'd left the Randalls' without telling Flossie, she jumped off the settee. There was a large thud as the anthology on demons and witchcraft fell onto the floor.

The blood drained from her face as the anthology opened up to a page depicting a horned devil sitting cross-legged on the floor. She stepped forward just enough to cover it with her nightdress.

"The most serendipitous thing has just occurred." Flossie was grinning like a cat.

"What is it?" Rua asked, trying not to look like she'd almost just been caught sleeping with a book about demons. She glanced at the clock; it was nearing midnight.

"The Madison Hotel has gone up in flames!" Rua was puzzled by how this excited Flossie. Reading her face, Flossie continued, "The Lord of Donore needs somewhere to stay. Fortunately, I was there when he discovered the news. He'll be residing with us for the foreseeable future."

Rua tried her best to kick the book under the settee before following Flossie out of the library. Foreseeable future?

"Is he here now?" Rua asked, moving her loose hair out of her face and smoothing out her skirt. She didn't want to see him, of course. He'd left her waiting in his carriage for twenty minutes too long. But she didn't not want to see him either. It was all very frustrating.

They continued down the hall toward Rua's bedchamber.

"We left the Randalls' together, seeing as you took his carriage for reasons I will not question. We were going to drop him at his door, but the road was blocked off because the whole building was on fire. He jumped out of the carriage to go help, the poor thing," Flossie answered. "Now, make yourself scarce or clean yourself up. The Lord of Donore could arrive at any moment. This is a chance to secure an advantageous match for you, a chance I wasn't sure we'd get. You will not mess this up." And with that final threat, Flossie flew down the stairs, shouting about curtains.

Rua waited until she was sure Flossie was downstairs, then she turned back to the library. She had to return Emma's books to their proper hiding places.

The entire house was abuzz, prepping for the lord's arrival. Everyone from the cook to the footmen had been woken up. Servants were dusting things that had been dusted a hundred times before, polishing silverware that wouldn't be used. It was a waste of time for all involved; Rua doubted the man would even notice.

The fuss was for Flossie alone, who apparently thrived in a constant state of agitation.

She wondered what business a lord had in putting out a hotel fire. What would prompt him to offer his assistance?

"Have you seen Mara?" Rua asked one of the passing chambermaids. She thought it strange that she still wasn't back yet.

The maid ignored her. Rua cursed under her breath.

Flossie's voice echoed through the marble foyer as Rua sneaked back into the library. She closed the doors behind her. The anthology was where she had left it, haphazardly shoved under the settee. She shut the text and put it back on the shelf.

Arms resting on her hips, she scanned the many shelves of the extensive library. Surely there had to be other books here on Irish mythology.

In no particular order, she began her search, bouncing from one shelf to the next, collecting anything that she thought might be of use and adding it to a growing pile in front of the fireplace.

When she finished, she assessed her findings. The majority of the books were unhelpful, even the one on Irish folklore, which was filled with tales of Ireland's mighty warriors—Queen Medb, Fionn mac Chumaill, and Cú Chulainn, to name a few. There was even mention of the Morrígan goddesses and their many conflicts but no real information.

At some point or another, the Morrígan had interacted with all the folkloric heroes. But the encounters were always brief, glossed over, and nondescript. Three goddesses, wicked adversaries, and protectors of the land who transformed into hags or crows and decided the outcome of a battle or foretold someone's doom.

She read the story about Cú Chulainn's death with interest. Tricked into eating cursed meat by the Morrígan disguised as three old women, he was immeasurably weakened. A sorry way to die. An unbeatable warrior, defender of the innocent, taken out by poisoned food.

Though it wouldn't be fair to say it was the food that killed him. A spear ultimately finished him off, spilling his innards. Even so, he refused to die on the ground and tied himself upright to a stone to face his final foes. None would approach until a crow tripped over his entrails, signaling his demise. Only then did a man come and remove his head.

Fascinating as they were, these ancient fairy tales served no purpose. It was not information Rua could use to better understand her current situation.

That kind of information likely wouldn't be found in the Harringtons' library at all. She needed more books like the ones she'd found under Emma's floorboard.

Rua threw herself on the chair, wondering where Emma had even gotten her hands on the anthology. Perhaps Flossie had given it to her in an attempt to offer her salvation. A book meant to scare her daughter away from the occult, not realizing it was her favorite maid who had introduced her to that world.

Rua sat up as another thought struck her.

Mara.

Already making her way downstairs, Rua hoped Mara hadn't yet returned from wherever she'd gone. Though if she hadn't, she would have to be returning soon; she'd been gone for several hours. But if Mara was a Morrígan enthusiast the way Emma supposedly was, then maybe she too had some paraphernalia hidden in her room.

Rua didn't think it wise to flat out ask Mara these questions about the Morrígan. She'd shared her memory loss with her, and while Mara was more than understanding, it made Rua uneasy.

Rua used the back staircase, a regular staircase made of wood and lacquer that was reserved for the staff. Three flights down and Rua was outside the staff sleeping quarters. The walls were white and cold, the hall long and narrow. Apprehensive, Rua walked forward. She hadn't a clue which room belonged to Mara. And there was no one to ask, because Flossie had all the servants upstairs doing needless tasks.

Rua's footsteps echoed down the whitewashed hallway. The first room she checked was empty apart from a crucifix hanging between two beds and a slim dresser. She continued her search, quietly shuffling in and out of the servants' rooms. All of the rooms were like the first, barren save for a few smaller personal items on the dressers. Most notable were the crucifixes, all visible from the door and always shared between two beds—except for one.

Rua walked inside. Above the cot on the left side hung the crucifix. The one on the right had no holy adornments whatsoever.

She thought about Mara's quick lie about spending time praying with Rua when Flossie had caught her on the floor in her room. Blasphemous, really. None of these devout maids were going to lie about their god to protect Rua. Unless, of course, it wasn't their god. And she knew Mara worshipped three.

Rua hurried over to the shared dresser, riffling through the limited personal effects. One Bible, a few letters, and one plain gown for each occupant. No Morrígan accoutrements. There was nothing under the beds either.

Rua sat on what she assumed was Mara's, thinking about where she could look next. The mattress was terribly thin; the bed frame pushed uncomfortably into the backs of her thighs. She didn't know how anyone could sleep like this. Curious, she lifted the light mattress and found a journal.

Pulse racing, she took it from its hiding spot and set the mattress back down. She checked the hallway, listening for sounds of anyone coming, but it was silent.

Rua flipped through the pages and found more than half of them filled, scrawled with what she assumed was Mara's handwriting. She shut the book, feeling like a terrible sneak, and tossed it on the bed.

She was going to put it back where she found it, she swore she was, but the journal landed open to a page with words she couldn't unsee.

23 May 1870

The Mother was not there today. I have yet to understand her pattern. She comes as she pleases, but I will be there, always, ready to do as she asks. And so I will wait for her direction. She will be pleased to learn that Emma has come around to the idea. She struggles with her mother, her anger driving her away and into the Morrígan's arms. I do not know what she wants with Emma, but her purpose will be revealed in due time.

Rua flipped over to the next page.

25 May 1870

I have no news from the Mother. I brought Emma to the hell-mouth while Mrs. Harrington was away. She was amazed that such a place existed so close to her home. She's taken her expulsion hard, mostly for the trouble it has caused with her mother. But she's grown more faithful because of it.

Rua tried not to sensationalize what she'd just read in Mara's diary, not to make more of something she didn't understand, but as she reread the passages, she drew the same conclusion. Mara and the Morrígan had lured Emma into the hellmouth, but why?

She tore through the numerous pages, urgently trying to find August.

31 July 1870

It happens tonight. She's more excited than I am. Whatever the Mother has in store, our lives will be forever changed.

Rua turned to the next page. The handwriting was frenzied. Tearstains blotted the words.

1 August 1870

I waited for her as long as I could, but the house will be waking soon. I'm sick with worry. And the guilt! What have I done?

She went in good spirits. I don't know what went wrong. We were able to communicate at first. She told me how dark it was, and cold, but she wasn't afraid. Brave girl. And then she stopped talking. I called for her over and over, but only my own voice called back.

Oh, I fear I've made a grave error. It's been hours. What have I done?

*

She's back. She's back! And unharmed. A little confused but physically unharmed. I should never have doubted the Mother's intentions.

A door opened down the hall, letting out a long screech. Rua froze, heart pounding, as she listened to cabinet doors opening and closing. "If you can't find it, Mrs. Smith'll have you scrubbing the chamber pots."

Time was up. Rua stuffed the diary back under Mara's mattress where she'd found it. She could always find a way to sneak back down here, but she would never be able to explain it to Mara if it were caught in her possession.

Besides, she'd found out what she needed to know. All of this was Mara's doing.

Rua fled down the hall, past the servants rummaging in the storage room, and back upstairs.

Thirteen

Finn hesitated, holding on to a bucket of water as he watched flames ravage the once-luxurious Madison Hotel, wondering if this was a sign of things to come.

The fire department was out in full force with their ladder trucks and hoses. They commanded the scene as they worked to clear the area and put out the flames.

He was surprised at the turnout of civilians offering their assistance. Crowded onto the street in front of the burning hotel, panic-stricken faces shouted orders, all trying to contain the spread. Saving the neighboring stores and homes had become the priority.

Of course, there were those who had simply come to watch. Tragedy so often did bring out the curious. Young children huddled in groups, staring at the flames in bemused horror. Men and women shook their heads, sorry but not surprised; wooden structures were prone to fires.

Wiping the sweat from his brow, Finn focused on the bucket he was holding, handing it off to the neighbor next to him. One by one they passed them forward, dousing out a flame just for another to rise in its place. It wasn't enough. The hotel was coming down.

"Help!" He heard a desperate cry through the roar of the flames. He looked around for the source.

"Help!" they cried again.

He tossed his empty bucket aside and moved toward the hotel entrance. A tremendous wave of heat licked his skin. It was like walking into a furnace.

"I think it's coming from that window over there," a fireman said, gesturing to the window on the ground floor. "We can't send anyone in. It's too dangerous."

A burning piece of debris crashed on the sidewalk.

"Please, help me!" a woman cried. Before anyone said another word, Finn ran into the burning building. There was no thought beyond helping that woman and his belief that he could save her.

"Where are you?" He coughed as he inhaled the smoke, his eyes burning. What remained of the hotel lobby was covered with fallen debris and charred furniture. He looked up at the beams buckling with the heat. The ceiling was going to come down.

"Here!" she cried.

Finn cursed when he saw her. She was trapped under a large beam that had already fallen from the ceiling, and he wasn't sure how he was going to lift it on his own. She knew it too. The look of disappointment that crossed her face when she realized he was the only one that had come for her was gutting.

"It's all right. I'm going to get you out of here," he said.

She nodded, but the fear in her eyes told him she didn't believe him.

He reached for the part of the beam that wasn't burning and tried to lift it. Judging by the size, it had to be triple the weight of him, more than any man could ever dream to lift on his own. The bones in her leg, if she ever got out from underneath, would no doubt be crushed.

Finn took a deep breath and squatted down, placing his hands beneath the corner of the beam. His skin burned against the scorched wood as he pushed upward, using the force of his legs to lift it off the woman. He let out a roar as he did it, feeling raw strength course through his veins. The woman cried as the wooden shaft rose off her leg and was cast aside, and then she fainted.

Chest heaving, he picked her limp body up from the floor, his eyes stinging as he tried to find the nearest exit. Through the flames and wreckage, Finn barreled his way outside.

The crowd rushed toward them, trying to help. Finn set the woman down far away enough from the blaze. Her leg was man-gled, and she was still unconscious. "She needs a doctor!" he shouted between gasps as he tried to clear his lungs of the smoke.

"How in the name of God did you do that?" a man asked, laying a blanket on the ground for the woman.

The shock and confusion on the man's face mirrored what Finn felt inside. His skin was hot to the touch, sensitive where blisters should've formed and hadn't. He glanced down at his garments, which were utterly destroyed by soot and flame, not understanding how he'd made it out unscathed.

"There was a path," he lied.

They both glanced at the hotel, the entrance nothing but a burning pile of remains, then back to each other.

Finn stood up and walked away from the man and the other prying eyes along the cobbled footpath. They were as surprised as he was, but he didn't need any more questions. Questions that felt like accusations.

He made a fist and released it, feeling that familiar buzz of strength. In no world should he have been able to lift that beam on his own, and yet he had done it. Lifted it as though it were nothing but a twig.

Away from the heat of the fire and the swell of the crowd, he found relief.

He thought back to when this had started, the unexplained strength he'd experienced when he knocked out the man at the ath-letic club, and his mind went to Rua. Everything had changed the day he met her.

In a daze, he glimpsed the street signs, realizing the direction he was walking—toward her.

In no time at all, he stood outside the Harringtons' home, won-dering about the decision that had led him here to this wealthy Manhattan neighborhood, mixed up with these titans of industry.

He'd been so blindsided by the news of the hotel fire that he'd hardly understood what he was agreeing to when Flossie offered him a place to stay. Come to think of it, he didn't think he'd agreed to anything at all, but as it was, he did need a place to stay.

At the far corner of the building, a window lit up. He could make out the slight shadow of a figure behind the curtain. Expectantly, he wondered if it was Rua.

He let out a sigh, crushing a pebble underfoot. Things were becoming complicated, and he didn't know when it had gotten this way. Perhaps it was precisely because he had been cautioned against her that he was so intrigued.

Nothing to do with the intense longing that plagued him night and day. A longing not pure and unfettered but marred and torturous, filling his quiet world with worry.

Resolute, he walked up the steps, straight into the belly of the beast.

"Good evening, my lord," the butler said as he opened the doors. His voice did not betray the shock in his eyes. Finn understood he must look like a depraved monster walking through the doors of the beautiful home. His shirt was undone, and he was covered in sweat and soot.

"Evening," Finn replied, exhausted and ready for sleep.

"I will show you to your suites straightaway. Mr. and Mrs. Harrington have retired for the evening, but if there is anything at all you require, do let me know."

"Thank you," Finn said as he followed the butler up the staircase.

The entire home was lit up, he assumed for his arrival, despite the late hour. Truly a magnificent display of opulence. It must infuriate the Harringtons to have so much money and still have to fight for acceptance.

"Someone will be available to assist with the collection of any personal belongings that might've been recovered."

"That won't be necessary," Finn said. "The damage is too widespread. There'll be nothing left but a pile of ash when it's done burning."

"Such a pity that is." The butler shook his head.

When Finn reached the top step, he heard something crash to the floor. He looked up to find Rua standing in the hallway, a pile of books at her feet. At this hour, she was the last person he'd expected to see. Her eyes widened at the sight of him, a slight flush in her cheeks.

She'd changed into her nightdress, free of her torn orange gown. A pity, he thought, as his mind wandered to their moment in the Randalls' front garden. To the curve of her breast as her body pushed against his and the feel of her hands digging into his torso. The familiar longing was once more building inside him. Though if he were being honest with himself, it was always there, simmering under the surface.

She bent down for her books, and he moved to help her, but by the time he reached her, she had them gathered. Without a word, she disappeared behind a set of mahogany doors.

"I do not want to overstep, my lord, but I fear I must warn you," the butler started.

"Go ahead," Finn said, already knowing what he was going to say.

"Best to keep your distance from that one. She's quite troubled. Spends all hours in the library, so it shouldn't be too hard to avoid her. Rather unstable."

Finn nodded. He was tired of everyone telling him that.

"Well, here we are, my lord. Do let me know if there's anything else you require." The butler stopped outside his new bedchamber and opened the door for Finn.

"Thank you."

Five minutes ago, he had been uncertain of his ability to make it up the stairs to his new room, his exhaustion was so extreme. But now he was alert, filled with the knowledge that Rua was awake and only a few doors away.

He entered his latest accommodations and was thoroughly impressed. Spacious and clean, everything like new. As he tossed aside his jacket, he wondered what book was so important that Rua needed it at this hour.

Restless, he sat in the chair, only to rise again a moment later. Curiosity, or something like it, got the better of him.

He made his way to the library, hoping she was still there. What he was going to do if he found her was another story entirely.

The double doors had been left ajar. He pushed them open and found Rua leaning against the settee, a book hidden behind her back. She was talking to her lady's maid. "If your mother knows you're out of bed at this hour," the maid warned.

"I told you I would be right there—" Rua stopped talking when she saw Finn. The maid looked startled. He understood; he was still wearing the clothes destroyed by the fire.

"What are you doing in here?" Rua asked, giving him a once-over.

"I was . . ." Lost for words, he thought, *What* am *I doing in here?*

"Please, Mara, I'll meet you in my chambers in a moment."

"But, miss," the maid protested.

"It's fine," Rua said.

Begrudgingly, the maid left, but not before shooting Finn a dirty look.

"No manners on the servants either, I see," he said, though he wasn't sure why he was needling her.

Rua stiffened.

A moment of quiet intensity lingered around them as they waited to be sure the maid was gone, and then she charged him, wagging her blasted little finger.

"You're quite bold for someone in a predicament such as the one you're in," she said, poking him in the chest, letting her finger loiter a moment on his bare skin. The sensation was invigorating, like a jolt to his heart. She snatched her hand back as if feeling the same thing. He glanced quickly to see that she hadn't left a mark.

He bent his head toward hers. "And what predicament might that be?"

Her gaze moved slowly from his mouth to his torso and back up to his eyes. "The one in which it's a quarter past two in the morning, you're bare chested, slicked with sweat, and in the library looking for me." She smiled.

He pressed his lips together. She had him there. "Your point?"

"Glass houses, my lord. Your manners are questionable at best."

Before she could speak again, he took a step forward off the wall. He would not allow this unruly woman to question his character.

She moved in response, losing her footing, and he contemplated letting her fall. There was no doubt she deserved a good thump, but he grabbed her around the waist and lifted her upright, electrifying the air around them.

She steadied herself, pressing her arm against his chest. The light touch, devastatingly tempting, left him certain that this time she'd burned right through him.

Eyes full of mischief and sparkling gold, Finn stared at the woman before him—so passionate, so willful, so wrong. The feel of her body awakened a primal need within him. Her luscious lips, full and pouting, dared him to touch them. He needed to know every part of her. Even the part that warned him away.

Hungrily, he studied her, desperate for any indication she was feeling the same. But she was unreadable, too clever to be caught. Stealing his breath, she turned her hand over. Both of them watching as she trailed the backs of her fingers across the upper part of his abdomen.

"Rua," he heard himself say.

Her eyes flicked upward, and he knew he'd broken the spell, severing all tension with his reckless plea. She pushed herself out of his arms, and the loss was immediate.

"You may dress in their clothes, you may use their words, but you are no gentleman, Lord of Donore."

She had no idea the truth of her words.

With that, she picked up her books and slipped through the library doors, not giving him a second glance.

Now alone, Finn went to the bar cart and poured himself a glass of whatever was in the decanter. He sat down in the brown leather chesterfield chair and put his legs up on the ottoman.

He rolled his head back and forth against the deep buttoning, trying to understand how he had ended up here. He glanced at the side table and spotted a book: *Legends and Stories of Ireland* by Samuel Lover.

Shocked that the Harringtons had it in their library, he reached for it and flipped through the pages, wondering why someone, presumably Rua, was reading up on Ireland. He'd hardly made it through the preface when he started to doze.

Finn wasn't sure how long he'd been asleep when he woke with a fright. He sat up and looked around the unfamiliar room. Recognizing it as the Harringtons' library, he leaned back in the chair.

The fire had dwindled to nothing, the candles on the mantel burnt to the ends, and he looked at the clock. A quarter past five.

He closed his eyes, trying to remember his dream, but all he could recall was the glowing eyes. Stranger and more frequent, his dreams were a new addition to his life. He thought back to when they'd started, to his new feelings of strength, and drew the same conclusion.

Rua.

Twinned feelings of aggravation and exhaustion battled within him. He let out a yawn; it was time to retire, though he doubted he'd get back to sleep. He left the library and went to find his room.

Fourteen

The breakfast room was the last place she wanted to visit at nine o'clock in the morning, considering she'd fallen asleep only a few hours ago.

"If you're not downstairs in two minutes, Flossie will be up looking for you," Mara said, looking tired. It was the first time Rua had noticed bags under her eyes. She wondered if Mara's lack of sleep had to do with Flossie or her own late-night excursion.

She hadn't had the chance to catch up with Mara after Finn interrupted them.

"She's never joined me for breakfast before." Rua let out a yawn as she rose from her vanity. Just another way the Lord of Donore's presence was inconveniencing her. The first being that she couldn't stop thinking about him.

"Where were you last night?" Rua asked as she walked into the empty hallway.

"What do you mean? I was here." Mara shut the door behind them.

"No, while we were at the Randalls', you went somewhere."

"I was running errands," she said.

"What kind of errands require you to be out until after midnight?"

"The important kind."

"You're being coy," Rua said. "Did you go to the hellmouth?" Now that Rua knew Mara had conspired with the Morrígan to send Emma in, she didn't trust that she wasn't still up to something now.

Mara shushed her, stopping at the top of the staircase. "You need to keep your voice down."

"Is that where you went?" Rua asked, lowering her voice.

Mara nodded, and they continued down, noting the lovely smell of bacon as they descended.

"I want you to take me with you next time," Rua said.

Mara shook her head. "No."

"Why not? If it can help me get my memories back, then I want to try."

"You can't just go there and get your memories back. There has to be purpose, careful planning, and a Sabbat. Samhain is the next one."

"At the end of October?" Rua had seen the date in Emma's journal. She couldn't wait until October; that was still almost two months away.

"Everything will work out the way it is supposed to. The Morrígan took your memories for a reason. When you are meant to have them, they will return. You cannot force it."

Like hell she couldn't. But she had to tread carefully and figure out a way to bring up what she'd read in Mara's diary without letting her know she'd read it. Besides, she needed to worry about handling both Finn and Flossie at breakfast.

Flossie's matchmaking schemes were tiresome, and Finn was the last person she wanted to be matched up with. Broad shoulders and a strong jaw would never be enough to compensate for his arrogance.

I'm not interested in the Harrington girl. Finn's words still ate at her.

"Any word on the hotel fire?" Rua asked, through her chagrin.

They kept a leisurely pace as they walked through the marbled foyer toward the breakfast room.

"They managed to contain the blaze, but the hotel is beyond repair," Mara said. "I heard the Lord of Donore ran straight into the flames and rescued a woman."

"Ran into the flames?" Rua looked at Mara.

"Yes." She nodded.

"Suspiciously heroic, wouldn't you say?" Rua thought back to the way he'd entered the library like a virile beast in need of taming. She'd

almost let herself entertain the idea. He was different in his unkempt-
ness, lacking his usual pretension, but then he'd opened his mouth.

"What do you mean?" Mara asked.

"How many members of the upper class do you know running
into burning buildings or doing anything at all that might prove to
be an inconvenience?"

"Well, it's in the morning papers."

"So it must be true," Rua quipped.

Mara shook her head. "They said he lifted a wooden beam the
size of a tree trunk off her leg without any assistance at all."

"I doubt that. Something is not quite adding up."

"Because he antagonizes you is not reason enough to question
his character. You of all people should understand that."

Rua let out a huff.

Mrs. Smith emerged from the breakfast room in a flurry, bark-
ing orders at Mara before they'd even entered. "All is in order for
his lordship. Keep an eye on her." She glared at Rua.

"Excuse me?" Rua was taken aback, but Mrs. Smith was already
gone.

Rua entered the breakfast room and was surprised to find she
was the only one there.

"Where is everyone?" she asked as she took a seat, annoyed that
she was the first to arrive to a meal she did not want to attend.

"I'll find out," Mara said.

Rua's stomach growled as she examined the contents of the
table. It was the most luxurious breakfast spread she'd ever seen
from the Harringtons'.

There were baskets filled with apples, pears, plums, and peaches.
Multiple plates of berries, sliced bananas, watermelon, and sugared
pineapple. Silver platters with bacon and another with scrambled
eggs, though there were also egg cups offering the option of hard-
boiled eggs. French toast with maple syrup and cinnamon. Hot
cakes and waffles.

Most days she was only offered berries and oatmeal. Maybe the
lord's presence had some perks after all. She helped herself.

A few minutes later, Mara returned.

"The Lord of Donore had previously agreed to morning tea at
the Fitzgeralds'. Apparently, you just missed him."

"That's too bad," she said, dropping a sugar cube in her teacup.

She didn't know why it bothered her. This was what she wanted, wasn't it? Breakfast alone, as usual. And if Finn lacked the necessary intellect to avoid the nasty brat and her surly mother, then so be it.

"Your mother is quite peeved. I would advise avoiding her if possible," Mara said.

Speaking of surly mothers, Rua thought, stirring the milk. "How is this my fault?"

"Well, she thinks if you'd come downstairs sooner, then he might not have left."

"That's ridiculous." Rua reached for a strawberry, then remembered Emma didn't like them. She opted for a waffle instead. "My presence would not have altered his plans."

"Your mother believes otherwise," Mara said, watching her.

"Flossie believes the moon and the stars were placed in the sky so that she might have something to look at."

"Flossie sounds quite the nitwit."

Rua almost agreed aloud until she realized who had spoken. Flossie was hovering in the doorway. Mara's cheeks went scarlet before she fled the room through the servants' door.

"I—"

"Save it," Flossie hissed, sauntering into the room. "I hope you're happy with yourself."

Rua shrugged. "I'm not sure what I could have done to prevent this."

"Shrugging is a despicable habit."

Rua straightened her back and lifted her chin.

"Better." Flossie continued, "Let me put it to you in a way that you might understand." She approached the table, her large skirt preventing her from reaching it fully. "The only reason you are still here in this house, in this city, is because the Lord of Donore escorted you out of dinner after your horrible little tantrum. And now he is living in our home because I had the foresight to arrange it." Flossie's tone blew past condescending and was teetering on disgust. She truly despised her daughter. Rua felt a stab of pity for Emma and what she must've endured. "Your presence in society will only be tolerated so long as the Lord of Donore appears interested."

Rua swallowed back her rising anger. She hated that she was letting Flossie talk to her this way. Hated that her acceptance hinged on that man's interest.

She was certain, just as Mara was in her journal, that Flossie's crossness was what had driven Emma into the arms of Morrígan—a refuge outside her mother's patronizing grip. And Mara had been there to capitalize on it.

"Have I made myself clear?" Flossie asked.

Jaw clenched tight, Rua nodded. Flossie would make good on her threat to send her to the asylum. She was sure of it.

It was time she started making other plans. She would not be collateral damage in this war between mother and daughter.

"Now go and find Mara. You're going for a walk in the park," Flossie said.

For the remainder of the week, Rua's routine was exactly the same: wake up for breakfast with the lord, come downstairs to find he'd already left, avoid Flossie's anger, then promenade in the park with Mara.

Nothing changed. No one spoke to her while she went for her promenade. She never saw the Lord of Donore, because he either kept exceptionally odd hours or he was dodging her. Regardless, Mara was the only one who would talk to her.

Being the debutante daughter Flossie wanted was exasperating. Rua spent hours getting dressed up, only to be ignored by everyone, and was then expected to smile. But her stunt at the Randalls' dinner the week before had set her back and slowed their social calendar considerably.

It wasn't permanent, Flossie assured her. They were too important, but for now, Rua was demoted to strolls in public places.

"The weather is getting a bit cooler," Rua said, appreciating the lack of humidity as they walked down the steps to the arcade.

As was her daily routine, they walked from the mall up to the fountain at Bethesda Terrace. She looked forward to it immensely, as it was the only part of her day that allowed her a true moment's peace. Today, however, she saw something at the fountain that made her chest ache.

Panicked, she stopped short and hid behind one of the arcade arches.

"What is the matter?" Mara asked, looking around.

"Shh." Rua pulled Mara beside her.

"What are you—Oh," she said, following Rua's gaze. "Will we go a different way today?"

Annette and Finn circled the fountain, arm in arm, desecrating Rua's favorite place.

She had no claim to Finn, nor had he any claim to her. But she certainly didn't like seeing Annette get what she wanted.

"I don't need another confrontation with Annette. Let's just turn around before she sees me."

"Are you sure that's why we're turning around?"

"Does it really matter?" Rua asked, looking to Mara.

"If you did fancy him, perhaps you and your mother could put aside your differences and work together?" Mara suggested.

"Work together to catch his interest? I will do no such thing. And besides, I don't fancy him. He is far too arrogant for my taste." And much, much too handsome. She'd never be able to concentrate.

"Whatever you say," Mara said.

Americans were loud, but Miss Harrington was louder.

While Annette prattled on about who had worn the wrong gloves at last night's dinner, he was being entertained by one red-headed socialite trying to hide in a gown twice the width of the pillar she was ducking behind.

He'd seen the look on her face the moment she spotted them. He felt a pang of guilt at the distress it seemed to cause her, like he'd taken the last piece of her favorite pie, then spit it onto the ground. He was surprised to see her grab her maid and go the other way. Disappointed, even. Though he wasn't sure why. It was his fault that they were becoming strangers.

She'd gotten under his skin with her clever tongue and striking beauty, and he had enough common sense to know that if he didn't put some distance between himself and Rua, he would lose himself entirely. But the distance didn't stop the longing.

He'd catch little glimpses of her. Sometimes in the mornings, groggily coming downstairs for a breakfast he was never going to attend. He'd love nothing more than to sit across from her and watch as she came to life with her morning tea.

Then there were his favorite quiet moments, when she'd sit by the window of the library reading. He'd often see her there on his way back to the house, illuminated by the firelight. How many times had he stopped outside those mahogany doors, threatening to join her, only to walk away before it was too late.

"I have it on good authority that she purchased it at a department store," he heard Annette say. "I mean, how are we to distinguish ourselves as their betters when they are able to dress like us? Though the quality is a dead giveaway."

"Indeed," Finn muttered, paying her little heed.

"If only there was something we could do about Emma Harrington," she said, finally managing to catch his attention.

"What do you mean?" he asked.

"You cannot tell me you didn't notice how peaceful the last week of events have been without her?"

He had noticed, all right, but rather than peaceful, he found them dull and loathsome.

"Not to mention how dangerous her reputation is for business," she said, parroting something she must have heard her father say.

"Madame Webster's dressmaking business seems to be faring well," Finn added. Perhaps he was too close to the situation, he wasn't sure he would have noticed otherwise, but in every ballroom he saw ladies imitating Rua's gown, down to the color. Annette included.

"Really?" Annette asked, sticking her nose in the air, "I hadn't noticed."

Finn said nothing as he guided Annette away from Rua.

"How much longer are you planning on residing in the Harringtons' home, my lord?" Annette asked, her voice a tad shaky.

"I hadn't thought about it," he lied. The Harringtons had offered for the season, and everyone knew it, thanks to Flossie. Had she not said anything, he would've moved into another hotel and no one would have batted an eye. But if he left now, it would further damage the Harringtons' reputation—further damage Rua's. Word would get out, and it would be twisted and warped in the scandal sheets. They would find some way to blame her for it, and so he'd decided he would stay.

Fifteen

After Mara had unceremoniously awakened her earlier that morning to let her know she was attending a lady's luncheon later that day, Rua arrived with Flossie at Delmonico's exactly on time.

The glamorous restaurant was located in Union Square near the Academy of Music. Flossie was frenetic. Her ascension to society would not be complete until she dined at Delmonico's for dinner after enjoying the opera from a box, but today she would settle for lunch. One more rung up the ladder.

They walked upstairs to a richly decorated room with a dozen or so white-clothed tables with place cards. Three-tiered porcelain serving trays had been placed at the center of each table, bearing varying sandwiches and pastries. At least sixty different women, none Rua could recognize, were gathered around the tables, mingling with each other.

She couldn't tell one scowling face from the next, except for the Fitzgeralds, of course.

"Say hello to our host, Mrs. Stevens," Flossie whispered.

"Good afternoon, Mrs. Stevens," Rua said.

Mrs. Stevens gave her a curt smile and turned to Flossie.

"Flossie, I'm so glad you mentioned the luncheon last night, and I do apologize. Your invitations must have gotten lost in the post."

"Think nothing of it," Flossie said, oblivious to the obvious or too desperate to care that she had been deliberately left off the list.

Mrs. Stevens moved on to the next guest. The Stevenses, according to Flossie, could trace their lineage in New York back to the Dutch settlers. In other words, they wanted nothing to do with the Harringtons or anyone else who made their money through trade.

Rua hadn't realized how important the Stevenses were. Up until now, the fuss had been made about the Fitzgeralds. Perhaps she should consider Lily's invitation.

"Come, let us find our table," Flossie said to Rua. Flossie walked to the front of the room, weaving in and out of all the tables, looking for theirs.

Rua noticed Mrs. Stevens and Mrs. Fitzgerald snicker and exchange glances in the corner while Flossie searched.

Eventually, Flossie figured it out. Their table was right by the door.

"Unacceptable." Flossie's nostrils flared. "I'm going to find out why we're seated in the back like lepers."

Rua considered telling Flossie that she was seated exactly where they wanted her to be, but she didn't think she would listen.

"Why don't you go and find Annette?" Flossie suggested senselessly.

Rua ignored her, unsure of what fairy world Flossie inhabited where she thought she and Annette were on speaking terms. She sat down and stared into the throng of women gathered around the head tables. The tables that Flossie was coveting.

"I see you made it after all." Lily sat quietly beside Rua, her back straight as a rod. Rua adjusted herself, trying to do the same.

"We did," Rua said, not bothering to mask her displeasure.

Lily smiled. "I understand how difficult these events can be."

"Especially when you weren't invited in the first place," Rua added, though she doubted Lily had any idea of what someone like Rua was dealing with.

"You're very forward," Lily laughed. "It's refreshing."

"I'm glad someone appreciates it," she said, and took a sip of the lemonade placed in front of her. She hoped Lily wouldn't bring up the social club again. Ignoring her offers was growing awkward.

"No one here besides me, I can assure you," Lily said as she stood.

Surprised, Rua laughed. Lily was charming and sociable; her mother must be so proud.

"I'm looking forward to seeing what you have to say at our next meeting." Lily winked and seamlessly joined the rest of the women at the front. Her secret society of strong-minded women sounded too good to be true.

"Well, there's nothing we can do. This is where we're sitting." Flossie huffed as she found her way back to Rua. "I saw you talking to Lily Stevens. What did you say to her?"

"Nothing," Rua said, bothered by the insinuation that she couldn't engage in small talk.

"Somehow I doubt that."

"Banal platitudes." Rua shrugged and sipped her watery lemonade.

"It's one thing to shrug at home, but in public, I will not stand for it," Flossie muttered.

No one else joined them at their table for the remainder of the luncheon, and for that, Flossie blamed Rua. Flossie would not entertain the notion that the Harringtons were simply not supposed to attend and the other women had added a table at the last minute only because Flossie was rude enough to ask for one.

Despite their seclusion, news of Finn and Annette's courtship managed to reach their ears. A stunning success; a proposal was imminent.

It soured both their moods.

"The lord's having dinner with us this evening. I tell you, it's about time. To think, we open our home to him, and I can't get him to sit down for one meal. What is the point of having a lord in the house? At any rate, this will likely be your last chance to impress him and make him reconsider," Flossie said.

"Reconsider what?" Rua asked.

"His courtship with Annette. With all the time they're spending together, I assume we truly are but an announcement away."

"I don't see how I'll make him reconsider anything." She couldn't remember the last time they'd spoken. Days? Was it weeks?

"For whatever reason, his lordship's taken some kind of an interest in you. Perhaps he doesn't even understand it himself, but we must use it to our advantage before it wanes."

The fact that Flossie thought Finn's interest was nothing more than morbid curiosity was sobering.

Rua knew Finn wasn't interested in her. Despite living in the same home, he'd done nothing in the last week to indicate he even knew she was there. But she would do what Flossie wanted, if only to buy herself more time. Because if Mara was right and she couldn't go into the hellmouth until Samhain, she had a few more weeks left of pretending to be Emma, and she'd prefer not to do it from the inside of a sanitarium.

"Now, let us leave. We've endured this disrespect long enough."

They said goodbye to no one and made their way to the carriage.

"I am utterly disgusted. The Stevenses might be New York royalty, but we've more money than that room combined. That should be enough. Perhaps it's your presence that has embittered them. You will sit out the next ladies' event, and we'll see how I fare."

"I think that's a wonderful idea," Rua said as they pulled up to the Harringtons' enormous home. Flossie would never consider that she simply wasn't well liked and her new money was unwelcome.

Mrs. Smith rushed to Flossie the moment she walked through the front doors. The conversation seemed tense as Flossie rattled off a list of demands.

Mara met Rua at the bottom of the staircase. "He's here," she whispered feverishly. "The Lord of Donore. He arrived only a few moments ago." Finn had made himself so scarce over the last few days that it was a shock to them all. Like finding a rare bird among the trees.

Rua tried not to be affected, but a wave of nervous flutters washed over her. "It doesn't matter. I'm going to change."

"What do you mean, it doesn't matter?"

"He's all but announced his engagement to Annette Fitzgerald." And it didn't matter, because she wasn't Emma. This wasn't her life, and she didn't need to make things any more complicated by forcing a man into the picture.

"But he hasn't announced it, and he escorted you out of dinner. That has to count for something."

"Over a week ago," she reminded Mara, "and it counts for nothing. He assured Annette's father that he wanted nothing to do with me, and he is proving just that." Irritated, Rua marched up the stairs.

"Don't take too long to change," Flossie called after her. "Dinner will be served promptly at five."

Rua let out a sigh. She would have to suffer a mortifying dinner with a man who didn't want her, all so that she might convince Flossie she shouldn't be sent away.

Finn shuffled around his new bedchamber, trying to get settled. But he knew Rua had returned, and he was anything but.

He couldn't shake it, couldn't explain it, but he wanted to see her.

He always wanted to see her.

There was a knock at his door. Part of him hoped it was her.

"Good evening, my lord."

Disappointed, Finn opened the door for the butler. "Dinner has been moved up to five this evening."

Mrs. Harrington had been trying to get him to agree to dinner, and up until yesterday, he'd been able to avoid it. Between events, he'd been taking his meals at the club and spending his evenings volunteering at the orphanage. Every day there were more and more displaced children in need of safe housing.

But last night she'd caught him coming in the door, and he'd had no choice but to agree. Now he was having second thoughts.

"I am afraid that does not suit. I've had a change of plans."

"Very well, my lord." The butler looked deflated.

Finn forced down the guilt as he lied to the butler. He had no other set plans, but he could not sit down for an intimate meal with Rua. Just like Mrs. Harrington, he knew that the more time he spent around Rua, the more he might like her. A truth he was trying to escape.

Tomorrow, he was going to officially ask Richard for Annette's hand. The decision had been made. His life needed contentment and routine, and neither of those things would be found with Rua.

He grabbed his coat and rushed out the door. He made his way toward the back staircase frequented by the servants so that he might avoid an awkward run-in with Mrs. Harrington, or worse, Rua.

When she was around, his thoughts were muddled, his heart beat wildly, and he was reminded of things he didn't even know he'd forgotten.

He had almost kissed her the night he moved in, proof that he couldn't trust himself around her, and why he stayed away.

He flew down the first set of empty stairs, but as he rounded the banister to make his way down the second, he stopped short.

Coming up the stairs was Rua wearing a lovely pink gown. Her head was down; she hadn't noticed him yet.

He contemplated turning right around and running back up, but he was glued to the spot.

When she finally looked up, her eyes widened, her mouth making the shape of an O. There were only a half dozen steps between them. She hesitated, her gloveless hand gripping the railing. No more than him, she looked as though she might have preferred to run the other way.

"Good evening," he managed to say.

"Hello, Finn," she said with a smile.

He loved that she had no qualms about using his given name.

She looked him over, noticing his hat and coat.

"Something has come up. I'll not be able to make it to dinner," he said, the lie scratching at his throat.

Her face fell, disappointment overtaking her smile. He hated it.

"But of course, my lord," she said, continuing up the steps. The sweet smell of meadowsweet hit him as she moved and lingered long after she left. His favorite smell. It reminded him of home.

He almost went after her. Almost found Mrs. Harrington and told her that he was able to attend dinner after all, but he didn't. His survival instincts were too strong, and Rua would be the death of him.

Finn left the Harrington house and made the long walk to Castle Garden. It took hours, but what else did he have to do?

By the time he'd reached the Battery, night had fallen. He could see the glow from the Castle Garden dome above the Rotunda, where, below, hundreds of immigrants spilled out through the gates despite the late hour.

After disembarking from their ships, those who arrived at Castle Garden entered the Rotunda. It was loud and frenzied and overwhelming for someone on their best day, never mind someone who had just spent weeks traveling to a foreign land.

Inside, they were separated between English speakers and non-English speakers and able to find all the corresponding offices to help with their arrival. Once they were registered, they collected their luggage, visited the currency exchange, and were checked at the hospital. Those looking for work went to the labor exchange. Others who already had plans and family waiting for them could wait inside the Rotunda until their families came or they left through the gates into Battery Park.

Unsuspecting new arrivals were often taken advantage of or left to fend for themselves. This was where Finn had met Sister Mary and the other nuns at St. Brigid's. They'd come down frequently and offer assistance to any and all who needed it.

Finn spent hours directing families, giving them the names of reputable housing and people they could contact for work.

When he returned to the Harrington household, it was after ten. Dinner would be long over. The sting of Rua's disappointment rearing its ugly head, he poured himself a drink and had the valet prepare him a bath before bed.

Sleep evaded him as thoughts of Rua spun round and round. In and out of consciousness, his mind conjured delightful images of them lying in the grass, her head on his chest, while he stroked her wild hair. Then they were dancing, spinning around the ballroom, while the room clapped and cheered.

In another dream, there was nothing but darkness and an ache burrowed so deep in his chest that he sat up gasping for air. The pain was so real, the betrayal so raw, he couldn't shake the feeling it was real.

"I've missed you," he said, knowing her absence meant only one thing.

She looked at him, eyes wild. There was a battle waging within them, the gold overtaking the green as she tried to control it.

Disappointment flared. He had so hoped she could control it, hoped she could choose him.

She grabbed his shirt with exorbitant strength and pulled him toward her.

He searched her face, desperate to find her, but the rise and fall of her chest gave her demons away.

She closed her eyes for a long moment, her head pressed against his.

He soaked her in, memorizing her. "Whatever may come"—he breathed the words into her mouth—"know that I love you."

Her response was visceral as their lips crashed together. In a silent plea, she clung to his neck. But tear-dampened eyelashes and a hungry kiss betrayed the truth she would not share.

They were not going to make it.

Hurried and hopeless, they fell to the grass.

He wrapped his arm behind her back, pulling her closer to him.

"I'm sorry," she said, a broken whisper.

Lost in the sadness, he said nothing.

Face-to-face they lay until they could wait no longer. She rolled onto her back and pulled him above her. He obliged her readily, kissing and teasing until there was no part of her left unexplored.

She took her pleasure and gifted him his.

A fleeting moment of ecstasy laid waste by her choices.

He rose from the bed, pulled on his pants, and threw a shirt over his head.

He sat down again, devastated and confused. He'd had a dream of Rua. Was that Rua? He rubbed his hand up and down his face.

It felt like Rua, or it felt like what he imagined she would feel like. Christ. He shook his head.

It was only a dream, he reminded himself. None of it real.

He shut his eyes, remembering the details, finding himself wishing they were true.

He couldn't stay another minute in his room, so he went to the library.

Sixteen

When she was sure Flossie was asleep, Rua left her bedchamber. Flossie had been on the warpath after Finn canceled dinner. No one was safe. To spare the servants, Ned had poured her three glasses of wine and taken her up to bed.

Per usual, Rua had eaten by herself, only this time she was sore about it. It was one thing for Finn to sneak around and avoid her, another to lie to her face about why he was canceling dinner.

If there was a wedding announcement in the papers tomorrow, she would toss him from the Harringtons' residence herself.

She pushed open the doors to the library. The lights were off, but the room was warm and smelled of firewood. Her favorite chair was pushed directly in front of the fireplace. She untied her robe and bent down to take the books from their hiding place.

She lit another candle, rested a cushion in her lap, and nestled into the armchair. She started with the small leather journal. The pages were almost translucent, and they were filled with symbols and words she couldn't understand.

She wondered if this was Emma's handiwork. Or had this been passed down to her, perhaps from Mara?

The sound of glass clanking on a shelf pulled her face from the pages. She snapped the book shut.

There across the room, stood Finn, leaning against one of the bookshelves, his gaze fixed on her.

Her heart came to a stop.

She stuffed the journal into the cushion behind her and kicked the rest of the books under the chair, hoping he wouldn't notice.

He stepped forward, his massive frame blocking the light. He was untidy, relaxed, and assertive all at once. Enough to turn her into a puddle on the floor.

"Good evening, Miss Harrington," he said as he swirled the golden contents of his glass.

"What are you doing in here?" She hadn't quite caught her breath yet.

"I like it in here." He shrugged.

His casual manner was as rousing as it was unnerving.

"So, you'd rather hide in the library than sit for dinner with me?"

Amusement flickered across his face. "I hardly thought you'd mind, Miss Harrington."

"I don't." She glanced out the window at the street below and back to him.

"I'm sorry I didn't make it," he said, moving closer.

"Are you?" She looked back at him, accusing.

"More than you know." His voice was earnest.

It was the last thing she'd expected and the only thing she wanted to hear. But she couldn't take the chance that he was just placating her. Her pride couldn't stand the blow.

"Didn't we agree that you would call me Rua when there was no one around?" Her words came out more delicate than she'd intended.

"Mmm." Finn nodded, placing his drink on the table. "And here we are again, with no one around . . . Rua Harrington." Her name rolled sweetly off his lips, like he was sampling the syllables. And there she was hanging, on to every last one of them.

The effect he had on her in the dwindling firelight was baffling. She couldn't think; she couldn't breathe. She needed to get herself together. But how could she when he was staring at her like that?

She opened her mouth, but she was unable to think of anything clever.

"Would you like to play a game?" He disappeared back into the darkness, not waiting for her answer.

"What kind of game?" she asked, struggling to keep her voice even.

Her heart raced as her eyes searched for him. She would have done anything he asked.

"Draughts," he said, reemerging with a box.

"I don't know how to play." And she had no interest in learning.

"How curious," he said as he put the box set down and dragged the armchair directly across from her. Next, he lifted the round wooden side table and set it down between them. He sat down, his size overpowering the suddenly tiny-looking chair.

"What?" she asked, watching the long fingers of his hand set up the black-and-cream checkered board with ease. They were rough and covered in little cuts, remnants of his heroics at the Madison Hotel.

"You freely admit that you don't know something. I'd have wagered you'd fake your way through the entire game." He looked up then, giving her a roguish grin.

Her heart gave a little squeeze. That smile was going to kill her.

"There are a number of things I have to fake my way through these days. I'm not interested in adding another to my list."

"Care to explain?" he asked, sliding a draught into the next square.

"Not particularly." She kept her eyes focused on the board. They were so close to each other. Inches apart, hovering over the game.

"Tell me, then, what books are so scandalous that you've hidden them all away on a dusty shelf where no one else would bother to look?"

Rua looked up slowly, eyes narrowed. "Why?"

She didn't know how long he'd been in the library before she entered. For all she knew, he'd been standing over her shoulder, reading the pages with her.

"Merely curious. I imagine a woman like you has scintillating taste in literature."

She smiled, hoping that's all it was. Regardless, she saw an opportunity to pivot. "Are you wondering if it's a naughty romance novel, my lord? Filled with notorious rakes bedding timid wallflowers?"

He remained stone faced, but she saw the lump form in his throat.

"You're very bold," he said, more of an observation than an insult.

"And I'm bored," she said, needing to get herself and that little journal with all its sacrilegious symbols out of the library before anyone else got their hands on it.

If anyone saw it, they would immediately assume it belonged to Rua. They would see the repetitive scribbles and illegible words and believe it proof that she was a deranged sinner.

Rua rose from her seat, taking the journal from its hiding place behind the cushion.

Finn watched her closely. "Read me the first page." He nodded toward the journal.

"What?" She gaped.

"Read it."

"Why?" Her eyes narrowed.

"I want to know what keeps you up at night," he said in a low voice that made her whole body warm. She met his eyes. If only he knew.

Willing to play along, she cleared her throat and opened to the first page.

Folding his arms across his chest, he waited with a smirk.

Pretending to read, she started, "Once upon a time, there was a man who fell in love with a woman who was his better in more ways than one. She was beautiful, of course, but also whip smart and cunning, with a keen eye for nonsense."

Peeking up from the page, she found Finn on the verge of laughter.

"As much as he wished it so, she did not return his affections. He tried and tried. So insistent was he, he even moved into her home. Eventually . . ." She trailed off, her fiction teetering too close to truth.

"Eventually, what?" he asked.

The air in the room shifted, so thick with desire she couldn't breathe.

"Eventually, nothing," she whispered, closing the book.

Unsatisfied with her answer, he stepped closer.

"Eventually," he said, his gaze moving to her lips, then back to her eyes, "his efforts paid off."

She sucked in a breath, unsure of what to say, and surprised at how she felt.

A silent prayer passed between them as they stood, wistful and wanting.

With a heady gaze, he reached toward her face. Cautious and deliberate, his knuckles glided across her cheek. She leaned into his caress, fearful of ever being without it. His touch was unhurried as his fingers left a scorching trail atop her skin, not stopping until they found her mouth.

And with the smallest amount of pressure, he let his thumb linger against her bottom lip, pulling gently until her lips parted, releasing a debauched shallow breath.

And then he pulled back, imploding her fragile existence.

Flushed with need, she'd gotten caught in her own web. A glistening maze of invisible strings, twisting and tangling, until she'd relinquished control and succumbed to the temptation.

Needing to regain her composure, she took a devastating step away from him.

"If there's something you wanted to tell me, Finn"—her words were a breathy whisper—"you only need say it." She was tired of waiting, and desperate for more, but she needed to hear that he wanted her. Her pride demanded it and wouldn't settle for less.

She had enough to deal with, never mind a man who wouldn't make up his mind. A man who so clearly wanted her but would never admit it. Not to himself and certainly not to their peers, because she was, according to them, a heathen.

"Rua," he said, his voice breaking, burdened with lust. He was the only one she wanted to hear say it. That name was his.

She swallowed hard, refusing to get sucked in again.

"Tread carefully, Finn," she said with all the nerve she could muster.

Confusion registered on his face.

"I know." She offered a pitying frown. "It must be confusing for someone like you to have fallen so easily for someone like me—the heathen Harrington girl."

Shock and anger waged war on Finn's face.

"Good night, my lord," she said, hurrying out of the library, book in hand. She stopped behind the door, out of breath, and more conflicted than ever. What was she thinking?

Rua shook her head and returned to her bedchamber.

Finn hadn't slept a wink last night. Another strange dream kept him up, though it didn't feel like a dream at all.

He raised his sword, blind with rage, and landed it down on his opponent's neck. One by one they came to him, and one by one they died.

He never tired, never weakened. There was no man on earth who could defeat him.

Sword gripped, he watched as a woman approached the ford. A great beauty with raven hair and the look of an angel.

Surely she could not mean to fight him.

"Halt!" he warned her.

She stilled, a smile creeping up her lips. "I've only come to declare my fealty and my love to the fearsome warrior."

"I've no interest in your charms, woman. I am in the midst of a war."

She resumed her approach. "Let me help you."

He bristled, mistrustful of her intentions. "I have no need of your assistance, pernicious woman."

The woman's face darkened, but her eyes glowed brighter. Warning bells rang in his head. He raised his sword, feeling her malice.

Before his very eyes, the woman disappeared. Upon the branch above his head sat a crow, and he realized his mistake.

Finn stood in front of the mirror, staring at the man in front of him. The man from his dream looked like him, felt like him, but that man wasn't a man at all. He closed his eyes, feeling the thrill of battle coursing through his veins.

He shook his head, moving from the mirror. It was nothing more than a fantasy.

But the conflict with the woman, the pernicious one—that part of the dream reminded him of a story he'd once heard, though he couldn't recall which.

There was a knock at his door.

"The carriage is ready, my lord."

"Thank you," Finn said, "but I won't be needing it."

"Of course, my lord," the groomsmen said before taking his leave.

Finn paced around his room a few more minutes before deciding to go downstairs to have breakfast. He'd sent the carriage away, after all. Wasn't that his intention? A chance to see Rua?

He made his way down, second-guessing himself every step of the way. A glutton for punishment, he thought back to those final moments in the library before Rua walked out, leaving him gasping.

Their chemistry was undeniable. A perfect combination of attraction and curiosity; he'd never experienced anything like it. A desire so raw, he'd let the world burn for the chance he might satiate it.

He ran his hand through his hair, trying to collect himself, wishing he could read Rua's mind. She'd pulled away to prove a point, but he'd wager it had taken everything she had to do it.

He entered the breakfast room, disappointed to find it empty.

He let out a deep breath. This was his sign to let this go. He and Rua, whatever connection they might have, was nothing more than a spark. There was no need to let it kindle.

He sat down at the table while breakfast food was laid out before him along with the morning paper.

As he read about the advance of the crown prince of Prussia, he couldn't help but feel detached from such affairs.

"What are you doing in here?"

Finn looked up from the paper to find a surprised Rua standing in the doorway. Her face was scrunched, eyes still sleepy. Bloody adorable.

A sweet smell drifted upward, almonds and wintergreen. The familiar meadowsweet scent caught hold of him and upended every last one of his senses.

He folded the paper and set it on the table. "Good morning, Rua."

"Shouldn't you be at the Fitzgeralds' or somewhere else that isn't here?" she asked, sitting in the seat across from him, letting out a yawn.

"On the contrary." He leaned forward. "I have no plans and thought I might spend the entirety of the day with you."

"You're not serious." Her eyes widened.

"No," he said regretfully, wondering what it might be like to spend time with Rua that wasn't stolen or tainted by society's harsh glare.

"Good," she said, buttering a scone. "I wouldn't want you getting any ideas about me. I have a reputation to uphold. Unmanageable and dangerous, as you well know." She waved the butter knife at him.

Finn let out a laugh, and she smiled as she set down the utensil. A rare armistice. After the way they'd left things in the library, he wasn't sure where they stood.

"Your reputation is well intact, I can assure you," he said, watching her take a bite of the pastry, mesmerized by her mouth. He cleared his throat. She raised a quizzical brow. "At any rate, I have things to do downtown today. I'm building a hospital." As he said the words, he realized how much of a braggart he sounded. All in a bid to impress Rua? Christ. He busied his hands, folding the napkin in front of him.

"A hospital and a hotel?" Rua asked in a mocking tone. She might as well have rolled her eyes.

"What?" he asked, feeling self-conscious.

"You're a walking contradiction, my lord."

"How so?"

"You want into their world, yet you can't let go of your own."

"My own?" The implication that he belonged anywhere else was unwelcome.

"I'm merely suggesting that you don't behave like the other men of your rank. Running into burning buildings and building hospitals for the poor. The rich don't care for the downtrodden."

"That's not true," he said.

"Yes it is. They think the poor are responsible for their squalor." She took a sip of her tea. "And I have it on good authority that the upper tens don't take kindly to things that go against the status quo. Soon they'll start to wonder about you and where you came from." Her eyes narrowed.

"Where I came from? What are you getting at?" he asked, feeling exposed, as though she'd taken his very thoughts from his head and used them against him.

Everything he wanted boiled down to the acceptance of the wealthy New Yorkers. He wanted to continue his charity on a grander scale, but to do that, he needed income that would grow. Real estate was the way he sought to achieve that goal. But he couldn't deny that his charitable pursuits were dwindling the deeper he fell into high society. He was spending fewer days at the Battery and more in the clubs uptown, rubbing shoulders with the wealthy elite and the entrepreneurs.

Rua watched him as he worked all this out, and he got the stark sense she was baiting him. Saying all of that just to garner a reaction, and he didn't know why.

"What about you, then?" He turned the conversation on her. She'd spoken as though she weren't a member of the upper class all her life. "You're hardly one to talk about the status quo."

"The difference between you and me, Finn, is that you *want* to fit in. I, on the other hand, *need* to."

"What do you mean, *need* to?" he asked.

"It's just harder for women," she said, before moving on to her hot cakes.

He wasn't buying it. This had to do with the rumors and her mother's constant attempts at pushing them together. Rua couldn't win New York over on her own, and Mrs. Harrington wasn't receiving the social adulation she sought.

He'd heard the way women spoke of them when they weren't around, seen the way they whispered when they were. Mrs. Harrington wanted to use his lordship as a shield for Rua's conduct and a loophole to gain entrance into the higher reaches of society.

Before he could answer, an out-of-breath Mrs. Harrington rushed into the breakfast room. "Did I hear you are spending the day with Emma, my lord?"

He looked around at the staff lingering by the wall, wondering which of them had slipped out and alerted Mrs. Harrington to their conversation.

"You heard no such thing, Mother," Rua said quickly.

He wondered if he was the only one who called her Rua. She'd said it was her middle name: Emma Rua Harrington. It certainly didn't roll off the tongue.

"As a matter of fact, Mrs. Harrington, you heard correctly." Rua's mouth fell open as he spoke. "I apologize for the lack of notice, but my schedule just cleared," he said.

"Don't be silly!" Mrs. Harrington beamed. "Well, I'll let you two finish your breakfast. Do let me know of your plans."

"What do you think you're doing?" Rua asked.

"Helping you fit in."

Rua's face softened. "I didn't ask you to do that."

"I know," he said.

Seventeen

Still sitting at the breakfast table, Rua wondered what Finn would suggest they do. Bitterly, she doubted it would be something public. She was appreciative of his offer, though, on account of Flossie; it bought Rua some time and possibly even some goodwill. But what they did would determine everything.

"I was planning a visit to St. Brigid's. Care to join me?"

"St. Brigid's?" she asked, shocked that it was somewhere outside the Harringtons' residence.

"An orphanage."

Rua smiled. "You're joking?"

"I'm not." He laughed.

"Sure, Finn, take me to the orphanage. Perhaps on our way, we'll find a wounded bird that you could nurse back to health?"

"Emma," Flossie's voice called from the hall before she reentered the room. "There's a letter here for you."

"Are you certain it's for me?" Rua asked, not paying her much attention.

Flossie nodded, handing it to her, shaking with excitement. "It's from Lily Stevens."

"Lily Stevens?" Finn asked, sounding shocked.

"Don't look so surprised." Rua clutched the letter to her chest. "I'm very popular." She grinned, opening the envelope.

She'd given no further thought to Lily's invitation, nor had she really expected one to arrive.

Flossie attempted to reach for the note, but Rua turned away.

No. 139 Greene St., 5pm sharp. Tell no one the location, not even your lady's maid.

Rua read the words and folded the paper up. Five seemed early for a meeting that was supposed to be held in secret.

"Well, what does it say?" Flossie asked, fingers twitching.

"Lily Stevens has invited me to an event this evening." Rua held the letter behind her back.

"An event?" Flossie let out a delighted squeal. "Forgive me. I just never—well, never mind. It's all happening now, isn't it?" She nodded.

Rua grimaced.

"You must get ready straightaway."

"But I already have plans, remember? I'm spending the day with the Lord of Donore." Plans she much preferred.

"We will do it another time," Finn interjected. "No need to explain. I know who the Stevenses are," he said with an encouraging smile.

Rua couldn't help but feel disappointed. Finn was, of course, a lord and ranked high on Flossie's list, but Lily was old money, and she held the key to Rua's integration. With Lily's approval, the Harringtons would be set.

"A gentleman through and through," Flossie said, batting her eyelashes. Rua rolled her eyes.

She stood up and placed her hand over Finn's. "Thank you," Rua said.

He squeezed her fingers in response. Her breath caught as they both stared at their hands on the table. She yanked hers back, remembering they weren't alone. He cleared his throat.

"Pardon me." He rose to his full height before her. She could see nothing but him and had to force back the urge to place her two hands on his chest and run them over his broad shoulders. She had a feeling he'd let her if she wanted to.

"Are you ready, miss?" Mara asked from the doorway. Flossie was grinning beside her, no doubt hearing wedding bells.

"I'm coming," she said, and hurried out of the breakfast room.

"This is excellent news," Mara said as they entered Rua's bed-chamber. "I haven't seen your mother this excited since the *Daily News* article came out."

Rua laughed in agreement.

An evening with a Stevens might be the answer to all of her problems.

"Where are you meeting Lily?" Flossie came to check on her after her hair was set and she'd had her bath.

"I believe it's a tearoom in the Iron Palace," she said, trying to sound convincing. She'd heard the Iron Palace mentioned more than a few times and hoped it was a place Flossie would believe Lily Stevens might visit. Retail shops were one of the few venues where women were allowed to gather unaccompanied by men. Hopefully, it wouldn't be a stretch to believe they would host events there too.

"How lovely. What gown are you wearing?" Flossie asked.

"The sapphire one," Rua said, relieved she didn't question her lie.

"Excellent choice. Now hurry up so you're not late."

For a brief moment, Finn was disappointed that Lily Stevens had inadvertently canceled their plans. But then he realized it was another sign—an act of mercy before he got in deeper with Rua and lost all his good sense.

He left for the orphanage as soon as Rua had gone upstairs and then spent most of the day repainting a fence while trying to keep his mind off her. The children were a good distraction, but it wasn't enough.

Rather than going back to the Harringtons' when he was done with St. Brigid's, Finn thought it was time he had that conversation with Richard. Make clear his intentions with Annette and put this matter to bed once and for all. A plan he thought he'd settled on last night. How quickly he'd cast it aside for Rua.

This decision did not come with clarity or excitement but rather an inexplicable sinking feeling, like he'd tied a rock around his ankle and jumped into the sea.

He checked his watch. By now, Rua should be on her way to meet with Lily Stevens. He was truly happy for her. After so much turmoil in such a short amount of time, it was nice to see her succeeding. A friendship with Lily Stevens would do more for her reputation than he ever could—though part of him wanted to be the one to save her, or at least the one to try. A selfish desire, no doubt, as he was about to propose to another woman. But to have Rua look upon him with admiration? There could be no higher praise.

Resolute, he rapped on the Fitzgeralds' front door. The footman answered and brought him into the parlor, where Richard and Gloria were entertaining.

"My lord." Annette ran up to him. "I'm so happy you called." He hadn't the slightest inclination to tell her to call him Finn. It felt like a secret shared only with Rua. Though if Annette were to be his fiancée, it was about time he did.

"Here," Richard said, jovially handing him a drink.

As he went around the room greeting Richard's guests, he almost spit out his whiskey when he spotted Lily Stevens.

"Good afternoon, my lord," she said to him, courteous as could be.

"Miss Stevens," he said with a nod, trying to come up with some explanation as to why she was here and not on her way to wherever Rua was going.

"Come, sit." Annette patted the floral-upholstered chair beside her. "Miss Hanworth is going to play us a tune on the pianoforte."

Finn endured forty-five minutes of poorly performed ballads while his mind worked to understand Lily's presence. Had she canceled her plans? Or perhaps Rua had gotten the date wrong? It shouldn't matter to him, but it did.

He'd just decided to ask Annette about it when she turned to Lily, wearing a grin, and asked, "Shouldn't you have left by now?"

Lily let out a big laugh. Finn stiffened.

"Do you think she will actually show up? Could she be that desperate?" Lily asked.

He bit back his rising anger, knowing they were talking about Rua.

"I certainly hope so," Annette said. "She should be arriving about the same time as the columnist." Both women burst out laughing.

"What are you ladies talking about?" Finn asked with a smile, trying his best to keep his voice even.

"Promise not to tell," Annette said to him, doing her best to look innocent.

He nodded, grinding his teeth together. "Of course."

"We sent Emma Harrington to Greene Street." Annette could hardly hold back her laughter.

"You did what?" He rose from his seat.

Greene Street was a notorious sex district. The block was littered with brothels. If Rua was seen entering one of those buildings, she'd be ruined. Never mind the danger she could be in—a woman of means walking alone in a neighborhood like that.

"It was Lily's idea." Annette shifted the blame.

"Don't be sour with Annette, my lord," Lily said, sounding bored. "I'm sure Miss Harrington will find herself right at home."

"Give me the address," Finn demanded.

"Surely you don't mean to leave and go after her?" Annette jumped up, looking dejected.

"The address, now."

"Number one thirty-nine," Lily said, wearing a wicked grin.

"Lily!" Annette whined.

This was all part of Lily Stevens's game. She'd given the address up willingly because she liked seeing Annette squirm. Nothing but an evening's worth of entertainment at the expense of a woman's life.

Finn made his way toward the door.

"Leaving so soon, Donore?" Richard walked over, noticing something was amiss.

"Ask your daughter," Finn said, not waiting for a response.

Knowing he was faster on foot, Finn took off in a run. He needed to get to Rua before the columnist got to her, or worse.

Rua wasn't as familiar with Manhattan as she would like to be, but she knew enough to know that she'd never been in this neighborhood before. She wished she could have brought Mara with her.

It had taken some convincing to get Mara to agree not to follow her. Mara didn't understand why she couldn't accompany her inside, but Rua figured if she had to go to this secret meeting, she should do it as Lily requested: alone.

"I'll be fine," Rua assured her. "Enjoy some time to yourself." And she exited the Harringtons' carriage on Ninth Avenue, outside the Iron Palace—alone. When she had walked far enough out of sight, she found a cab to take her to Greene Street.

The journey was longer than she anticipated. The road was crowded and backed up with traffic. Multiple times she wanted to get out and walk.

None of the shops or restaurants looked familiar. The streets were narrower and the sidewalks smaller and congested, but not with the type of stiff, aristocratic people she was used to seeing. She assumed this was all part of Lily's secret society—finding unique locations to maintain their anonymity.

And then she saw the sign for Greene Street.

"I will be done in an hour. Don't go anywhere," she warned the cab driver.

Rua stepped onto a block of well-kept row houses. It seemed quiet save for a few gentlemen exiting the houses. One of them stopped a few houses down and made eye contact with her. The hair rose on the back of her neck before she turned away and kept walking up the block, counting the numbers until she found the one she was looking for.

She did her best to pretend she didn't feel the man continuing to watch her. Even when he crossed the empty street at the same time she did, she told herself it might just be the direction he was headed. But her efforts to convince herself she was being paranoid fell short.

Quickening her pace, she glanced over her shoulder. Even as her stomach tightened in fear, she hoped she was overreacting. Not everyone was out to get her.

She sighed. This one was.

She smelled the liquor on him before she heard the footsteps come up behind her.

"Well, well, where have they been hiding you?"

Rua jumped at the sound of his voice. Refusing to look back, she continued toward No. 139, hoping if she just ignored him, he'd go away.

"You one of Whalen's girls?"

Rua said nothing as she opened the front gate to the house.

"You answer me when I'm talkin' to you," he shouted.

"I'm afraid you're mistaken, sir," she said, running up the steps. She was so close; she only needed to knock.

Before she could get there, the man grabbed hold of her ankle and yanked her off the steps. *The prick*, she thought as she fell to the ground, skinning her palms and elbows in the process.

She tumbled down to the pavement, and he grabbed hold of her once more.

Dragging her by the hair, he pulled her behind the gate beside the front staircase, where she'd be hidden from view. When she tried pushing herself upward on her side, a heavy boot caught her shoulder, forcing her down on her back.

"I would've paid extra for you." He stood over her, kicking her legs apart. "Now it appears I won't have to pay anything at all," he said, brandishing a small blade.

Rua closed her eyes, unable to summon the fear necessary to call for help. Deep in her core, rage was all that called to her—a sanguine song, melancholic and violent. Resolute in her hate, she opened her eyes, meeting the animal's above her.

"What the hell?" His words were slurred, his reaction delayed.

She sprang to her feet and let out a terrible scream. The man didn't expect it; she could see the confusion plain on his face. He stumbled backward, taking a panicked swipe as he did, managing to catch her forehead with the tip of his blade. Touching her head, she saw the bloodstain on her fingers.

The blood trickled down her face as she ripped the blade from his hand. With lightning precision, she slid it across his scruffy neck, letting out a satisfied breath as he lost his.

He slumped against the stone facade, legs sliding out from under him and a bright-red line of blood trailing down his collar.

She wondered if murder was a topic they'd be willing to discuss at Lily's social club, though she was beginning to suspect there was no such club.

"Fucking hell."

Rua spun around at the sound of another man's voice. Gripping the hilt of the blade, she was ready to kill anyone who approached her with malicious intent. At the sight of Finn, she dropped the knife, which hit the ground with a clatter.

"What are you doing here?" she asked, unnerved and skeptical.

He looked up from the bloody knife, shocked by the allegation. "Are you hurt?" He reached for her, his eyes scanning her for injuries. He saw the cut on her face and cupped her cheeks in his hands as he took a closer look.

"I'm fine." She jerked her head free. "How did you know where I was?"

Ignoring her questions, Finn walked over to the dead man's body and crouched down beside it. He said nothing about the gaping wound running the width of the man's neck as he checked his wrist for a pulse. He sifted through the man's pockets, coming up empty.

"How did you know I was here?" she asked once more.

All business, he rose and walked back to her.

"I'll tell you on the way, but, Rua, we have to get you out of here. If anyone finds out you were here, especially after . . ."

He didn't need to finish. He understood the situation for what it was.

Rua turned back to face 139 Greene Street. It might've been a lovely home furnished with all the trappings to make it so, but now it was spoiled, the blood of a dead man seeping into the cracks of the foundation while people lived their lives just upstairs.

She lifted her hands to see if she had his blood on them. She couldn't tell. The world spun around her and her vision began to cloud.

Rua glanced down at the knife resting comfortably in her palm.

There was no other choice. Her hand had been forced. She looked at the willing person standing before her. Blood dripped from her neck as the pressure of Rua's blade wore on her skin.

The drumming in Rua's ears grew louder. This was the only way to get him back, to undo what she'd done. The strength of the knife left her hand as it glided across her victim's throat.

And another piece of her soul chipped away.

"Rua, are you all right?" Finn's voice coaxed her back to reality.

"What's going on out here?" a woman shouted from the top window.

"Rua." Finn spoke softly. "We must go."

Wrapping his arm around her waist, he practically carried her as he hurried them down the block. She was in another world, trying to make sense of what she'd just seen. Of what she'd seen herself do. It couldn't be true.

"Oh god," she groaned, putting her hand across his chest to stop him, then she bent over and retched onto the cobbled road.

Hovering behind her, Finn's gentle hands gathered the strands of hair from her face while her body tried to expel the images from her mind.

Finn hated to see her this way.

"It's going to be all right," he said as he held back her hair while looking around for anyone who might prove a threat. It was still early enough in the evening that there weren't too many pleasure-seekers about.

But Annette had mentioned a columnist. If she was serious and they'd gone to the same address Rua had been given, she'd have a lot more to worry about than being excluded from parties. She'd wake up tomorrow on trial for murder, and given her reputation, the fact that it was self-defense would not even be considered.

Finn was gutted that he hadn't gotten to her sooner. He'd heard her scream, run as hard as he could, but he was too late. He was thankful that that was the scene he'd come upon instead of the other way around.

For once, none of this was Rua's fault, but bloody hell if she wasn't going to live with the consequences. A nasty trick played by two rotten girls and they were going to get away with it.

When Rua finished being sick, she was in a stupor, completely unaware of her surroundings. There was no color in her cheeks, and she was cold to the touch. Knowing she wasn't well, he scooped her into his arms to carry her the rest of the way.

He waited until they were far enough from Greene Street and away from Houston to hail a cab. The last thing they needed was to be recognized.

They traveled uptown, stopping a few blocks short of the Harringtons' residence. He wouldn't take the chance that the cabbie might put two and two together and recognize Rua.

She slept the entire way, finally waking when the transport stopped.

"We're here," he whispered.

Slowly, she opened her eyes. She glanced up at him, eyes wide, like she'd seen a ghost.

"I will take care of everything," he assured her.

She nodded, taking his hand as he helped her down from the cab.

"Are your mother and father home right now?" He needed to know what entrance to use.

She said nothing, not appearing to have heard him at all.

"Are your parents at an event tonight?"

"Um, yes, I think so. A private exhibit at the Metropolitan."

"Right, of course." He nodded. He was meant to be attending the charity tonight himself.

But that made things easier. Rua could walk inside without issue. He didn't know what was going on between Rua and her mother, but he knew it was best she didn't see Rua like this.

"How did you know where to find me?" Rua asked him.

"I heard Lily and Annette discussing what they'd done earlier this evening."

Rua muttered a handful of expletives under her breath.

"Ready?" he asked her, daring to interrupt.

She nodded, taking a deep breath. "Yes, I'll be fine."

This was the first time he'd ever thought to doubt her. She'd been formidable, even when she'd been raked over the coals by their peers, but right now he was concerned for her.

He opened the front door, guiding Rua over the threshold.

She grabbed his arm. "Mara. I left Mara at the Iron Palace," she muttered. "Is she here?"

"Left her where?" he asked. "Wait here a minute," he told Rua while he went to look for Mara.

He rushed to the dining room, thinking she might be there, and then he checked the parlor and the billiards room. No luck.

Assuming she would turn up eventually, he thought it best to see Rua to her room. He returned to the foyer only to find Rua halfway up the stairs.

"Miss Harrington, where is it that you're returning from?" The housekeeper's meddlesome voice echoed through the entryway.

Rua held tight to the railing as she continued upward.

"Miss Harrington, I am speaking to you."

The nerve, Finn thought. He was about to step in when Rua answered. She was at the top of the stairs, looking down on them both, a glow in her eyes.

"Mrs. Smith, I advise you never to speak to me in that tone again."

A chill crept up his spine. He could only imagine how Mrs. Smith felt. He thought about going after Rua, making sure she was all right, but something told him he shouldn't. Instinct, perhaps? He knew she would not be served by his presence, but he would find Mara for her if that's what she needed.

Eighteen

Rua didn't remember getting home; she only knew that she couldn't have done it without Finn.

Her head was an absolute wreck. She stood by her bed, wearing another ruined gown, and stared at the wall.

Terrible flashes of darkness and the blurred memory of another victim, intermixing with the man she'd killed at Greene Street, left her reeling. Not from regret but because what she'd just done appeared to have unlocked something deep within her.

No details, only the distinct feeling of profound loss and a desperate wish to undo it. Incapable of remembering, she fell to her knees, burying her face in her bloodied hands.

Undo what? she wanted to scream.

Her answers were there, trapped inside her wretched mind, if only she could break through the wall.

But the loss was with her now, unfathomable and ravenous, clinging to her soul and shredding it to pieces. So fresh and raw, every breath a serrated strike to her hollow chest.

Unable to stomach the pain, Rua crawled over to the wastebasket and vomited once more.

When she was finished, she went to the washbasin to clean her face. She stared in the mirror at her reflection, tears streaming down her face. Her eyes were not her own. Flecked with gold, they belonged to someone she didn't recognize. A monster.

She plunged her hands into the ceramic washbowl and splashed the cold water onto her face. It did nothing to rinse away the guilt. She splashed and scrubbed, again and again, until she'd done nothing but reopen the cut on her forehead.

As the blood trickled down her face, a malevolent calm settled around her. This was who she was. A cold-blooded killer.

She slumped to the floor and lay on her back. She stared up at the ceiling and hoped it would collapse on top of her.

When word got out about what she'd done, she'd be tried for murder. There'd be nowhere she could run. She'd missed her chance to flee.

There was a knock on her door.

Rua jumped upright, noting all possible exits. The window. The servants' entrance by her closet. If she had to, she could charge past whoever was opening the door, possibly catching them off guard. Imprisonment was not where her story ended.

"Emma, my goodness, are you all right?" Mara asked, taking in Rua's defensive stance.

"Yes, I'm fine." She might've missed her chance to run, but that didn't mean she'd go without a fight.

Mara sat down beside her. "Tell me what's happened."

"I can't," Rua said, the adrenaline leaving her, making room for the heavy weight of her consequences. She'd killed a man in broad daylight. There was nowhere to go from here.

"You can tell me anything, you know that," Mara said.

Rua shook her head, hugging her knees into her chest. She was exhausted, physically and mentally drained. Everything had spun so wildly out of her control.

Mara's arm wrapped around her shoulders, and Rua began to cry. "I should have gone with you," Mara said.

She didn't know how long they sat like that, but when she woke, she was in her bed in her nightdress.

The faint light of the day slipped through the curtains, but Rua didn't want the light. She turned over and fell back to sleep.

"What do you mean, she's still in bed? I've had enough of this. It's been two weeks." Flossie burst through her bedroom door. "Get up, Emma! Get up!"

"I'm up," Rua groaned as she shook off her covers and sat up. She had convinced Flossie that she was ill while she wallowed in her guilt and waited for news of Greene Street.

"The Lord of Donore invited us to use his opera box this evening, and I told him it was—oh, good heavens!"

"What's wrong?" Rua looked around the room.

"Your face! Your beautiful face! What happened?" Flossie shouted. "That's it. We're ruined!"

Rua assumed she was talking about the cut that still lingered on her forehead, but she didn't care to look in the mirror. This was the first time Flossie had seen her since the incident. She'd said she had too many social engagements to risk coming down with whatever sickness her daughter had. But the truth of it was, everyone was better off when Rua stayed home.

"So help me, you will tell me what happened this instant!"

"Well . . ." Rua tried to think of something. "The other night, while you were out . . ."

"Yes, I am aware of the general time frame," Flossie snapped.

Rua gave a quick glance toward Mara, who'd just entered her bedchamber, and continued trying to come up with something that Flossie would believe. "I was in the gold room, and I tripped. I tripped on my skirt and smashed my face against the little golden lion next to the fireplace. Perhaps it's why I've been so out of sorts."

"You tripped and fell on the little golden lion," Flossie repeated slowly.

"Yes."

"Is this true?" Mrs. Harrington looked to Mara.

"Yes, Mrs. Harrington," Mara answered.

Flossie shook her head. "Do you feel as though you're not getting enough attention these days? Or is it your intention to single-handedly fuel the scandal sheets for the entirety of the year?"

"I'm sorry," Rua said.

"I'm sure," Mrs. Harrington said, and turned back to Mara. "You've got a tremendous amount of work to do. We're leaving for the opera in six hours, and that face needs to be covered completely. Perhaps Madame Malvina has thought to fashion you a face cover to go with one of your gowns?"

"A face cover?"

"We are so fortunate to have a seamstress of her caliber design-
ing your gowns." Mrs. Harrington riffled through the closet and
pulled out a gown the color of fuchsia. "A small fortune but well
worth it. I've heard it's near impossible to get an appointment with
her now. She's booked through December! All thanks to us."

Rua rolled her eyes. The idea that the seamstress's massive success was all due to Flossie, who hadn't been welcomed through the
doors prior to this summer, was nonsense.

"It's true. They might despise you, but they adore your wardrobe. Madame Webster's started a new trend with you at the helm.
I can't tell you how many girls I saw with an exact copy of your riding habit."

"But I didn't even ride that day."

"No, but they did see you with the Lord of Donore," Flossie
said. "I'm not sure you're grasping the kind of impression he's left
on the ladies of Manhattan. I don't know how many times I have to
tell you." This time Flossie rolled her eyes. "He's the one they all
want to marry. And certainly it's not your charm that's gotten his
attention, so it must be the dresses. Simple as that."

Rua didn't have the energy to be offended.

"Yes, this is the one," Flossie said, pointing to a gown. "No one
will look at your face if you remove the décolletage."

"Are you sure?" Even for Rua's tastes, it was a bit much.

"They're already primed to talk about you. Better your chest
than a battered face, hmm? I imagine the Lord of Donore will
appreciate it nonetheless."

Rua took a deep breath.

Flossie appraised her as she headed for the door. "You should
get ill more often, my dear. You've lost some weight," she said, as
though she were paying her a compliment.

Rua wanted to throw a shoe at her.

"I'm so glad to see you up and about," Mara said, once Flossie
had left.

Rua turned to Mara. "I don't have much of a choice. Finn invited
us to his opera box. It's all that woman's ever wanted."

"Speaking of the Lord of Donore. He's been checking on you
regularly," Mara said.

"He has?" Rua asked, surprised.

She nodded. "He's quite concerned. I've never seen him around the house more than I have these last couple of weeks."

Rua lifted the gold-plated hairbrush from her vanity and ran it through her hair. She needed to find him and make sure he hadn't told anyone. She wasn't sure what she'd do if he did.

"Are you ready to tell me what happened? I've been so worried," Mara said.

She couldn't tell Mara the truth of why she was hiding in her room. Not the whole truth anyway.

"Lily Stevens tricked me. There was no event."

Mara gasped, covering her mouth with her hand. "I can't believe it. How cruel. Is that why you won't leave your bedchamber?" she asked.

"I can't bear the thought of my mother finding out. She'll send me away."

"She doesn't know! I promise you. Not a word has been uttered," Mara assured her.

Rua couldn't imagine Flossie not using Lily's invitation as a talking point. The Stevenses were the crème de la crème of the social set. Flossie would want everyone to know that her mangy daughter was mingling with one, if only to prove the Harringtons were worthy. Perhaps she hadn't been to any of the same events and that's why word hadn't gotten back to Flossie that Lily had tricked Rua.

But why had Lily and Annette not said anything yet? Clearly, their plan was to humiliate Rua. What reason could they have to delay, other than to prolong Rua's torment? If that was their plan, it was working. Her days were fraught with worry, waiting for the moment Flossie burst through the doors and declared she'd been so thoroughly embarrassed that enough was enough.

But since killing that man, Rua hadn't had the energy to do anything about it. She'd been plunged into the cold depths of sorrow with no reasonable explanation for her feelings. Flossie's indignation felt secondary.

She didn't care about the man she'd murdered. He didn't deserve her sympathy. But she wondered if he belonged to anyone. Did the bastard have an unknowing wife waiting at home who would alert the police? Was that what Lily and Annette were waiting for? The police?

Her life had gone to pieces; she had no business going to the opera. She should be planning her escape, but instead she was trapped in this gilded cage like a rat begging for its next meal. She gripped the base of the hairbrush tighter.

She couldn't take it any longer. She was tired of not knowing anything and living at the whims of Flossie Harrington. Tired of living a life that was not her own.

Letting out a frustrated cry, she fired the gold brush at her mirror. It shattered instantly, thousands of little pieces raining to the floor.

"Emma!"

Rua scowled at Mara. She wanted to scream that Emma was not her name, but she held her tongue.

"What has gotten into you?" Mara asked.

Rua let out a harsh breath and sat on the settee, her head hanging low. "I'm sorry, Mara. I think I'm losing my mind."

Mara came over and sat beside her. "It's going to be okay. Your mother isn't going to send you away. She doesn't know about Lily Stevens; she thinks you still met her, and she's delighted that the lord has been about the house."

"I feel terrible about the mess." Rua gestured toward the mirror.

"Don't worry. I'll tell Mrs. Smith it was knocked over. Come along, we must begin setting your curls."

Layer upon layer of powder went onto her face before she was permitted to leave her bedroom. Her hair was pinned in the front to help conceal the cut.

Rua turned back to a mirror that she hadn't shattered and added a little black to her eye shadow. She wasn't in the mood to be lighthearted.

"There now," Mara said as she clipped the front of Rua's shawl. "Although Mrs. Harrington will probably make you take this off."

"Thank you."

"A word of advice? Cheer up. Your mother has been looking forward to the opera box, and in truth, it wouldn't have happened without you. Enjoy the evening. You deserve it."

Rua nodded as she closed her eyes, allowing herself to fill the role she was supposed to play. "All right, I'm ready," she said, holding her head up high as she made her way downstairs.

She gripped the railing as she rounded the last staircase.

Standing at the base of the stairs was Finn, in full evening dress, wreaking havoc on her heart rate.

They locked eyes, and she felt the color rush to her cheeks. Even after everything that had happened, the sight of him filled her with happiness. An odd sensation, considering she'd spent the last two weeks ignoring one very specific detail from her memory. *The only way to get him back, to undo what she'd done.* There was no reason for her to think that version of herself was referring to Finn, but what if she was? What if that explained the strange pull when she was around him? The sense of familiarity and ease?

"What are you doing here?" Rua asked in a bid to hide her excitement, almost forgetting that he had borne witness to the brutal murder she'd committed.

"Emma, don't be rude!" Flossie shouted.

"I wasn't being rude," she protested.

"I understood perfectly what your daughter was asking, Mrs. Harrington. Please don't worry, and, might I add, you are looking wonderful this evening," Finn said, distracting Flossie.

Three long seconds passed before Flossie stopped fluttering her lashes and spoke. "Be that as it may, I will need to borrow my daughter a moment."

Finn gave Rua a wink.

Flossie took her by the arm and dragged her into Mr. Harrington's study. "What is the matter with you?"

"Nothing." Rua shrugged.

"For the love of god, stop shrugging," Flossie said as she swiped her finger along the shelf and checked it for dust. "You've been so difficult, and I had hoped things would have picked up by now."

Rua said nothing, knowing that things had, in fact, gotten significantly worse.

"We would not have been permitted into a box without the Lord of Donore's invitation. And who knows how much longer he will tolerate you. I can't imagine very long, what with your fragile physical condition. I mean, really, too ill to get out of bed and have breakfast? No doubt he's written you off for breeding." Rua gaped. Flossie continued, "We must take the opportunities where they come. Thank the heavens, there has been no announcement in the papers. There's still time for you to delight him."

Rua was happy that Finn wasn't engaged to Annette, but Rua was never going to be the one he proposed to. She was leaving. If it wasn't this week, it would be the next.

But Flossie's inability to see how humiliating her behavior was made Rua sick. She was no better than the beggars she'd so quickly mock and turn away.

"Money is not enough when you have a daughter like you." Flossie reached for the doorknob.

Rua felt the sting as though Mrs. Harrington's hand had just left her face.

"Come along. Don't forget your gloves," Flossie said, walking through the door.

Finn waited by the front door while Mrs. Harrington presumably scolded Rua.

Rua looked wonderful, all things considered. But he saw where they had tried to hide her cut. Her face was gaunt, but it was her eyes that gave her away. They shone with the indelible knowledge that only comes when taking a life.

She had killed a man, and that wasn't something that could be disguised with clever makeup. It was a mark that would last forever.

He paused, wondering how he thought he could know that. He'd never killed anyone, not in this world anyway. He shook his head. Dreams were not to be mistaken for truth.

Mrs. Harrington walked toward him, Rua following close behind. "Will you be riding in our carriage, my lord?"

"No, but I will meet you before the doors open. I have something I need to take care of." He checked his watch. He needed to meet a man on Mulberry Street.

"Very well, my lord. We will see you shortly."

Finn walked into the Lower East Side Five Points slum, where thousands upon thousands of the city's residents were packed into tenement housing. The conditions were so horrific and overcrowded that the people overflowed onto the streets, living in shanties and back alleys.

These roads were narrow and dirty, veering off to the right and left, filled with rubbish and refuse. The sidewalks were cramped with vendors selling rotten food, beggars, and all kinds of folk just trying to survive.

The homes were no better, falling apart at the seams, with broken windows and rotting wood, and small to the point of being unlivable. If the poor conditions weren't bad enough, the neighborhoods themselves were swarming with criminals and run by gangs.

His heart broke at the sight of two young boys playing about and splashing in a dirty puddle. No doubt the water was infested with bacteria. But there was nothing he could do about it now. He had something he needed to take care of.

Finn approached the infamous Mulberry Street bend where the gangsters convened. The Whyos were in charge down here. Hardened criminals and violent offenders, they backed the politicians, forcing votes to make sure they won their elections, and in turn they were allowed to run the districts as they saw fit.

St. Patrick's was on his left, and he was meeting a man in the churchyard.

"Oy," someone shouted as he came upon the gate.

"I'm here to see Connolly," Finn said to the man lounging against a headstone. He had a bowler hat in his lap and looked to be no more than eighteen.

"Who's asking?" the man grumbled.

"I know him," Connolly said, stepping out from behind an elm tree.

He was a young Irish American man, clean shaven and just as desperate for money as he was to prove he was a big gun. Wearing a bowling hat and a dirty day coat, he sauntered up to the spiked iron gate.

The Whyos had a laundry list of crimes they would commit for a fee. "The Big One" was murder for a hundred dollars. Finn only needed him to cop to a murder, not actually commit one, but somehow that was costing him triple.

"Here's the rest. That's three hundred, like we agreed upon." Finn handed the man an envelope.

He had given the man all the details—date, time, and location—but he'd left Rua's name out of it. If anyone came looking, Connolly was going to claim he was the one who had slit the man's throat on Greene Street.

It wouldn't be too hard to believe, based on the other murders he had committed. As far as Finn knew, the man Rua killed was new in town, just started work at a lumberyard. It wouldn't be the first time a transplant wandered into the wrong part of town or found himself caught in a brawl over a lover. No one was looking for him yet, and if anyone did try to claim him, they'd never connect it to Rua.

"Are we good?" Finn asked. The young man gave a nod.

He wasn't sure it would work, but it was the best he could think of in the moment. It hadn't yet reached the papers, and, at this point, he doubted it would. All he needed to do now was confirm Annette and Lily hadn't mentioned their trick to anyone else.

Nineteen

"Oh, just look at everyone!" Flossie pointed toward the Academy of Music as they stepped down from the carriage.

It was a colossal square building with hundreds of people waiting to enter in their finest clothes. Suits and ball gowns galore.

"Perhaps you shouldn't point, Mother. People might think you've never been to the opera before."

"Heavens, you're right. I forgot myself." Flossie tilted her chin higher and glided toward the Academy. "You know, your father tried to get us a box. Offered quite a large sum for it, but they wouldn't take it. I don't think you understand the opportunity this is, and for opening night, no less."

Rua didn't bother answering. Flossie wasn't expecting a response; she just wanted to hear herself talk.

As they shuffled indoors to the waiting area, Rua took in the faces of the guests and wondered if any of them knew the man she'd killed. Did they know what she'd done? Someone must want justice.

Perhaps the police would come and arrest her here. She would deserve it, of course. She was a killer, after all.

Rua took a deep breath and followed Flossie's lead. Mentally, she was prepared for the chilly reception, but as she walked past the clusters of women showering her with contempt, she realized it was an entirely different thing to endure it.

She was out of practice and ill prepared. Women spent years learning how to behave in social situations like these. Rua had been given a few weeks, and she'd spent most of them hidden away in the Harringtons' house.

"Pay them no heed, my dear. You must remember we are sitting in the Lord of Donore's box. We belong here."

Rua couldn't tell if the words were meant for her or if Flossie was trying to convince herself.

The opera house was one of the more lavish venues she had visited. Lush red carpet lined the staircase, and sparkling gold sconces covered the gold-plated walls. Adding to the glitzy effect were Manhattan's most moneyed residents brushing shoulders, trading stories, in their impeccable evening wear.

"May I take your things, miss?" an attendant asked.

Rua passed him the cape that hid the breasts trying to burst out of her gown. Embedded into the seams of the fuchsia fabric were tiny crystals that shimmered when she moved. She quite literally sparkled. She knew she looked glorious, but it was going to give people even more reason to talk.

She and Flossie moved deeper into the waiting room. It took her only seconds to find Finn in the crowd. He was a standout among the mere mortals as he waited with Ned by the refreshment table.

Not paying Flossie any attention, Rua went to greet them, but she was strong-armed backward.

"Where do you think you're going?" Flossie whispered harshly.

"To say hello?"

"Please do remember your manners. We are in public," Flossie hissed. "They will approach us when they are good and ready. Here is Mrs. Fitzgerald and Mrs. Stevens now."

"Forgive me, I almost forgot I was just a woman," Rua said bitterly.

Mrs. Harrington ignored her comment. They walked slowly toward her peers as though the most important thing in the world to her wasn't to breathe the same air as them.

"Miss Harrington, I wasn't sure you'd grace us with your presence ever again," Mrs. Fitzgerald said. Mrs. Stevens grinned.

Rua said nothing, wondering if either of them knew what their malicious daughters had done to her. She wouldn't be surprised if they all sat around laughing about how they'd sent naïve, desperate

Rua down to a brothel. Perhaps tonight was the night they'd expose her.

"She's well recovered from her cold, I assure you," Flossie answered for her.

"It's true, I'm feeling much better," Rua said.

"I'm sure you are," Mrs. Fitzgerald said, not bothering to hide her disdain. No doubt she was peeved that Finn had allowed the Harringtons access to the coveted opera boxes.

Like the Stevenses, the Fitzgerald family was New York royalty, and Flossie was fortunate Mr. Fitzgerald liked Ned so much, or she'd be dead in the water. She was even more fortunate that she had the Lord of Donore trapped in her home. She had something that these women wanted, and it was for that reason alone that Mrs. Fitzgerald and Mrs. Stevens were bothering to talk to her inside this busy theater.

As the women chitchatted about who had done what at dinner the evening before, Rua's mind wandered back to Greene Street. Would that man have been at the opera tonight had he not met her? Maybe.

She felt an elbow drive into her arm. She looked up; Flossie's eyes were pleading. "Isn't that right, darling?"

"Most certainly," Rua answered, hoping she wasn't agreeing to another luncheon.

"His lordship is looking marvelous this evening," Mrs. Fitzgerald said.

Rua couldn't have agreed more. He was smoldering. His navy jacket, tailored to perfection, suited him.

Mrs. Fitzgerald continued, "It's so kind of you to offer him lodging, though it seems he spends most of his time with Annette." She let out a little laugh. "He stopped by earlier to bring my daughter flowers. Roses, her favorite."

"Odd, since he's been at our home for every meal this week," Flossie said. "He was concerned for my daughter's health, you see."

Rua was at a loss for words as she watched the two women fight over the Irishman's attention.

"I wouldn't be surprised if there was something more nefarious going on in that house of theirs," Mrs. Stevens muttered to

Mrs. Fitzgerald, as though she and Flossie weren't standing right there.

"You're quite right, Marlowe," Mrs. Fitzgerald replied.

"Because Finn hasn't proposed to your daughter, you think something is amiss?" Rua questioned.

"Emma!" Flossie made sure to scold her before turning back to the women. "He and Emma are on a first-name basis."

No matter what Rua did, they would always think the worst of her, and Flossie would let them. Finn could declare his love for her and whisk her away to be his wife, and no one would believe that she hadn't tricked him into the marriage.

She stopped listening to the women, and her eyes somehow drifted back to Finn.

As he spoke with the men, his mouth tilted up to the side, revealing his perfectly placed dimple. She moved her gaze upward to his dark-brown eyes, which held more depth than she'd realized. She still hadn't thanked him for taking her home that night. More importantly, she hadn't asked if her secret was safe with him, though she already knew that it was.

With a start, she realized he was looking back at her now. He broke his gaze and excused himself from the men.

Her heart stalled.

Flossie and her faux friends' chatter reached a feverish pitch.

Rua angled herself toward Finn as he moved closer. He was smiling at her, and she found herself smiling back. Somehow, in this congested room, they were the only two people, connected by something well beyond her understanding. She wondered if she shouldn't just give in to it.

And then a shoulder hit her hard in the back, and she stumbled forward.

"Move out of my way, witch," Annette spat as she darted for Finn, leaving Rua mortified.

Finn had been looking past her—no, through her—to see the vile Annette. And everyone that mattered in New York had seen it. She didn't have the strength to look back at Flossie and those women.

Wanting to scream, she kept her eyes on the red-carpeted floor. Maybe if she stared hard enough, it would open up and swallow her.

She loathed everyone in this room and their pathetic attempts to make her feel inferior.

"Miss Harrington, are you all right?"

Incredulously, Rua watched as a pair of large men's shoes stepped into her limited view of the floor.

Lifting her head, she found Finn standing in front of her, looking at her like she was the only woman in the world.

"Are you all right?" he asked.

All she could muster was a nod.

"Would you allow me the pleasure of escorting you upstairs?" He offered her his arm.

She bit down on the insides of her cheeks in an effort to control the grin aching to spread across her face. "I would like that very much." She locked her arm with his.

Her satisfaction profound, she peeked over her shoulder at Flossie as she and Finn walked through the room. She wanted everyone to see her. Especially Annette. It was easy to find the brat dressed in an orange gown. *Not too harvest-like now*, she thought.

"You're looking rather magnificent." Finn's eyes dropped to her bare neck and back up again.

"Do you think so?" She laughed.

"You know bloody well I think so," he said, resting his hand on her back as he guided her toward the main stairway. She shivered at the touch.

Dirty looks and whispers followed them as they made a sharp right. "Under here," he whispered, pulling her into the space beneath the stairs.

"What are we doing under here?" she asked. "Someone might've seen, and I'd hate for them to think poorly of me." She smirked for good measure.

Finn frowned.

"Rua, how are you doing?" he asked. "I've been so concerned."

"I'm fine, Finn. Really." She smiled, never having thought of how her silence might've affected him.

"I have news," he said.

A pit formed in her stomach. Sensing her panic, he shook his head, reassuring her. "I've taken care of it. No one will ever know."

He didn't need to explain; they both knew what *it* was.

"How—" she started to ask, relief washing over her, but he put a finger to her lips, shushing her.

"Don't speak," he whispered, wetting the top of his index finger as he pulled her lip down and his hand away.

Never far from wanting, heat rushed to her cheeks.

He leaned his forehead against hers. "Let me savor this rare moment of appreciation." His mouth was so close she could almost taste it.

"You should learn to better control your emotions, my lord," she said, brushing the tip of her nose against his, their mouths close but never touching. "Or one might mistake your concern for something more."

"Like what?" he asked as they exchanged heavy breaths.

She arched forward, pressing her body against his, and he slipped his arm around her waist. She looked up through her lashes. "Desire."

She felt the heavy rise and fall of his chest.

Knowing herself—craving too much—she set her hand upon his chest, intending to create a barrier, but all it did was cement his hold.

With a rueful grin, he released her, but not before pressing his mouth to her ear. "I would've thought someone as clever as you would have discerned the extent of my desire ages ago."

Rua blushed, letting out the breath she was holding tight to, and Finn stepped back, straightening his coat.

"So." She smoothed out her overskirt. "Have I really nothing to worry about?" she asked, a little skeptical.

He nodded.

"But Lily and Annette just get to get away with it?"

Finn frowned. "Their actions were reprehensible."

"They need to be punished," she said. "I'll tell everyone."

"All that will do is put you at the scene of a crime in a neighborhood they deem morally bankrupt," Finn said, squeezing her hand. "You will have to settle for no one knowing it happened."

It wasn't enough, but it would do.

"How can you be so sure they won't tell everyone?" she asked.

"I have it handled," he said, leaving no room for question, but there was nothing she could do about it tonight anyway.

"Are you ready to find our seats?"

"Yes," she said, taking his arm.

"Gounod's *Roméo et Juliette* is meant to be excellent," Finn said as they walked upstairs to the U-shaped auditorium.

Rua was too distracted with the splendor of the theater to respond.

Below them at the orchestra level sat hundreds of upholstered seats, all filled. Across were three tiered levels housing the most prestigious boxes, identical to the ones they were in now. Ornate gold molding outlined each box, including the railing. Each was decorated with more gold sconces and embroidered silk curtains.

Finn showed Rua to her seat and handed her a pair of small pearl binoculars.

Flossie and Ned were seated at the end of the row alongside a couple she didn't recognize.

From her position in the Lord of Donore's opera box, she understood Flossie's admiration for it—her intense desire to belong. They were untouchable, sitting on top of the world. Here they held sway over Manhattan.

"My daughter has a profound love of the opera," Flossie announced to everyone. Rua let out an exasperated sigh.

"Is that so?" an older woman dressed in a black mourning gown asked.

"Oh, yes," Rua said.

"It's so nice to see the young ones taking an interest. What is your favorite aria?"

"My favorite aria?" Rua nodded with narrowed eyes, unsure of what an aria was.

Her eyes flicked to Finn, who looked like he was trying not to laugh.

"Tell her," Flossie urged.

"Well." Rua struggled to find the right words. "I love them all equally. How can one choose?"

"Your top three—"

"It's beginning," Finn said loudly, pointing to the well-timed curtain rise and the simultaneous dimming of lights.

"Thank you," she mouthed, lifting the binoculars to her face.

The curtains opened to a darkened ballroom in the city of Verona as the orchestra blared. Her heart skipped a beat, the dramatic notes overwhelming her with their intensity.

"Rua?" he whispered.

"Yes?" she answered, peeking out sideways from the binoculars but never taking her eyes from the stage.

His hand covered hers and pushed the binoculars down. "We're not staying."

"We're not?" She looked at him, her interest piqued.

Taking her hand and guiding her from their seats, he hurried her through the curtains into an empty stairwell.

"No one will take any notice of our absence now," he said.

Unlikely, she thought, but her eyes lit up. "My lord, I daresay my good sense cannot allow for behavior of this sort."

Finn paused. "Would you like to go back?"

"No," she laughed, playfully pushing his shoulder.

"Good." He smiled. "This way."

They traveled down four flights of stairs out into the street. The night air was cool—a chilling reminder of her limited time. October was here, and Samhain was on the thirty-first. Wistfully, she glanced at Finn, wondering how it had gotten so complicated.

"Here," he said, removing his jacket and slinging it over her shoulders. The lining was still warm. She rolled her shoulders, settling into it.

"Where are you taking me?" she asked, knowing she would have gone anywhere he wanted.

"I want to show you something. It's not far."

Side by side, Finn's attentive hand on her back, they walked through the streets. No one paid them any mind. Anonymous in the dark, they could be anyone they wanted—a newly married couple, lovers sneaking off for a tryst, or simply two people with the time to explore the complexity of their feelings. Rua sighed, knowing the last option would never be them.

A few short blocks later, they stopped in front of a large three-story brick building. A single lit candle rested in each of the windowsills. "St. Brigid's Home for Boys and Girls," Rua read aloud from the sign. "Is this the orphanage?" she asked, recalling one of their past conversations.

"Yes," Finn said, fiddling with the latch at the front gate.

"So, is this where you take all the girls, then?" she teased.

He glanced sideways at her as he swung open the gate. "Only one."

Rua grinned, trying to hide her satisfaction.

"Come on," Finn laughed, guiding her down a path that wrapped around the building.

"It's so quiet," she said.

"The children are at evening mass, but they should be back soon," he said.

They walked up the steps through the side entrance. The hallways were bright, covered in arts and crafts. She'd expected a gray, oppressive atmosphere in a city orphanage, not this.

"This is lovely, Finn, but why are we here?" She knew it wasn't because he wanted to show off.

"I have a standing date with St. Brigid's every Monday night. When the children return from mass, I read them stories for an hour before bed. I'll have to cut it short tonight, but I thought you might like to participate."

The hallway erupted into chaos as two lines of children burst through the doors, boys and girls of all ages.

"Fáilte! Finn!" Rua heard them shout.

"Finn! Sure, I told ye he would come," shouted a taller boy. The Irish accents were pronounced.

The older children walked past, offering quick smiles and nods. A few giggles erupted from the girls as they gazed upon Finn. Rua didn't blame them.

One little boy ran up to Finn, stood on his foot, and wrapped his arm around Finn's leg. He wasn't half the size of it.

Finn made a silly groaning noise, pretending to be a monster as he walked. The child clung to his leg in a fit of laughter.

The rest of the children screeched in delight, begging to have their turn next.

Finn took them on two at a time while Rua watched adoringly. He was carefree and lighthearted. She hadn't known this side of him to exist.

Feeling a tug on her skirt, she glanced down. A little girl, no more than four, was staring up at her through bright-blue eyes.

"An banphrionsa tú?" the girl asked.

She was going to ask Finn to translate, but somehow, she realized, she already knew what to say.

"Ní mé," Rua said, shaking her head at the little girl who'd asked if she was a princess. Finn watched her closely, listening as the Irish slipped from her lips. "Agus cad fútsa?" Rua asked back.

The little girl nodded, pulling her uniform skirt out wide and doing a twirl before running away.

"I didn't realize you spoke Irish." Finn's tone was accusing, as though this were information he should've been privy to.

"I don't . . ." She trailed off, knowing her memories hadn't returned. But perhaps embedded between the loss were the core parts of her—deeply inherent and impossible to shake. The language had come to her on a whim, surprising her with its ease. "And so what if I do speak it?" she asked, recovering herself. What was it to him?

"Ah, my lord, ye made it." A smiling woman in a nun's habit walked up to them, pulling a child off Finn's leg, effectively tabling their conversation.

"Sister Mary, this is Rua." Finn put his hand behind Rua's back. Rua smiled.

"Pleasure to meet you, Rua."

"Likewise," Rua said, thinking it was the first time someone had met her with a genuine smile upon their face.

"I've only time for a quick visit now, but I'll come tomorrow night, if that suits?"

"Ye are welcome anytime."

"Pardon us a moment?" Finn said to Rua, stepping off to the side with Sister Mary.

"Of course." Rua busied herself looking at the pictures on the wall while they talked. She tried not to listen, but there was only so much she could do. She heard the nun thank Finn and saw her stick an envelope into her skirt pocket. He was the reason these orphaned children had a comfortable and safe place to lay their heads.

"Go on now, the both of ye," Sister Mary said. "Get back to your evening."

"Tomorrow, then?"

"Tomorrow." Sister Mary nodded. "Lovely to meet you, Rua," she called, walking in the opposite direction. "Fergus, ye wee skitter, get back in there!" She pointed at the little boy who'd just opened a pair of double doors, letting the sound of boisterous chatter fill the hallway.

Rua laughed as Finn came to her side, taking her hand without a second thought, like he'd done it a hundred times before. Her heart skipped a beat, hoping he wouldn't let go.

"Thank you for coming with me," he said.

"I'm happy you thought to bring me."

He held the door open for her with one arm, holding her tight with the other.

Under the light of the moon and the blurry light of the streetlamps, she was so far removed from her counterfeit existence. One elegant brownstone followed another, their only differences being the designs of the balustrades and the flower boxes on the windows.

She counted her steps, wishing they didn't have to go back to the opera.

Rua wondered what he was thinking. Wondered if it would be hard to leave him behind. Of course it shouldn't be. Their connection was nothing more than a series of sparkling flirtations. Perhaps if she were someone else . . . She looked away, a sting in her eyes.

Abruptly, Finn stopped, pulling his hand from hers. Affronted, she turned to face him.

War waged on his face, tearing him between who he was and who he was trying to be. She swallowed hard, knowing which version of him would win. She could see it there in the depths of his eyes, pooling with an inexplicable need that matched her own.

Her breath deepened as she anticipated what would come next.

Finn took a step toward her; they were toe to toe.

His eyes met hers and, finally, he found his answer.

Breath ragged, he cupped the side of her face, working his fingers through her hair.

Her heart thundered as she absent-mindedly licked her lip, his hands anywhere on her body enough to drive her mad.

He responded with a guttural groan, pressing himself into her.

There was no reeling it back now. This was ecstasy.

His palm settled on the side of her neck while his thumb lingered at her mouth. The movement was unhurried as he traced her bottom lip. She trembled under his touch, desperate for more.

"Rua," he breathed, lowering his forehead to hers.

"Finn," she whispered back, tilting her face up to his, their lips almost touching for the second time tonight. She could endure the teasing no more.

Seeing the glow of her eyes reflected in his, a sharp rush of clarity shot through her. She felt like herself—clear, powerful, strong. If he wasn't going to kiss her, she would take matters into her own hands.

And then his mouth crashed down on hers. Urgent and yearning, he set her world on fire. Her fists knotted into his shirt, pulling him closer, but it wasn't enough.

Messy with wanting, they bumped up against a cemented wall. She let out a little gasp. He grinned and bent forward, burrowing his face in her neck, torturing her skin with his lips.

Pleasure ripped through her as his hands gripped her tighter, holding her for dear life. She melted into his embrace, feeling his strength.

Moving her hands to his face, she traced the outline of his lips, his eyes, his jaw.

He groaned his pleasure. Her pulse quickened at the sound. He kissed her mouth once more, then tragically pulled away.

"I don't want to go back," she said softly.

"Neither do I," he agreed, nuzzling against the top of her head.

They stayed there a moment, silent and reveling. Their kiss had changed things, inevitable as it was. She wanted to know every part of him, despite the feeling that she might already.

He inhaled deeply and stepped back, looking at her thoughtfully. "The scent of meadowsweet torments me night and day."

"Crios Cú Chulainn," she said, pleased that he'd noticed.

His face darkened. "What?"

"It's what the perfume is called," she answered, not understanding his reaction. "There's a story to it, I think. Something about the warrior Cú Chulainn using it after battle." She thought about it a moment. "I suppose the perfumer could have just been selling me a story to entice me. I would have bought it either way." She wasn't sure why she felt like she needed to defend her purchase.

He nodded, softening a bit, but his demeanor wasn't quite the same. "I'm afraid your mother's attention can only be diverted for so long. We must return."

A pang of disappointment swelled as they walked in silence back to the opera house. They did not hold hands or acknowledge each other's presence. They might have never kissed at all.

Regret was a tedious emotion, but it was all she could feel as her mind replayed over and over what could have gone wrong in the minutes since they'd last embraced.

The mention of Cú Chulainn—it was the only thing she could think of. She wondered what it was about her perfume that had him perturbed.

Unless, of course, it went deeper than that. Perhaps his lordship was dealing with a bout of regret himself. He was intending to marry Annette, was he not? And yet he'd kissed Rua—an earth-shattering, bone-melting kiss.

She let out a frustrated huff, thinking about Annette and how she was getting everything she wanted—Finn and a sullied Rua.

They stopped at the back entrance of the opera house where they'd originally sneaked out. The door was wedged open with a small piece of wood, letting the sounds of the performance drift outdoors.

Rua passed in front of Finn, chin up, as he held the door open for her.

To go from such a high to such a low in the span of ten minutes was infuriating. What was the point of inviting her to the opera, sneaking out to the orphanage, kissing her in the moonlight, if he was going to recede back to his churlish ways?

"You know, Finn, for no reason, you ruined a perfectly good—"

He grabbed hold of her arm, swinging her back to his front, and shushed her with a mouthwatering kiss.

His lips were soft as they melted into hers, his tongue gently coaxing its way past her lips.

It was quick. And it was subtle. And it meant everything.

Twenty

When the show was over, Finn and the other men bid the ladies farewell as they got into the carriages and went home. Custom dictated a cheroot at the club or, for some of the other men, an evening with a courtesan.

Ned was drunk in the corner of the room while Richard sat up front like a king.

Women filed into the club one by one, dressed in their late-night best, unencumbered by societal standards. The men in the room roared their cheers as the women paraded in front of them. Any one of them could've seen what happened on Greene Street, could've spotted him and Rua as they fled.

He moved behind one of the room's large white pillars, not wanting to be noticed.

He was still waiting for news of the murdered man. Waiting and listening to hear if any of the men had brought it up after spending some time with their women. The sad truth of it was, crime was on the upswing, and the police didn't bother to meddle in the affairs of the sex district.

All Finn really wanted to do was follow Rua home and find out all the ways he might have known her. He swirled the contents of his glass, thinking the color was the same as Rua's hair. He swallowed it in one sip.

She'd thrown him for a loop with the name of her perfume, Crios Cú Chulainn.

It was true what she'd said, that after battle the famed warrior had been known to bathe in the flower, its properties being the only thing that could return him from his battle frenzy. Unimaginable to think that the dainty white flower could stave off the ríastrad and subdue the beast that he became. What were the odds that she would pick out his favorite smell? What could explain it, other than coincidence?

And bloody hell, the sound of the Irish words when they'd left her lips. Spoken perfectly. He was in awe. Another layer she had revealed.

"Donore, I have a friend I'd like you to meet." An acquaintance named Fredrick peaked out from behind the column, disrupting his thoughts.

"Who?" Finn asked.

Fredrick pointed to a woman wearing a red satin gown with her skirts slipped up to her thighs. Flirtatiously, she offered him a wave, hiking her skirt up a bit more.

That was his cue. He put his empty glass down on the table and left the club.

His return to the Harrington home was greeted by muffled shouting. Curious, he followed the noise upstairs.

"Whatever were you thinking, sneaking out of the lord's opera box?"

He could hear Mrs. Harrington's raised voice coming through the library.

"I swear, young lady, I've had enough of your nonsense. Sneaking off into the curtains with a man like some trollop. If you were gone any longer . . ." She paused. "Well, I should hate to think of the rumors that would churn!"

"It wasn't just any man, Mother, it was the Lord of Donore. I thought you'd be pleased. Then we'd have him good and trapped, no?" Rua said brazenly.

"The cheek of you!"

"Surely, you could have stopped me if you thought it was an issue."

"I was watching the performance," Flossie snarled. "If you don't start acting the way a decent woman should, oh, so help me, I'll more than make good on my threat. Your behavior is a reflection on this family. You've left me with little choice."

Guilt washed over him. It was he who had lured Rua out of the opera house.

But Mrs. Harrington continued her assault. "Do you think the lord will want you now?"

If anything, Finn wanted her more.

"You've shown him how loose your morals are. Why would he bother marrying you now?"

Bloody hell.

Rua's silence broke his heart.

"When he gets what he wants from you, he'll return to wherever he came from with Annette Fitzgerald in tow. Now get to bed."

Once upon a time, he had shared Mrs. Harrington's sentiments. He felt monstrous for it now. Rua was a welcome diversion to the tedium—necessary, even.

As footsteps approached the door, he retreated into the dark corners of the hallway.

"Mara, I require a cup of tea before bed," Mrs. Harrington barked.

Finn's eyes darted to the shadowy nook concealing Mara. Apparently, there were two sneaks lurking in the corridor tonight.

"She's not right in the head. Positively hysterical. Imagine, sneaking out in front of everyone!"

Mara glanced toward Finn and back to Mrs. Harrington. He wondered why she wasn't giving him away.

"My husband's business prospects, my acceptance at social events—oh, heaven forbid it. We'll be forced to move out of the city. Live like lepers somewhere up north. We must keep her contained until it can be resolved. And it will be soon."

Mara whispered something too low for him to hear.

"And that's exactly where she is going. She'll stay home for the remainder of the week. Possibly the one after that, too. I can no longer bear it." There was a pause. "I'm going to bed. Bring me some tea."

He wondered if Rua understood the seriousness of her situation. Her cheek was sure to catch up to her at some point.

When Mrs. Harrington and Mara had gone, Finn moved into the library.

Rua was draped over the armchair, her face covered by a small book.

"Still reading that?" he asked.

"I've just gotten to the part where the man thinks his efforts have paid off."

He laughed as she lowered the book just enough for her lovely green eyes to show, though sometimes he was sure they were gold.

He shut his eyes, a terrible pain in his head.

He gripped the base of his blade, wary of the golden eyes that approached him.

"You should try and relax," she teased.

He heard the smile in her voice, but it did not ease his worry. For there could be no trust in a woman who did not trust herself.

"I've only come to find someone to enjoy the stars with," she said.

A true chameleon.

She reached for his hand. He gave it willingly.

Finn looked at Rua, trying to understand it. Trying to connect this woman before him with the one he saw in his mind. Were they one and the same?

Then what did that make him?

It had never occurred to him that he could be anyone other than who he'd always thought he was—a man from Ireland, with a good heart and a need to thrive. But meeting Rua had unraveled his meticulously curated world.

"Are you all right?" Rua asked, squinting and tapping the book against her nose.

"Yes, it's just—I feel terrible for the predicament you're in. It is entirely my fault," he said, casting his troubling thoughts aside.

"So you heard?"

"I heard enough." He walked over to her, stopping beside her chair.

She tilted her head back, exposing her slender neck as she stared at the ceiling. Sounding bored, she asked, "Do you think me a trollop, Finn?"

She brought her focus back to the room—to him.

"Of course not," he said. "But I never should have taken you from the opera. It was reckless." He should've had a care for how her mother would react, even if Rua didn't.

"I got up and walked out on my own two legs," she said, sitting up, reaching for his hand.

The light touch set his pulse racing. She was soft and delicate but wild and passionate at the same time. Truly unrivaled. How could he have ever thought he'd find contentment with someone else? Rua was who he wanted.

"And anyway, my issues with Flossie have nothing to do with you. I certainly don't care what you think of my morals." She grinned, then added, "I enjoyed myself tonight, and I would do it again."

He returned her smile, despite his concern. "Are you not worried about your mother's warning?"

She shrugged. "I have more pressing things on my mind."

"Like what?" He sat down in the chair beside her.

She stared at the floor for a long moment before she looked his way. "Can I trust you?"

"With anything," he answered without hesitation.

She smiled, thoughtful, as though she could hear every labored beat of his heart, but she did not speak. Her secrets meant too much.

But he could wait no longer. They'd existed for too long in this limbo, skirting around hard truths, and now he needed answers. "This is going to seem strange," he started, the words heavy as bricks, "but I need to know."

Rua's head cocked to the side, her expression menacingly unreadable. He almost reconsidered broaching the subject. "Do you ever get the sense that we've met before?"

"Before when?" Her voice was cool as she appraised him.

And then he saw it flash, the gilt in her eyes. A predator circling its prey. He batted down his alarm and pressed onward. "Before Manhattan. I cannot explain this feeling that I somehow know you."

"Well," she said, her words like slow-moving lava, "wouldn't you know if you'd met me before?"

"I suppose it doesn't make much sense," he said, regretting the conversation.

Rua sat unmoving. She might've been a statue.

He was immobile, too, realizing his life hung in the balance. He wondered if she would ever speak again. He hoped she was trying to think of the right words to tell him he wasn't mad and she knew exactly how he felt. But hope was a fool's fancy.

Abruptly, Rua got up and walked to the mahogany double doors. For a brief, humiliating moment, he thought she might leave. That she thought him too ridiculous to be worthy of a response. But she stopped, pushing them shut before turning her sights on the dark corners of the room.

When she was satisfied they were alone, she sat back down, leaning toward him.

"I need to get something from Mara's room," she said.

"Your maid's room?" he repeated.

"Yes."

"Why can't you just ask her for whatever it is?" he asked, realizing she was going to ignore everything he'd just said. He'd misread the situation and felt foolish for it now.

Rua shook her head, grinning. "She can't know."

He watched her a moment, a playful look in her eyes. He couldn't imagine what she might need to steal from the maid, but he didn't have the strength to refuse her.

He sighed. Perhaps it was enough that he'd brought the subject up. He'd unburdened himself, and how she responded was not in his control. "What do you need from me?"

"I need you to be the lookout," she said, scrunching her face.

He smiled. "I suppose it's the least I could do."

"I agree," she said, rising to her feet.

"I happen to know that Mara is making your mother a cup of tea as we speak," he said, happy to be able to provide her with this small piece of information.

"You'll prove useful yet, my lord." She laughed, hurrying toward the door. "What are we waiting for?"

They crept down the back stairs like two thieves in the night. He found being in cahoots with Rua to be thrilling, though the stakes weren't very high. But he was slowly realizing that if it mattered to her, it mattered to him.

"What is it that you need from her room?" he asked, keeping his voice low.

"A book."

He frowned, following her. "Your taste in literature is quite eclectic."

She glanced back at him with a cheeky grin.

"What are the contents of said book?"

She didn't answer.

They reached the bottom of the staircase and stared down a long corridor of white walls and many doors. There were no servants to be seen, but he could hear the distant clatter of dishware.

"Wait here, and don't let anyone by you."

"Simple enough," he said, watching Rua tiptoe down the hall into a room she'd clearly visited before. He checked his watch, noting that it was a few minutes past midnight. Perhaps the halls were empty because the servants were in bed. "Rua?" he whispered loudly to warn her.

Not twenty seconds later, there was a scream, and out barreled Rua, book in hand. "Go!"

He waited until she was ahead of him, and they both took off back up the stairs.

"What happened?" he asked.

"I forgot Mara had a roommate," she gasped, taking the stairs two at a time. "She saw me and got a fright."

They kept running until they reached the top. Rua plopped down on the step and lay on her back. He sat next to her, watching as she laughed and caught her breath. He'd never met anyone so beautiful. Giving in to the impulse, he lay back beside her, resting his hands on his stomach.

He stared up at the ceiling, thinking about all the ways he was amazed by her. "Rua, when did you learn to speak Irish?"

She rolled her head to the side to face him, and he did the same. "I don't know." Her voice was quiet.

He watched the delicate pout of her lips and the crinkle in her brow, and believed she was just as surprised as he was. But *I don't know* wasn't an answer.

"I don't understand," he said. Irish was a complex language. Not something one picked up on a whim. His mind grudgingly went to the rumors about her and the laborer's comments about the hell caves, Oweynagat. How did a young woman from the upper echelons of society wind up at a supposed hell cave? Something wasn't adding up.

"Neither do I," she said, her words final.

Finn sat up, propped against his elbows. "Mara's roommate will tell her that you were there, no?"

"Perhaps," Rua said, "but I got the book." She sat forward, pulling it from behind her back.

"That looks like a diary," he said.

She looked up at him through thick eyelashes, not an ounce of remorse. "It is."

He frowned. What on earth was she doing stealing her maid's diary?

"Well, if I told you what I was taking, you, with your strict moral code, wouldn't have helped me."

He'd like to believe that was true, but when it came to Rua, the lines were blurring.

"Surely you could've talked to her about whatever answers you're searching for?" he asked.

"No." She shook her head. "I had no other choice."

He believed her.

She tossed the journal over in her hands a few times. "What time is it? I should probably get to bed. I need to read this and put it back before she knows what I took."

Agreeing, Finn checked his watch. "Twenty past twelve," he said.

He stood up and offered her a hand up. She took it and didn't let go. The warmth of her small fingers wrapped around his own was agonizing.

He turned to face her, longing to pull her lips up to his. To experience one more moment of her exquisiteness. For a split second, he thought he might.

Then Rua spoke. "What about Annette?"

His chest tightened, knowing what she was asking. His heart or his head?

He stroked the back of her hand with his thumb, and she leaned into him.

Rua had upended his life, his very existence. He was set aflame, willing to burn his careful world to the ground for the chance to be with her.

"What about her?" He kissed the top of Rua's head, and they walked down the hall, hand in hand.

Twenty-One

The following Friday, Finn slipped out of the Harrington household before he could lay eyes on Rua. He hadn't seen Annette since the opening night of the opera and thought it best not to arrive to her birthday party in the same transport as Rua and potentially instigate a situation in which Annette felt it necessary to expose the trick she and Lily had played on her.

Things were going well, and he wanted to keep it that way.

But deep down he knew that wasn't the only reason he wanted to travel without her. A part of him clung to the version of himself that could still have everything this city had to offer, if he would only propose to Annette. He could do a world of good in this city with the Fitzgeralds' connections and a strong reputation. It was hard to let go of that dream, one he had chased for so long.

But as he thought about life without Rua, he couldn't imagine it. Christ, he had even paid a member of the Whyos to take the blame for a murder she committed, such was the depth of his desires.

"Donore." Richard raised a brow, greeting him inside the entryway. "I wasn't sure you were going to make it." His way of saying he'd noticed Finn's distance as of late.

Annette was standing next to her father. "Happy birthday, Miss Fitzgerald. You are looking splendid, as always."

By all standards, Annette was very pretty—ideal, even. She looked every bit the part of an aristocratic wife. Perhaps it was the illumination under the sparkling candlelit chandeliers, but now he saw her for who she truly was: a vapid brat.

"I am so pleased you could join us, my lord," Annette gushed.

"I would be honored to request a dance," Finn said, more out of duty than of want. "But first, might I have a word?"

She looked excitedly toward her mother and father, who nodded their approval.

They were a few paces away from the parlor room. Dozens of eyes were peeking over decorated fans; mothers were whispering in their daughters' ears. They were at dinner, and he was the main course.

He brought her to a quiet corner away from prying eyes.

"I was so worried you wouldn't come," Annette started. "I haven't seen you in quite some time." Because he was spending his free time with Rua.

Getting right to it, he said, "I need your word that you will not mention the prank you and Miss Stevens played on Emma Harrington to anyone."

"Why?" Her eyes narrowed.

"Because it is the decent thing to do," he warned.

Annette raised a brow, and it was then he realized he had misjudged the way this conversation was going to go.

"My lord, did my father tell you about the visitor we had earlier in the week?"

Finn didn't like the sharpness in her tone. "Of course he did not tell me, Miss Fitzgerald."

"Well, it was a reporter from the *Daily News*." Finn's stomach tightened as he remembered the columnist they had mentioned in regard to their prank. "He thought my father might be interested in what he learned."

Bloody hell. He knew what she was going to say before she said it.

"Apparently, there was a murder on Greene Street some weeks back," Annette said, feigning surprise. "Now, the reporter did not witness the murder, but"—she grinned, looking up at him—"it just so happens to be the same address we sent darling Emma Harrington. I daresay the conjecture alone would be enough for an arrest."

"Make your point," he growled, glancing around the room at the guests laughing and drinking, wondering how he could have ever wanted any part in it. They were despicable, every last one of them.

"You have embarrassed me long enough. Declare your intentions, announce our engagement, and this remains our little secret."

Finn scoffed. The chit was blackmailing a proposal out of him.

"Do we have an understanding, my lord?" Annette asked, impervious to his anger.

He could not speak, so ready was his rage to spill over. To think he had ever thought them worthy of his time. Richard was behind this, he was sure of it. He scanned the room, searching for the bastard.

"I'll need an answer, my lord." Annette's voice faltered. "I believe the reporter will be covering the party tonight."

Finn looked back at her, showering her with contempt. Cornered into a marriage. He couldn't believe it. "It will be an engagement in name only," he said darkly.

Annette flinched but nodded. She'd gotten what she wanted.

"I'm warning you," he said, "not a word of this gets out. Do you swear it?"

"Why do you care what happens to her?" she dared ask him.

His eyes grew wild. He knew his reasons, and they were none of Annette's concern.

"I need you to swear it," he said, hardly able to look at his betrothed, the hateful young woman who'd forced his hand, who'd torn him away from the one he truly wanted.

The realization hit him hard. He'd wasted so much time avoiding his feelings, and now it was too late.

"Yes, I swear it!" she screeched, too immature to hide her glee. Too self-absorbed to understand the depths of his disdain. "One more thing, my lord."

He was at his limit with her petulant demands. Distraught for the life he could never have with Rua. A life he hadn't even known he wanted until it was ripped away. Losing even the possibility of her was gut wrenching, and he'd never forgive the Fitzgeralds for taking it from him.

"You cannot tell her about the conditions of our arrangement," she said, smugly.

He bent his head down so that his eyes were level with hers. "And how the hell would you know if I did?"

Tears welled in her eyes. He didn't care.

She hadn't cared when she'd allowed her jealousy to alter the entire course of his life. If she wanted to play with the adults, then she'd better learn fast.

Leaving a whimpering Annette in the corner, Finn swiped a drink off the refreshment table and headed toward the veranda. How the hell had this all gone to shit? He took a sip of his drink. Had his affection for Rua been so obvious that he'd allowed himself to be cajoled into a marriage? He shook his head and leaned against the banister.

And where was she now, his harbinger of turmoil? He faced the ballroom, hoping for a glimpse, but stopped himself. He would have to move on. There was no other choice. Everyone would be better for it.

He took another sip of his drink, dreading the thought of returning indoors, but return he did. After all, there was an engagement to announce.

By now, most of the guests had arrived and were trickling into the ballroom. In no mood for pleasantries, he disregarded all who greeted him as he made his way back inside the foyer.

He spotted Annette by the front door with her mother. Through the angry haze, he reminded himself that a union to Annette was what he *had* wanted. He had to be practical—he used to be practical. This was the union that would open this city's doors to him and bring him the success he sought.

And yet here he was, the world at his feet, and he was watching the door with unbridled anticipation. Waiting for the one woman who had not arrived and could offer him nothing but scandal. A woman who had been lost to him the moment he laid eyes on her.

He tore his eyes away.

Finn thought back to the dream he'd had last night after leaving Rua.

The three women gathered below him, bloodied and jovial after wreaking their havoc. He remained unseen upon the cliff above the hellmouth.

The raven-haired monster, the one who'd come to him earlier, was washing the blood from her face. The cruelest of the three. He wondered what she'd destroy next.

Hate burned in his veins. They were the enemy to end all enemies.

The second sister, a brown-haired woman, sat upon a rock, braiding her hair.

He glanced up at the sky. The moon was almost at its peak.

He'd lost sight of the third, redheaded monster. Perhaps the cursed water they were so keen on bathing in had finally devoured her, doing his job for him.

Finn refocused his attentions on the people in the room around him, so far removed from the thoughts rattling around in his head. It was impossible to reconcile those memories with the life he had now.

The similarities between Rua and the redheaded monster from his dreams were chilling. Once again, he thought of the laborer's warning about the cursed waters and the first man Rua was supposed to have killed. It had happened near a hell cave. He almost laughed at the ridiculousness of it all.

A collective gasp filled the room, followed by a rush of murmurs. He didn't need to turn his head to know that Rua had arrived.

Somehow, he could feel her presence. Like the pull of a tether, he was drawn to her. And deep in the very fibers of his soul, he knew she had laid claim to him long ago.

As he turned to look at her, he found there were no words appropriate to describe her. Larger than life, she was an ethereal goddess. A vision cut from ancient Italian stone.

Her gown was a subtle shade of green satin that matched her eyes perfectly. The bodice appeared as though it were sewn onto her body. The neckline, sinfully low, exposed the curve of her breasts, which were instrumental in supporting the colossal diamond necklace that dangled from her neck.

The sight of her made his chest tighten, knowing they were over before they ever began. To think they'd spent every morning since the opera in a state of wide-eyed indulgence, enjoying breakfast and each other's company. Even Flossie had laid off a bit. He'd given in, set down his walls, allowing himself to believe it could work.

He didn't know how to tell her that it was over, that he was leaving her to pick up the pieces.

He wished to whisk her away to another world and show her all the ways he might adore her.

"Shall we move to the ballroom?" Mrs. Fitzgerald addressed the room, ripping Finn from his reverie, reminding him of what he had lost.

Annette moved through the crowd and grabbed hold of his arm. With no other choice, he escorted her to the ballroom.

"Try not to look so terrifying, my lord. People might think you are opposed to this match," Annette whispered with a smile as they crossed through the foyer.

"But I am opposed to this match," he said, devoid of all emotion. He looked down at her, seeing that she was altogether too plain for his tastes. He didn't know how he had ever thought otherwise. No matter how hard she might try, she didn't have Rua's natural albeit fiery charm.

When they had all gathered in the ballroom, Richard stood atop a dais to address the room. "It is time we let the birthday girl and her charming suitor share the first dance." Finn wanted nothing more than to pummel him.

Richard responded to Finn's glare with a wink.

Finn extended his arm to Annette, hating that Richard was pulling strings behind his back. Any chance for an amicable arrangement had gone out the window the moment they threatened Rua.

Annette was oblivious to his thoughts as they ambled toward the dance floor. She cared only that everyone saw her with the Lord of Donore.

His mind went to Rua and what she might be thinking. He pushed down the rising lump. It could no longer be his concern.

Not a word was uttered during the dance. Annette would rue the day she set her sights on him. From this day forward, he would offer her nothing but cold indifference.

He looked around the room at the other dancers, at the crowd watching them, forcing himself not to search for Rua. All the faces he met were smiling, no doubt discussing what a lovely pair they'd make. His stomach turned at the thought.

At the conclusion of their dance, Finn returned Annette to her mother. Gloria offered him a smile, which he did not reciprocate. He wondered how much she knew. Had Annette had the chance to fill her in and let her know their coercion had gone swimmingly? That they had deduced the lord's affections for Rua correctly and now had him up against a wall?

"Might you fetch me some lemonade?" Annette asked sweetly as one of her friends approached. She flashed him a warning look.

"Of course," he said, already tired of the charade.

He leaned idly against the table, forgetting about Annette's drink as he scanned the ballroom for Rua. How did he even begin to tell her the predicament they were now in?

"Looking for me, Finn?"

He turned around, pulse hammering.

"Hardly," he lied, because he was always looking for her. In every room, at every party, and all the places in between.

She was gloriously exquisite and fast approaching. He could not keep his eyes from appreciating every bit of her.

"I couldn't help but notice you looking forlorn," she said, wetting the corner of her lips with a flick of her tongue.

His eyes captured the movement.

She moved closer, her gloved arm reaching toward him. His heart beat faster as he imagined sliding the fabric off her hand, one delicate finger at a time. And the way her body might shiver if his mouth left slow, purposeful kisses from the tips of those fingers to the nape of her neck.

He'd never wanted someone more. Her scent alone was driving him mad. If she took one more step toward him, their bodies would touch and there'd be no saving them then. There'd be no time for decorum. He'd abandon it all just to taste her lips one last time.

He was balancing on the edge of madness and exultation. One wrong move and he would slip.

But then Rua slid past him, taking with her a glass of champagne and the last of his pride. He could not mask his own foolish deflation. She'd bloody baited him, and he'd fallen for it.

"Don't look so disappointed, my lord." She turned back with a smirk. "Apparently, I'm not your type after all."

She was talking about his dance with Annette. His heart ached as he thought of how much had changed in the space of an hour.

Unaware of their impending destruction, Rua pulled at his restraint as she tipped her head back to take a sip of champagne. All he could do was wonder what sound she would make if his mouth kissed the space where her jaw met her ear.

He adjusted his waistcoat, wondering when he would be free to breathe again.

She smiled at him, placing the empty flute on a passing server's tray. "You know, my lord, I think this was one of the best conversations we've ever had. You were quite amenable." She winked and walked away.

He gripped the edge of the table, trying to comprehend what he'd just endured. Never in his life had he been so handily stripped of the ability to speak.

"I thought we had this squared away?"

Finn turned to find Richard watching from the other side of the table.

"You're a foul bastard," Finn said, stepping up to Richard.

"Mind yourself, Donore. If you want to keep your pet safe, you'll keep that temper of yours in check."

He knew nothing of Finn's temper. Before he could respond, Ned approached.

"I hope my daughter's not troubling you too much, my lord," Ned said.

Troubling wasn't the word he'd use.

"The new contracts have arrived," Ned said to both him and Richard, but Finn didn't know what contracts he was referring to.

"Very good," Richard said, grabbing Ned's shoulders, "very good. You've done the right thing. Let's discuss this in my study."

Ned nodded, looking grave.

Richard turned to Finn. "Why don't you go and give my daughter her lemonade, hmm?" he said with a dismissive nod. "Come join us after."

"I should think my involvement necessary if you're discussing contracts," Finn snapped.

"I assure you, Donore, it's not." Richard didn't wait for a response and guided Ned out of the ballroom.

Finn was fuming, but what was he going to do about it other than exactly what Richard said to do? It wasn't enough for him to force the marriage; he had to let Finn know he could still destroy Rua if he wanted to.

Twenty-Two

"**I** think tonight is going rather well, don't you?" Rua asked Flossie. She didn't know what the Fitzgeralds had put in their alcohol, but no fewer than four gentlemen had asked her to dance.

"Two out of the four are notorious gamblers, the third is a nobody, and the fourth, well, he isn't very handsome, now, is he?" Flossie pressed her lips together while her eager eyes scanned the ballroom for her next victim. Rua wondered if all the other mothers in the ballroom were this horrible.

Flossie continued, "I must say that I'm most disappointed in the resurgence of the lord's interest in Annette. I had hoped that he might focus his attentions elsewhere." Her eyes fixed on Rua.

Rua had hoped so too.

She'd be lying if she said she wasn't utterly shocked to see the attention Finn was paying Annette this evening. She supposed it was her birthday, but it didn't ring true.

She'd thought they had turned a corner, even with Mara thwarting their efforts for privacy in the evenings. That their flirtations were turning into more. Their mornings at breakfast were her favorite part of the day.

"Did you really think moving him into our home was going to make him want to marry me?" Rua asked bitterly. Marriage to Finn wasn't what she wanted, but that wasn't the point.

"I certainly didn't think it would hurt. It doesn't matter now, does it? Mrs. Fitzgerald is telling everyone that he's proposing. Tonight." Flossie shook her head.

Rua sucked in a harsh breath. "Tonight?" After everything that had happened, after everything Annette had done to her? Finn's duplicity enraged her.

Flossie nodded. "And I assume she only wanted you here to stick our noses in it. I never would have let you come had I known."

Rua glanced over at the new couple sipping their lemonade but couldn't tolerate the sight of them. She cursed, wondering how she'd allowed herself to become so involved.

"You'll just have to try harder, hmm? You could do with being a bit more pleasant. Now, give me your dance card." Flossie stuck out her hand.

Rua forced down the lump in her throat, ignored the throbbing in her head, and handed over the ridiculous card that declared her desirable.

It disturbed her that if this little piece of paper was filled, she would not be scorned as a wallflower. Even more disturbing than the misogyny was her own delight that it was filled. She hated that it mattered to her and hated even more that Finn was not on the card.

The lines between her life and Emma's were blurring beyond recognition.

"I'm going to sit over there. I need a little break." Rua pointed to the collection of chairs by the window.

Flossie nodded, too busy hunting down Rua's next suitor.

She couldn't bear to look at Annette smiling up at Finn while they floated around the room.

The anger bubbling up in her chest was enough to take down an army. The same anger she'd felt before she'd killed that man, it came easy to her, filling her with purpose.

Rua forced herself to take a deep breath, her eyes wandering to the chandeliers above them. She'd love to have them shake and shiver before crashing down in a dazzling explosion on the floor, sending everyone scattering. And if a particularly large shard happened to impale Annette, then so be it.

She didn't mean that. She took another deep breath and counted to ten.

Yes she did.

Everything about this life went against her core instincts. Rigid and harsh, it allowed no room to live. She wanted to scream and throw things and tell everyone how absurd they were. But that was a one-way trip to the asylum. She had no choice but to be on their version of her best behavior. At least for a few more days, anyway. Samhain was almost here.

Flossie hurried over to her with a man in tow.

Rua forced a smile and took his hand.

A rag doll passed from one child to the next, Rua hung onto the man's arm, never bothering to get his name. Only a few more hours and the night would be over.

They danced until she was given to the next man, but never the one she truly wanted.

Finn bent down and lifted the sparkling piece of shattered crystal off the floor. He glanced back up at the chandelier it had apparently fallen from. Odd, he thought, tossing it on a side table.

Every time he turned around, Annette was there, waiting for him, making it damned near impossible for him to find Rua. But perhaps that was her intention.

It had been an eternity since they last spoke, and there was so much that needed to be said. He felt unhinged as he watched her move between dance partners. Men who didn't deserve a moment of her time. His heart ached with the loss of his future, knowing that only his deal with Annette stopped him from lining up like the rest of them. He would have to settle for the stolen glances and little snippets of conversation she granted him in public.

Without much forethought, he turned and asked Annette for another dance. It was a mistake, to be sure, but the orchestra was play-ing a quadrille. And it was an opportunity to be near Rua.

"I will accept, my lord, but for propriety's sake, this will have to be the last time. At least until we've announced, of course," she added with a bright smile.

He looked at her hopeful face, aggravated by her vacuity. As though their engagement were a decision borne of mutual attraction or love. He ground his teeth together to avoid saying something he'd regret. He would never love Annette, but he would not let himself become cruel.

They walked onto the floor, and there was a murmur from the crowd, who were no doubt speculating as to why the Lord of Donore would be dancing with Annette again.

For once, he did not care. His only thought was to be near Rua in whatever capacity.

"We meet again," he said as Rua came around to face him. He paid no attention to the scowl on Annette's face as she was passed off and spun in a circle.

"How predictable," Rua said, looking bored and beautiful.

"What?" he asked, though he already knew. Annette had kept him close the entire evening.

"You and Annette. Truthfully, I thought you a *bit* more interesting than that." Her gaze was penetrating, sending a necessary jolt to his wilted heart.

"What if I told you I was only dancing with her now so that I might get closer to you?" Her hold on him was innate and it was mutual, he was sure of it. He would not survive this world without her.

Surprise flittered across her face.

She recovered quickly, a gleam in her eye. "Then I'd say you should've just asked me yourself."

Their bodies synced as they spun on the dance floor, their movements fluid as they moved as one.

"If only it were that simple," he said.

They switched partners and spun around the floor until finally meeting again.

"What are you doing with her, Finn?"

The hurt in her voice was unmistakable. She wasn't playing games with him now.

Hands clasped together, they moved forward, meeting the others, then stepped back, facing each other.

He couldn't explain it to her here. There wasn't enough time.

"It was not my choice—" he started to say, but a strong tap on his back ripped his focus from Rua. He turned, ready to flay the man who had dared interrupt him.

As he glared at the gentleman, understanding came over him. There was no longer any music playing. A furious Annette stood at the man's side, along with a dozen or so other dancers.

Too focused on Rua, he had left Annette partnerless in the middle of the set.

Rua gasped, trying to free her hand from his, but he couldn't let go. Not yet. He wanted to stand beside her and declare his devotion, guard her from whatever was coming next.

But he saw the threat in Annette's eyes for what it was and released Rua, knowing that if he didn't, the fallout would be catastrophic.

All eyes were on them. The silence louder than any orchestra.

Rua would be raked over the coals for his mistake, Annette would make sure of it, but this was better than the alternative. Annette knew that as well.

These were the consequences of letting one's emotions lead. In one fell swoop he had ensured that Rua would never acquire the acceptance that she sought so desperately for her mother's sake. She'd never stood a chance.

"It seems as though I have forgotten the steps!"

Finn cringed as he heard Rua address the ballroom. He shook his head, willing her to stop talking. Her smile was forced, though not enough to mask the trepidation—something he'd never expected to see.

Rua's skin blanched as she watched a mortified Mrs. Harrington bury her face in her hands. He hated to see the panic in Rua's eyes as the enormity of the situation sunk in. It sickened him more to know that it was his fault, and he could do nothing for her.

"Miss Harrington can hardly be blamed for my subpar dancing skills. Do forgive me, Miss Fitzgerald?" he interjected, mortified.

He longed to shield Rua from their criticism and hurry her out of the room, but he knew it would only infuriate Annette.

"I do blame her!" Annette snapped. "It is obvious that she has put you under some sort of spell in an attempt to undermine our relationship—the wicked little witch."

He glared at Annette as she approached his side, forcing Rua to move.

Looking disoriented, Rua assessed him and Annette, side by side, a seemingly united front. Then her eyes darkened.

"There's something not right about her. Something evil, if you ask me." Annette hooked her arm around his, putting the final nail in Rua's coffin.

Rua stood alone in the center of the room while the other guests glowered and nodded their agreement.

"That is enough," he said sharply, freeing his arm from Annette's grasp. Her eyes went wild, but he didn't care. He'd had enough of this farce. He couldn't watch as Rua was hung out to dry, mocked and ridiculed.

"Take one more step," Annette hissed, "and I'll tell everyone, right now. Everything and then some."

The hair on his neck stood upright.

Rua was still watching them, watching the room, riddled with contempt.

Rua's dance partner stepped forward. Finn presumed he was going to do the gentlemanly thing and escort her from the center of the dance floor before the situation worsened.

He would do the same. "Annette, shall we get some fresh air?" Finn asked, knowing the sooner he removed her from the ballroom, the sooner things would deescalate.

He prayed Rua would understand that it was for the best. That Annette would only continue to hurl her vile insults, riling the room up.

Finn took Annette's arm in his, and as he did, he saw a violent shudder rip through Rua's body.

Rua met his eyes then, her own expression bold and self-reliant. He could see the betrayal raging.

He paused, reconsidering what he'd done.

"You may escort me to my mother, my lord." It was too late, he thought, as Annette took him in the opposite direction.

And then Rua's dance partner stomped off the dance floor, leaving her to fend for herself.

Twenty-Three

*D*eep *breath*, she told herself as she glanced around the room. *Just breathe.*

Cold, angry faces stared back at her, their loud whispers dull against the blood pounding in her head.

She searched the crowd. There was no one she knew. The Harringtons, Finn—they had all abandoned her, fleeing before things got worse, before the pitchforks were taken out.

She was more alone in this crowded room than she'd ever been on her own.

The accusations had no merit, but they resonated with the guests all the same. They were delighted to punish her because she was new and she was different.

She took one small step forward and then another as the room threatened to close in on her.

People shuffled and pushed each other so they could move out of her way. As if breathing the same air would prove fatal. Every last one of them spewed bitterness. So pathetic. Feeding off one another's uncertainty.

A familiar roar of anger, too long kept at bay, flared deep inside her, and it was reaching precarious heights. She was going to snap.

"Oh, just look at her eyes, the witch!" a woman shrieked.

"Pure evil, I say!"

That was the moment fury took over. She stepped forward and glared at the crowd, daring another to speak out.

In her anger she was free. There was nothing she couldn't do.

She let out a strangled cry as she walked onto the battlefield. The sounds of war thundered around her. Rain pounded against the earth while the men clashed their swords, swinging and slashing without purpose.

She wore no armor. She sported no shield. She alone was enough.

Rua walked among the mortals, pulling their hearts from their chests and the eyes from their heads. When she was done, the battle was won.

Those closest to her gasped and jumped back, while the room divided leaving her path unobstructed. An insidious grin spread across her face. Cowards, all of them.

She didn't stop until she reached the balcony. She pushed past the curtains and slammed her fists down on the cool marble railing, not bothering to halt the frustrated scream that escaped her. Weeks of pent-up stress and failed effort boiled to a head. There was so much rage churning inside of her, she could see only red.

Everything went dark.

At first, she thought it was just in her head—that her anger had momentarily blinded her. But when she turned back around, she found the ballroom in complete darkness.

The guests screamed their panic.

"She did it! That wicked sorceress is responsible!"

"She'll kill us all!"

For a silly moment, she almost felt responsible. But it wasn't possible to will darkness into existence.

The cries in the ballroom intensified as the room descended into chaos.

She looked around for her options, realizing she'd chosen the wrong balcony from which to flee. She was trapped with no access to the small garden below.

Returning to the ballroom was out of the question, so she did the only thing she could think to do and hoisted herself over the balustrade. The cool limestone tore at her silk gown as she fell. It was farther than she'd thought it would be; she hadn't really considered the potential consequences. But she landed upright on her two feet, surprised she hadn't shattered her ankles. She ran through the garden, knowing there must be an exit to the street somewhere.

Like all gardens in this world, it was perfectly kept and large enough for a statuary and trimmed hedge. She wanted nothing more than to burn it to the ground.

Her hands shook as she thought of Flossie's face. They were going to send her to an asylum. There was no way Flossie would live with the shame. And Finn, he had made his choice, one that had cracked her heart wide open. Tears burned her eyes. She needed to get as far away as possible.

"Rua?"

The traitor's voice stilled her.

"What do you want?" she seethed.

"I came to see if you were all right." Finn approached her the way one might a wounded tiger. He stopped beside a marble statue of a naked Hercules. Tremendous in size, it should have towered over him. Instead, they were comparable, each one a specimen in his own time.

Incredulous, she repeated the words back. "See if I'm all right?" She wanted to rip his eyes out.

He grimaced but did not falter. "It's the truth," he said. "I'm sorry for what happened."

The moonlight offered little by way of light, but she could make out enough of his face to see that he looked genuine. Or perhaps it was just the guilt eating away at him. Either way, it didn't matter. The damage was done. He had broken her.

She took a step closer. "How dare you leave me standing there. How dare you! You are nothing but a coward, playing dress-up in a world you are unfit for," she spat. Her anger flowed through her, driving her movements, propelling her forward.

"A world I'm unfit for?" He raised his voice. "You flit about ballrooms like a tornado, destroying anything in your path. So long as your needs are met, you don't care who might suffer."

Fury rushed through her, unimpeded by rules and decorum. The stress of the evening, of the last few weeks, had worn her down to the bone. There was nothing left.

Wrath was her weapon as she reached upward, meeting Finn's worried gaze. Rather than wrapping her hands around his neck, she grabbed the statue, pulling at the side of Hercules's marble neck.

"What are you doing?" Finn shouted, though he did not stop her.

She was lost to the darkness, guided only by rage. An exasperated cry escaped her, and the cool stone crumbled under the stress of her palms. With one ruinous tug, she ripped the statue's head clean off. The statue wobbled, on the verge of tipping over, dislodged by her violent strength.

She stared at the once-glorious demigod, horrified by the damage, tears flooding her eyes.

Finn grabbed her by the waist, pulling her from the falling statue's path.

It crashed to the ground, and Rua shook in Finn's arms. She didn't have the strength to pull away. So drained and distraught, she was ready to collapse. Her body felt foreign, her strength and resentment a raw nerve.

She buried her face in Finn's chest and began to cry. He rested his palm against the back of her head, holding her tightly to him as the stress of the evening, of the last few weeks, spilled out of her. For a quiet moment they stood under the cloudless sky, pretending everything was going to be all right.

Finally, Finn spoke. "I'm sorry, Rua."

His words were a reminder of his treachery. She pushed herself out of his arms.

"I thought it was the best course of action," he said, trying to defend his mistake.

"Best for who?"

Finn didn't answer.

He didn't need to. He'd stood by the woman he was intending to marry, and Rua felt idiotic for expecting something different. She'd known from the start that he was courting Annette. But deep down, she had hoped he would choose her instead.

"I wanted to remove Annette from the situation," he said, "as I thought your dance partner was going to do with you. I didn't think he was going to abandon you. Please, forgive me. I misjudged terribly."

"Your apology means nothing." She could hardly stand to look at him.

He shook his head, rubbing his hand roughly against the back of his neck.

"What you did in there." She hesitated, her voice was barely more than a whisper. "Leaving me like that, it was so much worse than anything Annette ever could have said. You stood by while she called me a witch in front of an entire ballroom, and then you walked away with her. Your silence validated her accusations and confirmed my status as an outcast."

"Rua, that was never my intention."

"I don't care what your intentions were! It's what you did that matters." She stared at him. She could handle her status as a leper; she could handle their scorn. But she could not handle Finn picking Annette over her.

The pain of it tore at her insides and ravaged what was left of her soul.

Though she was loath to admit it, somewhere buried in the dark corners of her mind was the knowledge that she and Finn were supposed to be together. All of this, the struggle and the loss, all of it was so she could find her way to him.

But on the other side of that clarity was the truth, where the guilt and uncertainty thrived. Where her mind was still keeping secrets from her. A dangerous reality that she knew would threaten everything.

"Rua, I have something to tell you." Finn's face was grave. "It will explain the majority of my actions tonight."

Her stomach turned, thinking it could only be something terrible.

He loosened the cravat at his neck.

"Annette threatened to tell everyone about everything that happened at Greene Street." He stepped toward Rua again.

She tensed. "I thought you told me it was taken care of?"

He looked at her, pain etched in the lines of his face. "It is now. Officially."

"What?" She met his eyes and saw the truth. His sudden change of heart. "No. Finn, you can't."

"It's already done."

"No," she said, her voice stronger, more desperate.

Feeling the familiar pang of loss, she shut her eyes and held back her tears. Annette Fitzgerald had won and taken every last morsel of hope and crushed it between her gilded fingers.

Rua had to leave. Tonight.

Twenty-Four

The tension was leaving his shoulders and taking up residency in his head. Moments ago, he was certain that Rua was going to attack him. She'd have been well within her rights, but hell if it didn't send a jolt of terror coursing through him.

Instead, she'd knocked the head off a marble statue as easy as if it were made of sand. The sight of it left him astonished. And when he held her, that's when he saw it. The culmination of weeks of strange dreams and feelings of familiarity.

He watched as she stared up at the moon, exquisite and other-worldly, and wondered how he hadn't seen it before. She turned to face him, hair blowing in the wind, and the accompanying whiff of her meadowsweet perfume knocked him senseless.

Struck with the sudden truth, he shut his eyes. Flashes of green fields, charioteers and bloodshed, dark meadows, and Rua, as she used to be, filled his mind.

No longer a distant fantasy, Rua had unlocked memories long buried from a life he couldn't remember. It was devastating and enlightening, and he didn't know what to make of it.

"Conor, my friend, has it come to this?"

Conor wielded his sword. "It has, Cú Chulainn."

"I have no wish to kill you, but I will grant you a swift death," he said.

And before the other man had the chance to move, Cú Chulainn's spear drove with almighty force through his heart.

The warrior lifted Conor with ease. There was no triumph, no glory, only sorrow. He carried his dead friend to the edge of the ford to be returned to his men.

A woman stepped forward, curious and unafraid.

"Why kill him if it was going to bother you so?" she asked.

Cú Chulainn looked up in surprise at the divine creature. Not thinking her a threat, he continued cleaning his spear.

"I will kill any man, or woman"—he threw her a sideways glance—"that approaches me with ill will."

"You couldn't kill me." She smiled.

He stood up to his full height and walked toward her, spear in hand. He was almost double her size in both muscle and height.

"I could, and I would enjoy it." A smirk played on his lips. "What is it you've come for, rua?" He thought it the perfect endearment to describe the redheaded beauty.

"You." She grinned, taking the weapon from his hand. With cat-like speed, she jumped up and kicked hard against his chest, sending him stumbling backward.

Excitement flickered across his face.

He fired a blade at her heart. She caught it just as it pierced her tunic.

"It appears I underestimated you, vixen." He let out a hearty laugh, his brown eyes filled with guile. "So, have you come to bed the famed warrior, then?"

A wicked smile spread across her face. With a slight step forward, she launched the spear at his shoulder with exact precision. Not even a mighty warrior such as he could withstand the force of it.

"Your confidence is misplaced, great warrior," she laughed. "What could I do with half a god?"

Shocked, he remained pinned to the tree.

"Tell me your name!" he shouted as she retreated on her chariot.

"You can call me Rua," she shouted over her shoulder.

"Do you love her?"

He looked at Rua, trying to reconcile the woman before him and the one he saw in his mind. The one who called him Cú Chulainn. It was illogical and absurd, and yet it made sense.

In the life he had forgotten, he was Cú Chulainn and she was a Morrígan, but who were they now?

"Love who?" He cleared his throat, wondering how she could ask such a thing. He loved the version of Rua in his memory, and the one she was today.

"Annette," she said.

Not the woman he was thinking of, but perhaps the one he should focus on. She was to be his wife, after all. He pushed down the resentment.

If he had any intelligence at all, he would lie and tell Rua, *Yes, I love Annette*, thereby snuffing out the sparks flickering between him and Rua. Save them both from this burning path of destruction and loss. A path, it seemed, they'd been on before.

He wasn't sure how to acknowledge there was another part of him long buried. Or dead?

He knew the legend of Cú Chulainn well. He also knew how he'd met his end—mortally wounded and bound to a stone with a sword in his hand. Cú Chulainn had died, so how was Finn here?

How was she here? He looked to Rua. How could any of it be true?

Rua and Cú Chulainn.

She had his mind spinning. Past and present. Her mouth teasing him with sweet smiles and secrets. He didn't know how to let that go.

"I do not love her," he said, wondering if that would be enough to satisfy her. She nodded and looked away.

"But I suspect deep down this was what you wanted all along. I've only sped things up for you," she said, her voice heavy with resolve. "You should thank me."

He shook his head, knowing that everything had changed when they met. It was still changing now. He'd love nothing more than to call this whole thing off. But what would be the point? The past was the past. What did remembering he was Cú Chulainn do to change the life he was living now? Perhaps he had simply lost his mind. And he wasn't going to risk Rua's life because his was in disarray.

But if she asked him to? If she asked him to leave with her and never look back, he would do it, in a heartbeat.

"You never answered my question," he said.

"Which one?"

"Have we met before?"

Her eyes narrowed as her shoulders stiffened. "I'm not having this conversation right now." She glanced up toward the ballroom. Shouts of terror still lingered.

"When, then?" he asked her, needing to get to the bottom of this.

"Why does it matter, Finn? You're engaged to Annette," she said.

He closed the space between them, waiting to see if she'd step back. He heard her breath catch, but she did not move. Instead, she met his eyes.

"It matters because . . ." His voice was nothing more than a gravelly whisper as he lifted his hand to her cheek. His fingers burrowed in her hair, tugging gently, as his thumb hovered above her mouth.

Rua licked her lips, the tip of her tongue grazing his skin. He sucked in a harsh breath, his chest encumbered by the weight of his desire. He bent lower so that his forehead rested against hers, their lips mere inches apart, and said, "I must know how you've so effectively brought me to my knees."

Rua's breath was ragged as she shook her head against his, sniffled, and then pulled back, eyes watery. "I've never met you before."

He stood up to his full height, unsure of why she was holding so tight to her secrets. "I don't believe you."

"I don't care what you believe," she said with a chilling calmness. "Your future is in there." She pointed at the Fitzgeralds' ballroom. "I have to go." She started walking toward the street, but he caught up to her.

"Why are you running away from me?"

"I'm not running away," she said over her shoulder.

"Then tell me. Tell me when it was. Tell me what happened between us," he pleaded, softening his tone. She had answers, he could feel it. He needed to know how they'd ended up here, living different lives, without any recollection of the past.

"Us?" She spun around to face him. "There is no us. What don't you understand? You have made your choice. And I understand why you did it, truly, I do, but it doesn't change the fact that it's done, and we have to move on with our lives."

Once more, she turned and walked away from him. He couldn't let her go. He couldn't keep this inside any longer. He didn't know what she remembered, what parts of her she was keeping hidden, but he couldn't go another minute without knowing.

"I've heard the whispers of you being a devil worshipper or a witch," he said in a desperate bid to keep her from leaving.

She stopped, her head tilted frighteningly to the side. Intuitively, he took a step back.

"And?"

"There is talk that the Harringtons' daughter went missing and wasn't quite the same when recovered," he said to the back of her head. "And there are some that say you're a look-alike, a fetch, who took the place of their real daughter." He was poking a bear, and he was one wrong word from being bit.

"I am the Harringtons' real daughter." She looked at him, eyes gold, her voice cold and hollow.

Finn shook his head. "You're not." She was the woman from his dreams. He was sure of it. But how did one bring up the notion of a life other than the one they were currently living?

"Excuse me?"

"You're not a devil worshipper any more than you're Emma Harrington," he said, trying hard to hold on to his nerve but wavering under her harsh glare.

"What, pray tell, might I be, then?"

He wasn't sure if he was bold enough to say it or ready to open that door. A door that had, for some centuries, been closed.

"You are one of the Morrígan."

Shock, confusion, and understanding played out all at once on Rua's face.

"You are wrong," she snapped.

He wasn't wrong, but he wasn't going to win that battle. Though he wasn't sure why he even wanted to. What was the point? Would that knowledge change anything?

For so long, he'd been riding the fence, so what was he trying to prove by getting her to admit she remembered their past?

He'd thought it was unintentional when he'd walked out of the ballroom with Annette, but maybe on some deeper level, he'd known it was the safer option. He'd agreed to marry her to save Rua, but really, it was the convenient choice. The one that led to less scrutiny, that allowed him to live his life without confronting his past. The one that did not compromise his values by aligning him with someone suspected of devil worshipping.

Even his charities would suffer if he chose Rua. Those he helped would reject him if they thought he wasn't a man of God. There was no room to invite the devil in, especially among the downtrodden. They clung to their beliefs with a devout fervor, all in the hope of entry to eternal paradise.

But here, now, confronted with the choice, a bright future or Rua, he would choose Rua. He would always choose Rua. Even if it meant not being with her. If this was the life Rua was living now, he would not let Annette Fitzgerald ruin it.

"I have to go," Rua said abruptly.

"I'll escort you home, but we'll have to walk. Wait here just a minute. I'll tell your parents you're coming with me." He started toward the ballroom, though he wasn't sure he'd find the Harringtons in the madness.

"No, don't," she called after him. "I don't need an escort. I'll simply kill anyone that gets in my way." She continued walking alongside the hedge until she was at the gate.

He knew she was joking but also wasn't entirely sure. "Wait for me," he said, running to catch up to her.

"Why don't you just go back inside where you belong, Finn? I'm sure the birthday girl is wondering where you are."

"I'm not concerned with her. If you'll allow me, I would like to see to your safe return." He held the gate open as she passed under his arm to the sidewalk. He locked it behind them.

Rua's next words were cut off as they both slowed to a stop. Pandemonium reigned supreme on the streets. Carriages blocked the roads at every angle as throngs of screaming people spilled out of the Fitzgeralds'.

"Is that all because of me?" She gaped.

"People were in a hurry to leave once the lights were blown out," he said, trying to ease her worry, though there were more on the street than remained inside.

He guided them away from the congestion, thinking they might be able to slip around it, but as they moved, more and more people pushed onto the street. He turned around, his head towering above most of the people, and saw no other way out.

"We'll just keep walking this way," he shouted.

Rua nodded, allowing him to take the lead. Someone bumped into the back of her, sending her crashing into his side. Ruffled but unbothered, she stood up.

"Are you all right?" he asked, trying to find the person who had shoved her, wondering if it was an accident or if she'd been recognized.

His heart skipped a beat as Rua slipped her arm around his and held on tightly. The crowd was growing wilder by the minute. More than just the well-to-do guests of the Fitzgeralds', there were those who had come to gawk at the spectacle and those who had come simply because of the commotion.

They shuffled forward, with Rua tucked under his arm and him keeping watch above. So long as no one recognized Rua, they would make it through the crush unscathed.

Then he noticed a woman staring up at him. Her gaze moved to Rua.

"It's her!" the woman shouted at the same moment an object was thrown their way, hitting Rua in the shoulder.

"Ow," Rua groaned.

Heads turned, and the crowd began shouting, "Witch! Devil! Sorceress!"

Rua let out a terrible screech as someone took hold of her hair. He caught a glimpse of her face lit up with rage as the man dug his hand deeper into her hair.

Finn grabbed the man's hand, squeezing with such force that the man's bones crunched beneath his grip.

The man roared in agony, but Finn didn't care. Rua's safety was his only concern. A protective rage overcame him; she'd done nothing to deserve this abuse.

With brute strength, Finn pushed aside anyone in his way; even still, they did not get far. He couldn't drag Rua along while also manhandling the crowd.

"Enough of this," Finn said, and he scooped Rua up. She gave a little yelp but then nestled in, shielding her face in his chest. Under any other circumstances, he'd allow himself a moment to appreciate the feel of her in his arms, but his focus remained on getting her home.

"And you thought you didn't need an escort," he scoffed, glancing down at her and her still-golden eyes.

"How could I have predicted an angry mob forming right outside the most prominent household in all of New York?"

He could think of a million reasons why the residents of Manhattan might want to protest Mr. Fitzgerald and his wealthy counterparts, the blatant wealth disparity and utter disregard for the poorer classes, just to name a few, but none involved getting spooked by a young woman when the candles blew out.

After a few minutes of aggressive effort, they'd made it through the madness. He kept walking until they were well away from any danger. Neither of them had spoken in quite some time. Perhaps it was enough to simply exist with their secrets, knowing they would be revealed in due time.

They were nearing the Harrington household, and he went to set Rua down.

"We're almost there," he said.

She didn't answer.

"Rua?" He adjusted her, and her head bobbed backward. "Blast." If it hadn't been for her shallow breaths, he might've thought she was dead.

He ran the rest of the way inside. Rua's maid, Mara, was waiting by the door.

"What happened?" She rushed toward them.

"She seems to have fainted," he said. "There was a bit of a scene at the Fitzgeralds', but she was fine."

"Where is Mrs. Harrington?" Mara asked.

"We left before her. There are delays with the carriages leaving the party. I don't know when she'll be back," he said.

"Quick, let's get her up to bed before she returns," Mara instructed, leading the way.

Finn felt awkward pretending he hadn't helped Rua steal her diary, but it wasn't his business. He only hoped that Rua had had the sense to hide it somewhere Mara wouldn't come across it, especially now that she was unconscious. Perhaps it would be best if he waited with her, if only to make sure Mara didn't go searching. There was no doubt in his mind that she knew Rua had been snooping in her room that night after the opera.

"Thank you for your help, my lord. I'll take it from here," she said.

"I'd like to wait with her, make sure she's all right."

Mara frowned. "My lord, may I speak freely?"

"Go ahead." He nodded.

"You have no intentions of marrying her." She stated it like it was fact. "So why must you be here when she wakes up? Your presence will only further confuse the situation."

Finn had no logical reason for wanting to be here when she woke up other than it was what he wanted. But perhaps Mara was right.

He was marrying Annette, as much as he wished it weren't so.

Twenty-Five

Sunlight crept in through the curtains as Rua sat up, unnerved and out of breath.

They were her curtains, but she didn't remember getting home. Her hand grazed over her nightgown. She didn't remember changing herself either.

She drew the covers up to her chin. Her mind felt like it was being yanked apart from the inside.

She rolled off the bed and rushed to the water basin. Her body trembled and her legs gave out.

"I'm coming in there!" she heard Mara shout.

She wiped her face with a towel and ran back to her bed.

The door swung open, revealing Mara with Finn on her heels. They both looked at her disheveled state with vastly different expressions.

Mara was chagrined, but Finn was red with appreciation, his eyes lingering a moment too long at her ankles.

"You are not decent, miss!" Mara pounced on her with a robe. "Begging your pardon, my lord, but I demand you leave this instant."

He ignored her.

"Rua—Miss Harrington," he corrected, "are you well?"

She tightened the robe around her waist, trying not to sway.

Mara's eyes darted back and forth between them before landing on Rua. "You will tell me what is going on this instant, or so help me, I will send for your mother."

Rua rubbed at her temples and let out a heavy breath, trying to understand why the two of them were standing in her room. She barely remembered leaving the party.

And then it hit her all at once. The party. The scene afterward. Fainting in Finn's arms.

"What time is it?" Rua asked. "Is Flossie in bed? Has she said anything to you?"

Rua remembered wanting to leave the Fitzgeralds' so she could get home, pack a bag, and run. Her conversation with Finn didn't matter. His accusation that she was a Morrígan had no bearing on the situation at hand. She knew that after what happened in that ballroom, Flossie would be livid, and she no longer had a place to stay.

If only her being a Morrígan actually meant something. For now, it was just a theory. A possible explanation for the lack of memories, but until she had all the pieces, it did nothing to help her current situation. Flossie was still the one with all the control.

"What time is it?" Rua asked again. She would have to figure out where to go. The park perhaps? The northern most part, far away from the clutches of high society. And then she could enter the hellmouth on Samhain, the same way she'd come out of it, and return home. Wherever home was.

"It's a quarter past eight in the morning," Finn responded. "Perhaps you should sit down. You've been through quite an ordeal."

"I don't have time." She closed her eyes, clutching her head, trying to plan her next move. "Please, leave. The both of you."

"Are you certain?" Mara said.

"Mara, I'm fine." Her words were final. Mara left with a solemn nod. Finn said nothing. Rua turned her back, waiting for the sound of the door to shut behind her.

When it did, she shoved the plainest gown she could find into her valise. She grabbed a shawl and a cape. They were lighter garments, meant for only the mildest fall breeze. Her heavier winter outfits were arriving later this week. Her throat tightened at the thought of not having somewhere to go as the cold weather moved in. The October days were perfectly comfortable, but the nights were noticeably nippier. She shook the thoughts aside. It would only be three days; she could handle the cold.

She bent down on the floor, pulled back the rug, and lifted the floorboard. She took out Mara's diary, preparing to pack it in her case. She needed the other little journal from the library, the one with all the dates, in case there were any details she'd missed.

"Are you packing?" Finn asked.

Startled, Rua spun around, dropping the book. "I thought I asked you to leave."

He lifted the diary off the floor and handed it to her, then looked at the valise haphazardly stuffed with clothes, worry in his eyes. "What are you doing?"

"Please, go." This time she opened the door for him. Leaving before Flossie knew to send anyone after her was crucial to her escape.

He didn't move.

"I went back to the Fitzgeralds' after you were safely in bed. Your parents hadn't left. They were talking to the Fitzgeralds. I let them know I brought you home."

"And what did Flossie say?" Rua braced for the inevitable. "Was she furious?"

"No." He shook his head with a crinkle in his brow. "The opposite, in fact. She thanked me and insisted we all have dinner this evening."

"We? As in all of us?" Rua asked, pointing to herself. Was Flossie so absurd that having Finn take her home was enough to make up for Annette's disastrous ball? Even Rua wouldn't have blamed Flossie if this was the event that tipped the scales. It was a calamity through and through.

"Well, I don't think she was extending the invite to the Fitzgeralds, but, yes, the four of us."

Rua let out a breath and set her valise down.

"Where were you going to go?" Finn asked her, concerned.

"I don't know," she said honestly. "But it doesn't matter now, does it?"

"I suppose not," he said, though she could tell he would have liked her to elaborate. He walked through the door, then stopped.

"Thank you again for getting me home," Rua said.

She was overwhelmed and full of mysteries. Last night was the first time she'd felt truly close to unhinged. First with Annette, and then with Finn in the garden. She thought of the marble statue and its severed head. Severed by her hand.

She glanced down at her hands, her weapons. A solid block of marble. Then at Finn, her intended target. He was the one she was mad at. What would she have done if the statue weren't there? Though she had the feeling Finn wouldn't have gone down so easily.

She'd seen the way he'd crushed that man's hand, pulverizing his bones as though they were no more than powder. She had never put a name to it and she'd been dancing around it for weeks, but could it really be true what Finn had said, that she was a Morrígan? What did that make him? The mysterious man from her dreams?

"Don't thank me. I set this in motion. I bungled the dance. Getting you home was the very least I could do."

To think that all of this chaos was the result of Finn not returning her to her dance partner. How stupid.

"Well," Rua said, "I'd better get myself sorted. I'm sure I have some explaining to do before dinner this evening." Though if it was true that she was an ancient Irish goddess, she wasn't sure what she was still doing pandering to Flossie.

Finn's face was serious. "Rua, if anything like this ever happens again, please, come to me. Or, if you ever find yourself in need of a safe place, you can go to St. Brigid's. Tell them I sent you. Sister Mary will take good care of you," he said, and then he left.

Rua lay back on the bed, drained. She hoped Finn was right, that dinner tonight meant that Flossie wasn't too mad. But the more she thought about the angry mass of people, the more she realized someone would need to be blamed. That someone would most certainly be her.

She didn't think Finn's interest would be enough for her to withstand that level of public villainy. Especially not if he were to eventually marry Annette. Rua sat up, plotting her next move. Flossie might have stayed her execution, but the people would want someone's head, and it was only a matter of time before Flossie gave them hers.

She couldn't live like this anymore. She was getting out while she still could.

She racked her brain for the pieces to the puzzle, but she was still missing a few. Who was Finn, with all his strength and this magnetic pull? Someone of great importance, the key to her past. The one she yearned and felt sorrow for. It was him; she knew it. But she didn't know what to do with that information.

Mara returned a short while later. "I've been informed that your mother is up and about. I imagine she'll want you downstairs shortly."

Rua grumbled and nodded.

"What happened?" Mara asked. "All the servants are talking about it. Did you really attack Annette?"

"Mara, of course I didn't. This is all so silly. Finn didn't return me to my original partner during the dance, and Annette got jealous. She turned the entire ballroom against me, telling everyone I was a witch and had the Lord of Donore under some sort of spell. Oh, I was so mad." Rua shook her head, remembering.

All of this felt so trivial in the face of her returning memories, but that was all they were. Memories of a life long gone. She couldn't understand how they connected to her future. For now, placating Flossie would remain her priority until she could sneak out of the house.

Mara winced.

"Yes, and then when I left the ballroom, I was on the balcony and there was a gust of wind, and it must have blown out all the candles. That's it. That's what happened. You can ask Finn." Though she realized then that Finn might tell another story. One in where she was responsible because she was a Morrígan.

"Well, I tell you right now, that's not the story that's in the papers."

"The papers?" Rua groaned, rubbing her temples. It had been less than twelve hours.

"Did you do it, though?" Mara asked.

"Do what?" Rua looked up.

"Darken the ballroom?" Mara said, lowering her voice as though someone might hear her. "Is that what caused you to faint after?"

Rua shook her head, not knowing what made her faint. Everything had happened so quickly. She was flooded with emotions. Rage, confusion, hatred, even love—thanks to Finn and his heavy conversation in the garden. *Love.* She sighed. "How could I have?"

"You said you were angry. Perhaps you were channeling the gifts the Morrígan bestowed upon you."

"What gifts?" she scoffed.

"You went into the hellmouth and returned. It's not something to take lightly. Over the summer, with such proximity to the Morrígan's power, you fainted. And it happened again now. Perhaps you're unlocking your blessings."

Ridiculous as it sounded, she thought this was a more plausible explanation than the one Finn had come up with. The Morrígan were mixed up in all of this, but to suggest that she was a war goddess was outrageous, comical even.

But as she recalled certain memories, snippets of moments from a different life, she found it harder to dismiss the notion.

"I need to go to the hellmouth." Her answers were there; she could feel it. The buzz in the air, calling to her, pulling her forward through the woods. She could find it again, and she could switch back places with Emma.

"That's not at all what I was suggesting," Mara said, her eyes worried.

"I'm out of sorts. I need some answers, and I think the hellmouth is exactly where I'll find them. Will you bring me?" Rua asked, thinking it'd be easier to have Mara show her the way.

"I don't think that's a good idea." Mara shook her head.

"I'm going tonight, whether or not you show me," Rua said.

"No," Mara said quickly, "not tonight. If you can wait until tomorrow, I will bring you myself."

"Why not tonight?" Rua asked, suspicious.

"You have dinner with the Lord of Donore, and your parents will be out and about tonight. It's too risky that we might bump into them," Mara said.

"Fine," Rua agreed. If it was true what Mara said, that the hellmouth only worked on a feast day, going tonight would only put her at risk of being caught by the Harringtons.

Flossie wanted rid of Emma, but on her terms. A runaway daughter wouldn't be enough to satisfy her. She'd need to know her problem was never coming back. They'd likely send out another search party, find her, and lock her up.

One more day of discomfort in the Harrington household wouldn't kill her and then she would leave for good.

As Mara dressed her, Rua thought back to Annette's ball and how she'd brought it to a screeching halt. The look on Flossie's face; the way the room sneered and screamed. Their attempts to humiliate and shame her were ill advised. All they'd done was incite her rage. As if that meant anything.

But maybe it did.

They had all thought she was behind the darkness in the ballroom. Was it possible? She supposed so; she was living another woman's life. Anything was possible.

Rua sighed and looked to the dwindling sconce beside her bed frame. She thought about the flame going out. Willed it to quench.

She focused, waiting.

Nothing happened, and she was embarrassed for trying.

"There we are," Mara said as she fastened Rua's last silk button. "You should really let me pin up your hair."

"No, it's fine." She didn't think her head could support the weight of her hair right now.

They made their way downstairs to breakfast, one marble step at a time. The magic of the morning lost now that Annette had strong-armed Finn into marriage.

"Get in there now." A fuming Flossie was waiting, arms crossed, at the bottom of the next set of stairs.

Rua held tight to the railing as her stomach did backflips. Finn was wrong. Dinner was an event she would not be attending tonight, because this was it: the moment she'd be tossed out of the house and sent to the asylum. She should have left earlier when she had the chance.

"You caused quite the stir last night," Flossie said, her eyes raking over Rua. "And how many times must I tell you that only children and harlots wear their hair below their shoulders?"

Rua took a deep breath and continued on to the breakfast room.

"Fortunately for you, everyone that matters saw the Lord of Donore carrying you safely through that ghastly crowd. Not only that, but he also came back inside and apologized to your father and Richard. Everyone's talking about it. Heavens me, I think he fancies you. I can't understand why. There might not be an engagement after all." She smiled, but Rua knew otherwise. There would be an engagement, or else the papers would read something different very soon, and then there would be police at their doorstep.

"Richard is truly miffed. He was hoping to win favor with the Tammany Hall crowd by bringing an immigrant into the family. I'll sort that out; don't you worry. We will assess the damage this evening and act accordingly."

"What's this evening?" she asked, not understanding half of what Flossie was talking about or how things had turned around again. She didn't trust it.

"The Houlihans' ball."

"No." Rua smoothed the folds of her dress. "I can't go to another party."

"I should think not," Flossie laughed. "A missive arrived promptly at nine informing me that you were disinvited. Can't say I blame them. On all that is holy, if I am disinvited to any forthcoming events because of you, heads will roll. It is thanks to Richard that you haven't tarnished my name."

Part of her was delighted to be allowed to stay home for the evening; the other part was terrified that she had to stay home for the evening.

Her exile had commenced.

Twenty-Six

"Thank you," Finn said, adding sugar to his tea.

"Good morning, my lord," Mrs. Harrington said, waiting for Rua to greet him the same.

"Morning," Rua grumbled. Mrs. Harrington shot her a scornful glare.

"Good morning, ladies," he said, rising then sitting back down when she and Mrs. Harrington were seated.

He was a moth and she the flame, and he was going to get burned. There was no doubt about it. The pull was too strong, the danger too real.

Rua's face was grave as she settled into her chair. Mrs. Harrington sat beside him. He supposed after the trauma of last night, it was to be expected. Mrs. Harrington had no doubt scolded Rua. Perhaps that's why she was packing a bag. Could it be so bad that she'd run away?

They all sat quietly and watched as the tea was poured.

"My lord, I must thank you for coming to my daughter's aid last night. It would seem we are indebted to you once again," Mrs. Harrington said.

Rua's mouth fell open, but she closed it before Mrs. Harrington noticed.

"It was the least I could do, considering my gaffe."

"Nonetheless, we will have an early dinner this evening as thanks. That way you can still attend the Houlihans' party. I assume you'll be in attendance?" Mrs. Harrington asked.

Finn nodded. The Houlihans were good friends of Richard's. Important friends. He shouldn't miss it.

"Unfortunately, my daughter has been disinvited and will have to remain home alone for the evening. It's terrible the way people talk." Mrs. Harrington stroked the side of Rua's face. If he were Mrs. Harrington, he would be removing that hand before Rua bit off her fingers. "As if my daughter could have blown out every candle in that massive ballroom. I mean, really, it's utter nonsense."

Rua let out an exasperated laugh, which was met by a terrible glare from Mrs. Harrington.

"Gossips are a blight on this world," Finn said, taking a drink of his tea.

"It's quite generous of you to be assisting Richard with his run for office."

"I beg your pardon?" Finn gulped down the hot liquid.

"Well, a few of the ladies and I were visiting with Mrs. Fitzgerald the other day, and she told us all how her husband is going to be running for office. With your help, he's sure to win over the Irish votes. Surely there's enough of your kinsmen running around lower Manhattan for that to mean something."

Finn remained tight lipped, but he was certain he'd turned a nasty shade of white. This was the first time he'd heard of Richard's political aspirations. And the boys at Tammany Hall were a corrupt lot. What the hell was Richard doing getting involved with Tweed?

"Well, I have many things to do today. It was so nice of you to join us for breakfast," Mrs. Harrington said, rising from her seat after being in the room only five minutes. "Your presence is quite appreciated," she said to him before she turned to Rua, who had just put a piece of pineapple in her mouth. "Your dresses were measured to fit your figure exactly as it was. They are not designed to stretch." And then she left.

Rua's lips curled in disgust as she stared daggers at the back of Mrs. Harrington's head. Then she rose from her chair, taking one final sip of her tea, and brushed any crumbs off her gown.

"Are you finished already?" he asked, hoping she'd stay.

"Yes," she said. "I'm in the mood for chocolate, and there is none here."

"It's nine thirty in the morning. Certainly, there are better ways to start the day," he said.

"Yesterday, I had one of the worst days I can remember, and do you know how I started it?"

He shook his head, hiding a smirk.

"With eggs and toast." She leaned across the table. "So save your nutritional advice for someone that wants it—your fiancée, perhaps?"

Finn winced. "I'd like to talk to you," he said, rising from his chair. "Can we go somewhere more private?"

"I have to work on my sampler," she said. "You can join me in the sunroom if you like."

He followed her through the halls, maid in tow. Rua didn't strike him as someone who embroidered.

She sat down on the green settee by the window and lifted her needlework off the coffee table. He sat across from her.

"Some more tea, please," Rua said, nodding to the maid as she wove the needle into an unfathomable shape. *Wove* was a generous word; *stabbed* was more like it. Her movements were too hurried to be effective.

He looked at her face, haloed by the sunshine. There was nothing but deep concentration despite her lack of skill.

"Tell me, Finn, do you find the sight of a woman doing needlework attractive?"

"Enormously," he said.

She grinned. "Would you care to see what I'm working on, then?"

He nodded.

"It is at Flossie's request that I complete one sampler per week." She turned the embroidery out to face him.

"You're not very good," he said, noting for the hundredth time that she referred to her mother as Flossie. She was all but confirming his suspicions.

"What is it supposed to be?"

"A sunset." She laughed the most delightful sound.

"I can assure you, with the utmost confidence, that what you have created there bears no likeness to any sun that has ever set in any sky."

She laughed again, and so did he. It was natural, just like it was in his memory of that meadow. Seeing Rua here now, he wasn't sure how he had ever forgotten her.

"What did you want to talk to me about?" She was acting as though he hadn't accused her of being a Morrígan last night. Perhaps she didn't remember, or she was simply giving it no credence.

"I had a dream of you," he said.

She set down her sampler, glancing nervously around the room. The closest servant was waiting by the door; the other had not yet returned with the tea.

"A dream of us," he continued. "We were together in a wild meadow. You were beautiful, and you were wearing a flower crown made of meadowsweet."

Her breathing slowed.

"Perhaps it's why meadowsweet is my favorite and why you wear it now? I don't know." He closed his eyes, remembering.

"I'd like to go somewhere else," she said, rolling over so that her chest rested atop his.

"Where?" He picked his head off the grass so that he could reach her lips. Her kiss was rushed.

"Anywhere but here," she sighed.

She'd been different the last few days. Distant, skittish.

Pushing off of him, she stood up to her full height. She pulled loose the ties on her dress, letting it fall to the ground in a heap at her ankles. Kicking the dress up with her foot, it landed on his face. Laughing, she ran to the lake wearing only her crown.

He sat upright, watching as the meadowsweet bushes tickled her bare skin.

"Catch me if you can," she sang.

He lost sight of her in the sunlight, its glare deceptively warm. He knew better than to trust its light.

Struck with a sudden feeling of impending doom, he ran to find her.

"Rua?" he called, feeling the heavy beat of his heart. "Rua, where are you?"

But when the gentle wind blew, his heart stilled, for it carried on its breeze the sweetest scent.

He opened his eyes again.

He needed to know for certain if the woman he loved in his dreams was the same woman before him now. He needed to know if it was worth risking the life he had built for the one that had been taken from him.

"Have you called off your engagement?" she asked.

"I haven't." He'd love nothing more than to tell the entire Fitzgerald family to piss off, but he had to be sure Rua was going to be safe if he did so.

"I don't need you to fight my battles, Finn," she said.

"That's unfair and you know it."

"Is it?" Her tone was sharp. "What is to stop Annette from telling everyone my secret the moment you're wed?"

"We made a deal," Finn said, though his argument felt thin.

Rua laughed. "Oh, please. Don't be so naïve, Finn."

Perhaps he was too trusting. Too willing to take people at their word. But that didn't change the fact that she was avoiding the truth.

Bit by bit it was returning to him. A profound connection coupled with the unsettling feeling that it could never be realized. Soul mates destined to be torn apart. That was the part he remembered and the part he wished he could forget.

She shook her head, refusing to look at him.

"What is it that you're so afraid of?" He paused. "It's because I'm right, isn't it?"

"You are not right," she whispered harshly, glancing around the room. "I can't help that you have embedded me into your fantasies."

"Embedded you into my fantasies?" He rose from the chair, feeling the sting of her words. He would not sit while she made a mockery of things he knew to be true.

"Oh, pardon me, my lord. I didn't expect to find you here," Mara said, coming to the entrance of the sunroom. Mara's interruptions had grown frequent, borderline deliberate.

"I was just leaving." Finn rose and moved toward the door.

Part of him wanted Rua to protest, but deep down he knew she wouldn't.

He checked his watch as he stormed into the foyer.

"Donore, I'm glad I caught you." Ned stopped him at the door. "Richard wants us at the Union Club in an hour."

"Fine." He didn't like being summoned, but after last night, there were things to discuss. "I'll meet you there." Finn gathered his coat and left immediately, needing a walk to clear his mind.

He didn't know why he was worrying so much about Rua when he was marrying Annette. But it seemed that the more things came to light, the further he felt from his life in Manhattan.

He stared at the footpath ahead, watching as men and women went about their day. He wondered what it would be like to be a person who hadn't met Rua. Who didn't understand the thrill of knowing her. How boring that must be, and yet so peaceful.

The leaves had begun their subtle change. Finn reached up and grabbed one from a low-hanging branch. He crunched it in his palm, sprinkling the debris as he walked.

He spotted the Union Club and wished to turn right around. Nothing good was going to come of it.

"Donore, right on time," Richard said, acting as though he hadn't coerced Finn into a relationship with his daughter.

Finn gave him a curt nod, noticing Ned hadn't arrived yet.

"Last night was a bloody disaster, wouldn't you say?" Richard handed him a billiards cue.

Finn took it without response. He wasn't sure he had the capacity to keep the conversation civil. He'd worked so hard to make a name for himself, and all of it was tainted. He'd been so caught up in his admiration for Richard's business acumen that he couldn't see he was being manipulated the entire time.

"No matter," Richard said, hitting his break shot, "there'll be an announcement in Sunday's paper. It's all sorted. I owe a man a favor." He winked.

Finn gripped the base of his cue, imagining breaking it over Richard's head. So this was the agreement he'd come to with the columnist. One headline for another. He had no doubt paid a hefty sum to keep it hushed.

"I want your word that the story stays buried," Finn said, Rua's words fresh on his mind. He needed to make sure he wasn't doing this all for nothing.

"You're not really in the position to be making demands, Donore. The way I see it, I've got you on all sides." Richard smiled. "Your shot," he said smugly.

Finn set the cue down, still at a loss. "I'm not in the mood, Richard." There was nothing he could say to change the situation. These were the consequences of his actions, the path he'd laid for himself.

"I warned you to stay away from her," Richard said. "Look at the mess she dragged you into, hmm?"

Finn hated that he'd let Richard get the upper hand, that he'd allowed this dynamic in which Richard was the wise elder and he the wayward son.

"You'll thank me yet." Richard let out a laugh. "I see those articles they run of you in that weekly you're so fond of, *The Irish World*. Donore saves woman from burning building. Donore donates large sum to underfunded orphanage. Donore this, Donore that. An Irish hero is what you are. They're proud to claim you. How long do you think that would last if you ran off with Miss Harrington, a known Satanist?"

Finn knew Richard was right, especially after last night. "You should've had a conversation with me. We're business partners. Instead, you sent your daughter to blackmail me."

"It worked, didn't it?" Richard said.

Finn had nothing else to say.

When Ned finally arrived, they moved into a private room.

"We've much to be thankful for this day, gentlemen," Richard said, cheerful as he motioned for them both to sit.

A servant placed a round of drinks on the table.

Giving nothing but a vacant stare, Ned nodded.

Finn wondered if perhaps Richard was going to fire Ned and that's why they were here. He'd only given him the contract for the first two floors of the hotel. The rest of the floors were contingent upon Rua's reputation, which had been one disaster after another, last night the worst of them all. If that were the case, Richard was a cruel bastard to bring him out here to fire him.

"I'll get right to it. We've dealt with a problem that's been troubling us all for quite some time. But the removal of said problem has opened you both up to better opportunities."

Ned looked like he was going to be sick all over himself as he tipped his head back, letting the contents of his drink pull him further away from the room.

"Ned, I'm looking forward to working together for the totality of the project. The countersigned contracts have been sent back to your solicitor as of an hour ago."

Ned looked at the floor. Finn didn't understand the issue, nor what contracts could have been negotiated without his presence.

"Donore, as an early wedding present, I've cashed in on a favor owed, and I've gotten an associate from Dartmouth to agree to a residency in your new hospital, whenever it should be ready. Funded by me, of course."

It was too generous an offer to be without a catch. "What the hell is going on?" Finn asked, but Richard ignored him.

"Ned, cheer up, will you?" Richard said. "You've done the right thing. The only thing you could do. You'd never get out from under your own two feet otherwise."

Ned let out a muffled sob.

"What the blazes is going on?" Finn asked, his voice rising with irritation.

Richard laughed. "Now that I've got you by the balls, Donore, there's no need to say it any differently: get me the votes I need, or your little enchantress's neck will wind up on the chopping block. That story gets out and an asylum will seem like a holiday compared to where she'll end up."

Finn looked at Ned, the pathetic man, guzzling his whiskey, too cowardly to speak up for his daughter.

"You're a bastard," Finn said.

"I'll see you round the house for dinner tomorrow. Seven o'clock sharp," Richard said.

Finn stormed out of the club, swearing never to return.

Miraculously, Ned caught up to Finn just as he was about to turn the corner.

"My lord, you have to understand, she's not our little girl anymore." He grabbed Finn's shoulder for balance. "Our daughter died in those woods. I'm sure of it. I don't know who came out, but it wasn't Emma."

Finn's stomach clenched. This situation was beyond comprehension. He knew for certain that Rua was not their daughter. So what had happened to the real Emma?

He pushed away his disappointment. "You'd better sober up, Ned. Your family is expecting you for dinner."

Twenty-Seven

L etting Finn leave the sunroom like that didn't sit right with Rua, but what was her alternative? How could she admit to him what was going on in her head? How could she admit she wasn't Emma Harrington?

That admission would lead to questions she didn't know how to answer, leaving room for doubt and speculation. She didn't want to be blamed for Emma's disappearance. Mara and the Morrígan were responsible, not her. She was just as much a victim as Emma.

At least, that was what she told herself.

But she couldn't go on pretending that Flossie might change her mind and allow her to stay. She couldn't rely on Finn; engagement aside, he was pressing her for details he shouldn't be. How had he even made the connection to the Morrígan? Whatever their past, she knew there was something keeping them apart, and she wasn't sure she wanted to know what that was.

Her mind was made up. She would go with Mara to the hell-mouth, and she wouldn't come back.

Until then, she would pack a proper bag and stay out of Flossie's way.

She had hours before dinner. While she waited, she took out Mara's diary, flipping through the journal, scanning the pages for any mention of Emma's name. Mara's handwriting was neat, her entries organized and concise, and there was one for every day of the year. Most of it was quite tedious, making it a chore to parse through.

Rua let out a sigh and skipped to August, after her arrival in Conleth Falls.

August 5, 1870

I hope that she does not continue to insist that she is not herself. Her mother does not have the patience for it. She won't last the week.

So, that entry was about Rua. Stretched out on her bed, she rolled over onto her stomach, her head propped up by her elbows.

She turned the pages back, dozens at a time, until she was in May. She wanted to understand who was contacting Mara and how they had convinced her to send Emma into the cave. But there was no specific mention. One day Mara was at the hellmouth praying, and the next she was talking to the Mother.

So why did the Morrígan want Emma to go into the cave?

She skimmed the pages, not learning much of anything. She couldn't bring herself to read in chronological order, though she knew that she should. The days were too monotonous, and she felt she'd cover more ground if she bounced around. She was wrong.

"How are you feeling?" There was a light knock on the door, and before she had time to move, Mara was standing in her bedchamber.

Heart racing, Rua closed the journal and shoved it under her stomach. She put her full weight on the mattress, praying Mara couldn't see it beneath her.

"What are you doing?" Mara gave her a funny look.

"Oh, just trying to nap," Rua lied, placing her head down on the bed and her arms at her side. She imagined she looked like a seal.

"Without any pillows? In your day dress?" She laughed.

Rua smiled. "Last night was exhausting."

"Well, it's time to get ready for dinner," Mara said. "Up you get."

"I'm not ready yet," Rua groaned, feigning that she was just too tired to move. She would die if Mara caught her with her journal. It was one thing to steal it, but to be caught reading it? The shame would be unbearable. She hadn't meant to keep it for as long as she had, but it was a slog to get through.

"Fine," Mara laughed. "Ten more minutes, but no more or your mother will have my head."

"Thank you," Rua grumbled, and shut her eyes. When she was sure Mara was gone, she slid off the bed and shoved the diary under the floorboard.

Mara returned exactly ten minutes later with the chambermaids by her side. They readied her bath while setting her curls. Getting ready for dinner in the home was just as extravagant as getting ready for a grand dinner somewhere else.

She wondered if Finn would still show up to dinner after their exchange in the sunroom. It wouldn't be the first time he had skipped out on a meal, and this time he would have good reason. Anxiety twisted in her stomach as she imagined the meal without him. Flossie would be insufferable.

By the time dinner arrived, Flossie was seething. It was after four and there was no sign of Finn.

"What did you say to him?" she snarled. "You were alone with him at breakfast. What did you say?"

"I didn't say anything," Rua lied. She had wounded his pride and dismissed his feelings for the sake of her own.

"Darling, no need to panic. It's only a quarter past four," Ned said.

He was as useless as any man could be. His gentle constitution did far more harm than good. In his effort to avoid any and all conflict, he had allowed Rua to be berated and bullied by his malicious wife. She wondered if Ned would care if she was sent away. Would he wake up then?

Rua looked anxiously at the door, willing Finn to arrive. She shouldn't have brushed him off this morning. She should have been smarter. Told him what he wanted to hear, if only to keep him on the hook until she could ensure her own safety.

But didn't he know how important this dinner was?

He was the one who had told her about it in the first place. He'd assured her that Flossie wasn't angry and had invited him to dinner to thank him. Sure, he wasn't privy to the inner workings of her and Flossie's relationship, but he wasn't a fool. He knew it was important.

Rua slipped a finger under the collar of her gown, trying to loosen its hold around her neck. She let out a deep breath, reasoning that he couldn't have known because she hadn't told him anything. She'd remained tight lipped and therefore was in a mess of her own making, once again.

"She said something to scare him off. Our disgrace of a daughter. I just know it." Flossie's vitriol spewed with such efficacy the dining room was no longer habitable. "I think at this point she's deliberately trying to ruin things. She won't be our problem much longer."

Ned rubbed the top of Flossie's hand in a lame effort to calm the wicked beast.

Hearing Flossie's threat for what it was, she took a deep breath. Rua was the beast that needed calming. Deep down, she could feel her rage flaring. She'd had enough of Flossie. Another deep breath. It was almost over.

With a slight tremor in her hand, she reached for her glass. She took a sip, tasting nothing but bitterness.

If Finn did not darken their doorway soon, she was going to do something she'd regret.

As the minutes wore on and Flossie continued to hurl insults, Rua forced herself not to hear them. It was all she could do not to fire the ceramic pitcher across the room.

"It's four thirty. I think it's time we eat," Ned said. "We can't be late to the Houlihans'."

Flossie and Ned exchanged a look that chilled her.

"May I be excused?" Rua asked, gripping the base of her glass.

"No, you most certainly may not be," Flossie spat.

Rua's head pounded, her vision clouding; she couldn't catch her breath. She closed her eyes. Panic had settled into her bones. She was like a caged animal, stronger than her captors but disadvantaged in a world that wasn't her own.

Rua stood up. She was done.

"Please forgive my lateness." Finn rushed into the dining room. "I am terribly embarrassed, but I was trying to procure a treat for your daughter, and the line was around the block."

Stunned, Rua leaned against the table. She'd almost let her anger get the better of her, and Finn was out buying sweet treats.

"Please do not think on it, my lord. We've only just sat down," Flossie said, lying through her teeth.

"Miss Harrington, I hope tomorrow morning is better," he said, placing a gold box on the table that read *Maillard's Chocolate.*

Rua looked at the box and then at Finn, overcome with gratitude for this unassuming gesture. "Thank you," she said, unable to keep from smiling.

"You are very thoughtful, and with exquisite taste, I might add." Flossie gushed over the gift from the popular confectionary shop.

Finn sat down beside Rua, whispering, "Sorry I'm late. I hope it didn't cause you too much trouble."

"Nothing more than usual," Rua said, still smiling. Her anger had receded to a manageable level at the sight of Finn. Shaken at the thought of what she might've done to Flossie, she shivered, letting out the sordid thoughts.

Dinner was uneventful and embarrassing, but by now, she and Finn were used to Flossie's attempts at forcing a relationship. If only she knew how far that ship had sailed.

After dinner, everyone but Rua was going to the Houlihans' party.

She trudged up the stairs with her box of chocolates as she listened to the conversation below her.

"Would you like to join us in our carriage?" Flossie asked Finn.

"That won't be necessary," he said.

Rua wondered if Finn always walked to parties. As much as society dictated that the proper way to appear was by carriage, Rua always thought that given the proximity of all the mansions, carriages only delayed things. It was another tick in the box that set Finn apart for things that rich men didn't do. If he thought Rua was an Irish goddess, she wondered what he thought of himself. Did he think he was a god? Rua let out a laugh. Probably.

She lost the sound of their voices as she turned up the next set of stairs and returned to her room. One way or the other, this was going to be the last night she spent in this house.

She packed her bag with more care, arranging additional gowns and capes. So many had arrived since Malvina had fitted her that the maids wouldn't notice any were missing, at least not right away.

She wondered if the dressmaker had heard about what a disaster Rua turned out to be. Did she regret fashioning her entire wardrobe? Or perhaps she had always known Rua was going to crash and burn. But the attention she'd receive while going out in a blazing heap was enough to make people stop and admire her gowns while doing it.

Before putting her packed bag back in its hiding place, she took Mara's diary out, continuing on with where she had left off.

July 9, 1870

Emma has agreed to the Mother's request to enter the hell-mouth, but I do not know the purpose. She is as devoted as ever. It is enough for her to know she will be doing the Morrígan a great honor, and I will be rewarded for bringing Emma to them.

Rua wondered what Mara's reward could've been. Had she known she wouldn't be getting her friend back, would she still have done it?

She skipped forward to August.

August 15, 1870

I dislike Manhattan very much. It's overcrowded and smelly. I fear we'll never get back to Conleth Falls. The only moments of peace I have are when we are in the park, and even then it is not the same.

I've found the stone chamber, but there are always others present. I've made a habit of visiting in the night, though I don't feel quite safe. We do what we must, I suppose.

My duties are tenfold here, mostly because Emma has become such a handful and Mrs. Harrington is worried. I don't blame her. The memory loss is unexpected and troublesome.

I have plans to return to the chamber tonight and every night hereafter. I must speak with the Mother again. I have to understand how to help Emma. If I cannot, I fear she will be sent away.

Rua hadn't realized Mara was so worried. Or that she was visiting the stone chamber so frequently.

August 30, 1870

The Mother has made contact. Her voice is different. Richer. She asks about Emma and the Lord of Donore. I get the sense she does not want to see them together, though Mrs. Harrington is doing everything in her power to arrange it. I don't understand the Mother's concern; I think they'd make a handsome pair. Perhaps she has greater plans for Emma than either of us realized and there is no room for men in the sisterhood.

Emma has been asking to visit the chamber, but the Mother does not want her there. She says she must be kept away at all costs.

If that was the case, why had Mara agreed to take her there tomorrow? What had changed since August that she would defy the Mother? Rua skipped forward a few pages, looking for more mention of Emma's name.

September 7, 1870

I am running out of excuses to keep Emma from the hellmouth. The Mother is adamant that she steers clear until Samhain.

I have told the Mother that her fears of Emma and the Lord of Donore are baseless. Emma is too outspoken, her behavior too unpredictable for a man like that. His engagement to the Fitzgerald girl is all but confirmed. I need not interfere. Emma will frighten him away on her own.

Rua balked at the insinuation.

There was a knock at her door, and she jumped.

"Just a moment," she called, stuffing the journal back in her case and the case back in her armoire, before running to open the door.

"Since when do you open doors?" Mara asked.

Rua eyed her supposed friend, thinking she was far sneakier than she'd ever given her credit for. She'd assumed Mara hadn't a clue about her missing diary, seeing as she hadn't brought it up, but perhaps she was keeping her knowledge to herself, uninterested in picking a fight with a volatile Emma. She thought that was more likely than her roommate not sharing with Mara that she'd seen Rua sneaking around their room in the middle of the night.

"I was just getting up to go to the library," Rua lied. She was always lying of late. Such was the state of her position in this house.

"Perhaps you'd like to spend the evening in a different room tonight," Mara suggested, apprehension plain on her face.

"Why would I do that?"

"It's the Lord of Donore."

"What about him?" Rua asked.

"He's stayed back from the party. I was trying to avoid you running into him."

"Why would you do that?" she asked, though she knew why. The Mother didn't want her to be with Finn.

"He's going to marry someone else, no matter what your mother tries." Mara reached for Rua's arm, her attempts at interfering now obvious. "I don't want to see you get hurt."

Rua smiled, wondering if Mara could tell her own wants from the Mother's.

"Don't worry. I'm aware of Finn's intentions with Annette."

"And even after that nasty prank she pulled." Mara shook her head. "I really think it best if you steer clear."

"Your concern is unnecessary," Rua said. "The lord and I are friends, nothing more."

"Would you like some company?" Mara asked, getting desperate.

"Is he in the library right now?" Rua asked.

"No," Mara said.

"I truly don't understand what you're fussing about," Rua said. "I'll be fine."

"Very well," Mara said reluctantly, adding, "I'll be downstairs if you need me."

The fire in the library was lit, and she welcomed its warmth. The temperature had steadily begun to drop in the evenings as they neared the end of October.

She looked around the splendid room that had become her solace. The one place Flossie usually didn't bother her. She sighed, knowing it would be her last evening.

And for that reason, she took a drink from the crystal decanter on the shelf by the door. She felt the burn trickle down her throat. And then she poured another.

"I thought I might find you in here," Finn said.

She spun around at the sound of his voice, the liquid in her glass sloshing out onto the floor. She hadn't heard him come in. He was standing beside the shelf with all her incriminating books.

"I thought you were going to the party," she said, wiping the liquid drops off her bodice.

"I changed my mind." He shrugged.

"And you've come to the library to find me?"

"Is that all right?" he asked.

She looked up at him, meeting his eyes. "Yes," she said quietly, butterflies filling her stomach.

Needing to settle her heart rate, she set down her glass, slowly and with concentrated effort.

When she turned back around, Finn was putting a novel back on the shelf. His coat was draped over the back of the chair, and his sleeves were rolled up to his elbow. It didn't appear he'd ever even dressed for the ball.

"What book was that?" she asked, not really caring.

"I don't know," he said as he slapped his hands together, brushing the dust off on his trousers. Her eyes followed the motion of his hands on his thighs. Strong, muscular thighs. She recalled the story of the woman he'd saved from the hotel fire and the way he'd carried her with ease through the frenzied mob after Annette's birthday.

He cleared his throat, and her eyes moved too slowly back to his face. The longer she stared at him, the warmer she felt and the smaller the room became. The truth was closing in on her; she only needed to let the walls down.

Embarrassed for staring, she took out another glass and offered him a drink.

He accepted. She watched as his mouth settled on the rim of the glass.

He swallowed, then asked, "So, what are your plans for this evening now that you've got the house to yourself?"

"You're looking at them." She lifted her arms, gesturing to the room.

"Care for some company, then?" His voice was assured, but his eyes said otherwise. He was testing the water, and understandably so. He wanted answers, and she didn't know how to give them to him. Her mind had yet to allow her the privilege of knowing.

She wanted the truth, but instinct warned her against it. If Finn was the man in her dreams, if she'd known him in another life, then he was here under false pretenses, just as she was.

"You can stay," she said, despite her reservations. Despite knowing in her gut that tonight would change things.

"Shall we play draughts?" he asked with a laugh.

She grinned, remembering the last time they had played.

"Dominoes it is," he said, after pillaging the game chest. One by one he explained the rules to her. "If there is any part that you're not following, let me know before we begin. Once we've started, I will not let you win."

She laughed at his seriousness, and she liked that about him. A lift of his chin and he could command a room.

There was an unforeseen effortlessness that existed between them. They were opposites in every way, but it worked. There was no pretending. Unapologetically, they were themselves.

Finn's glass clanked hard on the marble side table after he'd won for the third time.

"How do I know you haven't made up the rules in your favor as the game went along? Surely I'm not that bad," she said, looking at her pieces.

"I can assure you, you are," he laughed, rising from the chair.

Her heart sank as he stood. She wasn't ready for him to leave yet. Mara was right. She should have stayed away.

But then he held out his hand.

"Will you do me the honor of having this dance?" he asked.

She glanced around the room. "There's no music."

"Give me your hand," he whispered.

With bated breath, she gave it to him. His fingers laced between her own, and a rush of happiness swept over her. The effect was dizzying.

He guided her to her feet and wrapped his arm around her waist. Their closeness was intrinsic, vital to her existence. Without him, she felt nothing.

With expert ease, he began to sway. She closed her eyes and rested her head against his chest. The moment so beautiful, so perfect, she could *almost* hear the music. A slow melodic waltz, familiar and enchanting.

She looked up at Finn, and her heart skipped. He was humming the tune they'd shared their first dance to at the Fitzgeralds' ball. She closed her eyes once more.

Feeling the gentle vibrations as he lilted, she relinquished all control to him. The intimacy of the moment blew her away.

Minutes, maybe hours, passed. She'd been transported to another place and time, free of the pretension, a place only for them.

And when they finally stopped moving, the room spun around them.

The way Finn looked at her, like she was made for him, almost let her forget that he hadn't a clue about who she really was. Neither of them did. But maybe it didn't matter.

The passion was there. She could reach out and touch it if she wanted to. He had awoken a hunger inside of her, a primal need to have and be had.

Tired of waiting, she wrapped her arms around his neck and stood up on her tiptoes. She wanted his mouth on hers and couldn't wait to get it. He saw what she needed, and was happy to give it to her.

Hands resting on her back, he pulled her in closer. As his mouth came down on hers with an intensity that matched her own, she wondered how they'd ever thought they could survive apart.

Sliding her hands down the front of his chest, she worked to open the buttons of his shirt while he stole hungry kisses. Breathless, she slipped the shirt over his shoulders, letting it fall to the floor. The sight of his shirtless chest in the firelight caught her breath. He was sinew and muscle and covered in scars.

He sucked in a breath as she traced her finger across one of the many marks on his abdomen. And his chest—a six-inch jagged line lay above his heart.

He was so virile and wholly male.

"Come here," he commanded, his breathing labored. He tipped her chin upward, his mouth finding hers once more. She couldn't breathe with the need for him to never stop kissing her.

Letting him know she wanted more, she took his free hand and guided it to her chest.

"Rua," he groaned as his hand worked its way under the fabric of her bodice, cupping her breast. He lifted her up, her legs wrapping around him, and he carried her to the settee as she slowly slipped into blissful oblivion.

Lying on her back with him above her, she gave him full access to explore. His hands tugged and massaged her breasts free of their restraints. "Fuck," he said, admiring what he'd done.

He bent his head down and kissed the hollow space at the base of her neck, moving up to her throat, leaving a wake of devastation as his tongue traveled up to her ear. He nibbled tenderly on her earlobe while she writhed beneath him.

Hands grasping, she brought his face back to hers, and her tongue moved slowly and deliberately as she melted into his mouth. He let out a low growl, sending tremors throughout her body.

She was lightheaded with need, unable to comprehend the enormity of her feelings.

He was familiar and forbidden. Her own personal paradise. Nothing would ever compare.

He belonged only to her.

And then came the knock on the door, reminding her that he didn't.

"Ignore it," Finn whispered, kissing her neck, not ready to let go.

She couldn't ignore it. An impeccably timed dose of reality to remind her that they could never be. Like a dark cloud, it loomed high above in the distance, threatening her with its power. She pushed herself out of his arms, setting herself to rights. She closed her eyes, trying to catch her breath, her mind offering to reaffirm what she knew in her heart—they were doomed.

"I love him, Nemain. I do not wish to see him dead."

Nemain placed her free hand on Macha's cheek. "You cannot break the bond of our sisterhood. There can be no undoing what Badb has set into motion."

Macha left the dining hall.

"Where are you going, sister?" Badb stopped her in the arched doorway.

"To the water," she said.

Nemain shot her a warning look.

"I shall join you," Badb said.

Macha discarded her clothes and dove into the basin of water floating above Oweynagat, lethal to any mortal. Only she and her sisters were afforded the luxury of swimming in the mystical water.

"What troubles you?" Badb asked. "Do not tell me it is that dolt Cú Chulainn."

She didn't answer.

"Do you love him, Rua?" Badb snickered.

Macha looked up, shocked that she'd called her Rua. Only he called her that.

"You cannot trust a man, sweet sister. He is our enemy."

Macha did not answer. Their love was pure; he would not bring her harm.

"Of the infinite lovers in this world, you'd give yourself to him?" Badb gave her a disapproving look. "You should've known better. But do not worry, I will protect you. Always."

Macha dipped her head back under the water. There was no way to undo the oath Badb had sworn to Queen Medb. The Morrigan's word was a blood oath: the queen's third-born for victory over an insurmountable enemy—Cú Chulainn.

When Macha returned to the surface, Badb was waiting, inches from her face.

"We meet the warrior tonight. He dies tomorrow."

Rua's legs gave out as she collapsed into Finn. His large frame surrounded her as he wrapped her protectively in his arms.

"What's the matter?" he asked her, noticing the severe change in her demeanor.

She fought hard to keep from crying. This latest memory so devastating.

Macha, Badb, Nemain. She'd heard those names before.

They were the triple goddesses of the Morrígan: mother, maiden, crone. The women from her dream. Finn was right. Her stomach hurt with the threat of the truth.

And Cú Chulainn. The goddesses killed him. She'd read that story, but this wasn't a story. This was a memory.

She was Macha. Macha to her sisters and Rua to the one who loved her most—Cú Chulainn.

She loved him and she'd killed him.

He stroked her hair and held her tight to him.

Burdened with this knowledge, she still didn't know why she was here in Emma's place. Why take her memories all away only to let them return in dribs and drabs, past the point of usefulness? What was the reason?

Perhaps this was hell. Punishment for killing her soul mate. She'd found him again, just in time to lose him to another.

Another knock.

She had to go.

Twenty-Eight

The universe demanded balance, and their kiss in the library only confirmed it. Rua's mouth, warm and inviting, had brought him to a level of ecstasy he'd never thought possible. With that kiss came a revelation, an answer to a question gnawing at the back of his mind.

He and Rua were at odds. Enemies in the truest sense of the word. And he was Cú Chulainn, though he hadn't the slightest idea how it could be possible.

Perhaps her kiss had driven him to madness.

His thoughts were unmanageable, but a larger question remained, one he wasn't sure he'd ever get an honest answer to: How much did Rua remember?

She held tight to his hand as she guided them toward her bedchamber. Something had changed with her in those final moments before leaving the library, something that had shaken her to her core.

He didn't know what was going to happen next; he only knew he couldn't leave her. He felt like he'd been given a second chance at life but that it could be taken from him at any moment.

He shut Rua's bedroom door, and she glanced up, her bright eyes hooded by her lashes. She studied him, her expression thoughtful.

"Do you remember loving me, Finn?"

Her question caught him by surprise. He ran a hand up and down the back of his neck as he considered his words.

The soft heart in him wanted to say *Yes* and *I love you still*, but the part of him that knew better said nothing. It was a question so profound it could only be a distraction. She had been so resistant to his inquiries up until now that this abrupt change could only mean Rua was trying to learn all she could before deciding her next move. A move typical of the Rua from his memories, confirming she remembered their past.

A reminder that she could not be trusted. Not yet, anyway. Maybe not ever.

"I'll take that as a yes, then." She smiled.

"Why?" he asked.

"I'm trying to decide if I can trust you." Another smile.

"You and I both," he said, and sat down on her little lilac settee. "And if I said that I remember?"

"Then I'll know that I can't trust you."

His eyes narrowed. "So you were lying when you told me you didn't remember anything." Whether or not she would admit to it, she remembered enough to know they weren't supposed to love each other. That when they did, it had cost him his life—Cú Chulainn's life.

"I've seen little fragments of moments I don't remember living."

He nodded. "I've had as many dreams as I've had nightmares. I don't understand any of it, only that I know this isn't the first time we've met."

Rua moved to sit beside him on the settee. There wasn't much space, but he didn't mind.

He knew she was still trying to decide where they stood. But he was tired of it. He hated waiting in the dark.

"Rua, tell me. Tell me everything. We're connected, you and I, whether you want to admit you know it or not."

Rua pursed her lips. She was so close to opening up; he could see it in the subtle crease between her brows. But Rua needed her secrets to survive. Perhaps if he could somehow show her that he was safe?

"I don't remember all of my past," he volunteered, "but I remember that I love you."

He sat at the edge of the basin, watching her. She was both goddess and warrior, beholden to only her whims. Furiously free.

She slanted her head back, basking in the sun. In this light, she looked like an angel. And maybe she was. Maybe she wasn't the devil who'd been foretold. There were three of them. Perhaps she was the exception.

"Do you think me so lovely that you can only stare, great warrior?" Rua called down to him, her voice like honey.

"Why don't you come down here so that I might tell you?" he shouted.

In one breathtaking movement, she dove from the cliff, her body one with the cascading water.

Exception, the rule—it did not matter. He was already gone.

Lost in a memory, he hadn't realized his mistake. Her hand covered her mouth, her eyes wide with shock.

"Loved you. I loved you once." He looked away from her, mortified that he'd said it like that. Why couldn't he just admit it? He should say it to her properly, but he wasn't sure it would matter. They weren't going to work, not in that century nor in this one.

When he looked back, she too was lost in another world, a distant gleam in her eyes.

"Rua?" he asked, watching a single tear roll down her face.

She looked at him, her expression tormented, heartbroken even. "Finn," she whispered.

He reached for her hand, and she gave it. The worry he'd seen on her face in the library had returned. He wasn't accustomed to seeing her discomfort.

She squeezed his hand and leaned into his chest.

"I'm only trying to put the pieces of my life back together—pieces that I hadn't even known were missing until recently—and coincidentally, it involves you." He sighed. "So much of it involves you, and if this is news to you, then I'm happy to be the one to share what I know."

He was going out on a limb here, but perhaps her memories hadn't all come back. His certainly hadn't. He hadn't even realized he'd lost any memories until they'd entered his dreams, revealing little details with explosive consequences.

He'd thought he was living the life he was always meant to until he ran into Rua that fateful day. From that moment onward, nothing had been the same. Not the way he felt nor the way the world seemed to work.

"I remember you," she said finally. "Well, I wasn't entirely sure it was you until now. It's all very vague, but usually we're in a meadow, nearby water, smiling and laughing. But there's always this sense of urgency, like we're on borrowed time."

So she hadn't remembered as much as he'd thought or hoped, but it was something. Unless, of course, she was lying.

"I've had similar dreams," he said.

"Are we together in them?"

He thought about his answer, not knowing if she'd accepted what he'd told her: that she was a Morrígan. If she did accept his truth, he didn't know what version of Rua he was going to get. The one that loved him, or the one that had teamed up with her sisters and killed him.

He knew the stories of Cú Chulainn well. And to think that he, Finn, was the renowned warrior and demigod, born of the god Lugh and mortal Deichtine. How did he end up here?

"Are we together in the memories I have?" he asked, trying to understand her question.

"Yes," she said.

"Many of them." He didn't understand what she was trying to learn from this information.

"And are we happy?" she asked.

Rua was pulling details out of him, disguising her interrogation in obscure questions. His answers would tell her everything she wanted to know. But they also told him that she knew about the Morrígan, and probably Cú Chulainn.

"In some of them, we are," he answered.

"You're being coy. Is it on purpose, or is being thickheaded a part of your charm?" she asked.

He laughed. They were dancing around the truth, neither willing to give in and accept defeat.

"I'm leaving tomorrow. Will you come with me?" she asked.

"To where?" he asked, surprised.

"I don't know, but I'm not going to pretend any longer that I am who they say." Rua looked at him, head held high. She'd lifted the veil.

"So you're not Emma Harrington?" He wasn't sure how this worked. He was Finn, but he was also Cú Chulainn. They were not two people; they were one.

"I'm not," she confirmed with a smile, "but you already knew that."

"I did," he agreed, a sense of unease overcoming him. A worry that the rumors might have been true about one thing. "Where is Emma Harrington?"

"I haven't a clue, but it's not my problem. I remember who I am, to an extent, and I will not let that nitwit mother of hers put me into an asylum."

"And what about your maid?" he asked.

"What about her?" Rua's brows furrowed.

"Well, I helped you steal her diary, and now I want to know why."

"She had information about the Morrígan. I thought she might know how I got here."

"Did you find anything?" He found it incredibly odd that an American maid would be so well versed in Irish mythology.

"Nothing of consequence. She's mentioned the hellmouth in Conleth Falls, and there's one in Central Park. I think that's where I need to go."

"A hellmouth? Like the one in Rathcroghan?"

"I don't know." She shrugged. "I haven't remembered that much yet."

The mention of the hellmouth reminded him of their differences. Differences that were so frightfully exposed. They could pretend here in this room that they were on the same side, working together to unravel the mystery of their past, but outside, in the real world, they were enemies. She had killed him once, and he had somehow ended up here in this time period. Had she come at the behest of her sisters to finish the job?

He wondered if she remembered that part yet. But it was only a matter of time before she would make her choice. The same choice she'd made all those centuries ago. An oath made by one was an oath made by all. He doubted that her sister Badb would so easily let him roam free.

"Rua, I don't think you should go anywhere."

"I can't stay here, Finn. Flossie's one wrong look away from committing me; Annette's party has tipped the scales. To them I am nothing more than a dispensable daughter and I am at their mercy."

"I will delay my engagement to Annette, give her something to hang on to."

"Delay your engagement?" She recoiled. "You can't seriously still be thinking of going through with it?"

"Why wouldn't I be? I gave my word." And Richard had him backed against a wall. Whatever had happened in the past, it was in the past. They could not go back and undo it. They had to play by the rules of the life they were living now.

"To hell with your word. My secrets don't need protecting anymore. This isn't my life!"

"Rua, I don't think you've thought this through. You need a plan, somewhere to live, funds. All of that can't be done in an evening's time. I will help you, whatever you need. Just . . . don't run."

"I've already packed, Finn. I'm going."

"A suitcase is not a plan."

He thought of her attempt to leave last night after Annette's birthday. Haphazard and impulsive. This was no better. "Why not wait until you've gathered all the information?"

"Why are you still going to marry her? After everything we've just learned. After all that we . . ." She trailed off, but he knew what she meant.

"Because whatever that life was, it ended. It's over." *You killed me*, he wanted to say. "This is my world now."

He could spend the rest of his life chasing the pleasure of their moments in the library and never come close. But he might also do the same if he chose Rua. For the moment, their interests aligned. What about when they didn't? There was no guarantee that she would ever stay. He had to protect himself.

Weary, he looked at the woman who'd handed him the last piece of meat. As his body drained of power, he couldn't help but notice the tear sliding down the old woman's face. It was then that he looked in her eyes and knew who it was.

A mighty gasp escaped him as he lost the power in his left leg. More than the loss of his limbs was the sorrow in his heart. He wanted to ask her how she could do this to him, but he could not speak. Weakened and betrayed, he limped to the battlefield, knowing that nothing that waited for him out there could be worse than what he'd just endured.

"You should go," she said, her tone chilling.

He stared at her gilded eyes and found that he recognized her. In the glow of the lamplight, she was the dark shadow, the monster, come to devour him.

Without another word, he left, wondering if he'd ever see Rua again.

Twenty-Nine

Rua couldn't sleep. Her mind kept replaying her conversation with Finn and all that she had learned, trying and failing to put it all together into something coherent for her mind to process.

She was a Morrígan, Finn was Cú Chulainn, and they'd both arrived in New York, memoryless and wanting. The only difference was that Mara had facilitated Rua's arrival. So how had Finn gotten here? And why? What were two immortals doing in Manhattan?

She'd gone back to the library and reread the anthology on demons and witchcraft, searching for any pertinent information. According to the author, the Morrígan were nothing but vicious aggressors who wreaked havoc on the world. Ireland's mightiest hero was struck down by the goddesses out of spite.

Rua tried to understand where her and Finn's love story fit into that narrative. From everything she remembered, it didn't. But it was there, and it was stronger than everything else.

He'd even slipped up and almost admitted it earlier. "I remember that I love you," he'd said. Her stomach fluttered, then soured as she remembered that he tried to take it back because he was still engaged to Annette.

More potent than their love was the betrayal. It came to her after he said that, and it would stay with her forever.

Their fire was only a short distance from Cú Chulainn's camp. It was there that the three beautiful sisters transformed into old hags, masters of deception. The demigod would never see it coming.

Macha's mind was in pieces. She was bound by blood to her sisters, and her love for the warrior meant nothing.

"It is him or us, Macha," Badb reminded her.

Given the choice, she would choose him. But Macha had no choice. Badb had taken it from her.

"His chariot approaches," Nemain said.

Badb's delight sickened Macha. She would never forgive her for this.

"Would you care for a bite?" Nemain called out as the warrior neared.

Cú Chulainn's gaze swept over the three old women. Macha held her breath. He wouldn't recognize her like this. He'd never know it was she who'd betrayed him.

The warrior looked at the meat they were roasting on the open fire, his lip curled in disgust.

"The champion is too used to dining with kings! He would never lower himself to eat with us," Badb scoffed.

Macha knew that Cú Chulainn was a humble man despite his conquests. He would take the slight personally.

"Forgive me, I did not mean to offend you. I should love a piece," he conceded.

"Go ahead, sister, cut the man some meat." Badb nudged Macha, wearing a malicious grin, and offered her a knife. Macha took the weapon, her hand shaking.

"Are you all right?" Cú Chulainn asked.

Macha looked at him, her eyes begging him not to see her for who she was.

She turned to Badb, thinking she should plunge the knife into her conniving sister's neck. How long had she been planning this?

"Cut it. Unless you want his suffering to endure a lifetime," Badb whispered.

"Go ahead," Nemain urged her gently.

A single tear fell from Macha's eye as she sliced the meat and handed it to her lover.

"Thank you," he said, taking it. Her heart was in tatters. So kind was Cú Chulainn that he would eat the vile meat to spare the old women's feelings.

She watched in horror as he took a bite, the confusion and pain registering as the strength in his left arm disappeared. It dangled lamely at his side, the piece of meat falling from his hand, landing on his thigh. Cú Chulainn roared as his left leg was stripped of its ability to walk.

Macha turned away, drowning in her shame as Cú Chulainn limped away to his inevitable death.

"On the other side of that hill, an army of five thousand approaches. He'll not survive the day," Badb said triumphantly. "We've made good on our deal with Queen Medb. And we couldn't have done it without you, Macha."

It was no wonder he wouldn't leave with her.

She stared at the ceiling as though the solution might suddenly appear. Every bone in her body wanted to run and never look back. Be free of the cage she was never meant to occupy. But Finn and his sensibleness had gotten under her skin.

Something wasn't sitting right with her, though she couldn't quite put her finger on it. Assuming everything she remembered was true—and it had to be, because, well, as inexplicable as it was, it made sense. The Morrígan connection had always been there, through Mara, the hellmouth, and then the more obvious fact that she was living another woman's life.

But if Cú Chulainn had died—and he did die; she was painfully certain of that—how had he come back? More importantly, why?

She was going to take Finn's advice and gather more information, which was why she would still go to the hellmouth with Mara tonight. Something there might trigger the rest of her memories, and she could find out once and for all why she was here.

Stomach growling, she looked at the clock. It was five thirty, though she doubted breakfast would be ready yet.

Rua opened Mara's diary to an entry from earlier in October. She was past the point of feeling any kind of guilt for stealing it.

October 9, 1870

She hasn't left her room in days. The girl she hoped to befriend played a nasty trick on her. She is putting in a poor effort, and Mrs. Harrington has all but given up on expecting her behavior to be different.

Poor effort? Rua scoffed at Mara's words. Although, she conceded, she had killed a man. She continued reading.

I am concerned she might be sent away and not make it to Samhain at all. And to make matters worse, the turmoil is driving her and the lord closer together. I don't know how to stop it. Mother will not be pleased. But she has stopped asking to go to the hellmouth. Less than a month until I get Emma back.

Get Emma back. So Mara knew Rua wasn't Emma. She wondered how long she had known.

It was a strange realization that the "mother" Mara was always referring to was likely Rua's sister.

She skipped forward, wondering why Mara had agreed to bring her today, on the thirtieth.

Well, that was fine with Rua. Finn wanted nothing to do with her anyway. She pushed down the pain. She couldn't blame him. She wouldn't be so quick to get over a betrayal like that either. Though she wasn't so easily killed.

"There you are." An out-of-breath Mara burst through her doors.

Rua shoved the book under her dress. "What's wrong?"

"We're going to the hellmouth. Now." Mara turned to Emma's armoire, searching for something.

Rua moved to her side table and slipped the book in the drawer. When she turned around, Mara had picked out a cape.

"Right now?" she asked as Mara threw the dark-green cape over her shoulders. "I thought we were meant to go tonight."

"Yes, but things changed," Mara whispered urgently. "Let's go." She hurried Rua down the hall.

"What happened?" Rua asked. They paused at the top of the staircase. Voices echoed from below, which was odd; it was too early for a social call.

"I'll explain on the way." Mara yanked her toward the servants' staircase.

"What's going on?" Rua asked, trying to come to a stop, but Mara kept pulling. "Who's down there?"

"Probably something to do with the hotel."

Rua remembered how early the men had been at the worksite the first day she'd arrived in Manhattan, and she herself wasn't accustomed to being awake at this hour, so it wasn't for her to say if it was out of the ordinary.

But as Mara pulled her along, a feeling washed over Rua, telling her that what Mara said about the hotel wasn't the truth.

"Why can't we go tonight?" She struggled to keep up with Mara, who was practically running.

Stopping abruptly, Mara looked at Rua. "Do you want to go to the hellmouth or not?"

"Yes," Rua answered, though now she was unsure. Mara knew she wasn't Emma. Perhaps she was just desperate to get her friend back and didn't want to miss the opportunity.

"This will be our only chance. Mrs. Smith made a comment to me about my nightly habits. I don't want her to catch the both of us and tell your mother," she said, out of breath.

Rua appraised Mara's flustered appearance—the sweat beading at the top of her forehead, the unusual flush of her cheeks, the high pitch of her voice. Perhaps she really was worried they wouldn't get another chance to get out of the house before Samhain and she would lose her opportunity to bring Emma home. But what was the plan? To camp out in Central Park all night?

"All right," Rua said, guarded but willing. They continued down the back stairs and then out through a door she'd never used before. It opened to the garden at the side of the house.

They moved through the garden and through a side gate with ease. The fog was thick and the air was cool. Rua pulled her hood tight.

They crossed Fifth Avenue, Mara nervously looking over her shoulder, and made their way toward the park.

Rua glanced back at the Harringtons' tremendous home. She wouldn't miss a bit of it.

"How far is the walk from here?" Rua asked, realizing she had only her slippers on and the seams of last night's gown were beginning to dig into her skin.

"Trefoil Arch is only a short bit away," Mara said, stuffing her hands within her cape.

"In relation to what?" Rua asked. "I wasn't expecting it to be so chilly." She rubbed her hands together and shoved them in her cape like Mara.

They passed none of the familiar landmarks as they walked, not that Rua would have been able to see them anyway. The fog was so dense that her outerwear was beginning to feel damp.

Mara didn't answer her as they continued walking north on Fifth Avenue alongside the park.

There was a shift in the air. Rua looked around, but there was no visible movement as the fog pressed in on them. Still, she couldn't shake the feeling that they weren't alone.

Mara didn't seem to notice, nor did she slow her pace.

They had walked so far from the Harringtons' that Rua's feet were blistering. It was impulsive to leave with Mara like this. She should have waited.

"Rua?" Mara broke the silence. "Were you searching through my things? I seem to have misplaced my diary." She sounded more curious than annoyed.

Put on the spot, Rua's heart stalled. Focusing on the familiar clicking of a horse's hooves on stone and the slow roll of carriage wheels as they crept to a stop, she tried to come up with an answer.

"I . . ." She looked up then, realizing what Mara had said—what Mara had called her.

Rua.

Rua looked beside her, but Mara was no longer there. "Mara?" She turned around, finding a horse and carriage waiting on the road. The Harringtons' carriage.

Her chest tightened as confusion gripped her. What was going on? She looked around for Mara, for help, but she was alone on the foggy street.

A sharp stab pierced her skin. She screamed, pulling a syringe from her neck.

"What have you done?" Rua's words felt heavy on her tongue as she began to wobble. She fought to remain conscious as a figure emerged from behind the carriage.

Despite the weight of her eyelids, she managed to blink. It was enough to let her see the face peering over her as she slumped to the ground.

"I want my friend back," Mara spat.

Thirty

Finn stood watching in the window as a black carriage rolled out of the drive. *Awfully early for visitors*, he thought.

The fog was dense and the streetlamps were still on, casting a murky glow over the footpath.

He hadn't slept after leaving Rua's bedchamber. Leaving in the first place had been a mistake. He thought about returning, but on the chance she'd fallen asleep, he didn't want to wake her. After what she'd endured publicly, she deserved a respite.

But his memories, returning to him piecemeal, would not let him rest.

He found himself smiling at the memory of what was likely the first day they'd met. The day she had driven a spear through his chest and changed everything. She had been clever and mysterious, much like she was now. But she was tied to her sisters, goddesses of sovereignty and war.

Rua was unlike anyone he'd ever met. A free spirit in the truest sense, torn between her desires and her instincts, he could never be sure which part of her was winning. Even with the uncertainty, he didn't know how to let her go.

After all this time searching for validation in Manhattan, he'd found it in her. She was the missing piece, but she wanted to go home—to her home—because this wasn't her life.

But what reason did Rua have to come to New York, centuries later, if not to find him? He would be a fool to think it a coincidence.

Finn checked his timepiece and noted that it was just after six in the morning, still wondering who was in that carriage.

He walked out of his bedchamber, down the long corridor, past the library and the grand staircase. Mustering up the nerve, he stood outside Rua's room. The door had been left slightly ajar.

He was about to knock when he heard Mrs. Harrington speak. "My lord, what are you doing?" she asked, looking alarmed.

It was highly inappropriate for him to be visiting Rua's bedchamber, especially at this hour. He wasn't sure what to say, knowing that whatever he came up with would reflect poorly on Rua.

"I thought I heard crying. I wanted to see if she was all right," he said, grimacing at his poor excuse of a lie.

Mrs. Harrington stared at him with pursed lips. "I assure you, my lord, she's fine." Then she forced a smile. "I think it best we let my daughter rest."

Finn nodded in agreement, wondering what Mrs. Harrington was doing up. She didn't look tired; rather, she looked energized. Perhaps she hadn't gone to bed after last night's event.

She stood in the hallway, waiting for him to leave Rua's doorway. Reluctantly, he moved, saying nothing as he walked past her and descended the stairs.

Feeling unsettled, Finn continued through the foyer and out the front doors. He crossed the street and walked north. The fog added to his general sense of unease, which increased tenfold as he traveled. He rarely traversed the area north of Seventy-Third Street. The last time he'd been past here was when he had followed Rua into the woods during the promenade.

There was no particular reason why he stayed away from the area; his aversion was innate. Even that day, when he'd stopped Rua, he'd felt all sorts of wrong, like something terrible would happen if they went any deeper into the woods.

In the distance, he could make out a carriage pulled to the side of the road. As he approached, he recognized it as the same one that had left the Harringtons' driveway.

What were the Harringtons up to? He walked faster, feeling like he needed to find out.

As he approached, the carriage rolled away, seemingly unaware of his presence.

Finn stood on the footpath, wondering what about this carriage had him so curious. Fretful, even.

Or maybe it was the lingering feeling of his last conversation with Rua clouding the rest of his morning. He wouldn't feel right until he talked to her and told her he'd been mistaken. This world had given them a second chance. It was the only one in which they could work, free and clear of her sisters.

So, if Rua was leaving, he wanted to go with her, if she would have him.

The hour was ungodly, but Finn didn't care. His mind was made up, the engagement was off, and he was going to tell Richard now.

"Good morning, my lord." A surprised butler greeted Finn at the Fitzgeralds' door.

"I must speak with Richard at once," Finn said, knowing that he'd be up. For all his faults, Richard was a hard worker and rose with the sun.

"Just a moment," the butler said.

A minute later he returned, instructing Finn to follow him into the breakfast room.

Suddenly, Finn regretted his hasty decision to come and speak to Richard. What if Annette was up having breakfast with her father?

It was too late. It had to be done. Bracing himself, Finn entered the room.

His shoulders relaxed when he saw that Richard was alone.

"To what do I owe the pleasure?" Richard asked with a cocked brow. "Come, sit." He gestured for Finn to sit down.

"I'm not staying," Finn said.

"Is that so?"

"I've come to let you know I will not be proceeding with the engagement."

Richard's eyes narrowed. "Why?"

"Well, I'd rather not start a marriage on threat of blackmail, and to be frank, I'm not interested in your daughter."

Richard rose to his feet. "And what? You think you're going to ride off into the sunset with the Harrington girl?" he jeered, shaking his head. "That ship has sailed, Donore. That ship has sailed." He sat back down, unable to get a handle on his emotions.

"What I do is no longer your concern."

"You can't renege," Richard said, holding his hands up as if to say it was final. "I've already sent the announcement. It'll hit the papers later today."

"I suggest you find a way to undo it," Finn said as a distant thought crossed his mind. Why hadn't Richard yet threatened to expose Rua as a means to make him agree, as he'd done so many times before?

"Do you know what it'll look like if you walk out on my daughter?" Richard asked, the veins in his neck starting to show.

"I imagine it'll look like your family has a problem."

"You're finished in this town, Donore! You hear me? Finished!" Richard roared.

Finn kept his face neutral as he imagined everything he'd worked so hard to build vanish into thin air.

"Goodbye, Richard," Finn said, and walked out the door. The relief he'd expected did not come. He'd gambled his life away on a chance. He didn't even know if the woman he'd done it for wanted him.

Finn gave the butler a nod as the man opened the front door for him.

He heard Richard's heavy footsteps following after him.

"Donore?" he called. Finn turned around to face him.

"I'll take pleasure in knowing that you'll never see that worthless whore again." He laughed, raising his arms in the air. "You've thrown it all away, and for what?"

Before he uttered the last syllable, Finn landed a punch on Richard's jaw, sending him flying.

"Go to hell," Finn said, and he left.

His heart was racing, not from the adrenaline but from the fear of what Richard meant. He'd said he'd never see Rua again. What could he possibly have meant by that? How could he possibly know something like that?

Something was happening to Rua. He could feel it in his bones. He cursed, knowing he should have checked in on her this morning. It had been too much of a coincidence to find Mrs. Harrington hovering in the hallway at that hour of the morning. She was in on it. They all were. He started to run.

Minutes later he barged into the Harrington household.

"Ned?" he shouted. "Ned?" He stomped toward Mr. Harrington's study.

"For heaven's sake, what is the meaning of all this shouting?" An annoyed Mrs. Harrington hurried toward him.

"Where is Ned?" he asked, thinking he might be able to put a stop to whatever it was they were doing to Rua.

"He's indisposed," she said coldly. He should have known better than to ask for Ned when Flossie had always been the one in charge.

Finn glared at her. "Where is she?"

"I don't like your tone." Mrs. Harrington tilted her chin upward, believing she had the upper hand. And for now, she did. If Finn wanted answers, he was going to have to acquiesce.

He swallowed back his distaste and said, "Surely there's been some sort of mistake?"

"My lord, I assure you there has not. This has been in the works for quite some time."

Flossie dared to look at him with a pitying expression. He took a deep breath, trying his best not to lash out at her. He would never allow Rua to be abandoned to this fate.

"Let us go sit down, hmm?" she asked, guiding him toward the gold room. A lavish room he had previously avoided at all costs. "My daughter is being sent somewhere to get well."

He and Mrs. Harrington sat by the massive arched window, on two different dark-green embroidered settees. Separating them was a narrow table with a gilded edge.

He turned back to Mrs. Harrington. "Rua is well," he insisted.

"There! You see? Rua." She repeated the name with disgust. "I haven't the slightest notion where she came up with that little pet name for herself. That should tell you how well she is," she scoffed. "My daughter's name is Emma. No one has ever called her Rua. She made it up!"

Finn let out a little laugh that Mrs. Harrington mistook for shock. Rua hadn't made it up; he'd given her that name a thousand years ago. What would Mrs. Harrington think about that?

She nodded, thinking he was finally coming round to her side. "Perhaps you didn't spend enough time with her to know that she had become positively unhinged. I shall tell you something that will put your mind at ease once and for all. I am sure you have heard the stories of her disappearance over the summer?"

He hesitated, and she noticed.

"Despite my efforts, they spread like wildfire, so there's no point in denying it."

"I heard them," he conceded.

Mrs. Harrington nodded. "Well, all of them are true. I'll deny this if you ever mention it to anyone, of course."

"Of course," he said, sensing that Mrs. Harrington was in the mood to talk, excited to be ridding herself of her problem. And Finn was too involved not to want every last detail.

"I'm not certain if you're familiar with the town of Conleth Falls? It's a good bit north and quite the picturesque little place despite being home to Boa Island."

He shook his head.

"Well, what they don't advertise is that it is a haven for the lowest kinds of people—devil worshippers, heathens, and the like. They lie in wait, hiding in the fringes of polite society, waiting to capture your unsuspecting daughters. Of course, I was warned of the legends detailing the history of the woods, but as a God-fearing woman, I wouldn't dare entertain them. Alas, it is those very woods where our daughter disappeared to, and that is where she died."

"Died?" A pit formed in his stomach.

"So to speak. We searched all night and day until finally we found her. She just walked out of the woods and up the stairs to the house like nothing had happened. Well"—she dropped her voice lower, brows raised—"we found someone. Certainly not the daughter I knew. It has been quite a struggle for some time. Nothing about her behavior is normal, but we pretended it was, and she pretended to try."

Finn wondered if she was going to mention the man who had lost his life in the process of trying to find Rua. He could only imagine what Mrs. Harrington would do if she knew there were two murdered men attached to Rua's name.

Despite the deceit of it all, he felt more assured that he had done the right thing in covering up the murder on Greene Street. If only he knew a way to help Rua now.

Mrs. Harrington paused and put her teacup down. "I should have known she was gone the moment she refused to answer to Emma, but the doctor assured us it was a temporary setback."

"So, then what changed in a few days?" he asked.

"Try as you might, you cannot reduce my decision to a single event, my lord. From the moment we returned to the city, she has been tormenting me with her poor behavior. I lie awake dreaming of whom she might offend next. Everyone was turning on her. Can you imagine if Ned were to lose out on such an investment because of a nonsensical young woman? And heaven knows how it would have affected your good name as well. I should hate to think on it."

"Mrs. Harrington, let me assure you, there is no world in which you could have the slightest effect on my reputation." Though that was a lie, apparently.

Her eyes widened, her voice feverish. "Well, did you know that she told Mara she murdered that man on purpose?"

Finn's stomach tightened. "What man?"

"The one that I hired to find her in Conleth Halls and bring her home. Mara finally felt comfortable sharing with me the truth. God only knows what happened in those woods. I couldn't risk any of it being true. She belongs behind bars, but I'll settle for Boa Island."

"Mara told you this?" he asked.

"A few weeks ago." Mrs. Harrington nodded, a satisfied smile returning. "Don't tell me that wasn't enough to send everything toppling to the ground. I did this to save the hotel. The Fitzgeralds insisted upon it—the contracts required it."

It was all beginning to make sense, the way the Fitzgeralds appeared to overlook scandal after scandal. Ned Harrington must have made assurances, and, at the expense of Rua's life, Richard had used Finn's affections for her against him.

"Mrs. Harrington, I implore you reconsider."

"This has been in the works for quite some time. Weren't you there when the contracts were amended?"

Had he been, he never would have allowed it to happen. His silence was answer enough.

"My lord, you are quite out of the loop, it seems. I understand that my daughter's brash manner has a certain allure for those unfamiliar with American social customs, but she was a liability through and through. A dangerous one at that."

"Where is she now?"

"On her way upstate to Boa Island. She left early this morning with Mara and Mrs. Smith."

The black carriage. His heart sank, and his hands balled into a fist. He was so close; he could have intercepted her.

Finn rose to his feet.

"Where are you going, my lord?"

He was going to find Rua. He would burn the world to the ground before he let her spend a minute inside an asylum. How quickly he'd succumbed to a life that was morally gray.

"Naturally, that's none of your concern," he said with a smile, thinking of all the times he'd asked Rua the same thing. "Though I thought you might like to know that I called off my engagement this morning."

Mrs. Harrington's face fell.

"I was going to speak to Ned today about it. I wanted to marry your daughter, but alas, she's gone now."

All color drained from Mrs. Harrington's face. None of this meant anything, of course. Rua's murder on Greene Street had truly ruined all hope for a redemption arc, assuming that Richard would release that news if he got a whiff of a happily-ever-after for Finn, but it was worth it to see the look on Mrs. Harrington's face. For her to think she might've sent her daughter away all for naught.

Thirty-One

Rua wafted in and out of consciousness as the world rattled around her. She was in a carriage, but she hadn't quite figured out why.

Her body was no longer hers to control. No matter how she tried, she couldn't lift her head or her limbs. Reminded of how Cú Chulainn had died, tricked by the three sisters into eating the cursed meat that drained him of his strength, she knew that this was retribution.

Rua had killed the love of her life, her soul mate, all because her sister wanted to, and she could do nothing but participate.

Rua had almost drifted back into her unsettled slumber when the carriage jerked and startled her awake.

She tried to sit up, but her head was still too heavy to lift.

A hand touched her shoulder. "There, there," came Mara's voice. "We've a good distance left to travel before we arrive in Conleth Falls."

"Conleth Falls? Why?" Her words tumbled out of her mouth.

"That's enough questions," a stern voice cut in.

Dopey, Rua rolled her head to look at her. Mrs. Smith.

"What's going on?" Rua slurred.

Mrs. Smith clucked. "Your mother has finally come to her senses."

Rua's mind raced to catch up, and then it hit her—the asylum on Boa Island.

She closed her eyes, the pain of trying not to cry mounting in her head. But she wouldn't give them her tears.

When they thought she'd dozed off again, they spoke.

"We'll spend the night and be rid of the wretch by morning." Mrs. Smith let out a big huff. "I don't know what Mrs. Harrington was thinking, letting it go on this long."

"I suppose she put too much stock in the Lord of Donore's interest," Mara said. "For a time, I thought he was truly interested in her."

Mrs. Smith laughed. "You're naïve, girl. That wicked child never stood a chance against someone like Miss Fitzgerald."

Rua's chest burned with hate. She wanted to throw Mrs. Smith from the moving carriage, but she was too weak, her body reduced to nothing but a lump of unusable appendages.

"I suppose," Mara said quietly.

This time Rua did slip back into oblivion.

"Careful she doesn't stir. Lord knows what she'd do to you," Mrs. Smith shouted over the howl of the wind.

Rua shivered as a bitter gust whipped her hair into her face. She wasn't in the carriage anymore. She peeked through the hair in her face to see that it was nighttime and she was being carried indoors.

They had reached the Harringtons' estate in Conleth Falls.

"They'll be around to collect her first thing in the morning." Mrs. Smith voice echoed in the foyer.

"We'll keep her in the staff's quarters tonight. Good enough for her." Mrs. Smith laughed. "It'll be luxurious compared to where she's going."

"Put her in the room with me," Mara offered. "It'll be easier to keep an eye on her."

"You must be joking if you think I'm going to fall for that," Mrs. Smith snapped. "Don't think I don't know that you're no better. I don't need the pair of you sneaking off into the woods in the middle of the night. She'll be in my room, and I'll hear no more about it."

Mara said nothing as they continued downstairs. Rua presumed it was the driver who was carrying her, as their voices floated away.

Their footsteps echoed through the empty house. The cold had seeped into her bones and tightened its grip on her heart. There was no warmth, nothing to coax her from this icy void.

Impressed that Flossie had followed through on her threat, she wasn't bothered by Mara's betrayal. It wasn't really a betrayal, after all. Mara was friends with Emma, not her. What she was bothered by was Finn and the last conversation they'd had. Would they truly never meet again? They'd learned what they'd learned and then parted ways. Again? Though she'd wager she was getting what she was owed.

Even still, there was unfinished business between them, perhaps because she had never told him how she truly felt. But maybe, if she had told him she loved him instead of quizzing him and asking him to run, he wouldn't have walked out of her room.

Had she shared anything worthwhile with him, he might've seen Mara's farce for what it was, and she wouldn't be a few hours away from a lifetime of imprisonment.

She heard shuffling while they paused a moment, and someone opened a door.

They traveled down an endless hallway, the Harringtons' house being too large for anyone, until finally, a door creaked, and she was set down on a bed.

She kept her eyes closed, not wanting them to know she was awake. Not that it mattered. She couldn't do anything to them, despite how much she might wish it.

"Give her another dose now, and it'll last through the rest of the night," Mrs. Smith said to Mara.

"I'll be right back," Mara said, and Rua wondered if Mrs. Smith noticed the strain in Mara's voice. Maybe she was having second thoughts.

Rua kept her eyes shut as she waited miserably for the sting of another needle. She smelled the light of a match as she focused on planning the demise of everyone who'd had a hand in delivering her to Conleth Falls.

She was a far cry from the girl she was when she'd murdered the man on Greene Street. That was an act of survival. This would be payback.

Now that she had regained many of her memories, she knew all the divine ways she and her sisters had killed before. First, she would kill the driver. His suffering would not be prolonged, as he was likely just doing his job.

Next would be Mrs. Smith. Or perhaps Rua would stick the old bully in the asylum, since she seemed absolutely giddy at the thought of Rua in one. In truth, that would be the best place for every last one of them. Flossie and Mara especially. Death was too kind. They deserved to know that crossing her had consequences. They deserved to suffer for their actions.

"Ah, there you are," Mrs. Smith muttered as someone opened the door. "I—"

There was a sputtering sound and a great thud.

Confused, Rua turned her head to the side to see the commotion, only to find a terror-filled Mrs. Smith slumped on the floor, held up by the wall. Her hands clutching her throat as the life bled out of her.

Rua propped herself up on her elbows and found Mara standing beside Mrs. Smith's dying body, holding a knife, looking lost in the firelight.

She wasn't frightened of Mara, merely curious. "Why did you do that?"

"You're not going to the asylum," Mara answered, her eyes never leaving Mrs. Smith. Rua watched as the hand holding the knife shook uncontrollably and the other worked to stop it.

"I-I had no other choice," Mara said, her voice breaking.

"I'm sure. And what of the driver?" she asked, suspecting Mara's list was growing.

Mara spun around, her deranged eyes on Rua. "He's dead too."

Her strength not having returned yet, Rua's elbows gave out and her head fell back on the bed. Still, she asked, "What is your plan here, Mara?"

"When I get Emma back, I'll figure it out," she said, pacing, her words riddled with anxiety.

"And when you do get Emma back, do you really think Flossie is going to let her come home? She's supposed to be in the asylum. And never mind how you're going to explain Mrs. Smith to her. She'll think Emma did that too."

"Stop talking." Mara waved her arms in the air. "I can't think in this room." Mara glanced sideways at the slain Mrs. Smith, and her body lurched. "Are you well enough to walk?"

"No." Rua's body felt like jelly.

Mara came over and put her arm around her, pulling her upward. She groaned as she lifted Rua off the bed.

Rua's head was heavy and her legs wobbled, but she could stand with Mara's support.

Not trying to make things easier for her, Rua did nothing to help, letting her full weight to rest on Mara's shoulders. She dangled around Mara's neck as they shuffled around Mrs. Smith into the hallway.

"If you stick another needle in my neck, I'll rip your throat out," Rua warned.

Mara said nothing.

Together they hobbled down the dreary hallway, back upstairs to the grandeur of the summer home.

"How do you know where you're going?" she asked Mara, who was guiding them without any light.

"I've worked for the Harringtons for years. I know my way around," she said spitefully.

"Where are we going now?" Rua asked. "I'm starving."

"Stop asking me so many questions," Mara snapped. "Feeding you is the last thing on my mind."

The moonlight filtered in through the windows, providing enough light for Rua to recognize that they were in the foyer. The air was cool. The furniture was covered with sheets. There were no servants milling about. The house was hollow.

"You seem a bit frazzled, Mara. Perhaps you should have thought twice before you committed a double murder."

Mara let out a whimper. "I had no choice." Her voice dropped lower. "Really. I had no choice. This is the only way. It will all have been worth it once I bring her home. Mother will reward me."

"Do you think so?" Rua asked sarcastically. From the small bits she could remember, her sisters were not the gifting kind. They were vengeful and vindictive and always had an ulterior motive. "Can you imagine if you did all of this and Mother was lying?"

Rua didn't know which of the goddesses Mara was talking to, but regardless, it was not going to go the way she hoped. She'd be lucky if she even found a way to get Emma back, but Rua didn't care. She was going through the hellmouth one way or another; what happened after was not her concern.

Emma and Mara had meddled in affairs so far beyond their purview that the consequences could only be cataclysmic. Though Rua did feel a bit sorry for Emma, who likely never would've gotten involved with the Morrígan had she not been influenced by Mara in the first place. In truth, wherever Emma was, she was probably better off. Her homecoming would be met with a fierce manhunt once Flossie realized she'd never arrived at Boa Island.

"She's not lying," Mara grunted, adjusting her grip on Rua as they began up the stairs.

"I can do it myself." Rua shrugged her off, leaning against the thick marble railing. She remembered her shock that first day she'd walked out of Emma's room and gazed upon the stunning opulence of the well-appointed mansion. Now it was nothing more than the vacant remnant of the Harringtons' ruinous aspirations.

By the time they reached the second landing, Rua could hardly stand. Mara noticed and propped her up once more, and they walked down the hall, past the pedimented doors to Emma's room.

Mara set Rua down on the chair and lit the sconces.

Rua hated this room and its pink upholstery and flowered walls.

"Let's get you into bed," Mara said, helping Rua.

"When are we going to the hellmouth?" Rua asked.

"Tomorrow," Mara said. "For now, you can rest."

Rua didn't trust it, but she was too exhausted to fight.

"Do you know who I am, Mara?" Rua asked, realizing that they'd never discussed it. Mara had acknowledged that she wasn't Emma, but where did her awareness end?

"Do you?" Mara rebutted.

That was answer enough. Whichever goddess Mara had been conversing with, whichever of Rua's sisters, they'd told her how to handle her.

"No matter," Mara said, pulling the chair up beside the bed. "I'll tell you a story, since you seem to have forgotten everything."

"I'm not interested," Rua warned.

Mara ignored her. "Centuries ago, there lived a warrior born of man and god, the bravest in all of Ireland. His name was Cú Chulainn."

"I don't want to hear this." Rua cut her off, shaking her head side to side. The one thing she had remembered, she was trying hardest to forget.

"But you must," Mara continued. "He was handsome, blessed with all the gifts of the gods. His conquests drew the attention of a most fearsome adversary, the Morrígan. Badb sought him out, thinking to get him on her side. You see, she liked to collect special things."

Mara was telling the story as though Rua hadn't lived it. Hadn't felt the sting of the very details Mara didn't want to leave out.

"In the meantime, Cú Chulainn continued winning battle after battle, fighting on the side of the righteous. The warrior was good hearted, but he was arrogant. One eve, Cú Chulainn was woken to the sound of roaring cattle, and he went to investigate. He found Badb on her chariot and a man driving a cow. He accused her of stealing the cow, but a goddess cannot steal what is already theirs.

"Badb taunted Cú Chulainn and told him that his opinion meant nothing to her. Taking great offense, the warrior leaped onto his chariot and threatened Badb with his sword. She turned herself into a crow and landed on a branch. Cú Chulainn realized then who she was, but it was already too late.

"Amused and unfazed, Badb returned to form and recited a poem to the hero, foretelling his doom at the Táin. Cú Chulainn did not take kindly to learning of his death and threatened to defeat Badb.

"Thinking only of her own interest, Badb did not intercede when she found out that her own sister, Macha, had fallen in love with the hero. In fact, she thought it would only sweeten her victory over him when he found out that the woman he loved had a hand in killing him. Because an oath made by one sister is an oath made by all."

Rua felt ill. Her breath slowed, the sweat beading on her forehead. She didn't want to hear anymore.

"One day, Cú Chulainn found himself fighting a Goliath of a man. True to her words, the Morrígan attacked three separate times. Cú Chulainn just barely survived his first opponent thanks to the Morrígan's violence. Macha was torn apart by her guilt, but she could not bring herself to leave him. Her love for the warrior was too strong. Never once did she consider that her sister had deliberately instigated her torment."

Mara's words played out in Rua's mind as if it had happened only yesterday.

"On his final day, the warrior was tricked into believing that there was a great slaughter of innocents underway at Emain Macha. Cú Chulainn, being the valiant hero of the weak, rode out against Queen Medb's army. He was almost at the battlefield when he was stopped for a final time. And who did he meet?" Mara paused as if Rua might answer.

"The three Morrígan sisters disguised as hags, cooking taboo meat over an open fire. They offered Cú Chulainn a bite. Seeing tears in one of the women's eyes, he took the meat and bit into it. But as the food touched his lips, the strength in his limbs disappeared. Confused, Cú Chulainn left the old women, immeasurably weakened."

Mara's voice softened. "Poor Macha, bound by the ties of her sisterhood, was forced to participate in the slaying of her one true love."

"Stop," Rua whispered, not wanting to hear any more. The pain was overwhelming.

"As the hero traveled down the road to Emain Macha, he came upon Queen Medb's army. He knew he wouldn't survive, but he refused to retreat. He still managed to strike down a great number of men, but Cú Chulainn was struck fatally by a spear, his intestines spilling out of him onto the ground."

Rua's tears slid down her face, onto the pillow.

"Cú Chulainn tied himself upright to a large stone so that he could die upright and face his enemies. His enemies did not approach the warrior until a crow—Badb—landed on the shoulder of Cú Chulainn. It was only then that the men knew he was dead. And so they came and took his head."

The ache in Rua's chest was unbearable. "Why couldn't I remember any of it?" she breathed.

"Perhaps because you don't deserve to?"

"Excuse me?" Rua's irritation overtook her sadness.

"You're a disgrace to your sisters," Mara said. "Look at you." She gestured toward Rua in her weakened state. "Utterly powerless. It's disgusting."

"You would think someone as devout as you would speak to me with a bit more respect," Rua snapped.

"Anyone who would renounce their life as a Morrígan to chase after a mortal is not someone deserving my respect."

"What do you mean, chase a mortal?" Rua sat up on her elbows.

"You killed Cú Chulainn, yes? He was then expelled from your realm, as was deserved. And now you're here for Finn, the earthly version."

"But what am I here to do with him?" Rua asked, wondering who Mara was getting her information from.

She watched as Mara realized she might've said too much. "Well, it doesn't matter now, does it? It was a fool's errand. He chose someone else. You failed," she backtracked.

Rua bristled at the reminder. He had made a choice, but he needn't try to protect her any longer. As she thought more about his selfless decision to save her by marrying Annette, she wondered now if it was just as much a decision that saved him from Rua. His subconscious protecting him from their past. Choosing Annette wasn't a choice at all; it was an out.

"What happens now?" Rua asked.

"You go home. Let Emma return. Simple as that."

Nothing was ever that simple.

Rua laid her head back down with the disquieting feeling that something important was being left out. A pivotal piece of information, like the conditions under which she had come to New York in the first place.

She must have known—made the conscious decision to come to a place where she would not have her powers. That was a risk she was willing to take for Finn? To what end? To appease her guilt? There had to be more.

She didn't feel ready to leave him yet. She'd only just gotten him back, but not in the way she wanted. She wanted all of him, and she wanted him to be selfish with need for her. She didn't want his noble sacrifices any longer. They had never been for her anyway. It was Emma's reputation he was protecting, but now she needed him to focus on her. The real her.

But how was she going to get to him now? He was in Manhattan, and Samhain was tomorrow.

As if reading her thoughts, Mara said, "If you stay, you'll be stuck here without your powers, locked away in an asylum, or you'll be out on the street. Do you know what choices there are for women of limited means? Servitude or prostitution."

Rua shivered at the reminder of her run-in with that animal on Greene Street. Mara could add prison to her list of choices. Was staying for the possibility of Finn worth losing her freedom? Especially when he was going to marry someone else anyway?

He'd soon build a family with Annette and there'd be little Finns running around, and his time with Rua would fade from memory.

She shut her eyes, trying to block the pain of imagining his happy life with Annette, the hateful bitch.

What reason did she have to stay here, then, if only to make herself suffer?

"What about you, Mara?" she asked, staring up at the bed canopy.

"What about me?"

"What was the point?" Rua asked. "I've read your diary. What was it you wanted from the Morrígan that was worth dragging your friend into it?"

Mara didn't answer for a long while and then said, "Sisterhood. A powerful sisterhood that could in turn make me powerful. And I wanted that for Emma." She sniffled.

"You did all of this for magical powers?" Rua was incredulous.

"You don't what it's like to be me, born to cater to the whims of the wealthy," Mara said. "And Emma, well, she's much softer than you. Kinder and more open hearted. She wouldn't have lasted a week in the city after those devil-worshipping rumors spread. Flossie was harsher than ever; Emma would have crumbled." She shook her head. "I should have caught on sooner when you didn't."

Rua was not insulted by her description of Emma. It was the same one she'd conjured in her mind for the young woman too. The only difference was that Rua wasn't sure Emma was coming back.

Thirty-Two

Rua didn't know how long she slept, but she could see the day's light peeking through Emma's curtains.

Groggy from the sedative still running through her veins, she sat up. Her dreams had been plagued with images of her cutting a woman's throat. Or maybe it was a memory; she couldn't tell the difference anymore.

"Are you ready?" Mara asked from the doorway. Her face was gaunt, and the bags under her eyes told Rua she hadn't slept a wink.

"You let me sleep?" Rua wished she hadn't.

"I didn't want to carry you the whole way," Mara answered, stifling a yawn.

"What time is it?" Rua asked. Samhain began at sunset.

"Time enough," was all Mara said as she helped Rua out of the bed. "We'd better get a move on. Flossie is expecting Mrs. Smith and me home on the first train out. She'll come looking when we don't arrive."

Rua, feeling more like herself after her rest, followed Mara out through the veranda and was struck with a terrible sense of déjà vu. The splendid summer home cast a long shadow over the earth, its gilded grasp not willing to let go.

They walked down the steps, and Mara hesitated by the fountain, looking out at the untidy lawn, dreary with the fading daylight. The grass was uncut, the bushes overgrown, the limestone pathway unkempt. "It's all so different now," Mara said, dropping her head. "I brought this on, invited you into our lives."

Rua didn't answer, though she wasn't sure she agreed with her. How much of this was Mara's doing and how much was predetermined? There were too many things at play here, and she doubted someone like Mara had any real influence. Mara was likely nothing more than a puppet on strings.

They continued through the garden, finding the place where the bushes bowed and granted them entrance. A ringing in Rua's ears and the low thrum of forest told her where she needed to go. She found the source and walked against the flow of the creek as it curved and bent around the earth until finally she found where the water pooled.

The hellmouth.

When Rua looked back, Mara was a good distance away. The look on her face was one of reverent trepidation.

"What are you waiting for?" Rua shouted. Had Mara lost her nerve? She had led the horse to water, but she was too afraid to watch it drink.

Rua looked at the small opening in the ground, the entrance to the cave. She didn't like the idea of crawling back inside the narrow hole. There was a horrible smell coming from inside it.

She walked past it, kneeling beside the basin of water. She cupped her hands and dipped them under the water. The temperature was frigid, and still it invited her. Hungrily, she brought it to her mouth, letting it dribble down her chin and arms in the process. Over and over, she repeated this, drinking the water, letting it fill her with life.

Little moments flooded her mind. Flashes of blood and battle, grassy fields and gentle hills, warm fires and laughter. But it wasn't enough to complete a picture.

Rua stood up, discarding her garments. The harsh wind whipped around her, bitterly cold, but as she stepped into the water, warmth shrouded her.

"What are you doing?" Mara asked, still at a distance.

Ignoring her, Rua dove into the water. As her body was enveloped fully by the hellmouth's water, her mind exploded, flooding her with images of her scattered life. All the pain and the suffering, the love and the betrayal. Her sisters, Cú Chulainn, but most of all, her power. She felt it all, writhing inside her, begging for release, and still she could not free it.

Frustrated, she rose to the surface, steam rising from the water with her. Taking a deep breath, she lay back, letting herself float atop the water. She closed her eyes and listened.

"You have a choice to make, but know once you do this, I cannot stop her," Nemain said. *"She is well within her right to retaliate."*

"She has no right!" Rua cried. *"I have lived a lifetime without him because of her demand for retribution. The pain never dulls."* She clutched her chest. *"It grows wild with every passing minute."*

Nemain stroked Rua's hair, consoling her.

"You will have three months to find him. Three months to rekindle what you've lost and bring him back. But in that time, if you do not succeed, he will die a mortal death at the hands of Badb."

"Why does she get the final say?" she asked, brimming with hatred.

Nemain gave her a knowing look. "You know why."

Rua did know. It was Badb who'd sworn the oath to kill him. Cú Chulainn was only half god. And Nemain had gone behind her back to undo it.

"How did you find him?" Rua asked, but Nemain shook her head.

"You only get one chance to undo death. This is yours."

"What if he rejects me?"

"Sweet sister, your love is pure. Trust in that. His death was not your choice," Nemain said, but it did not help ease her worry.

She would not be so quick to forgive if it were the other way around and Cú Chulainn had killed her. But Cú Chulainn was not her. He did not mirror her bloodthirst nor her penchant for revenge.

"I will keep this from Badb for as long as I can, but you have only till Samhain. He must remember who you are and choose your love before then. Sundown, not a minute after. Once the veil is lifted, she will come and finish what she started."

"He won't remember me?" Rua asked.

"Cú Chulainn has moved on. You must find who he is now and reconcile. Come back without him and it will all have been for nothing. His death will be permanent. This is your only chance."

"*Show me where he is.*" *Rua had no doubt that she could find him and explain. Their love truer than any oath. She would make this right and bring him home.*

Nemain smiled, thoughtful, almost pitying. "Are you ready?"

"Yes." Rua nodded as they walked to Oweynagat.

"Go ahead." Nemain gestured toward the entrance. "There's one more thing," she said as Rua entered the cave. "You won't remember any of this. You will lose yourself and succumb to the mortal realm. If you do not return before Samhain, with or without him, Badb will kill you both."

"What?" Rua spun around.

"You must decide if your love for the warrior is worth risking everything."

There was no question in her mind. She'd spent centuries wrapped in a haze of grief, but no more.

"How will I find him?"

"I've taken steps to ensure you are started on the right path, but there is no more I can do," Nemain said. "I've already done too much. Badb will react, and her wrath will be unrelenting."

Rua threw her arms around Nemain. "Slán agat."

"Slán leat, a Mhacha."

Gasping, she jolted upright, standing neck deep in the water.

She had to get back to Finn before it was too late.

Rua ran through the water, approaching the mound of grass where Mara sat before the cave. It looked as though she were talking to someone, but Rua could hear nothing.

She put on her clothes and slipped the cape back over her shoulders, all while trying to think of a way to get back to Manhattan that didn't require Mara's help.

Mara was no longer useful, her information lacking and skewed in her own favor. She was wrong to think she could bring Emma back. These must have been the assurances Nemain talked about. She'd lured Mara into the woods and had her bring her a sacrifice. Wherever Emma was, she wasn't coming back. Rua shoved the lingering guilt aside and started walking back toward the Harringtons' estate.

"Stop!" Mara shouted. "Where are you going?"

"To find Finn," Rua said.

"You can't go! You won't make it back in time. She is coming."

"Who?" She turned around.

"Who do you think?" Mara shouted.

Badb.

"Is that who you've been talking to when you go visit the hellmouths?" Rua asked, knowing that could mean only one thing. All of this—getting Rua up to Conleth Falls, separating her from Finn—was Mara's doing at Badb's request. Nemain had told her that Badb would retaliate. This was it. Mara was keeping them apart long enough so that Badb could kill them both.

"As a matter of fact, it is. The better sister." Mara smiled.

"What is your point?" Rua asked.

"I'd heard the rumors about the hellmouth. About the tales of disfigurement and unholy possession. I'd heard the rumors and still thought I knew better." Mara was shaking now. "I, the devoted fool, brought my best friend into the fold. Promises of rewards greater than I could ever imagine. I was selfish, and now she's trapped in there because of you." Tears streamed down her face. "Because of you!" She lifted up a jagged knife and waved it at Rua.

"Because of me?" Rua laughed. "Mara, this matter is well beyond your understanding."

"Badb told me you would dismiss me! But I understand everything. She told me of how you betrayed your sisters for a man. A man who does not want you!" Those last words pricked her, and Mara knew it. Emboldened by her weapon, she took a step closer. "He knows who you are, and he's chosen someone else."

"And you betrayed your friend because a voice in the woods told you to."

"I did not betray her," Mara said. "Emma was happy to do it."

"You wanted favor with the Morrígan, and you used your friend to get it."

"Get in." Mara's voice was cold as she used the knife to point to the hellmouth.

Rua didn't move.

"I will return your body to Badb. Dead or alive, it doesn't matter," Mara said, coming unhinged.

"You can't kill me," Rua said, though she wasn't sure that were true. Nemain had bent the rules to get her to this realm, and she might very well die if stabbed.

"I can!" Mara charged her, swinging violently without a care.

"Mara, stop!" Rua shouted, trying to grab hold of her wrist, but she missed. At the same time, Mara's knife cut through Rua's forearm.

Both of them froze, looking down at what she'd done. Blood soaked the pale-green sleeve of her arm, spreading as quickly as the pain set in. Mara made eye contact with her then, and like a fresh-lit match, her eyes glowed with the reflection of Rua's.

Panic-stricken, Mara dropped the knife.

Rua bent down to pick it up, enraged by Mara's audacity. As she took a step forward, Mara moved backward.

"Why do you want to stay here?" Mara asked, her words flowing with fear. "There's nothing for you here. You've driven Emma's reputation into the ground. You can't go back and live with the Harringtons as if none of it happened. Your time is done here."

Mara was right, but it wasn't going to stop Rua. She owed it to Finn to try. She couldn't enter the hellmouth without letting him know what she remembered and warn him of the dangers. But she was running out of time and had no resources to get to him.

Rua took another step toward Mara, contemplating her next moves. Mara raised her arms in defense.

"I'm not going to kill you, Mara. Why would I do that when I have you to thank for the return of my memories? I never would have gotten here if it weren't for you."

"Then what are you going to do to me?"

"Get in," Rua said, pointing toward the opening of the hellmouth.

Mara shook her head. "What?"

"I said get in."

Mara knelt down, trembling before the black hole. "It's not time yet." They both glanced up at the sky, the sun slowly fading from view. "Nothing will happen to me."

"You don't really know that for sure, though, do you? If a goddess puts you into the hole, maybe that trumps the holy day." Rua shrugged. "Maybe nothing will happen. Or maybe you'll meet my sisters. Hopefully not Badb, though; she's not really the forgiving sort, and I think she was expecting you to deliver me."

"Please," Mara begged. "I don't want to die."

Rua bent down so that her face was level with Mara's. "If you make it until sunset tomorrow, feel free to come out. Not a minute before, or I'll know," she lied. She just needed Mara to stay out of the way long enough for her to get back to the city and find Finn. As she was now, uselessly mortal, she had no discernible connection to the hellmouth's powers, but Mara didn't know that.

"Don't be fooled into believing that you're the innocent here just because Finn is stupid enough to put you on a pedestal. He doesn't know who he is. How can he know who you are? Even with his memories, he could never really *know* you. No one could."

Mara's voice was strained, full of pain and anger.

"Finn won't go with you," she continued, "and you'll have missed your chance to return home. If Badb doesn't find you, Flossie will, and she'll send you to an asylum for the rest of your days."

Rua didn't know if she could bear the pain of Finn's inevitable rejection, but she couldn't just leave him here, unaware of Badb's impending strike. Rua would rather live without Finn knowing he was alive then live safe in a world where he wasn't. She'd already done it. And she'd spent centuries mourning his loss.

"Get in, Mara," Rua said, noting the foul smell emanating from the hole. Sniveling, Mara lay flat on her back to go feetfirst.

Rua remembered the day in August she'd crawled out of the hole and the terror she'd felt at the unknown. Her clothes and hands had been covered in blood. *Whose blood*, she wondered.

Mara shimmied and inched her way in until she was no longer visible.

A few moments later, Mara cried, "Oh god! The smell."

Rua heard retching.

"There's something down here," Mara shouted through her audible gagging. "It's a body!"

Rua swallowed hard, remembering.

She studied the woman's face. A fetch. The likeness remarkable. Not an identifiable difference.

Nemain had planned this down to the very last detail. How long had she known that Cú Chulainn would return? And how long would it take for Rua to forget everything?

The hope was unbearable. A chance to find the love she'd lost— the love she'd killed.

"I am Emma Harrington." *The woman spoke, wide eyed and daft, all too willing.*

She handed Rua a knife and knelt down before her, tilting her chin upward. "It is my great honor to offer you my life, my home, my family, in exchange for a life in the god realm."

Rua looked down at the knife in her hand.

She pressed the blade against Emma's neck.

Guilt, sadness, anger, hate. All of it consumed her. But it didn't matter—she needed Emma's life.

Rua's hand shook with the heinousness of the truth. These were the moments before she crawled out of the hellmouth, before Mara and the men came upon her.

The blood was Emma Harrington's.

Rua had come to take her place by killing her.

It was amazing the way she'd allowed herself to believe she was a victim, that she and Emma, in some twisted way, were in this together. But the truth of it was, she was the goddess of death.

Resolved and ashamed, Rua left Mara and her dead friend in the hellmouth.

Thirty-Three

By the time Finn arrived in Conleth Falls, it was after three in the afternoon. He might've gotten here quicker had he waited for the next train, but he couldn't sit and do nothing all night. He needed to be moving toward Rua.

The quintessential summer town was glum and unwelcoming, and it had nothing to do with the grim light of day.

The moment he passed the WELCOME sign, he felt the subtle change in the air. He was an outsider intruding on well-kept secrets, secrets that would kill to be kept hidden.

There was no need for him to inquire about the hellmouth's location. Its presence loomed ominous over the sleepy little town. The distant howls carried on the wind, whipping through the trees, telling him exactly where he needed to go.

There wasn't a soul to be found on the cobbled streets. As he left Main Street, he made his way toward the forbidding woods. Beyond the graveyard beside the church, he could see the trail.

He hesitated at the cemetery's entrance. There was no way but through. The idea of having one's remains buried underground for all eternity had never much grown on him.

He took a deep breath, reminded of his own gruesome death, and crossed under the archway. He tried not to think about it as his horse's hooves sunk into the uneven, spongy ground.

The headstones and grave markers were broken and splintered, growing more neglected with every step closer to the woods. These souls had long been forgotten, lost to the darkness that reached out from beyond the trees.

As the woods grew around them and the light from the afternoon faded, he could sense the tension in his horse. His own lantern did little to light their way as the sun began to dip behind the trees. He ignored the voice screaming in his head, telling him there was danger all around him. His only focus was on finding Rua.

He was forever chasing after her, and she was always just out of reach. But even with all the uncertainty, he had hope. Maybe it was a weakness, but he would not betray her by giving up.

There was good in Rua. The Rua from today was not the same Rua from his past.

"But we are together now. There is nothing more she can do," he said, stoking the fire. *The night was cold and full of stars.*

"Nothing more she can do?" Rua's voice broke. "She will not let us be." He sat down on the stone beside her.

"Run away with me." She looked at him in earnest. "We could roam the world, do whatever we please, and truly be together." She rose, a faceless shadow before the firelight, then bent down before him. Her eyes were level with his as she whispered, "We could finally live."

"We would not live. We would be running for eternity."

He watched the rage in her eyes come and go—a burst of light, then sudden darkness. She'd spent too long with her sisters. Scheming and killing.

He was going to have to draw out the good—he just hoped he could do it in time.

She was, after all, just like the others.

Three sisters with a penchant for killing tamed only by their link to one another.

To expect her to do the right thing simply because it was right was too big a risk. It wasn't worth it to put forth the temptation.

Dread was the common thread woven throughout his broken memories. No matter which way he looked at them or how he tried to remember it all differently, disaster waited around every turn.

It was an eerie sense of recognition, the kind that made his heart stop and made him wish he could go back to how it was before, when he was unaware.

Slowly, he traversed the uneven ground. The landscape was unfamiliar, but he felt a familiar buzz in the air. A warning that he was somewhere he shouldn't be.

"Help!" He heard a shout.

"Rua?" he called, riding faster.

"Please, help!"

He followed the woman's cries deeper into the woods. Every part of him was on edge.

"Where are you?" Finn called, but as he approached the basin of water nestled among the rocks, he recognized it immediately. He slowed his horse.

The hellmouth.

"I'm over here," the voice called, spurring him to action.

He tied his horse and ran to the mossy mound with the triangular hole cut in the center, revulsion coursing through him. He hated this place and every other one like it.

"Who's there?" the woman shouted from the inside of the cave. He recognized the voice.

"The Lord of Donore," he answered. *Cú Chulainn*, he thought.

"My lord, oh, thank goodness. It's Mara, Emma's maid."

So they were both keeping up pretenses. For whom, he didn't know. They were in the middle of the woods at hell's door.

"Please, pull me out, my lord," she begged.

"How did you get in here?" he asked, noticing a terrible odor.

"Emma. She's gone mad. When she learned where her mother was taking her, she forced me out of the house and brought us straight up here."

Finn's stomach dropped knowing the maid meant Rua.

"Where has she gone?"

"I don't know, my lord. Please make haste."

Against his better judgment, he knelt before the hole to offer Mara his arm. Gods above, he didn't want to go inside. He couldn't. He just hoped his arm was long enough to reach hers.

As his hand crossed the threshold, between the world he knew and the darkness below, he felt an unfamiliar rumble in his chest. A frenzied vibration that sent his heartbeat racing and his world spinning. As his vision began to blur, clouded by rage, he yanked his hand back before it could go any farther.

"My lord?" Mara called for him.

Chest heaving, he looked down at the opening and the stone resting atop it. This was the Morrígan's lair, an invisible gate to hell, and it had unlocked something primeval inside him.

"My lord, are you still there?"

"I'm sorry, Mara, I can't pull you out."

Startled to find a woman in a hole who needed help, he was too quick to take Mara at her word. But what if Rua had put Mara in this hole for good reason?

Mara was the enemy. The enemy of a killer, he reminded himself.

The path to warping his morality, all in service of Rua's interest, was swift, to say the least. So blinded was he by his passion that he'd forgotten what she'd done.

He might not remember the life he used to live, but she certainly was the one who had taken it from him. Speared and beheaded at the hands of Rua and her bloodthirsty sisters. And it seemed Rua was going to take this life away from him too.

Gone was his contentment; in its place was intense yearning. Longing for the truth, and for justice, but most of all for her.

He cursed, knowing that in this life and the next, he would love her. No matter the pain she inflicted, intentional or not, he would be hers, always.

"Where is Rua?" he shouted down to Mara.

"I don't know where she's gone. Probably to the house to gather a bag. She's running away."

"Running away?"

"She's not Emma, you know." Mara's voice changed.

He knew this.

"Emma's right here, beside me, dead."

Finn swallowed the lump in his throat, noting the tightening in his chest. He'd danced around the possibility for ages, but he'd never allowed himself to fully consider it.

"Your precious Rua cut her throat." The last word came out like sob, but he had heard enough.

With almighty speed, Finn tore through the trees. Somehow he knew exactly where to go. He could sense Rua and the darkness hovering, leading her astray. She was fighting it, but he could never be sure what part of her was winning.

If only he had listened to her when she asked him to run.

Thirty-Four

Rua walked through the garden up to the Harringtons' home. She had to make a decision. Temptation called to her with its rich offer of power and eternal life, free from the tribulations of man. If she walked away from the hellmouth now, she risked losing it all forever.

Risking it all on the hope that she could find her way back to Finn and save them both. But how? She looked at the sky, knowing she had little more than an hour. She would only be able to choose one.

She walked up the steps of the veranda with all its marble statues.

She'd sat out here with Flossie on her very first day as Emma. Had she only known then how difficult it would be, she would have cut her losses and run, but then she'd never have found Finn.

Rua walked inside, down the long corridor toward the grand staircase.

The idea that a home as grandiose as this could be left abandoned for several months of the year was truly outrageous. She wondered if the Harringtons would ever return, or if the proximity to the hellmouth was now enough of a deterrent.

Rua climbed the familiar stairs to Emma's bedchamber. Guilt wrapped its hands around her throat as she opened the bedroom door. She looked around the pink room and could see nothing but Emma's rotting corpse.

Swallowing back her despair, she moved to the armoire to see if there was anything left for her to change into.

Was there anything more depraved than rifling through your murder victim's things? Rua didn't think so.

She wanted so badly to hate Flossie. To believe that she and Emma were on the same side. But Flossie hadn't killed Emma; Rua had.

Rua took out a black mourning dress. The only thing left. How appropriate.

She put the dress on and turned to the golden full-length mirror, finding she looked as miserable as she felt.

Rua focused on the gold of her eyes, remembering who she was supposed to be, but all she could see was the villain. She wanted the life she was owed, free of the decisions that had turned her into what she was now, a lovesick mortal who'd allowed guilt and shame to cloud her judgment.

A terrible scream escaped her, and she brought her fist to the glass, shattering it, sending shards of it to the floor. She didn't feel any pain, nor did she notice the blood as it dribbled down her arm. She could only stare at the fractured reflection that mirrored her soul.

Rua took a deep breath and wiped the tears from her eyes, looking at the mess on the floor. No one was coming to clean it up for her.

Remorse was not becoming of an ancient war goddess. She did not need to feel guilt for taking Emma's life. Emma had offered it; it was hers to take.

Resolved, she bid farewell to the pink room. The sun was beginning its descent, leaving way for Badb to come through the hellmouth. She needed to get to Finn.

As she walked into the hall, she heard the creak of a door that was meant to stay quiet. It came from the first floor.

Wondering if it was Mara, hoping by some miracle that it was Finn, Rua hurried down the brown marbled steps. She didn't need to slink and hide. There was no more watching her behavior and keeping herself in check. If she wanted something, she was going to get it.

Rua heard the clink of fine china against a table.

She rushed into dining room, shocked at who she found.

Flossie Harrington was sitting at the table like the queen herself. She didn't seem at all surprised to see Rua, her lip curling in disgust as she looked her up and down.

"I should have known you weren't done tarnishing this family's good name," Flossie said.

Rua's shock quickly wore off, melting into a razor-sharp hatred that was too excruciating to contain. There was no one she wanted to suffer more than Flossie. For months, this woman had tormented her with her criticisms and callous behavior.

"Look at you, in that hideous frock. Where is it that you were planning on going?" Flossie sneered. "You're a fugitive and a murderer, it would seem."

"Where I am going is no longer any of your concern," Rua said, taking the murderer comment in stride. There were so many, she didn't know which one she could be referring to.

"Soon enough, it won't be." Flossie shook her head, rising from her seat. "I mean, what did Mrs. Smith and the driver ever do to you?"

"That wasn't me," Rua said. "That was Mara."

"And where is Mara?" Flossie asked, arms raised as though she were merely disappointed and not at all horrified. "I have to do everything for this family. I hand you the lord on a silver platter, and still you failed. All you had to do was be likable." She shook her head. "We were so close. He was living under our roof, for Christ's sake," Flossie's voice reached a new pitch. "Well, Annette can have him now. Free and clear. Thanks to you." She grabbed hold of an empty vase, clutching it as she began muttering to herself.

"The gossip will be near impossible to avoid. Everyone will wonder what happened to the Harringtons' daughter. They will whisper and wonder, but they'll understand. They'll agree that we had no choice but to send you away. They'll probably even be relieved to learn of your death."

"My death?" Rua laughed.

Flossie rose and moved around the table, still holding the vase.

"What are you doing?" Rua asked, amused.

Eight chairs were all that stood between her and the overwhelming urge to silence Flossie forever. They were more alike than either of them had realized.

But Rua was a goddess, and Flossie was no one.

"If you take one more step toward me, I swear it will be your last," Rua said.

Flossie hesitated, eyebrow raised, and then she smashed the vase against the wall.

"Are you truly that demented that you would speak to me like that?" Flossie bent down and lifted a sharp piece of what was left of the glass vase. "I am your mother, and you will give me the respect I am owed."

Flossie walked slowly at first, then picked up speed as she rounded the table, knocking down chairs as she went.

"Are you meaning to harm me with that?" Rua nodded toward Flossie's hand while taking careful steps backward.

"What choice have you left me? You've made me a laughing-stock." Tears welled in Flossie's eyes. She continued to encroach while Rua edged toward the servants' door.

"You can never leave Conleth Falls. It's Boa Island, or it's this." She looked at the makeshift weapon in her hand.

"I'm not going to Boa Island," Rua said, throwing her body into the swing door reserved for staff, only to find it locked. She knocked her head as she bounced off the wooden door and stumbled forward, trying to get her bearings.

"Then it's this." Flossie grabbed her from behind, coiling her arm around Rua's neck, pulling her to the ground. Rua couldn't believe Flossie's aspirations had driven her to this.

With wild force, Rua swung her elbow into the matriarch's nose.

Flossie let out a howl, clutching her face as she fell backward.

Rua grabbed the glass off the floor and pinned Flossie to the carpet.

Flossie sobbed, staring up at Rua's face. "You look like a monster."

"That's because I am a monster," Rua said, raising her arm, ready to plunge the glass into Flossie's neck.

"Rua, stop!"

Not believing her ears, she looked up to find Finn in the door-way. Her relief could not dampen the stunning rage that wanted to slice Flossie from ear to ear.

"Rua, let her go," he cautioned, taking a step toward her.

Rua's hand shook with temper. Her grip on the glass was so tight that it cut into her palm. How dare he ask this of her? How dare he try to take away her vengeance?

"Why should I?" she shouted, looking down at Flossie's sniveling face. The blood from her nose had dripped into her mouth, out-
lining her teeth.

"Because you are more than this."

"No!" She closed her eyes, head shaking. "This is who I am."
Rua pressed her forearm harder into Flossie's throat.

"You can make a different choice now, Rua," Finn said, his voice
softening as he approached.

She looked at him, choking on a lifetime of regret, wishing
she'd been strong enough to make a different choice then.

He nodded, encouraging her with kind eyes and a face full of
forgiveness.

Could she trust it? Just like that, he would forgive her?

She'd spent so long doing the wrong thing, the selfish thing.
Countless crimes had led her here. What was one more body? This
was her way.

"Rua." Her name a gentle plea, a promise of more.

Pained, she held his gaze, believing his silent promise. This was
how she atoned.

Letting out a frustrated cry, Rua released the pressure on Flossie's neck and climbed off of her. Finn ran toward her.

"You're here," she sobbed, running into his open arms.

"I'm here, a ghrá," he whispered as he held her. Her heart lifted
at the endearment. The acknowledgment of the love that existed
between them.

She glanced up at him. "I love you, Finn."

He smiled and kissed the tip of her nose. "I love you always."

"Let's go home," she whispered.

"My lord, it would seem you are as demented as my daughter."
Rua had been so grateful to see Finn, she'd almost forgotten about
Flossie.

Rua looked back, thinking of a dozen different ways to maim
Flossie while Finn was busy being the bigger person. He wrapped
Rua's arm around his and guided her out of the room, away from
any further trouble.

But that wasn't good enough for the matriarch.

"How dare you walk away from me, daughter!" she screeched as
she lunged for Rua, taking hold of her hair.

"Enough," Rua yelled as her head was yanked backward. She spun around with a quickness that startled Flossie enough to release her hold. Flossie fell backward hard, her head landing among the shards of the vase she'd broken. Her eyes bulged with pain. Rua felt no pity. No pull to help. This was what Flossie deserved.

But as Flossie's blood pooled on the carpet, she felt a change in the air. A severe gust of hostility and an immediate sense of danger.

And then something growled.

"Finn?"

She looked up from Flossie's body.

"Finn?" she said again, turning to find him rising from the ground, slow and rigid like a bear waking from sleep. The muscles in his back twitched and contorted as the veins in his neck bulged. She could hear the rapid pace of his heart and the slow intake of breath.

A man she did not recognize turned around to face her.

His eyes were feverish, dark and soulless. Hate filled in all the parts of him that she used to know. Finn was no more. Standing in his place was the warrior Cú Chulainn, and this was his battle frenzy.

"Finn, can you hear me?" She approached him carefully. But he was more beast than man, and her words meant nothing. This was the famous ríastrad.

Somehow her crime against Flossie had triggered something within him, highlighting their inexorable differences. The defender of innocents versus the war monger.

His breathing grew frantic, like that of a wild bull set to charge. Up and down, his chest heaved as his body rattled with temper.

He looked at her, then, fighting to hang on to the last shred of his humanity, and growled, "Rua, run."

Not needing to be told twice and with only a split-second head start, she tore through the house, trying to find a door to the garden. Sounds of pure chaos erupted behind her as he tossed furniture aside and barreled through walls to catch her. Shocked by her own speed propelling her forward, she flew through the back doors down to the veranda.

As she ran past the dried-up fountain, she heard a terrible shatter. She looked back to find that he'd run straight through the window. Glass sprayed everywhere as he flew down the limestone steps. He moved like an animal, switching between running on his two legs and galloping on all fours.

Rua pushed harder as she disappeared through the tree line. She was running back toward the hellmouth, the only place he might not go. She could hear him behind her, his ragged breaths and monstrous groans, tearing through tree trunks as though they were curtains. He was practically on top of her. She wasn't going to make it. He was too fast, too deranged.

Thunder rolled above her, growing louder and more violent with every step until she realized it wasn't thunder at all. The sky boomed with the sound of hundreds of thrashing bird wings.

A massive swarm of crows exploded over the treetops, blocking out what little daylight the clouds offered. They mushroomed in a wild heap hovering over the woods before nose-diving. She blocked her hands to shield herself, but they flew past her, aiming for Finn instead.

He roared as he tried to fight off the swarm of birds, to no avail.

It was enough of a hindrance to get her to the hellmouth. She had two seconds to decide before he was upon her, ripping her limb from limb.

Cave or water, both with enormous consequences.

If she went into the cave, he might not follow her, and when the ríastrad was over, he'd be left here alone, susceptible to Badb's wrath. It would all have been for nothing.

If she chose the water, she didn't know whether or not he could enter. He might dive right under and kill her there.

She could hear the steady pounding of his feet growing louder and louder.

The sun was setting. The time to decide was here.

One impossible choice for another, but only one offered them a chance.

As the sun dipped below the horizon, Rua ran into the water, him on her heels. Braced for a fight, she turned back to defend herself. But he'd stopped, hovering by the water's edge, roaring like a beast. A beast that couldn't touch the water.

Apprehensive, her eyes darted to the hellmouth, wondering which was worse—Cú Chulainn's ríastrad or the inevitable arrival of Badb.

She had to admit, the timing of the ríastrad was fortuitous. Finn's body preparing for what his mind could not. He would destroy Badb the moment she crossed the threshold, leaving them free and clear to return home.

Rua took a deep breath and dipped under the water. Soaking it all in, she couldn't believe they were finally going back.

When she returned to the surface, Cú Chulainn was gone from the water's edge. Horrified, she found him atop the hellmouth, jumping up and down with such force that the earth around it began to shake.

"Stop!" she screamed, but he couldn't hear her. He scratched and he clawed at the hellmouth, shredding and tearing until there was nothing but dirt.

"Finn," she cried. "Finn! Please stop. We can go home together!"

The water began to bubble as the cave below collapsed in on itself, their chance of returning dwindling with every violent blow.

"Finn, stop!"

Over and over, his fists struck the ground until there was no more.

His thumping and digging began to slow.

Wading out of the water, Rua ran to him.

"Finn, can you hear me?"

The hulking man turned to face her, and she was afraid of who she might find.

She breathed a sigh of relief. "Finn."

Sickened, he looked around at the destruction he'd caused. "What have I done?" He reached for her. "Are you hurt?"

Rua offered a soft smile. "I told you before, you're no match for me." She nudged his shoulder. "Half a god, remember?"

A desperate laugh escaped him as his arms wrapped around her body. She melted into his embrace, feeling a familiar surge of energy coursing through her veins. Like warm honey, it soothed her, coaxing her stifled magic out of its long slumber.

"Is Mara still in there?" he asked, his voice strained.

Rua shook her head. "Maybe. I don't know." She stepped back, looking down at the obliterated hellmouth. If Mara had listened to Rua and stayed put, she was likely crushed. Or perhaps she'd made it to the other side.

"We have to help her," Finn said, crouching down, digging through the rubble.

"Why? So she can help my sister find us?" Rua put her hand on his shoulder. "She's gone, Finn."

Rua was more concerned with what they were going to do next and how they were going to get back. An uneasy feeling settled in her stomach as she realized she didn't know if Finn would be willing to leave New York with her.

"Do you think it's really destroyed?" she asked, not ready to ask him what she really wanted to know.

"I can't imagine it's functional now," he said. The entire mound of grass had caved in, laying waste to the cave below it. There were no visible openings. It would be impossible for Badb to come through at this point.

"What happened back there with Flossie?" Finn asked.

"She fell," Rua said, not feeling an ounce of pity for her.

"Is she dead?" he asked.

"I assume so. Does it matter?" She stiffened, wondering if that was one too many crimes for Finn. He'd come to Conleth Falls to save her when there was still hope for her humanity, but the bodies had since piled up.

"Of course it matters." He frowned. Rua held her breath, fearing the worst. This was his breaking point. A woman with murderous tendencies did not fit into nineteenth-century Finn's future plans.

"Look at what I've done." He pulled back to look at her. "I don't ever want anything like this to happen again. I don't know what I would do if I hurt you, Rua." Relief washed over her. How quickly he'd forgotten that she'd once killed him. He hugged her tighter, pressing the side of his face against hers. "I cannot lose you again." His lips left a kiss against her hair.

"You won't," she promised. "We have a second chance, Finn." She tugged on his ruined shirt. "We can be together, free of my sister. But we'll have to find another way back."

"Do we have to?"

She looked up at him, worried that she'd misread things.

"Do we have to go back, I mean."

"Finn, I can't stay here." She shook her head, though she didn't know how they would return now that the hellmouth was destroyed. "I thought you understood?" Life in New York was over for her. She was done pretending; she knew who she was.

She was Macha, the Morrígan goddess, affectionately called Rua by her lover, Cú Chulainn.

But if he wanted to stay, she would not take that from him. The choice was his.

"We could go anywhere else," Finn said, his hands moving to the base of her neck, his thumbs stroking her jaw. "I don't care about Manhattan. I don't care about any of it. You are my home. I choose you."

Rua's heart soared as tears filled her eyes. She stood on her tiptoes, and he bent down to meet her. She breathed him in, intoxicated by his presence. His mouth was warm as it found hers, teasing her with playful pecks until finally he slipped his tongue past her lips.

His kiss was careful and hungry, but most of all, it was hers. Alive with the knowledge that they could start anew.

"I love you." She smiled up at him. There were three months until Imbolg. "Where should we go?"

"Anywhere, a ghrá."

Somewhere between the light and the dark, a woman was found, and as her hand held his, she wondered what she'd done to deserve it.

Acknowledgments

First and foremost, I would like to thank my family for their unwavering support of my literary endeavors. Without them, there would be no book.

To my husband, Luis, who sleeps next to me on the couch when I am up all night writing, I love you, and I promise to name the horse after you in my next book. Ronan, you are my superhero, and my favorite person in the whole world. Mom, your dreams for my book are as big as mine. Without your encouragement, I might never have finished. Dad, thank you for pretending you didn't know that I was writing when I was on the clock. Pat, Sean, Michaela, and Kevin, thank you for always telling your friends to like my book posts. Nanny, thank you for thinking everything I write is wonderful. My mother-in-law, Mary, thank you for feeding me and making our house feel like a home. To my father-in-law, Enrique, I know you would be proud.

To those of you who read early versions of my book, thank you, and also, I'm sorry. It took many years for me to realize that firsts drafts were not meant to be shared, but your feedback and excitement kept me writing. I'm pretty sure there are at least ten different versions of this book floating around the internet, and you've all read multiple. Again, I'm so sorry. Mom, Coleen, Tara, Siobhan, Noelle, Grace, Sarah, Mary Jo, Nuala, Kristy, Val, Collette, Doran, Eileen—thank you for everything!

To all of my beta readers throughout the years, your feedback was invaluable. A special thank you to Hannah, Bailey, Kaitlin, Khaya, Nicole, Genevieve, Destiny, Amanda, Nisha, Ashley, Juniper, Melissa, Mikayla, Sara, Bridget, Anna, Christina, Allison, and Cat.

To all of my friends and family who checked in to see how things with my book were going, I remember, and it meant the world.

There's something to be said for people who know exactly what you're going through, and the writing/publishing experience is so uniquely unhinged that I couldn't have done it without any of you. I have met so many incredible writers, all of whom I admire and aspire to, but just to name a few:

Megan Jauregui Eccles, the day you slid into my DMs was the day my life changed. Raquel Valldeperas, the day I slid into yours was the day your life changed. Jokes aside, I don't know what I would do without either of you. You inspire me every day and keep me from getting into internet fights. I am so excited to be on this journey with you.

Angela Montoya, of all the strangers to find online, I'm so lucky I found you. Your words and stories are a gift to the world. It's been my privilege to watch you flourish, and I will not rest until *Kiss the Gods When I'm Gone* is on shelves.

Diana Rodriguez Wallach, your support and mentorship have meant the world. I wouldn't be where I am without your help. Rebecca Thorne, it was a really good effort. You almost had me, but the fickle beast that is traditional publishing pulled me back in. I appreciate every minute you spent helping me, and though I chose a different path, your guidance was instrumental. Breanne Randall, thank you for all of your time, your expertise, and your amazing voice notes. I have cherished them all. I promise one of these days I'll send one back. Avery, Cami, David, Lexie, Rain, you're the only people I ever want to picnic in Central Park with. George Jreije, thank you for your publishing wisdom. I hope your books take over the world.

To everyone on TikTok and Instagram, a profound thank-you for sticking with me. I've been talking about this book for years, and your continued excitement and support made it all the more worth it. I wonder if you'll miss that one book pitch I used over and over and over again because it was the only one that worked. Don't worry, I have a new one you're going to love! And to the algorithm, I have some concerns, but overall, you've been okay.

A massive thank you to my wonderful editor, Melissa Rechter. The care you put into my book went above and beyond. Working with you was a dream, and the final product is a testament to your craft and love for the story. To everyone at Alcove Press who worked to make this book a success, thank you so much! Corinne Reid, thank you for capturing Rua and Finn and creating the most stunning cover art I could've ever imagined.

To my amazing agent, Steffi Rossitto, I am so grateful this book brought us together. I couldn't have done this without you! Thank you to the team at the Tobias Literary Agency. Lane Heymont and Jacqui Lipton, you're awesome.

Lastly, I would like to acknowledge myself, because writing a book is hard.